HOSTILE
ENVIRONMENT

PATRICK C. CROWELL

HOSTILE ENVIRONMENT
PUBLISHED BY SYNERGY BOOKS
2100 KRAMER LANE, SUITE 300
AUSTIN, TEXAS 78758

For more information about our books, please write to us, call 512.478.2028, or visit our website at www.bookpros.com.

Publisher's Cataloging-in-Publication available upon request.

Library of Congress Control Number: 2006928111

ISBN-10: 1-933538-60-0
ISBN-13: 978-1-933538-60-0

ACKNOWLEDGMENTS

There are many people who I would like to thank for their support provided to me in relation to the writing of this book. Those are: Kim Brooks for her expertise provided years ago; Lynn Long for hers; Tom Mihok for his; Gord Henry for making great boats; Julia Mortensen, Pam Crowell and the Southwest Page Turners Book Club for their patience and dedication to an early version; John Foster for his expertise, friendship and support; Jim Rodriquez for his; my daughters, Julie (the cover rower) and Sharmin; Steve for inspiration; Tom DeWolf for inspiration; all my family members; Risa Reynolds and Kay Hall for much needed and trusted editing; my wife, Maureen, for her constant and devoted love and for how she lets me be me; and, last but not least, my deceased father, "Pop," for providing me with this and all opportunities.

CHAPTER 1

I'm so stupid! thought DeeDee Lane, as tears trickled down her cheeks in the bathroom stall. *Maybe I led him on somehow. But what did I do?*

The silent, air-conditioned place closed in around her like a womb. If only she could be back in there. She had sprinted down the hall after it happened, and the hollow sound of her heels tapping tile and the bathroom door behind her echoed in her mind. She'd glanced at her distressed image in the mirror then, and felt ugly.

Idiot! Moron!

The heat of embarrassment swelled upward from her chest and reddened her face. Turning away in disgust, she'd sought refuge in the stall. Its fake marble facade was bleak and austere, and it was ironic that she felt security behind the latched door. She slumped on the toilet with her legs spread, elbows on her knees, and head in her hands.

As she replayed the events and searched for clues, random thoughts jabbed at her. The more confusion set in, the more salty liquid flowed from her eyes as she pondered how she'd caused the situation. A part of her knew she'd been violated and her premise of self-blame was false, but there were deep-rooted, indoctrinated signposts. *This way*—the mental path trodden by legions of women unable to actualize they'd been wronged. Perhaps if she'd worn a burqa …

Gradually, her crying gave way to sobs, and her body shivered in the chilly booth. Her reddened eyes dilated, and she became numb. It seemed as though her world had been reduced to this tiny stall, spinning on an eerie tornado through scenes of her sheltered life. That is, sheltered until today. But her thoughts soon jolted back to the present, and she landed as abruptly as Dorothy's house, as her mind replayed what had happened in the office down the hall.

· · · ·

"Miss Lane, would you please come in here to take down a letter?" he asked through the intercom, as his pulse rose in excitement. He was delighted that his hunch was true—though it was late in the evening, she was still in the office. He'd been watching her ever since she had transferred to the legal department, stalking her like a hunter and studying her behavior.

Rising quickly, he darted across the room to rotate the switch on the wall, dimming the lights to just the right illumination.

DeeDee Lane was newer to Legal than he. At twenty-three, five foot two inches, and sporting shoulder length, towhead hair, he found her astonishingly cute. Her royal blue eyes reminded him of his mother's. But what he liked even better was her soft, voluptuous roundness. Slightly overweight about the hips and bottom, she was large through the chest and amply proportioned. Cute, young, blond, petite and voluptuous—a recipe he found irresistible.

DeeDee entered his office, surprised at the dimmed lights. *How can I take a letter*, she wondered. Her awe prevented her from speaking out. Although she'd done work for him yesterday, this was the first time he'd called her to his office. Her heart began to race.

She gathered up her voice. "Hi!" It came out high pitched.

It amused him, and he almost chuckled aloud. *She sounds like a cheerleader*, he thought.

"Hello," he said. "DeeDee, isn't it?"

"Yes!" *The executive vice president and general counsel of Western Town Production Company remembers me*, she thought.

DeeDee admired the cherry wood desk, chairs, and credenza. They were classic and tasteful, perfect for a man of his position. Along the opposite wall was a luxurious couch and Queen Anne coffee table, flanked by matching end chairs and lamp tables. The bronze lamps on the tables stood tall and elegant.

His spacious corner office was on the top floor of the administration building and DeeDee was dumbstruck by the panoramic vista provided by the long, horizontal windows forming two of the four walls. It was six stories up; DeeDee couldn't resist wandering over to the long panes for a look. Even after dark, the view of the Western Town theme park was spectacular. A million lights sparkled and shimmered as an army of maintenance workers cleaned the grounds like busy fairies in the night.

"Impressive view, isn't it?" he said, almost like a statement. His pride in showing it off had already become passé.

"Oh my!" she said as her voice squeaked, and she realized that people outside could see in were the lights not dimmed. She had no way of knowing that one of the first changes he'd insisted on when hired was the installation of a dimmer switch.

DeeDee took note of his immaculate attire. It made her uneasy. He wore a navy, pinstriped suit pants and a white, monogrammed shirt, crisp and generously starched, with dark blue suspenders adorned by tiny duck heads and a crimson power-tie. It gave her the impression that she was in the presence of tremendous corporate clout.

Her reverence overshadowed the fact that he wasn't that good-looking. His forehead was high, and a wave of dark, dangling hair draped to the side and back. The look was cosmopolitan and sophisticated in her eyes. As he fumbled papers behind his desk, her gaze settled upon his shadowy eyes and large, protruding nose. Forming almost a perfect quarter-circle, and flat on its underside, his nose projected like a carving on Mount Rushmore.

With pad and pen in hand, she eagerly sat in a chair facing his desk.

He became irritated. He'd intended to be waiting on his couch when she arrived, but she had come too quickly.

"Just a second, please," he said, and popped back to his desk. "I just remembered something terribly important." Still standing, he jotted down a fake note as he figured a way to maneuver her to the couch. He loved this game, and this was but a new challenge.

"Sorry about the dimmed lights. I've been here fourteen hours now, and my eyes hurt," he remarked, guessing she'd be impressed. He'd scoped her out and noticed she kept long hours. With a couple exceptions, it was odd for a secretary in his new department to ever stay late, let alone always. He added, "I need to move to the couch for my back—it's *really* been a long day. Do you mind?"

"No, of course not."

He moved spryly for one with so sore a back, but DeeDee didn't think of it—still dazzled by so important a man. He could say anything and she'd believe it; after all, he was the boss.

As he passed by the door, he shut it firmly. His excitement mounted, and with an unseen flick of his thumb he locked it. DeeDee followed him to the couch, and settled at the opposite end. Crossing her legs, she stared at him with her blue eyes big and bright, her pen poised.

Christ, she can't be playing hard-to-get, he thought. *She's very naive.*

"Oh, I forgot something," he said.

"Let me," she offered.

"No, it's okay, I can do it." He was already halfway across the room.

Grabbing a piece of paper from his desk and oblivious that it was blank, he skipped back to the couch. He positioned himself close to her as he sat, flipping the paper on the coffee table. He placed his hand on her thigh in the manner that touchy-feely people do; he grazed her a little high, and let it linger a little long.

"I've heard you have a two-year secretarial degree," he said.

"Yes, I do." She caught a whiff of his freshened Ralph Lauren cologne.

"And, you want a promotion to legal sec' here, don't you?" Again he moved his hand on her leg, higher, longer, relishing the feel of her. *Dare I squeeze just a little?* Pawing her excited him, and it was gratifying to get away with it. He remembered when he was a boy hiding in the woods with a box propped by a stick tied to a string. She was the rabbit underneath the box, and he was about to tug the line.

"Yes, I really do. It's my next goal."

God, she's such a little cheerleader, he thought, rubbing his hands.

8

She was self-conscious, her focus on impressing this man in order to gain her promotion, and she hoped the dim lights wouldn't thwart her ability to take dictation.

"Well, that's good. I have confidence in you. You'll make it. The next opening ... we'll take a hard look ... Uh ... no pun intended." He was delighted with his cleverness, but it was lost on her.

"Oh, thank you so much," she said brightly, still the unsuspecting naïf.

"You know, Peckinpah really needs this memo. But I'm beat. My eyes hurt, and my neck and shoulders are killing me. I think if I take awhile to relax, I'll be able to do it. Would you mind ... rubbing my shoulders a bit?"

He marveled at his nerve. It was nothing new, but thrilling nonetheless. He'd barely been introduced to the young woman, yet he could make such a request. *The power ...*

"Uh ... well, no ... I guess not," she said, taken aback.

"Just right up here with your hands," he said, turning his back to her and indicating. As she began rubbing his shoulders, he moaned while drowning in his sense of power. "Oh yeah ... that feels so good."

She continued massaging his shoulders.

"Now a little lower, if you don't mind," he said.

Dutifully she complied, but she sat more erect than usual, glancing about the room and feeling as though someone was watching. As she ostensibly relieved his stress level, she felt her own rising. She continued to massage his upper back until he asked her to massage his sides, and showed her where. Once again she submitted.

At last, he said, "Thank you, that's good. How 'bout you? ... You know, I'm impressed with how much time you spend here. But you work too hard. Here, turn around."

He shifted his body.

She turned her back to him timidly, her eyes glazing over and her brow furrowing. *Aren't I supposed to work hard?* Something wasn't right, but she didn't understand exactly what. She felt frozen in time, like a deer blinded by headlights.

He followed the same pattern he'd asked her to follow on him, but his hands didn't feel strong or patient. They seemed methodical and cold, like he was just going through the motions, until they reached her sides. Then she felt them broaden and flatten, and they became purposeful. His fingers stretched and fondled with each movement and she suddenly sensed his excitement.

The dim lights! At once she realized this just wasn't right. It wasn't at all what she'd expected, and now she didn't know what to do. Time became stuck in a modulating continuum between his hand movements and her confusion; and she wanted to make it stop, but didn't know how. Though pleasing this man had been her aim, it hadn't crossed her mind to please him in this way, and her awe was now swamped by fear.

Just when the groping began to resemble flagellating flounders burying themselves in the sand, she felt it stop. His fingers started a new movement—forward this time, until they reached the soft fullness of her breasts, and she couldn't believe it when he began to massage them.

DeeDee bolted off the couch and faced him. It was shock on her face, searching for intent on his. It was there—she saw it plain as day—clear and unabashed through the dim light. He gazed at her with a half grin as if to say, "What'd you expect? Come on back and accept my offer—play the game."

DeeDee turned and fled through the door. The reception area whizzed by as she shuttled past the legal department offices to the women's bathroom down the hall.

CHAPTER 2

Frustrated, the executive vice president of Legal buzzed a different woman—a legal secretary he knew would also be working late.

"Marta, come in for some dictation, please," he said.

Marta Delong snatched her pen and pad, wondering whether she'd really need them, and marched out of her office with purpose. *I was right to stay*, she thought. *He's going to be my way up the ladder.*

She thought about his former administrative assistant—he'd openly described her as eye-candy and, à la Trapper in M.A.S.H., a "sultry wench." *What a fool she was*, Delong thought, remembering how the woman had quit abruptly, without explanation. *I know why she left. So much the better for me. I'll land her job and it'll only be a matter of time before I convince him the legal department needs an office manager.* She thought back to her interview with him last week. *The other girls don't have a chance.*

Delong walked through his door, and he again locked it, this time not so subtly.

She looked at him in triumph. *He wants me again*, she thought. She didn't know, nor would it matter, that she was his second choice that night. *I want his power. Quid pro quo.*

He watched her strut in, but wished she were better looking. Her tall, frail body slouched as she moved to him. He focused on her pale, freckled skin and thin, jet-black hair, which always looked dirty to him. Sunken brown eyes made her look tired, and there seemed to be a perpetual longing about her. But it didn't matter. Perhaps that was it—he knew she'd latch on like a suckerfish to a shark, and clean up whatever.

He grabbed her to him and planted his mouth on hers. His hand molested her small breast and she reached for his groin, her dull eyes almost alive.

Some people make love, she thought as she endured his animalistic acts, enjoying her power. *Some have sex.*

CHAPTER 3

"Adel Blair! Will you come to the starting line please?" the elderly referee barked through his megaphone, as annoyed as any of the cantankerous, crusty old men in the sometimes stuffy sport of rowing. Because the racecourse contained six lanes and there were six female rowers on the lake water, each in their own single racing shell, he'd assumed Adel was in the women's race.

"I'm not in *that* race," Adel yelled, loud enough to be heard on the float-boat behind the starting platform.

"What do you mean?" he said, still irritated.

"Check your sheets; I'm in the *next* race!" she yelled, a little annoyed herself. An argument with an official was the last thing she wanted now.

"But that's the men's single race!" His face bore distinct incredulity. *Preposterous*, he thought.

"That's right. I'm racing the men today," Adel stated as though it was the most natural thing in the world.

"Thank God!" a female rower yelled to the laughter of the others at the line.

Adel looked around, trying to erase the conversation from her mind. The bright blue sky was laced with scents and sounds of the lake. A huge decorative fountain was off center in the lake, and gulls whirled about and screeched as though it were spewing French fries. The water was serene with a light, steady chop. The slight breeze would serve as a helpful tailwind for the rowers. Mallards and black swans mingled with spectators on the banks as the rowers watched the referee—each with quite different feelings on the issue.

There were eleven rowers in racing shells—five males and six fe-males—each waiting for their respective race, or so it had seemed. The females had all maneuvered their long, sleek shells into their lanes. They backed their boats to starting positions and began inhal-ing deeply, then forcefully exhaling as they made final preparations of their bodies. All, that is, except Adel Blair—she didn't go to the line. She placed her oar handles between her knees and abdomen and folded her long, muscular body forward on her sliding seat to relieve her ever-sore back.

Self-assured determination exuded from her unruffled face out-lined by wavy, golden-brown hair pulled into a ponytail. Were it not for her racing sunglasses, one would see the resolution in her eyes. That she was going to race the men that day was never in doubt, even if she had to row unofficially.

Adel could see the referee turn to the other officials on the float-boat. They were checking papers and speaking to each other with a variety of gestures and expressions.

"Outrageous! Absurd!" the referee protested to the others. "Who does she think she is?"

"There's no rule against it," the lone female official reminded him. "It's an 'open' event," she explained. "She can race."

After much turmoil, the referee turned to face Adel and raised his megaphone. "Have a good race, Ms. Blair," he said with deliber-ate emphasis, confident she'd be clobbered by the men. This was something he'd never seen in his forty-year association with the con-ventional sport of rowing, but she'd get what she deserved.

He turned to the five lady scullers and polled them to ascertain their readiness. "Are you ready? Row!" came his harsh starting com-mand.

Adel watched from the side of the course as her friend Annie Jakes predictably pulled ahead. Then she refocused, visualizing the effort she'd need to accomplish her own unthinkable challenge—beating the men.

CHAPTER 4

As the women raced down the course, Adel Blair sensed the remaining single shells around the starting platform pulling into their respective lanes. Checking her oarlocks to ensure they were tight, she spied out of the corner of her eye a couple of the male scullers glaring at her.

She never looked directly at opponents before a big race, in order to convey that she was as unconcerned about them as a hunting lioness about the birds in the sky. She was not about to change. This was about speed, and speed alone.

Hers was the only *Fluidesign* boat in the race, distinguished by its sleek lines, relative length and stiffness, and distinctive design with the rigger *behind* the rower rather than in front. The manufacturer's owner, Gord Henry, had convinced Adel that the boat's aerodynamics were better this way, much like an airplane. She knew she'd have to test Gord's theory, because today she would have to fly. With one powerful stroke her narrow *Fluidesign* glided into lane three, in the middle of the men.

It bothered some of them that Adel ignored their annoyance. The man in lane four said with a sneer, "Hey baby, why don't you save yourself some pain and go get me a beer for after the race."

"I'll have time after I finish," Adel said.

The rower in lane two smiled.

Adel wondered what it was—*was it instinctual fear that not only might they lose, but that they might lose to a woman?* She shrugged her strong shoulders, too focused on winning to let her mind be disturbed by anything.

Adel balanced her delicate, twenty-nine pound shell at her starting position and took a practice-start. The sleek, black, twenty-seven foot craft jumped forward with instant velocity. After her sixth quick and light stroke she moved her hands down to the gunnels, causing her oar-blades to rise, and glided with perfect balance upon the water until the fragile, carbon-fiber shell coasted to a dead stop. After a moment of controlled poise, she un-weighted her hands, causing her oar-blades to smack hard against the water. Then she pivoted her boat one hundred and eighty degrees in her lane, sculling it around with her oars. She paddled back, turned around again, and took her position at the line. The six rowers—five men and Adel Blair—readied themselves.

"Give me strength, Daddy," Adel said, summoning the personal drive and mental toughness of her deceased father as she drew her body to starting position and focused on the referee.

The aligner raised his white flag signaling to the referee that there was alignment. There was one person assigned to lean over and hold the stern of each shell from the platform, and through headsets he'd instructed each of them in order to align the bows perfectly. The referee polled the rowers, and the red starting flag went up.

Adel fixated on the flag. She always watched the flag because the sight of its movement was quicker than the sound of the referee's voice.

The rowers sat erect.

"Are you ready?" the referee yelled. The rowers stiffened.

"Row!"

The starting command bombarded their eardrums a split second after the referee swung the starting flag down. Adel took off on the flag's movement, gaining a slight jump on the men, but all six boats lurched forward with sudden speed like silent starships transmuting from inertia to instant motion and disappearing into warp speed. From the aligner's position on the side, he saw six bows jumping forward at differing cadences, each propelled by forceful drives of the rower's oars through the water. One in the middle of the pack seemed to take more leaps forward, grabbing shorter bites of water, but climbing away from the other boats at a higher stroke rate. It was Adel Blair!

Adel knew she had to row at a higher rate if she wanted to beat the larger, more powerful men. Bigger bodies would get more from each stroke at any rate. Therefore, she had to row high—higher than the men. She gritted her teeth as she sensed herself pulling to an early lead at forty-four strokes per minute. It was the kind of resolve that endurance athletes and soldiers know well—to perform through the most fearsome circumstances and pain. It was a small slice of perfection she served up, something few ever experience, as she heard the simultaneous catches of her oar-blades striking the water, felt each accelerating drive through the water, and pulled back to her chest, forcing her hands down and away quickly and smoothly. She pulled a full start and thirty strokes at that speedy rate, building a three-quarter-boat lead over the men!

Ten more high, she told herself, glancing down at her electronic stroke monitor. *Still at forty-two! Smoothness!* she thought, as her extra ten high-strokes netted a full boat length lead.

Settle now! She felt her bottom move slower with the sliding seat, without disturbing the precious speed she'd developed. *Power ten on the settle,* she called to herself, and her boat maintained pace without check.

Lactic acid in her long, sinewy legs began to build like mortar hardening between concrete blocks. *There's the pain!* she thought. *Accept the pain!* It was only to be her companion for a short eternity.

At the five hundred meter mark—halfway—she still led by a length, but she gained no more. The less taxing, lower rates of the men were becoming more efficient compared to her tiring thirty-six beats per minute—especially in lanes two and four. She knew the rower in lane two. He was a slow starter and strong finisher. He'd be coming on.

Smoothness, she thought. *Accept the pain! Drive it through! Smoothness through the two-fifty. Fast hands!*

The men were gaining, chasing her furiously. She didn't hear the announcer calling the race on the loudspeaker and lamenting with amazement at her lingering lead. She couldn't distinguish the astonished cheers, and jeers, of the crowd watching from bleachers and chairs on the banks of the lake. It was all suppressed by unmitigated focus. All that mattered in the world was that lane two on her left was back within a half-length and closing with each stroke, and lane four on her right was charging them both. Even the other three men were coming on.

Power ten! Adel commanded her soul at the two-fifty mark, momentarily holding off the horde. Pain exploded in her quadriceps. Her abs and hips seized up, hurting like an eight-cylinder motor running without oil. Even her powerful forearms and shoulders wanted to fail her now—but she wouldn't allow it.

She saw the rower in lane two take it up—increasing his stroke rate—then lane four. *They're coming at me!* she thought. *The men are coming. The men are coming!* Lane two moved on her again with one fantastic stroke. *He's within a quarter length! Gaining momentum! Lane four—within a half-length!*

"No pain!" Adel uttered. It wasn't a scream. It was the sound of unadulterated intent to compete, as though that was her single purpose in life. Her body transformed into sheer will power. Something visceral overtook her soul, and through force of mind alone she hung on, willing her boat forward through a murky gel of extreme pain.

Lane two—pulling even! Lane four—right behind! Up again!

She stroked with fury, minding nothing but driving force, blocking out the feverish burn as though by self-induced epidural. Feeling the boat, becoming the boat, her legs as hard as the carbon fiber hull, she stroked as fast as human ability allowed, knowing she was almost to the merciful finish. *Keep stroking!*

"Blap! Blap!"

The race was so close, the line judge could only trigger his horn twice for the three rowers, and the second sound fell late. The other men followed shortly after. It was over.

CHAPTER 5

Adel slumped in her boat like she'd been shot with a bullet. Her legs throbbed with rapid-fire beats of her racing heart. Her chest heaved to catch air, and then there was another sensation—her insides wanted out. It wasn't pretty or feminine, but then again, maybe it was.

As her nausea subsided, Adel wondered who won. The loudspeaker from the stands sounded.

"Ladies and gentlemen! In a most remarkable race, winning by the length of a two-inch bow ball, we have a *woman* victorious in the Men's Open Single event ... Ms. Adel Blair!"

There was a brief moment of gratification. Then she became oblivious to the line judge's praise as she wiped vomit from her mouth and chin. The female official on the float-boat that followed the race down was leaping about and causing the pontoons to rock. She slapped the elderly referee hard on the back, celebrating the triumph of her gender. Disgruntlement was his response as he grabbed the railing for support.

The ovation from the stands was ambiguous. Many women screamed, and jumped up and down and high-fived each other. Others remained seated and gave half-hearted applause, in some sort of polite shock.

One man, a tennis player there with his friend, looked over at his buddy. "Wow!" he said. "Does that happen often in your sport?"

"No," the friend said. "I've never seen such a thing. But I'll tell you what, that woman's awesome. I know those guys out there, and they're fast!"

The tennis player looked around. He noticed men down the aisle complaining that Adel Blair must have jumped the start. "Check it out," he said to his friend. "They think she cheated. Do you?"

"No way. The officials are all over stuff like that. She's just really good. Men will have to deal with it, just like Michelle Wie, or Lisa Leslie, or that woman that broke all records swimming the English Channel."

"You're right, but look. There's some other guys over there calling for a protest!"

"They don't even know why, other than the boys lost."

. . . .

"Nice race, Adel," the rower in lane two said. "I'm gonna get you back one of these days." Michael McKerrin drooped his six-foot five-inch angular frame over his oar handles while sweat dripped from his black hair into admiring blue eyes.

"Nice race, Michael," Adel replied, still breathing heavily. She sculled her shell around and sat quiet for a moment, reflecting on what she'd done. Then she began rowing toward the dock.

The male sculler in lane four said nothing to Adel. He scowled as he sucked air and watched her paddle by.

Ready for that beer now, buddy? she thought.

Michael watched Adel as she rowed away. *Typical,* he thought. *She's not even celebrating. She's probably already thinking about her next workout. What a case she is.* He stared at her, not upset like his beaten compatriots, though he'd at least come in ahead of them. His was a smoldering brew of different emotions.

He watched her perform the gentle motions of the rowing stroke, noticing her racehorse-like quads and sleek biceps and triceps as they contracted and relaxed through rhythmic gyrations. Her skintight shorts and sports bra exposed the subtle waviness of her flat abdomen, and Michael saw familiar ripples appear and disappear as she laid back into each stroke. Flashing to days gone by, he envisioned her streamlined figure.

She was "ripped" in the vernacular of weightlifters, though her sinews were not bulky or stiff. They were long, lean and flexible, like his, finely proportioned and stretching long distances between joints over her five-foot eleven-inch body. Although he knew he had no right, he was proud of her awesome physique and of what she'd done. But he also appreciated her femininity. He visualized the golden hue of her baby-smooth skin, and how after only a half hour of rays, she'd stay tan for weeks. Her wavy, calico hair was long and thatched, falling to the middle of her back. Her strong chin underlined full, pouting lips, and blended into high cheekbones. Her nose, a slight pug, was the logical extension of dark brown eyebrows that peaked and faded to fine points near her temples, rendering exotic beauty to her hazel eyes, shaped like the almond eyes of an Oriental cat.

Michael pondered his relationship with this quiet woman as he watched her row away, remembering how they met more than three years ago through his uncle, attorney David McKerrin. Uncle Dave was her boss and he'd taken her out to celebrate her first victory in trial as a fledgling attorney. She was a second year associate then at McKerrin, Smith & O'Donnell, a medium-sized but well-respected law firm in Orlando. Fortunately for Michael, he'd gone to the same jazz bar and restaurant that evening with some of his fellow assistant state attorneys. Smitten by the tall, athletic beauty sitting with Uncle Dave, he couldn't resist. Things looked even better when he discovered she was a rower.

He thought about how they'd dated "on again, off again" ever since, depending upon her dictates. They had a great deal in common between lawyering, Uncle Dave, and rowing. But the relationship never blossomed like he'd hoped. She wouldn't allow it.

He knew it was her ambition, so he didn't blame her or think less of himself. Just as she intended to be the best single sculler in the masters rowing circles, she also drove herself to be the best trial attorney. Like a two-headed dragon that consumed her, these were the focuses of her life. Her deceased father had been like that too, Michael had been told, as had been his mother before him. It was as though "drive" was an end in itself. Every time Adel achieved a goal, her insatiable oomph searched for a new one, allowing no time for celebration or resting on laurels. In fact, relaxation often seemed to be her enemy. She just wanted to do.

Michael admired that unfaltering motivation. He admired it, and hated it.

She's too aloof, he'd often thought. *Too focused, too self-centered, too driven. That's what beat me today and what beats me always with her. It's part of her charm though; she's like a beautiful machine, like a wind-up toy that never winds down. She's simple, consistent, powerful, and strong, but I wish I could refocus her to help people and their causes … and refocus her on me.*

"Mr. McKerrin, are you all right?" the referee asked through his megaphone.

Michael snapped himself back to the present. He waved in response and paddled his racing shell to the dock, behind Adel, where he found Uncle Dave waiting for them.

Dave McKerrin watched his favorite associate and nephew row in. It used to be that he wouldn't even have had time to come to the Saturday regatta, but he'd been practicing law for well over thirty years. A medium-sized man with a ruddy complexion and sandy brown hair, Dave had worked hard and was growing weary of the practice, and now chose to play more golf and travel with his wife.

He remembered how the partners in his firm recognized Adel's traits right off. As senior partner, Dave decided Adel would be his associate, and he exercised territorial jurisdiction over his precious find. He was proud of her, and soon learned to totally rely on her. He wanted to give her the opportunities he'd been provided, so he became her mentor, an unusual mix even in those days. Their relationship blossomed beyond boss and associate, and he now thought of her as his daughter, while she let him fill part of the void in her heart created by the premature death of her father.

She's perfect, Dave had thought. *Married to the law and rowing. Smart, well prepared and doesn't need any supervision. She works up the law and facts; I contribute my instincts and experience.* Together they analyzed cases and enacted their strategies, making a strong team and enabling him to work less while she learned her trade from a respected journeyman. It was a proper quid pro quo.

I should make her a partner, Dave thought, as she guided her shell to the dock. He'd come to watch his favorite nephew and surrogate daughter race. They'd been taunting each other for weeks. *Don't turn it into business,* he thought. *Besides, I'm not sure I should do that to her.*

Dave felt warm-hearted as he watched them being helped by the dock-master and her assistant. Like Michael, he'd hoped the relationship between Adel and Michael would develop into something more. But then he didn't.

A common impulse overcame him. "Michael, you oughta be ashamed of yourself, letting *a girl* beat you!" he yelled, enjoying a shot at both of them in one.

The female dock-master glared at Dave, misunderstanding the trio's bond or that teasing was how they displayed affection. Michael smiled as he and Adel removed their feet from the secured shoes, realizing the old man's intent and being too exhausted to give anything back. Besides, he figured Adel wouldn't let it go by.

"Next I'll be taking over your firm," she said without looking up. Dave smiled.

"Adel," said a female rower who carried an oar onto the dock. "Want to row in a four with Christine, Annie, and I, and stomp the men's fours?" The female rower was buoyed by Adel's remarkable victory and wanted some of the same for herself.

Michael and Dave perked up, both interested but saying nothing.

"No," Adel replied. "I row alone."

CHAPTER 6

"My God, the quality of men's rowing certainly isn't much down here," Louis Victor Scarlechek said after Adel Blair's victory had been announced. "That would never happen in Philly or Boston."

"Could it be that she's just that good?" Madeleine Wilbanks retorted, trying to be clever and flirtatious without believing her suggestion.

"Oh, come now," Scarlechek said. "Surely you don't believe a woman could do *that* against decent male rowers."

"A woman won, therefore the male rowers were lousy, is that your syllogism?" she asked with a smile.

Scarlechek's face turned sour. He didn't like being pegged so easily.

"It is," he said. "Do you have proof it's false?"

She realized he was serious and was thankful she didn't need to respond. The Mayor of Orlando, Millie Davis, was approaching. An attractive woman in her early fifties with short and stylish reddish brown hair, she was hard to miss in a crowd.

Wilbanks had planned to see her. It was, after all, the Mayor's Cup Rowing Regatta, part of an annual late summer festival of social events held in The City Beautiful for the past ten years. It was held on Lake Eola, a block or two from downtown and just large enough to hold a one-thousand-meter racecourse with six buoyed lanes. Every year, Public Works erected bleachers for the spectators, including a large "steward's enclosure" for Orlando's social elite with a perpendicular view of the finish line. The enclosure was constructed of white wooden rails that fenced in dozens of matching chairs. A massive green and white striped tent covered it, housing a perennial cash bar and awards stand. Closed circuit television allowed VIPs to view the entire race from this vantage point.

"Hello Maddie, how are you?" Mayor Davis said, resonating well-practiced social grace.

"Oh, I'm fine. It's so nice to see you again Millie. How are you?" Wilbank's voice also reverberated.

"I'm surviving," Davis said. "I'm sure you've read all about the referendum—"

Scarlechek broke in. "I have. I must say, I admire your fortitude."

Mayor Davis turned to him and smiled, grateful for any show of support. "Thank you so much. I don't believe I've had the pleasure."

"Lou Scarlechek, Executive Vice President, Legal ... uh ... Western Town." He said it like flashing a badge. The company was the largest sponsor of the event.

The regatta had turned into a "must attend" for those of any standing in the City. Gentlemen were required to wear coats and ties in the steward's enclosure, even in Orlando's humid environment. The more sporting men donned traditional straw skimmers with colorful bands. The ladies sashayed about in long, colorful dresses and wide-brimmed hats reminiscent of the Kentucky Derby. The event had become more than a rowing regatta. It was, as Dave McKerrin called it, a "yuppie happening" that mimicked the Royal Henley Regatta in England, the oldest and greatest rowing regatta in the world.

"Lou has just been hired as the executive vice president of the Orlando Legal Department and general counsel for Western Town Production Company," Wilbanks said.

Davis smiled, registering a new player. Western Town was a long time Fortune 500 company that had become the most exciting theme park and movie production conglomerate in the country. Anyone with power there was a force to be reckoned with.

"Well, that's quite a position," she said. "You'll no doubt be involved with us a lot. Very nice to meet you, Mr. Scarlechek."

Scarlechek stood erect and puffed out his chest. "Lou, please."

It was unwritten policy for executives like him to participate in community events and politics. He was determined to carry it out—it was extremely important. It was no accident he was accompanied by Wilbanks, Western Town's Director of Public Relations, over whom he'd usurped authority by explaining that legal proceedings and deals could be dramatically affected by improper public relations. He claimed no choice but to manage Wilbanks, carving broader turf for himself and Legal. There was the company's image to protect, and he didn't mind at all that she was blonde, five feet six and quite shapely, as well as acquainted with everyone in town.

Mayor Davis checked Scarlechek up and down. Besides a skimmer, he wore khakis, boat shoes and a canvas sailor belt, a crisp, blue-and-white striped shirt with an embroidered crest, a royal blue tie with a gold anchor, and a navy sports coat with even more anchors on the golden buttons.

"You must be a boater, Lou."

"I love boats. They're my escape … that is, when the company will leave me alone."

"What do you have?" she asked, making a natural assumption.

Scarlechek became sheepish. "Well, none right now."

"Oh … well what did you have?"

"Well …"

The thought occurred to Davis that he'd never done any boating at all, and she looked away for a moment. "I'm a patron of rowing," she said to change the subject. My husband rowed in high school and college, and my girls row at Edgewater High. Do you row?"

"No, I played lacrosse in school." It was high school, but he hoped she'd assume he meant college. Though he was a strong man, his athletic days had ended with a knee injury during his senior year. Now his five-foot, eleven-inch frame and sewn-in shoulder pads disguised a bulging middle, evidence of too many exquisite meals at fine restaurants.

"Well, did you see that last race? Isn't Adel Blair incredible?"

"Yes, she certainly is! What a race that was."

Maddie Wilbanks shot him a look. He ignored her, as though it was quite natural for a woman to win. He wasn't about to berate the quality of rowing in Orlando now.

"She's an attorney you know. I knew her father quite well," Davis said, feeling unspoken kinship with this woman who, like she, had beaten the men.

"Interesting," Scarlechek said though he wasn't interested at all. He'd never seen Adel Blair, and could care less that some woman beat a bunch of rowing wannabes from the Deep South. At the moment he was enthralled with speaking to the Mayor of Orlando in front of others. "Now, about that referendum," he said, steering the conversation.

Suddenly the announcer interrupted over the booming PA.

"Ladies and gentlemen, we have a special guest today, who's just arrived—the CEO of Western Town Production Company, Thomas Armstrong Peckinpah!"

Every head in the steward's enclosure, including Scarlechek's, turned to watch Tom Peckinpah enter the enclosure like a king entering court. His entourage—his traveling secretary, her assistant, and his limo driver doubling as a bodyguard—stopped short at the entrance. The gathering became abuzz with pointing and chatter, and people thrust their hands to Peckinpah. Tall and handsome, he was Mr. Corporate America. His image often plastered the covers of magazines like *Time, Money, U.S. News*, and he regularly played host to Western Town's monthly made-for-TV western drama. He was as much a household name as Disney.

Mayor Davis, realizing that she needed to greet the man, excused herself and abandoned Scarlechek.

Shit, I didn't even get to make my point, he thought.

By the time Davis crossed the crowded patio, Marlene Francis was already commanding Peckinpah's attention. Francis was the Orange County Manager and wanted Western Town to contribute land for a local affordable housing project. Chenoweth Taylor, the President of Orlando Community College, had also pounced on Peckinpah. Taylor was intent on persuading Western Town to donate $500,000.00 toward a new gymnasium. The gift had been sought through Western Town's Public Giving Program, but the sum was too large for local approval, though too small about which to bother Peckinpah. Like Marlene Francis, Taylor was charming, confident, and reasonably attractive in a forty-something, business-like fashion. She couldn't wait to get her hands on the handsome Peckinpah.

Scarlechek watched both women pursue the unexpected opportunity, with Mayor Davis not far behind. Having been left and disregarded, he let a familiar feeling wash over his spirits.

I'm nobody, he thought. Desolation swept over him like a great pendulum casting its shadow over feelings of importance when others showered attention on him. He felt only emptiness now. He flashed to Christmas when he was five and his visiting cousin got a bigger truck. He remembered the fit he threw until his mother offered her poor sister three times the money for the toy right then and there. He'd nearly suffered a self-induced seizure, but he'd gotten what he wanted.

Searching for solace as he did back then, he found it in the submissive brown eyes of Maddie Wilbanks.

"My, people come and go so quickly around here," she remarked, still trying to be clever.

"Yes, and I'm a newcomer. It's a little unnerving," Scarlechek admitted. He drew closer to Wilbanks as they leaned forward on the white rail overlooking the lakefront.

"Surely you know Tom Peckinpah," she said.

"Well yes, I do," he boasted, soaking in her approval like a sponge. "I met him at the last Executive Committee meeting. As a matter of fact, I need to say hello ... and there's something very important I need to tell him."

Suddenly his cell phone rang. "Uh oh, duty calls. Please excuse me ... Lou Scarlechek," he said into the plastic, feeling pride that someone needed him for something. "Oh, yes, absolutely ... yes, it's very important that you called," he said.

Wilbanks wondered why he was speaking so loudly.

A second ring emanated from a second cell phone in Scarlechek's breast coat pocket.

Perfect, he thought.

"But wait," he said to the first caller. "I'm getting another call ... hang on." Pulling out the second phone and flipping it open, he said, "Lou Scarlechek," to the second caller even louder, overjoyed that *two* callers were impressing his importance upon Maddie Wilbanks.

"Oh, yes, you must do that immediately ... I don't care that it's Saturday ... it's critical that it's on my desk by tonight ... of course I'll be there, they never let me get away ... all right, I'll see you then. Don't leave until I get there ... all right, ciao."

Closing his second phone, he returned to the first, his voice booming as though the caller was in Africa.

"Hello ... yes, I'm back ... yes, fax it to me tomorrow morning by ... six. I'll need some time. I'll call you at nine ... Church? ... You'll have to skip. It's imperative that it gets to Paris ... all right ... good job." He disengaged the first cell phone. The pendulum swung upward.

"So many people need me all the time, I have to carry two phones. Maybe I'll get some time off soon, huh?"

"Maybe," she replied, staring at him with a kind of amused sanction.

"Well, anyway, it looks like I'll be pulling an all-nighter tonight," he said, though he had no such intention. "They need me so damn much, I really don't know how they got along without me. I'm terribly sorry; I've got to speak to Tom about this too. Will you excuse me?"

"Go ahead. I'll stay here," she said.

"Yes, but there are things I want to talk to you about, too."

He turned his body to lean his hip on the rail and face her. "I know I can help your career," he said.

Her eyes opened wider.

He drew closer and extended his arm, grabbing the rail where her abdomen rested. His fingers touched her as they clenched the rail.

"Oh, excuse me," he said, his eyes gazing straight into hers without removing his hand.

She didn't move her body away, and measured her response. "It's ... all right."

He smiled. "I'll be back in a while."

Scarlechek deserted Maddie Wilbanks like a boy leaving his mom at the plunge. He sauntered up to the group hovering around Peckinpah.

"Tom! Hello, Tom!" He was speaking loudly again, hoping people would notice.

Peckinpah glanced up mid-sentence and smiled at Scarlechek. He recognized the man, but for the moment couldn't remember where they'd met, or why, let alone his name.

Scarlechek was undaunted and charged forward.

"Hello Tom!" Scarlechek extended his hand above the three women, who reluctantly parted to make room for the intrusion. They made no effort to disguise their irritation, although Scarlechek didn't seem to notice.

"How's Janis?" Scarlechek asked.

"She's doing very well, thank you," the aloof Peckinpah said. He tried to return to his discussion with Chenoweth Taylor.

Scarlechek pressed. "Tom, the Executive Committee meeting went well after you left, but there are some issues I must—"

Fully annoyed, Peckinpah squared to Scarlechek and said, "I'm sorry, what was your name again?"

The remark flattened Scarlechek, and the pendulum swung low.

"Lou … Lou Scarlechek," he said, feeling like one in a thousand at a soup line.

"Oh yes, I recall," Peckinpah said, scowling at Scarlechek for a long moment. "You're Landis's new man here in Florida." Peckinpah's killer instinct took control as he kicked the downed man with the attitude, confident of his power and ability to do so. "Good to see you again," he said with obvious insincerity.

After a moment, he decided to let up. "Let me introduce you, Lou," he said with a trace of compassion.

Scarlechek grinned throughout the introductions to Chenoweth Taylor and Marlene Francis, though inside, his emotions boiled in a kettle of embarrassment, anger, and envy. He'd been made a fool, and sensed Peckinpah's purposeful intention. It never occurred to him that he deserved it. Instead, he focused on Peckinpah's power and his intense desire to take away that for himself, just like his cousin's truck.

He remembered his first Western Town Executive Committee meeting. He'd entered the corporate world for power and status, a desire that knew no bounds. In Peckinpah he saw the modern embodiment of America's landed gentry, the epitome of the corporate autocracy—rich, ultra-popular, and ultra-powerful. It was then that Scarlechek became consumed by insatiable longing to have this for himself.

"Ladies and gentlemen!" the announcer bellowed over the P.A. "We have the medalists of the ladies' and … ahem … men's open singles races here for the presentation of their awards—the Orlando Cup and the Mayor's Cup. Fitting that we have a female mayor. Mayor Davis, would you come over for the presentation, please?"

All eyes in the enclosure turned to the awards stand, upon which already stood three women and only two men—one of them, Michael McKerrin. The announcer called for Adel Blair and when she didn't appear, Michael suspected where she might be and sent a young rower to find her. With much pomp and ceremony, Mayor Davis awarded the second and third place medals for the ladies event to their respective winners, and the Orlando Cup to Annie Jakes. The crowd applauded as Jakes took a bow.

But there was still no Adel Blair. The announcer called for her again over the P.A. and then began to stall.

"Ladies and gentlemen, I've been doing this many years now, and I have never seen what we witnessed here today … a woman winning the men's open single event and the Mayor's Cup …"

Just then, the young rower ran up to the announcer and whispered in his ear. They'd found Adel working out on an ergometer—a commonly used rowing machine known as an "erg," for short—in the nearby boathouse.

Adel was approaching the stand now, escorted by two other rowers. "Oh … excuse me ladies and gentlemen, but here she comes now! I give you the obviously female winner of the Men's Open Single race … Miss Adel Blair!"

Adel took her place on the highest block, the pedestal between Michael McKerrin and the male racer from lane four, who still didn't appear very happy.

"Thirsty?" Adel whispered to him as she took her place above him.

Michael jabbed her with his elbow as if to tell her to behave.

They'd found her training without giving a thought to the ceremony. She stood on the block in her skintight shorts and sports bra, wet from perspiration, and her untamed hair still pulled back in a ponytail. Her golden skin was flushed, and it glistened as subtle contours revealed themselves with the simplest movements as she accepted the Cup from Mayor Davis.

The crowd took in the modern version of Athena, many of them thinking, *no wonder she could beat the men.*

Some women transformed jealousy into criticism of her incredible gall. A spectator about Adel's age with a beautiful face and stylish clothing, but with a pear-shaped body, whispered to her mother. "I can't believe how tacky she is. I can't believe she didn't put something over that. Look, you can even see her nipples!"

The woman's mother replied, "To row against the men. For shame. And worse, to win! We'd never have considered such appalling behavior in my day. And you'd never dress like that at a social gathering."

The young woman's husband ignored them, for he was too busy lapping up every detail of the splendid view from behind his tinted Oakleys.

One row in front, a woman in her late twenties told her nine-year-old daughter, "You see, Julie, you can do anything you want in this world if you work hard enough. Don't let anyone, man or woman, tell you otherwise." The little girl brimmed with dreams as she studied Adel.

Next to her, a young, conservatively dressed man, the picture of athletic mediocrity in his youth, experienced a primal sense of inadequacy. His discomfort made him squirm in his wooden chair. His conservative Christian friend to the right breathed contempt as he watched Adel in her place above the men; it was an abomination of biblical morality.

Tom Peckinpah watched but didn't give Adel Blair any thought. Instead, he signaled to his secretary that it was time to leave.

While the photographers snapped shots for the newspaper, Adel picked Peckinpah out in the crowd. She'd heard that her friend and first secretary, Cookie Albertson, was working for Peckinpah, so she scoured the throng to catch a glimpse of Cookie.

"My word. What a woman!" Chenoweth Taylor said.

Marlene Francis agreed and mentioned that Adel was an attorney downtown.

Lou Scarlechek listened, filling his mind with lustful images. He heard men to his left rudely assessing Adel's form. He took in Marlene Francis's remark about Adel being a lawyer, and recalled Mayor Davis saying the same thing. His mind raced through the possibilities, and desire consumed him, so that he momentarily forgot about the scene with Peckinpah and his anger. His lip curled as he watched Adel's legs ripple when she stepped off the platform. His eyes narrowed and gleamed.

As she walked away he listened to the buzzing around him. She was the tallest, the smartest, the most athletic, and the most beautiful. She was suddenly the best of womanhood to him, because she was the best to the others. To possess her would mean that he would have what all others wanted. For Lou Scarlechek, the desire to have her went beyond conscious thought; it was something magnetic.

CHAPTER 7

"Just marry Dirk," DeeDee Lane's father had said. "He loves you. He'll take care of you. ... He's a great guy!"

"But Daddy—"

"I just don't understand you, DeeDee. Why would you throw away all that Dirk has to offer? He and I and his father will build you a house. We'll give you the land. You'll be right next door to us and we can even babysit."

Her mother looked on, knowing to say nothing.

"Daddy," she said, pleadingly, "I want to be a person ... my own person. That first, then maybe Dirk and I—"

"A person? You were a cheerleader! You were homecoming queen for crying out loud! We live in Iowa on the largest farm in the valley. You're the picture of wholesomeness. You're the envy of every girl in town! What more do you want?"

She looked down.

"DeeDee ... you're so cute. Are you just trying to be cute?"

I was trained to be cute, she thought. *It's almost like I practice.* But she knew better—she was incapable of anything so disingenuous.

"DeeDee, you've always avoided conflict and you're so well liked. Why don't you trust Dirk and me like always? We know what's best for you."

It's because of you two that I have to do this, she thought

"Daddy, I've never been a strong-willed person, and I've always been eager to please. I know I'm naive, and things bother me too easily. But I've realized that to be a person, my will has to have force. I want to be strong. I can't do like I always have, giving way to the

34

desires of others all the time. If I want to be my *own* person, I have to do this."

Over her father's protests, she had attended a two-year institute and enrolled in the legal program. Between her desires and her father's, an unidentified dialectic guided her to secretarial work. She became lightning fast and accurate with computers, and mastered the dreaded art of shorthand. A job placement specialist suggested Western Town as a possibility. Having grown up with the company, DeeDee saw it as the perfect choice. But Daddy still thought otherwise. Eventually, she announced she was leaving Iowa and moving to Orlando to work at Western Town. Her mother said nothing all along.

"But DeeDee, why?" her father asked, again pleading his case.

"Because, Daddy. I want to discover who I am. I want to make my own choices. I don't want to be the homecoming queen anymore. I hate the stereotype. I always have to be a certain way here. In a totally new setting, I'll have a choice. I don't have to be what everyone else expects. Especially with Dirk—it's always the same. I don't want to be the same. And it's not anyone's fault but my own. Here, in this place, I have to be what people expect. That's why I have to leave."

"At least let Dirk and me help," her father said, hoping one last try from Dirk could talk some sense into her.

"No Daddy. It's important. I need to do it alone."

Thus, she said goodbye to her family, her boyfriend, and the old DeeDee.

In Orlando, DeeDee took what she could get and set up life on her own. She found a secretarial job under four male supervisors in the Operations Division of Western Town. She enjoyed discarding wholesome habits, willingly giving up sleep and eating poorly. She was always at work, always fast and efficient, and always bubbly and cute and imparting spirit to her "boys." She did things her way while learning on the fly what that was; though her natural desire to please resurfaced. She gave up breaks and lunches—to her they didn't represent dedication. Instead, she labored long hours while sipping Diet Pepsi and nibbling baby carrots. The company took advantage of her dedication, but she didn't mind. She'd learned one thing about herself: she *could* please her bosses in the work force.

Aspiring to be promoted to senior secretary and eventually to be transferred to the Legal Department, she showed off her dedication and abilities in Operations. Her stellar performance didn't go unnoticed by management. A senior secretarial position in Legal finally opened, and she seized it, along with a boost in her self-image. Redefining herself with every small step, she began to think of her career and where it could go, perhaps even starting her own business. Although she didn't realize it in these terms, she was a rebel, because she wanted to escape the cultural expectations that had weighed her down. It was her own personal insurrection, and every small victory was a step toward greater opportunities.

Her characteristics were noticed soon at Legal. Once, after an attorney had already worked twelve, straight hours on a construction contract that still needed work, the VP in charge called on the attorney to put together a rush contract for a deal in France.

"Hey, I'm only one guy," the beleaguered lawyer explained to the VP. "Which contract is more important?"

"Both," the VP replied. "Do the best you can," he added before unceremoniously hanging up.

Frustrated, the lawyer wondered whether he'd ever be able to see his wife and children again. When he tried to find a legal secretary to stay late and type the second contract, everyone bolted. Everyone, that is, except DeeDee.

"Hey!" she chirped with the same spirit she'd shown at pep rallies. "You look pooped, silly. How do ya' expect to match wits with Clarence Darrow looking like a tired rooster in a henhouse?"

The lawyer gave her a double take.

"Go splash water on your face, Flash, and I'll get you something to eat while you dictate away. We'll get it done!"

Typing and editing his changes into the wee hours of the morning, she ended up alone in the office at two o'clock, until she finished e-mailing and faxing the finished contract to France.

The lawyer had found himself reminiscing about high school days while he watched DeeDee whiz through the document and chat up her home on the farm. He knew people in the department were talking about her. To some, her demeanor appeared too much, an act. To others, she was a bimbo. But he could tell she wasn't. He learned that he could count on her, and she was fun to be around. That was enough for him.

But just as she felt she was getting somewhere, after all she'd been through and all her struggles, DeeDee hit an unanticipated roadblock. DeeDee Lane had been sexually harassed. She'd been victimized, like a damsel raped by a pirate, and all she felt now was confusion.

Such a man in so great a company couldn't be to blame. Somehow, I must've led him on.

How she had done so was inexplicable, but she believed that she had. Inconsistently, she questioned the reason she'd been given her job, and it was a staggering blow to her self-esteem. A part of her had been taken and could never be returned.

Two days after the episode she returned to work.

I'll change whatever it was I did, she thought as she walked from the elevator to Legal's front door. As she entered, she glanced to his side of the complex. *Don't even look that way, stupid.*

Later that morning, one of her superiors dropped a file on her desk and asked her to run it down to his office. He rushed off before she could answer. DeeDee's palms began to sweat. She checked over her attire and tried to rise from her seat. She couldn't. Her heart raced as she thought of alternatives, and her face flushed with dread.

"DeeDee," a co-worker said. "Are you okay?"

"Oh my goodness, no! I've got to go to the bathroom! Will you run this to Lou's office?"

Sitting in her stall and blaming herself again, she didn't understand that her bubble had burst because the harasser had treated her as an object—a sex object. She didn't comprehend that it was only a side benefit that she tried hard and did a good job. Trying to break out of Smalltown, USA, she still didn't get it—that she couldn't break out without subjecting herself to the power of man and without bargaining with what was perceived as her only real and valuable asset, her sex.

CHAPTER 8

"So how'd I get so lucky?" the double-D-sized temp asked as she fixed her coffee in the break room.

"He likes busty redheads," her friend joked.

"No, I mean why'd his administrative assistant go AWOL?"

"No one knows. After two weeks and no calls, though, she's not coming back. She was really smart, you know, but she was from Southern California. I mean, what a flake."

"Who knows what motivates some people," said another woman stirring java at the counter.

"I heard Lou telling some of the lawyers that *he* didn't even know why she left," the friend said. "He said she just took off without even talking to him."

"He needed someone right away though," the second woman said. "I've heard that he claims he needs two secretaries, but they have to go through channels. That's why they brought you in to the rescue while Human Resources finds a replacement," she said to the redhead.

"Yeah, but I want to stay with this job," the temp said.

"You know who else really wants the job?" the friend asked.

"Who?" asked the second woman.

"Marta."

"God, that's all we need is to give her some power."

The temp turned from the coffee maker without realizing her friend had moved close, reaching for the cream. Her chest brushed against the woman's arm.

"Oh, I'm sorry," the temp said.

"Like I said," the friend said. "He handpicked you after taking one look at your ... qualifications. I'll bet the side view is his favorite. You passed the 'elbow test.' You know what they say about girls with big boobs: 'Hire her. We'll teach her to type.' You've always had that major pop-out factor, you know? That'll get you the win over Marta—she's flat as a fried egg."

"I don't break out these babies unless I have to," the temp said.

"My guess is you'll need some quick release Victoria Secrets."

"Oh, shut up and get back to work."

· · · ·

"You're late for your three o'clock, Mr. Scarlechek," the temp bellowed through the doorway, as she tugged on her tight blouse that had ridden up. "And Madeleine Wilbanks is holding on line two. John Waverly is on three."

I'm so lucky to be here, the temp thought as she adjusted her heavy-duty bra strap for good measure. *This is my big chance. Hmmm. I wonder why his administrative assistant left. Oh well, I hope I can land this job.*

"Tell Maddie to hang on," Scarlechek commanded. "Tell the meeting not to start without me. They'll just have to wait; it's *very important* that I hear it all." He held his hand over the telephone so Bruce Snavely, the Vice President of Finance, couldn't hear. "I'll dump Snavely and take Waverly," he continued, loving every second.

"Listen, Bruce, I've got to go," Scarlechek said, after removing his hand. "I've kept Waverly holding for too long." Waverly was the President of Western Town Production Company, Peckinpah's right hand man. It was a less-than-subtle name drop, glazed with the implication that he often received calls from the president and had the balls to keep him on hold. "Call me tomorrow and we'll talk more of this," he added, enjoying sloughing off a fellow VP and requiring Snavely to seek him out.

With a push of a button Snavely was wiped out, and so was that side of Scarlechek.

"Yes, John," he said, the two words meant to convey that he'd die to carry out Waverly's wishes. He snapped to attention over a two thousand-mile-long wire, kissing ass through cold plastic.

After the call ended, Scarlechek got up and walked to his expansive wall of windows and looked out over Western Town.

This is what I was born for, he thought. He spread his legs and placed his hands on his hips and laughed, imagining he was the hero in an Ayn Rand novel.

Damn teachers, he thought. *Making me read* The Fountainhead *and* Atlas Shrugged. *I'm on top of the world without that wordy tripe.*

Hearing his laughter, the redhead shuffled polyester and nylon into his office. "Lou," she said. "Ms. Wilbanks is still on line two."

"I know," Scarlechek said. *Let her hold,* he thought.

"God, this is marvelous!" he said. "They need me so badly here."

The temp looked at him and snapped her head back.

"They crave my pronouncements," he continued. "They can't make a decision without me, and they scurry around like ants to please me."

Not knowing what to say or how to react, she tried to do her job. "Lou, your meeting is still waiting also."

"Yes. Yes. You're such a slave driver," he said with a smile and a flip of his dangling hair. His desire for her breasts reminded him of something else he'd wanted to accomplish that day. "Listen, while I'm in the meeting I want you to track down a photo journal of Orange County lawyers for me. If the meeting goes late, leave it on my chair … unless you'll stay. We could accomplish a lot if you stayed late tonight."

He grinned at her like a schoolboy.

"I can't, I'm sorry." *Why does he always ask that?* she wondered. *He knows I have night school.*

Scarlechek was nonplussed. *You're blowing your chances,* he thought. *Too bad, with that rack. But like my dad always said, a small breast in hand is worth two large ones in the bush.* He pictured Marta Delong naked and smiled.

"Okay," he said. "Oh, about that directory, if anyone asks why I need it, just tell 'em I'm trying to learn the names of local lawyers. Understand? Good girl. Now, tell Maddie I'll call her later."

The temp shook her head. *Couldn't we have told her that five minutes ago?*

Scarlechek turned and swaggered out the door, puffing out his chest and pulling his shoulders back in case someone saw him. He took another glance at the redhead's profile and thought of his mother.

If Momma could see me now. Not bad for a boy from the Polish quarter of the Windy City.

He imagined his head nestled between his mother's bare breasts as he strutted down the hall. It was one of his favorite fantasies. He was her only child. While giving birth to little Lou, Carolyn Scarlechek had developed complications that prevented further pregnancies. She stayed home with him as much as possible, and little Lou became the sole focus of her life. He was her escape from everything unpleasant, including her chauvinistic husband, Paulo.

The anguish of his lower middle class life came back to Scarlechek. His problem was like his father's: cursed with brainpower greater than his station. *I'm carving my own empire,* he thought. *Something Papa couldn't do.*

Paulo Scarlechek had been a lower level management employee in charge of road inspections with the Illinois State Department of Transportation. He and Carolyn were descendants of immigrants from Warsaw. Paulo blamed Carolyn for not giving him more children. Not that he really wanted more, but chastizing Carolyn placated his feelings of inadequacy.

Scarlechek's hatred toward his father surfaced often, though he failed to recognize that he was just like the man. Despite Carolyn's doting, Scarlechek had become aware of what his family didn't have, and what others did. Without understanding why, he'd realized early on in life that everything about him, and his, was never as good as others and theirs.

He caught a glimpse of himself in a mirror as he walked the hall. All he saw was his nose. He remembered when he first realized his ugliness at eleven years old. A beautiful sixth grader refused to ride with him to a dance because she wouldn't be seen in his father's dirty, state-owned pickup. "Besides," she'd explained to her friends, "he has a snorkel nose!"

It was just like Papa's.

This is my domain, he told himself as he moved on, trying to make himself feel better. *They all have to do what I say.* Power had become his tool, and he really had it now. It was power measured through the eyes of others. It was the power to take anything he wanted, to not be jealous of what others had because he got it first or could take it from them. It was the ability to make others acquiesce to his desires simply because they were his. It was the arrogance to behave outside the moral side constraints of the rights of other men and women. It was superiority he felt over others when he treated them as lesser beings. Power made all this possible.

The pendulum was on the upswing and pride invaded him just as it had when he was fourteen and elected freshman class president. Then, he had devised a scheme to pool freshman lunch money so there would always be enough for all, even those classmates robbed by upper class bullies. Through fuzzy accounting, he lined his pockets. He offered the extra cash to poor females in exchange for copped feels behind block-wall bathrooms, the only way "Snorkelnose" could satisfy his raging hormones.

He remembered how he'd decided to become a lawyer. In high school, he witnessed a sizzling debate between two politicians, one of them a lawyer. The lawyer chewed up the other politician and left him juicy and cold in a spittoon. Scarlechek envied that power. It didn't matter *what* was said, he learned. It was *how* it was said. The envy gave him focus. The lesson sharpened him.

His intellectual ability grew to match the agility of a gecko, always alert, always quick. Scarlechek perceived, pounced, and ate everything up throughout his youth, and the more he did, the more he believed that life was about taking, as though he lived a modified Descartian credo: *I take, therefore, I am.*

Scarlechek saw his personal placards and framed diplomas that he had placed on the hallway walls. Notre Dame University. He'd obtained a full academic scholarship there where he studied business and finance. His participation in the debate society and the philosophy club fine-tuned his ability to beguile with words and facades.

After law school, he became a real estate and corporate "deals lawyer" with a high-powered Wall Street firm. Taking false pride in the idea perpetuated by Wall Street lawyers that New York City lawyers were the best in the country, and that Wall Street lawyers were the best of New York City lawyers, he played politics, schmoozed clients, and charmed, sold, and impressed by whatever means imaginable. He took note of what high-powered New Yorkers valued and assimilated those ideas into his own life, all the while incorrectly presuming that these same values would be important to everyone else. He learned to comply or die with the wishes of his superiors and clients, and to mandate that kind of delivery from his subordinates. But when he gave a directive, there was *never* an excuse for failure.

Scarlechek walked into his meeting, enjoying the looks of relief on the six participants gathered around the table. He remembered one incident at his former firm when he had flipped back his dangling locks and announced to his staff, "I'm the highest biller in the firm." It wasn't true—he knew it and his staff knew it. But that he could say it without having anyone summon up the nerve to challenge his assertion made him feel like a king.

What could he get away with in this meeting? If he stood naked before them, he bet he could get them to say they liked his new clothes.

CHAPTER 9

Scarlechek walked the quiet hall before returning to his office after the meeting. He smiled when he found the photo journal on his chair. Still drunk with self-importance, he let his mind race to a subject that would quench his thirst. Adel Blair.

He sat behind his desk and flipped open the journal, taking in the sea of faces. For a moment, he thought back to what it had been like to be on the outside, and appreciated his in-house counsel status. No more ingratiating games to retain and satisfy clients. No more worries about his partners.

I'm the prized client, he thought. *All these lawyers suck up to me.*

He thought of his old firm. It was nationally known and represented some of the biggest and most successful corporations in the country. The ties between the firm and its clients were historical, many having hired the firm's lawyers as in-house general counsel.

He recalled how he'd landed his position at Western Town. Geoffrey Landis, Western Town's general counsel at corporate headquarters in Phoenix, had hired his firm for a major real estate transaction in Canada. Landis, without truly knowing Scarlechek, had soon become convinced that Western Town needed Scarlechek's expertise in-house for its expansion to Paris.

"The French will be tougher than the Canadians," Scarlechek had told Landis while sipping champagne in a fancy restaurant after the Canadian deal had closed and Scarlechek had taken the credit. "But they'll still be pushovers compared to the Japanese, or worse, the Koreans, whom I've also handled by the way."

That night, Landis picked up the check. But not before offering Scarlechek the position as the new General Counsel of Western

Town, Orlando, and the Executive Vice President of the Legal Department. Scarlechek jumped at the opportunity. It couldn't have been better timing.

Those asshole partners of mine, he thought. *I'm a liability. I'll show them! We're down here in Florida and they're still up in the cold. I'm the department head of thirty people in one of the most exciting companies in the country. They won't have stock options when they retire.*

He remembered the rundown Landis had given about the company. Donald Town had started it in 1960 with a humble theme park on the outskirts of Phoenix. Modeled after an authentic town in the Old West, it contained a central avenue with shops, restaurants, and saloons, surrounded by rides, shows, and exhibits depicting scenes from American history. One of the main draws was its live rodeo. Western Town had become an overnight success, benefiting from the explosive growth around Phoenix. Landis reviewed the company's movie business, explaining that during the sixties in Hollywood it started with westerns—classics, with the likes of John Wayne, Alan Ladd, and Jimmy Stewart. The two businesses complemented each other well, and the creative company flourished. The company went public soon after, and the park grew into a resort with several three- to five-star western-style hotels.

Of course, Scarlechek knew all of this and had already decided to accept the position, but he enjoyed being solicited by Landis and Western Town, so he let Landis continue talking.

Landis related how the company had opened a second resort in the dry foothills of Van Nuys, California, in the early seventies, and a third resort in Orlando in 1982. Western movies decreased in popularity in the late seventies and early eighties, so the company expanded to other family-oriented genres to continue its high level of success. Planning resort expansion into the western Canadian market by the mid-eighties, the company created its fourth gate in Vancouver. It was now working on the fifth gate in Paris, and Scarlechek would be part of that project if he came on board.

"Our yearly gross revenues are several billions," Landis had explained. "Our operating capital is over one billion dollars and growing."

How much for me? Scarlechek had wondered.

"Our name has become a cultural icon, as you know, Lou, associated with high quality tourist experiences and family values," Landis had said. "Young men and women across the country dream of working for us. We are an institution of magical happiness that has meant much to people as they've grown up. Lou, you'd get to be part of that. And I can tell you, it's special."

Scarlechek leaned back in his chair and relished the memories and his new power. The life of the rich and famous was within sight.

Who knows, he thought. *Maybe someday I'll take over Landis's position. Me, general counsel for the entire company, or even company president. And that son of a bitch, Peckinpah. He'll need me then. He'll remember my name then.*

Scarlechek resumed flipping through the journal. He found the "Bs," and located Baldwin and Blalock, but no one in between. No picture of the marvelous beauty he'd seen at the regatta. Instead, there was a blank space with the scales of justice where Adel Blair's face would have been had she cared enough to have shown for her photo. However, her name was listed and Scarlechek learned that she worked at the firm McKerrin, Smith & O'Donnell, P.A., in downtown Orlando.

That's a step in the right direction. I need to find out what kind of work she does.

Lou Scarlechek pondered the bevy of Western Town women at his disposal. It was time to add another to his fold.

CHAPTER 10

Adel Blair strode down the office hall with a graceful gait, shapely lines rippling through sheer white stockings with each long step stretching the fabric of her dark blue tailored suit cut four inches above her knees. Unlike many tall women, she dared to wear two-inch heels, and so now she stood over six feet.

Out of the corner of her eye, she caught a female office worker staring her up and down. She suddenly wished she were rowing.

Adel had learned long ago that people stared at her. It didn't matter whether she slouched or dressed like a homeless person. People scrutinized her the same way toddlers studied a picture book, so she overcame any self-consciousness and dressed and walked to please herself. It had been tough for an introvert. But then, she never let herself take the easy way out.

She'd been in the break room perusing the Wall Street Journal and sipping French Roast. It was seven twenty-three when Dave McKerrin arrived and asked her to give him five minutes. He had called the night before and asked her to skip her workout. It was rare for Dave to come in so early. Usually at that time, he was cursing and claiming a Mulligan somewhere around the fifth green of his morning nine. But this day there was a new client.

Adel entered her boss's wood-paneled office and bid him good morning. Feeling comfortable in the warm room, she checked out the familiar artifacts and then sat down in front of his antique oak desk. Dave's wooden chess table displayed the survivors of an ongoing match with another lawyer, each making a move whenever the mood hit or the right gambit became clear. The wooden rack on his desk was filled with tobacco-caked meerschaum pipes, though on doctor's orders he no longer smoked. She enjoyed being there because it was cozy and safe in the same way her daddy's den had been, and it was a place where she gained knowledge from her respected mentor.

She daydreamed of her father while Dave reviewed a draft legal brief she'd written. Daddy had raised her on his own, she having been only six when her mother had died. He had been a successful man in real estate, and he and Adel had nurtured a close relationship fostered by the mounds of time he devoted to his motherless child. They'd learned to rely on each other for everything.

"All right, little girl," her father said one time. "Why'd you smack Billy in the nose?" They sat in his Porsche after he'd picked her up from the principal's office.

"Because he called me a bean pole," she said. Her face was red.

"Adel, you have to be smarter than people like that."

Mr. Blair had been an athlete too. He'd been a rower in college and stayed with it for years afterward. Adel would get up early every day and make breakfast in their house on the lake while he rowed, and then he would take her to class. Preaching toughness, heart, and dedication to her from an early age, he knew she was special when on an Indian Princess camp-out, she decided to trail him on a run. She would never have quit had he not forced the determined eight-year-old with long legs to stop for her own good after three miles.

As she grew, he gradually taught her to row and by the time she entered high school, she was already an outstanding athlete. With his help, she excelled in school. But he, a widower and confirmed bachelor, worried that she didn't have enough female influence in her life. Often on Saturdays they would rise together and row his double-seated racing shell for an hour and a half, and then complete the ritual with a monstrous breakfast. Afterward, they would clean up and he'd take her shopping and insist on buying her a dress. She would wear it, for him. On Sunday mornings, they'd row again and then go to church. But he could never convince Adel to attend the youth groups.

He was proud when his beautiful daughter obtained a rowing

scholarship to Rollins College in Winter Park, Florida, a small and exclusive liberal arts school that happened to have an extremely competitive rowing program.

It was while Adel was off to her first year of law school that he died from a heart attack while doing what he loved—rowing. His body, found by a fisherman, had collapsed in his boat with his feet still tied into the boat shoes on the foot stretcher.

With the insurance and inheritance, Adel suddenly became a wealthy but lonely, young woman.

Adel waited for Dave to finish his review of her brief.

"Checking your investments this morning, were you?" Dave asked without looking up.

"Yes," she said dryly, and it was true. "I'll be buying this building soon."

"Fine ... but you'll still work for me," he said with a touch of arrogance, mixing in a thinly veiled compliment.

"Not if you become so lazy you don't work anymore," she said, hinting at his mushrooming desire to hit golf balls into tin cups.

Dave ignored her remark. He learned long ago that she wouldn't quit, no matter how trivial the challenge. He saw it in everything she did. Whether it was teasing, rowing, or litigating a case, his associate would compete until she won.

"We have a famous new client," he said, looking up from the brief and flipping it to her. "They've been sued for sex discrimination by a woman named ... dang it ... I can't remember her name. Trial is imminent and they're displeased with their current lawyers. We're meeting their personnel manager ... John Moore—got that one right—at ten to discuss the case. I want you here. You remember a little about Title VII, don't you?"

"A little ..." Adel attended law school at the University of Florida where she had made law review and graduated in the top five percent of her class. Her paper had been about the evolving law of sexual harassment from the point of view of a harassed employee, and how to overcome the corporate and harasser's defenses. It was a perspective she favored, as she often rooted for the underdog. She had "booked" her social legislation course—receiving the highest grade—which included a study of the 1964 Civil Rights Act. Because of her academic excellence, she'd been sought after by many firms. She chose Dave McKerrin's firm because she liked him right off.

"Good. Read the file," Dave said, tossing a large binder at her with irreverence. "Meet me at nine and tell me about the law and any issues you see. Good job on the brief. See ya. By the way ... good morning."

She didn't say a word and left his office smiling, eager to dive into the new case. Not only did she love the subject, but also she knew the firm was struggling financially. Dave had confided this to her last week, though she wasn't a partner. The recession had hit Orlando hard and one of the hardest hit groups were lawyers. There were too many lawyers in the city. Adel was eager to pull more than her weight by racking up even more billable time.

CHAPTER 11

"But Mr. McKerrin, we can't have some young associate working on this case without supervision," John Moore said. "I'm coming to your firm because I've heard about you, not some young female named—"

Moore's sentence went unfinished. Adel had entered Dave's office, and Moore stared at her, stunned by her appearance.

"Mr. Moore, this is Adel Blair," Dave said, noticing her effect on him.

Adel offered her hand.

Recovering his composure, Moore said, "Hello, Ms. Blair. I'm sorry I don't mean to belittle you. It's just … my company can't afford to lose this case and we're in trouble. Our lawyers have botched it up procedurally for the last time. The judge is livid, so we're terminating their services."

Moore's company, River Ridge Defense Company, was a mammoth defense and space contractor, which bid billions of dollars worth of government contracts every year. It couldn't afford to be found guilty of violating Executive Order 11246, signed long prior by President Johnson, and which prohibited sexual discrimination in government contractors' work places. Although recent administrations didn't seem too interested in punishing such discrimination, it was still possible for NASA and other government agencies to "debar" River Ridge from competing for government contracts for at least one year. Besides the outcome of the case brought by Roberta Makinlon, the complainant, millions of profit dollars were at stake.

"We have to win or settle ... we cannot lose," Moore said. "But we can't settle because Makinlon wants way too much, and we can't set the wrong precedent. So we have to win at trial. We need ..."

A man, Adel thought. She gazed at Moore, waiting.

Moore suddenly felt asinine. "Someone with more experience," he continued, changing his thought midstream. "Someone like Mr. McKerrin here."

"That's understandable," Adel said. "Look, I know Title VII like the back of my hand. Dave needs me. I'll do the legwork and Dave can try the case, if that's what you want. Now shall we talk about the case?" she asked in her typically direct fashion, anxious to cut to the relevant issues.

Moore's frown eased.

Dave sat there watching. *By the time this meeting's over, he'll want her on the case,* he thought.

Moore explained the facts. Roberta Makinlon, a River Ridge employee, sued the company because she claimed that it discriminated against her based on her sex. According to her claim, the company allowed a male employee, Joe Collins, to "bump" her from her position as a computer operator.

Adel recalled the law review article she'd written in school. Title VII of the 1964 Civil Rights Act prohibited discrimination in the work place based upon race, color, religion, sex or national origin. The law had been enacted as a part of Lyndon Johnson's Great Society, and was regarded as a good piece of social legislation. However, the budget for the EEOC—the Equal Employment Opportunity Commission—which was created to enforce the law, was lacking sufficient funding during recent administrations.

"The matter isn't a harassment case as it's presented in the complaint," Adel said. "It's a simple disparate treatment case. Have there been any threats to raise harassment?"

"Not that I know of," Moore said, not knowing that harassment allegations had been tossed about in Makinlon's deposition and that these, ironically, might help win the case for River Ridge. The allegations may very well have been true. But at the time, harassment was often misunderstood or disregarded out of hand.

Adel regurgitated the law in her mind. Generally, there were two ways an employer could violate Title VII under established legal analysis. "Disparate treatment" of employees was one. Carrying out facially neutral policies or practices that had a "disparate impact" upon protected groups was the other. But in the mid-seventies a line of cases advanced the idea that sexual harassment, like racial harassment, also violated Title VII. As that case law developed, it established that there were two kinds of sexual harassment cases: "quid pro quo" cases, in which a higher level employee makes unwelcome sexual advances, making a subordinate's opportunities dependent upon his or her willingness to grant sexual favors; and "hostile environment" cases, in which an employee is subjected to pervasive comments, innuendos or other types of unwelcome sexual conduct to the point that a hostile or offensive work environment exists.

"Simply stated," Moore continued. "Makinlon was a computer operator who was bumped out of her position by Collins, the more senior employee, when a company cutback eliminated his higher position. Makinlon thinks we discriminated against her because we allowed Collins to bump her down even though he couldn't keypunch and she could. Keypunching is a menial task, similar to simple typing. But under the seniority system rules, Collins only had to be able to perform the stated job functions of the position into which he wanted to bump. Keypunching wasn't one of the stated job functions in the job description. So we actually could have been 'grieved' by Collins under the union's system, if he had not been allowed to bump Makinlon."

"Makinlon argues that this is all a pretext for discrimination because a month before the bump, one of the male directors in Makinlon's area who knew of the coming cutbacks allegedly asked her to consider taking a voluntary layoff in order to save a job for others," Moore explained. "Makinlon interpreted this to mean 'men'. The word around the workplace was that her husband has a lot of money and she didn't need to work."

As Moore continued, Adel pondered Makinlon's angle, discrimination through stereotyping. However, she was claiming sex discrimination simply because the union "bumping" system delivered an unsavory result. It protected senior employees under a collective bargaining agreement reached long ago between the union and River Ridge. It was a matter of choice by the unionized employees exercising desires to safeguard job security. What Adel had read of the Makinlon deposition transcript before the meeting made her suspect that Makinlon's lawyer might have sued under the wrong theory.

· · · ·

"Well, that event went well in spite of you," McKerrin said after Moore left, resuming their teasing as though it had never stopped.

"Only because you managed to hide your delirium" Adel said.

"It's the sobering effect you have on me. I want you to handle the case. I'll convince Moore. You already have … halfway. There are no technical legal issues that I see. She filed her charge on time, and filed suit within the statute of limitations. Those other lawyers were trying to make the case something it wasn't. It's pure and simple, discrimination or not. Interview your witnesses and prepare for trial. Two weeks is a short fuse, but you can do it. You know the drill. Have fun. See me if you have any problems. Don't screw it up!"

"Stay out of my hair and I won't," Adel said, as she walked out the door.

He smiled as she left, confident that she'd find a way to win the case and they'd secure a great new client.

Adel marched past her secretary into her office and asked to be undisturbed.

CHAPTER 12

"We've responded to all faxes and e-mails," Marta DeLong said, with the exuberance of one in a new position, loving the importance of her new boss. "Your memo to Phoenix is faxed. We've called everyone. Peckinpah and Waverly are out of the country, and ... oh! The Andrews memo went off, too! So I think we're done for—"

"Did Laughlin revise the Andrews memo like I told him?" Lou Scarlechek interrupted.

"Yes, I saw to it."

She smiled. She'd enjoyed riding herd over Laughlin, a lawyer and Vice President in the Department. As the boss's administrative assistant, Marta DeLong now wielded the power.

"And it went to Yates and his boys?"

"Yes."

Scarlechek leaned back in his chair and cracked a derisive grin.

DeLong saw his satisfaction and grew excited from watching her new source of vitality contemplating his move. She wondered whether they'd be staying late, determining he deserved to be rewarded.

DeLong had given Scarlechek sexual favors four more times in the last two weeks and—quid pro quo—had accepted the position of Scarlechek's administrative assistant.

Scarlechek's wife, Marsha, often found herself waiting for her husband's return from late evening "conference calls" with Phoenix, Van Nuys, Vancouver, and Hollywood. Marsha had her suspicions, but she was a material girl, and the good life was her reward. She turned a blind eye to any signs of Lou's behavior. *La dolce vita* was the opiate that blurred her vision, especially while driving her Benz to the spa for a day of pampering.

It was easy for Scarlechek to blame his absences on the demands of his position. He often claimed he was needed by Landis in Phoenix at five, six, or even seven o'clock Mountain Time. This unavoidably required him to be in his office two hours later, Eastern Time, standing by the computer, phone, and fax. Likewise, other matters could come in from Van Nuys, Vancouver, or Hollywood. Of course, the calls could last for hours; and he *always* needed an assistant on hand. Marsha didn't seem to care. For both of them, the illusions were enough.

I've earned getting laid, Scarlechek thought, reading Delong's mind. He checked her attire. *I'll bet she's wearing a thong.*

Marta DeLong was attractive only in a hard sort of way … or maybe it was that people felt she could be nice-looking. Whatever she had, it was negated by boastful pronouncements and her consuming desire to be a corporate player.

Once, in the break room, DeLong walked in on three lawyers milling about the coffee machine and discussing the procedural aspects of a large case that had been filed against Western Town in an Arizona federal court. The plaintiff claimed that Western Town stole his ideas for a sports complex constructed at the Arizona site in the eighties. Scarlechek had no role in the litigation, it being monitored by Landis himself in Phoenix. But when DeLong heard the lawyers speculating about who would get axed if the company lost, DeLong interrupted.

"You people don't know anything," she said. "It'll be Landis who'll get canned. Then, Lou and I'll have to get used to the dry climate in Arizona." She smirked, and then smugly looked over her shoulder as she strutted out. "Life's a bitch."

Now, she gazed at her boss with reverence. *Maybe tonight we'll—*

"Bring me my copy of the memo," Scarlechek commanded, wishing he could be a fly on the wall when its recipients perused Andrews's cannon shot across the bow. "I want to review it again."

The memo was a warning against "partnering," the methodology used by the Engineering Design and Construction Department, for a new theme park under construction in Phoenix. Western Town's construction lawyer in Phoenix, Lyle Andrews, with indirect reporting to Scarlechek, was its liability "watchdog." Andrews's memo lamented that partnering involved the company, as the owner, too much in the design and construction processes. This involvement could result in "untold millions of dollars in liability" to the public in personal injury cases, and would encourage "monumental construction claims" from outside architects, engineers, construction managers, and contractors. The young lawyer was new to the company and didn't realize there was no way the company, a show-oriented group, could stay out of these processes. It cut against the grain of Western Town to give up complete control of its own show.

Scarlechek had identified Andrews's naive fervor, and used it as a tool to carve more turf for himself. He urged Legal to stay involved in the special partnering deals to avoid opprobrium. Making Legal necessary in all company endeavors at all times was his goal, though anathema to the get-things-done business executives.

Andrews had written the memo after one meeting and two conference calls with Scarlechek. Scarlechek directed his construction lawyer to soften it, and then let Andrews send it to Sandy Yates and the other construction execs, copied to Andrews's direct boss and to Landis, Waverly, Peckinpah, and himself, all the right players.

"I think we're finished for the day, Lou," DeLong said with pride, as she handed him the memo. She walked around his desk and he smiled, anticipating her actions. She placed her hand on his monogrammed shirt and massaged his chest, and he flipped his hair and reread the memo with delight.

I'll bet they're shitting their pants, he thought.

How should I please him tonight, Delong wondered.

She had hounded Scarlechek with her desire to be his administrative assistant. She wanted to ride him like a surfer on a wave, milking him for every ounce of corporate rush he was worth. Having received her position in exchange for carnal consideration, a loyalty was developing between them that would last as long as the deal was of mutual benefit, as though they were business partners.

Scarlechek and DeLong kept their liaisons secret, but although Scarlechek was a lawyer, neither fully comprehended the reasons, moral considerations aside. This was not, strictly speaking, sexual harassment. The conduct was not "unwelcome," the gravamen of such a charge. But neither cohort realized that others could argue their behavior was evidence of a hostile or offensive working environment, an environment where a woman *had* to grant sexual favors to keep her job, or get it in the first place, in violation of Title VII.

She massaged with enthusiasm while he enjoyed her efforts and contemplated his expanding sphere of influence. He was quite pleased. More and more, people were responding to him. Vice presidents in the company felt unsure of his power source. Directors and managers wondered whether they were dealing with the future president of the company. Their uncertainty caused them to heed his dictates as he marked his territory like a dog.

To Sandy Yates, the highly favored Executive Vice President in charge of the company's construction processes, the Andrews memo came as a surprise attack. Yates viewed the memo as a shot out of the royal blue of supposed support. His power derived directly from Waverly, who had hired him. As part of the expensive deal to land Yates, Waverly granted his condition of autonomy, exempt from corporate politics, requirements, and niceties. As a result, Yates was renowned for singular management and direction style that tolerated no interference. It was as though he admonished the rest of the company, "You design and create the shows however you please; we'll build them and keep them running and clean, if you stay out of our way."

DeLong's hand was just lowering to Scarlechek's groin when the telephone line came alive. She sighed, but answered the call.

"It's Sandy Yates in Phoenix," she said, anxious and smiling. Delong watched her dark knight pick up the line, and a wave of excitement consumed her like water absorbed into litmus paper. Her pale skin suddenly radiated vibrant color.

DeLong could hear Sandy Yates' booming voice through the plastic.

"What the hell do you think you're doing? Don't you ever ..."

Scarlechek's face grew white, like a kid who'd overestimated his courage to watch scary parts of a horror flick. She waited for an eruption from her hero, but his continued silence meant he was on the receiving end of a tongue-lashing. Her heart sunk.

His eyes suddenly changed. They weren't forceful or fierce, but DeLong could now see they were no longer fearful. He was about to speak.

"Sandy, I had no idea. I haven't even seen it." He lied with the ease of an impudent teenager as he lifted the memo in his hand and gazed at it. "He's only dotted-line to me. He reports to Steve Florence. Of course I'm not trying to carve turf. I have no need of that. This kid's a maverick. Let me get to the bottom of it and I'll get back to you."

His facial expression changed again, like that of a scuba diver spying a Great White lurking in murky water.

"No, Sandy, I'm not looking for a battle with Waverly, I assure you. I'm just a lawyer; I'm not looking to run things. Please, let me find out about this. Rest assured, I'll speak to Andrews and Florence … Okay. Bye."

They hung up. Scarlechek turned to DeLong. He was angry and hurt, searching for a salve. He'd miscalculated and gone too far.

"Get your pad!" he commanded.

By the time she complied, he was calm again and turned to plotting.

"To Andrews," he said, dictating to her. "Paragraph. Have received your memo but haven't had chance to read. Period. Don't know if concur. Period. Hope you had presence of mind to speak to Yates first. Period. Strong feelings in this area, I would imagine. Period. Lou. Copy Florence and Yates."

"Will you sign?" DeLong asked, already accustomed to his methods.

"No. Put 'dictated but not read.'" It was an important addition that he often used, in case he needed to distance himself from his own written words. It also implied how busy he was. "Fax it all around. Do it now!"

DeLong complied and returned a short while later.

59

By this time Scarlechek had returned to his fantasy realm. His confidence and composure restored by a simple misdirection play—distancing himself from the memo—he was again desirous of sexual homage from his new chief aid.

DeLong, let down by his lack of machismo, had lost her desire.

"Lou, I forgot," she said. "My mother wanted to meet me for dinner. I'm sorry. I have to go."

CHAPTER 13

Lou Scarlechek took DeLong's departure as a biting criticism. It was as if she'd said, "You're not as powerful as I thought, and I'm disappointed." It upset him that she didn't succumb to his wishes. Her unspoken words stung, and left him with a throbbing desire that needed fulfilling. His thoughts turned to an alternative.

He'd been watching the cute typist since their first encounter. He noticed she'd begun to stay late again, and he occasionally positioned himself to encounter her. Each time, he carried her through the awkwardness by a display of perfect grace. He tested her, pretending nothing had happened and showing her how to do the same. His expertise at saving face and his unerring charm caused even those who mistrusted him to succumb to his act. He'd been attempting to win her back over, like a hypnotist lulling his victim to sleep.

Lou Scarlechek buzzed DeeDee Lane.

"Yes," she said, her voice bright and chipper.

"Will you come in please, DeeDee?" he asked. "Marta has left and I need to send a note to Peckinpah immediately. It's very important."

DeeDee's heart began to race. "Uh ... gee ..." *Excuse. I need an excuse. But he's the boss!*

"Okay," she heard herself utter, wishing she could reel the word back into her mouth. The intercom disengaged.

Why did I stay late tonight? Oh God ... I don't want to go in there.

She thought long and hard before getting up from her desk. Although she had convinced herself that the last encounter was her fault, DeeDee remained apprehensive around the man. She wanted

61

to go because, by God, she was determined to make it in the business world. If she couldn't make it in the wholesome atmosphere of Western Town, where could she? She wanted to confront and resolve this challenge, despite her inclination to run and hide. Something gnawing at her held her back. But finally, she drew a long breath and trudged down the hallway.

She opened Scarlechek's door and saw that once again the lights were dimmed. He sat on the couch, in the middle.

Here we go again, she thought, anger welling up in her. It felt amazingly good to have it seething through her veins.

"Come in, DeeDee. Close the door," he said. He let the lock go because he was quite sure everyone had gone home.

DeeDee complied, but this time she was going to let him know that what he wanted wasn't going to happen. She was going to stand up and be respected.

She mustered every dripping ounce of sarcasm she possessed and said, "Long day again, Lou?"

"Yes, you're catching on." He mocked her. "Come sit down, I want to talk to you. We'll *just talk.*"

Reluctantly, she complied.

"Lou," she said, "I don't want anything to happen. I only want—"

"DeeDee, you know it's time for you to grow up," he said, moving close to her. "You need to learn the ways of the world. This isn't some cornfield in Iowa. This is the big time, with big-time games and rules. Now, I like you and I hear you're good, too. But sometimes that's not enough. I know we have a legal secretary position opening up next month and I know you want it. ... You know what I want."

His voice echoed in her mind, like that of a drunken redneck in a topless bar. He moved closer, laying his hand on her thigh. His other hand began twirling a ringlet in her hair.

"Take some fatherly advice from me. I think you should grow up and recognize what's best for your career, and for what you want." At once his demeanor waxed impatient. "I'm not accustomed to doing this much talking about it."

He moved again, reaching for her waist and leaning over to kiss her.

"No, Lou! I don't want this!"

He leaned back and drew a slow, angry breath, exhaling so forcefully that she could smell garlic from his lunch.

"Then, DeeDee, you can kiss your future here goodbye, and I'll be very curious about your next review," he said, in a cold, deliberate tone. His voice had turned threatening.

She looked back at him helplessly. Fear rose from within—alarm that she could lose what had been providing so much satisfaction ... her job. It'd been the source of her first real feelings of worth. Tears welled in her eyes, and she became dazed and confused like a small animal in the clutches of a boa constrictor. Her choice was simple, yet complex. She could either fail herself here, or fall short in the eyes of her disbelievers back home.

He sensed his chance, bent over, and kissed her cheek. She surprised herself and allowed it. He did it again, this time longer, stroking her hair. She leaned back on the couch, at once resigned and disappointed.

He eagerly unbuttoned her silk blouse like a child grabbing candy out of a jar.

She rested her head back as he buried his face and nestled like a baby in the full and ample softness of her breasts. It continued and progressed, and she acquiesced, feeling as though she was falling through a long, inescapable tube and with each irretrievable inch that she fell, she knew she could never climb back.

She clenched her teeth in disgust, but it didn't matter to him so long as she stayed silent. Getting his way with someone new gave him more power. Power over another person, another soul.

When it was over and DeeDee had stumbled out of the room, Scarlechek smiled.

CHAPTER 14

The court clerk announced the case: "Makinlon v. River Ridge Defense Company."

The attorneys delivered their opening statements and the plaintiff's case was under way. Except for client John Moore at her side, Adel Blair sat alone at the counsel's desk. As always in trial, she felt some nerves. Dressed in a tailored navy suit and heels, and with her hair pulled into an elegant French twist, she cut a stunning figure in the courtroom.

The judge was a man, Federal District Judge Steven Raymond Livingston, III. Adel stared at him.

The judge's gender is presumed to be inconsequential, she thought with a slight smirk. But there was no denying his background. Judge Livingston was a southerner, born and raised in the Bible Belt's upper middle class. He had sat on the bench for decades, and was known for adhering to ultra-conservative Christian beliefs like a starfish to a rock. Adel knew he was pro-prayer in school, pro-life, pro-family values, anti-gay, and anything but politically correct. He was no mystery to Adel, for she had often argued before him in other cases.

She hoped Judge Livingston would listen to her for a change, and be swayed by the fact that she, a woman, didn't buy Makinlon's story. With him, she faced an uphill battle no matter *what* the issue or the strength of her client's argument; Adel felt that he believed she didn't belong in his courtroom. Her female contemporaries shared the sentiments. One friend had once explained that her first trial came before Judge Livingston, and that she had neglected to have her trial exhibits pre-marked by the clerk. The judge glowered from behind the bench while she labored to get them done, until he finally remarked, "You know, my wife keeps me waiting all the time, too … and that's why I leave her home."

Adel took delight in pondering the judge's painful dilemma: deciding whether to side with a female lawyer or a female civil rights plaintiff. In his estimation, they *all* belonged at home.

The courtroom was modern and austere, divided by a partition and swinging gate that separated the gallery from the staging area. There was an empty jury box with three elevated rows of twelve chairs each, where venires and juries sat in cases allowing a jury. To the left of the jury box was an attorney's podium for questioning witnesses in the witness stand next to the judge's bench.

Adel wondered what a jury would do with the case. There was no jury because Title VII didn't allow complainants the right to a jury trial. Title VII's "make whole" remedies were considered to be "equitable" in nature, historically the province of a judge, not a jury. It was anticipated that the right to trial by jury would soon be enacted into federal law by the President. A bill expected to pass both houses of Congress looked good, but a raging political football game continued over whether the new bill should be applied retroactively to existing cases.

Adel looked at Makinlon. *A jury might like her.*

Roberta Makinlon was a thin-framed woman of average height. She was pretty with her long, medium brown hair, delicate features, and feminine figure. But when Adel looked at her face, she got the distinct impression that Makinlon was perpetually mad. Her anger reminded Adel of a smoldering muck-fire, in which a raging inferno deceptively lies beneath the surface.

Adel studied the scene as Makinlon testified under direct examination.

He's coached her well, Adel thought. *She's not letting anger get the better of her.*

Adel also noticed that Judge Livingston seemed to be buying it. To win the case, Adel knew she needed to give him a reason to discredit and discard Makinlon's testimony. So far there was none.

Makinlon's lawyer brought his client to the close of her story.

"And this is your EEOC charge form that you filed?" he asked. After she confirmed its authenticity, he offered the key document into evidence.

"Any objection?" the judge asked, frowning at Adel.

"No, your honor," Adel said, rising quickly to her feet. There was no possible objection and, besides, she intended to use it.

"Nothing further, Your Honor," Makinlon's lawyer said.

Adel lifted Makinlon's deposition transcript from the table. She pretended to study it as she moved to the podium.

At the platform, she held the transcript up in her hand and focused on it more. Then she peered at Makinlon, still without saying a word. Leading Makinlon back to the transcript with her eyes, it was like a warning, as if to say, "Don't screw up, because it's all here and I'll make you look silly."

Everyone watched the exchange. The judge knew the silence was not stage fright, and just as his patience wore thin, Adel opened up.

"Now, Ms. Makinlon, your EEOC charge form that you just told us about … you signed that form, didn't you?"

"Yes."

"And your signature was sworn and notarized, wasn't it?"

"Yes."

"And that was under penalty of perjury, wasn't it?"

"Perjury? I don't—"

"Ms. Makinlon …," Adel interrupted, patronizing the plaintiff and raising the transcript higher.

"Well, yes, just above the signature space the form says I am testifying under penalty of perjury," said Makinlon.

"Thank you, Ms. Makinlon. Now, is that form complete and accurate?"

"Yes."

"And it's truthful and correct?"

"Yes."

"And it contains all the ways in which you believe you were discriminated against?"

"Yes."

There it was—the trap. Adel knew she had her.

"But Ms. Makinlon, do you recall giving your deposition on July 17 of this year?" Again, Adel held up the transcript.

"Yes, I do," Makinlon said, her anxiety rising. The deposition had been unpleasant.

"Now isn't it true, Ms. Makinlon, that you believed Steve Quincy was in love with you?" Quincy was another computer operator who had seniority over Makinlon.

"Yes, he was."

"And that was because he told you that every day?"

"Yes, he did."

"And isn't it true, Ms. Makinlon, that you believed Bobbie Beamans wanted you sexually?"

"Yes, he did."

"And you knew that because on a daily basis he either told you that, or he would pinch your bottom, or engage in other sexual contact, correct?"

"Yes, it happened every day!" she said, reliving her frustration.

"And once you thought he purposely bumped into you with his hand held up so that it touched your breast, correct?"

"Yes, yes, he did!" The tears began to well. "He said it was an accident, but I knew it wasn't!"

"And Jim Connagher, he told dirty jokes daily?"

"Yes."

"And once he suggested that you two drive off property for a 'lunch-quickie,' the subject of one of his jokes, correct?"

"Yes, he did that! We were friends, and he did that!" She turned to the judge as she began to cry.

He glared at her, unsettling her even more, for he doubted that all these good Christian workingmen could do such things.

"And isn't it true that your manager, Tim Arnold, once asked you to have sex with him in the storage closet?"

"Yes, that's true too. I was shocked! He said he was joking, but he wasn't. I could tell." Makinlon's tears were now flowing freely.

"Now, none of this is on your EEOC form that you stated was complete and accurate, is it?"

"They did do all that," she cried. "They all wanted me!"

"But none of that is on the form, is it?"

"But—"

"Just answer the question," Judge Livingston interjected, feeling impatience and growing animosity toward the woman.

"No … it's not, but it's all true!"

Adel continued the barrage. "And, Ms. Makinlon, isn't it true that you thought that your director, Mike Hall, had asked you to take a voluntary layoff not only because your husband had a good job, but also because Mr. Hall had allegedly been pressured by the wives of all your male coworkers to get rid of you, because they knew their husbands all wanted you?"

"Yes, that was true too! Just ask him. He told me so. And the way they all treated me at all the parties! They were afraid of me. All of them! Their men all wanted me! They all wanted me!" She bawled as she muttered the words.

"So, it wasn't discrimination … it was the wives of your co-workers, wasn't it?"

"It was discrimination! They didn't make him keypunch! But it was the wives, too!"

"But that isn't on the form either, is it?"

"No," Makinlon whimpered.

"But you just testified that your charge form was complete and accurate!" Judge Livingston interjected. His tone was incredulous.

"It was!" Makinlon sobbed.

Adel could see that in her emotional state Makinlon was incapable of explaining away the inconsistency. She glanced quickly at Makinlon's lawyer, who was grimacing. Then she checked Judge Livingston. He'd found his excuse.

It's over, she thought. *Judge Livingston won't believe another word she says.*

Adel knew she'd made the woman appear delusional in the judge's eyes. Makinlon had testified inconsistently. It was a risky but brilliant move, under the circumstances. Makinlon's lawyer was the key—he didn't understand sexual harassment. Adel's cross-examination had given the plaintiff seminal proof of a "hostile environment" harassment claim. Makinlon's lawyer could have moved to amend his client's claim and finished proving it up. But he didn't because, as Adel suspected, he didn't understand the issue. He could only comprehend that his client appeared psychotic.

Prejudicial judge, ignorant lawyer, emotional plaintiff—all factors in an equation securing yet another ruling for a big corporation, Adel reasoned. She merely had to coast through trial now, calling up witnesses to deny the allegations and confirm Makinlon's delusions.

She heard the courtroom door open behind her, and she turned to see Dave McKerrin leaving. Having snuck in without Adel's knowledge, he glanced at her with a hint of the wry smile that only she recognized. He, too, knew it was over.

"Your Honor, it was only the unbiased, preordained workings of the seniority system that rendered the result of which Ms. Makinlon complains," Adel argued in closing. "Her claims of sex discrimination are figments of her overactive imagination."

Judge Livingston announced his ruling right from the bench. "I find that River Ridge Defense Company did not discriminate against the Plaintiff. Counselor, please draft proposed findings of fact and conclusions of law and submit them to me ... copy opposing counsel, of course. Do either of you have anything further to discuss?"

"No, Your Honor," Adel stated, hopping to her feet. She watched Makinlon's counsel hesitate before rising slowly, disappointment washing across his face. She watched Makinlon sobbing with her head on her arms.

"No, Your Honor," the lawyer said, not wishing to prolong the agony.

"Fine. Good day, and thank you very much, ladies and gentlemen," the judge said.

"All rise," the bailiff barked as the judge got up.

Adel smiled as the judge exited the room, sensing Moore's delight when he hugged her. But it was strange; she didn't feel the usual jubilance of victory as her peripheral vision took in the image of a sobbing Makinlon being consoled by her lawyer.

CHAPTER 15

That evening Adel returned to her office loaded down with her briefcase and "bomb bag" filled with the case files. She sighed as she stepped into her office; it was a relief to be in familiar surroundings.

She reclined in her burgundy high-backed chair and gazed at the pictures on the wood-paneled wall across from her desk. Losing herself in a photo of her racing a single shell at a national competition, her mind turned to her father and his relentless will to compete. She turned her attention to the photo of him on her desk.

You were so tough, Daddy. I hope I'm like you.

For a fleeting moment she allowed herself contentment. But she couldn't help wondering how much of Makinlon's allegations were true.

Makinlon's attorney made a major mistake, she thought. *He should have sued for "hostile environment" harassment. When those allegations came out under cross, he wasn't prepared. I opened the door for him, and he didn't walk through.*

Exactly what did I accomplish today, she wondered. *All those wild accusations from Makinlon—they must not have been true. If they were, I certainly didn't do womankind any good today. Hey ... I did my job—I won. Now, I need to go home and get on the erg.*

As Adel prepared to leave, she noticed a paper star taped to her door. It was a firm custom to acknowledge trial winners in this fashion upon their return from battle. But this one had a note—"See me." It was Dave McKerrin's handwriting.

He's still here?

She discarded her bags and went to his office, where she found him waiting with a bottle of champagne.

"Congratulations. You managed to bumble your way through again," Dave said, as he grinned wide and poured her a glass of bubbly. "Moore called me from his car and raved. He wants you to speak to his personnel director's association on employment discrimination issues. It's a golden opportunity ... there'll be a lot of big companies there. "

"Great," she said, with hardly any emotion. "When?"

"You need to call him tomorrow and set it up. Now come on, let's toast, then I'll take you to dinner."

"Dave, I've got to train ..."

"Oh, give it a rest," he said, refusing to take no for an answer. "You're going to turn into a flippin' oar, you pull on 'em so much. You did a fine job today. Let me take you to dinner."

She hesitated. "All right."

. . . .

As they approached Maloney's, Adel could see it was packed as usual. It was Dave's favorite place because of the Stilton cheese-encrusted Irish Burger. As they entered and saw the gyrating crowd on the dance floor, she thought back to the time Dave introduced her to Michael three years before, and it warmed her heart.

Dave and Adel negotiated the turbulent throng and sat at the bar. She enjoyed talking to him about the trial and relaxing with a beer. After a while, over the buzz of the crowd enveloping them, she heard a familiar voice from behind.

"Uncle Dave, how ya' doing?" It was Michael McKerrin once again, like three years past.

Feeling déjà vu, Adel wondered whether Dave had arranged this. Her hunch proved correct when she noticed his shooting glance and guilty grin.

"Michael! How are you?" Dave blurted out. But before Michael could answer he continued, "Adel, this is my nephew Michael that I've told you about. You know ... the rower."

Adel picked up on Dave reenacting their first meeting, re-pushing buttons on the stifled relationship that she wouldn't allow to develop.

"Oh, hi," she said, rolling with the joke and feigning boredom.

She checked him up and down. Michael's tall, lean frame sported navy pants and a white button-down with his collar unbuttoned and tie loosened. Adel noticed a vibrant link of light between his dark blue tie and his cobalt eyes. His large, angular hand engulfed the bottle of Sam Adams Light, reminding her of her father.

"Michael, this is Adel Blair, my associate." The words were filled with a certain pride even as Dave continued his charade.

"Hello," Michael said. "Come here often?"

"After trial, like the one I just finished."

"Oh. What kind of case?"

"Title VII. Sex discrimination, of course."

"You win?"

"Yes, I did."

"*Not* representing the plaintiff, I suppose?" His voice turned judgmental.

"No, as a matter of fact I represented River Ridge Defense Company. Your Uncle is helping me celebrate."

"Ahh-h," he said, his tone contemptuous. "A big corporation snows another judge. Nice touch, using a superwoman like you to do it. Obvious ... but nice. The judge wasn't very smart, was he?" Not letting her answer, he continued, "You know, I'll love you even more, Adel, when you learn to fight for the little people."

"You're such a bleeding heart," she said, ignoring the casual declaration of his emotions.

"I only wish I had found you before my corrupt uncle, so I could have saved you from the loathsome practice of representing big corporations. Your talents are wasted on those who don't need them."

"Oh, Michael, me boy," Dave said in Irish accent. "You're nothing but a flamin' liberal who doesn't know his place. A state attorney with, of all things, a bleeding heart. The Public Defender's office wouldn't have you, so you join the prosecutors to go after big corporations, knowing they've always been the backbone of me practice."

Adel knew Dave was once again teasing his nephew. Michael had walked from the Public Defender's office on a matter of principle. The State Attorney jumped at the chance to hire a potential star.

"I wouldn't have them, you mean! They didn't want to fight. I want to fight for people. Now, in Economic Crimes I can do that. I wish you would represent the people, Adel. With your unyielding spirit, you'd do so well—so much good. And you'd make tons of money—more than working for Dave's clients who'll constantly chop your hourly rate. Most firms looking for corporate clients are struggling now, anyway, in this economy. It's too late for you, Uncle. You're locked in. But Adel, you and I could form our own firm and bring America's corporate autocracy to its knees."

"Oh my God, we've got him on his soap box, Adel." Dave said. "He's trying to steal you from me in more ways than one, now."

Adel listened, wondering how many times she'd heard this all before. It'd gone in one ear and out the other. She'd never leave Dave McKerrin.

Why does Michael think it's any different, she wondered. *There's no great moral purpose in shifting from representing corporations to "people." Corporations are, after all, nothing more than groups of people—big powerful groups.*

The thought made her muse over something incompatible, the subject having occurred to her before. She wondered why, when she watched athletic events, she always pulled for the underdog. *In fact, most people seem to do that. Why?* She remembered her law school paper, which she'd written from the perspective of representing the employee. *What happened?*

"Adel ... hello! Am I getting through to you?" Michael grabbed her shoulders and gently shook her.

"Your compassion is admirable, Michael," Adel said coolly, not allowing herself to give in.

Michael sensed it was time to change the subject. If she'd ever come around, it'd have to be on her own. No man could ever change her, he knew that.

"Okay," he said, "I'll leave you alone ... my little corporate kitten. Tell me about your trial today."

"She was marvelous," Dave interjected and told what he'd witnessed.

Somehow, to Adel, the words rang hollow.

CHAPTER 16

The passenger in the speeding vehicle feared for his life. The young construction lawyer clenched his arms to his side, acutely aware of his boss's red Swiss Army knife attached to the keys banging against the dash. Lou Scarlechek was driving through the streets like a maniac.

They were in no real hurry, returning from a meeting across the property. Hanging tight to the door handle with whitened knuckles, the lawyer gave thanks that Scarlechek at least slowed for the red light as he barked orders to Marta DeLong on his cell phone. The lawyer watched in amazement as Scarlechek's Mercedes swung a left turn from the right lane in front of oncoming traffic. Horns blared, tires screeched, and irate shouts could be heard, but Scarlechek showed no concern, as if he were the grand marshal of a parade.

Scarlechek continued barking orders to DeLong while his vehicle raced ahead.

Man, Scarlechek drives like a tourist, the young lawyer thought. *Only worse. Stop signs? Speed limit signs? Medians? Other people? Is there a reason Scarlechek should even begin to consider any of these things?* The young lawyer could tell Scarlechek never even asked the question. He couldn't care less. The Mercedes only knew two speeds: full out and stop, and the young lawyer was grateful that Scarlechek didn't pick up his second cell phone and try to drive with no hands. The Swiss Army knife continued clanging back and forth.

"When's the next Executive Committee meeting?" Scarlechek asked DeLong.

"January."

"Where?"

"Vail, at the corporate chalets."

"The company has chalets at Vail?" he asked. This excited him.

You didn't hear me? DeLong thought. "Yes," she replied.

"Are any of them better than the others?" Scarlechek demanded to know.

"I don't know. I've not been there."

"Find out. Get me the best."

"Peckinpah will get the best," DeLong said.

"Just the best one you can," he retorted, irritated. "One last thing, get me the phone number for the firm McKerrin, Smith and O'Donnell. I want to set up a seminar on that EEO crap."

"The company has an EEO specialist in HR who does that, Lou. We don't need—"

"Just get me the number!" he interrupted harshly. His tone softened. "I'm sorry, but I've heard there's a woman there who knows the stuff better than anyone. I want the best for my people. It'll be worth the expense."

"Yes, Lou," DeLong answered, suspicious of his motives. She didn't buy it, but it didn't matter.

After they disconnected, Scarlechek's thoughts fell to Adel Blair as he barged ahead of another driver at a four-way stop sign. He could still see her sweaty, half-naked, goddess-like body on the awards stand, like a slave woman about to be sold at auction. He intended to be the purchaser. His scheme had come to him over the weekend while reading a news article about the River Ridge case. The plan excited him.

His thoughts turned to Tom Peckinpah and the next Executive Committee meeting.

Corporate chalets in Vail, Colorado, he pondered. *Nice. Maybe a little skiing. But, Peckinpah. How do I get in tight with Peckinpah?*

The young lawyer shuddered as Scarlechek reached for his other cell phone. Wedging the Mercedes steering wheel between his knees, Scarlechek began punching numbers, looking at the keypad more than the road. The lawyer had grown up Catholic, and he started reciting Hail Marys for the first time since the bar exam. The pocket knife scratched the dashboard.

CHAPTER 17

That evening when DeeDee entered Scarlechek's office, she noticed the lights were dim as usual.

Good, she thought. *I don't want anyone to see me ... ever.*

She looked at him, but didn't smile. He was sitting behind his desk concluding a telephone conversation and gestured for her to come in, covering the mouthpiece.

"Hang on, sweet thing," he said. "This is very important."

He spoke into the phone, "Yes, Bruce, that's right. You never know who'll win a case like that."

He glared at DeeDee and snapped his fingers at her while he listened. Jerking his hair from his eyes, he motioned for her to lock the door, wondering why such obvious instructions were necessary.

DeeDee complied, taking silent position by his chair.

She wore gray pumps and a matching skirt and jacket over a white blouse that buttoned to her neck like a Sunday school teacher. If she'd ever worn clothes hinting at sexuality, she didn't now. A single black pearl adorned her outfit.

He finished his call and placed the receiver down. Without a word, he turned to her abdomen and unbuttoned her blouse like a kid opening a toy cabinet. He didn't look her in the eye, but pulled her blouse free from her skirt. He grasped her waist with both hands, lifted her onto his lap, and tugged her body close. He unhooked her brassiere and caught the heaviness of her breast. He fondled her, enjoying her softness and savoring her hushed obedience. Then his hand groped underneath her skirt to explore the softness of her hose-covered thighs.

I can't stand myself, DeeDee thought as she felt one of his finger-nails snag her nylons. *I'm so weak.*

She wondered how she'd come to this, while he slobbered on her neck. It was like she'd been on a plateau and was suddenly swept over the cliff.

I was a cheerleader, she thought. *A homecoming queen. I should've listened to Daddy.*

She blamed herself for leading Scarlechek on, but knew deep down it wasn't her fault. Regardless, she despised herself for letting it continue. She felt worthless.

She thought of her new job. She was to receive the new legal secretarial position, just as soon as the Legal Department found the right attorney to hire. She'd try to enjoy reporting to her family the second promotion within six months, knowing word would reach Dirk. But she was disgusted with herself.

On one or two occasions she'd tried to cope with her distaste by convincing herself that she enjoyed it with Scarlechek. After all, he was intelligent, rich, and powerful. But she quickly dismissed the preposterous suggestion, holding him in contempt. It might have been different if *he* was different, but that in itself was a contradic-tion. All that happened, all that *was* happening defined his character ... and her own.

Lou's so influential, she thought. *But he craves power. He's no better than a drug addict and I'm his pusher. He's a selfish faker ... and I'm no better.*

Her self-esteem plummeted. Gone was the perkiness. Her co-workers had noticed and begun to gossip. To them she'd become downright morose.

"DeeDee, let's go out," they'd say after work.

"No," became her standard response, barking it when they be-came insistent, losing her ability to like other people because she couldn't like herself.

Scarlechek moved her over to the couch.

As she lay back, she thought, *I'm just a common little whore.*

CHAPTER 18

Adel Blair returned to her office late that evening after visiting the corporate office of a new client. She planned a quick stop to check her messages and calendar, before heading home to cross-train on her stationary bike.

She found a message on her desk that excited her. The Executive Vice President of the Western Town Legal Department had called and wanted her to present a seminar on equal employment opportunity. She was to call him the next day to discuss it.

Another big corporation, Adel thought. *And what a prestigious client to land. It could be just the shot in the arm the firm needs.*

She thought about calling Dave, but decided it could wait until morning. Driving home, she wondered what Michael would have to say.

CHAPTER 19

"Marta! Has Adel Blair returned my call?" Scarlechek yelled as he rushed into his office at ten o'clock the next morning.

"No, she hasn't," DeLong replied, wondering why he was so concerned. *Good morning to you too,* she thought. *It's just a seminar.*

"Get her for me, now!"

DeLong was fumbling for the number when another secretary who happened to overhear remarked, "Adel Blair, eh? I know why he wants her."

"Why?" DeLong inquired.

"She's absolutely gorgeous—all six feet of her. Has the body of one of those aerobics instructors, too. I used to work at the firm across from hers. Everyone, men and women, gawk at her whenever she's around."

DeLong didn't respond, but her eyes narrowed as she dialed the number. *That's why he's so concerned about her call.*

DeLong was coming to know Scarlechek rather well. Each day brought more insight and she was able to pinpoint his motives. *The man's prehistoric,* she thought. She knew she wasn't his only consort. She could tell DeeDee was involved, and she sensed its effect on DeeDee. DeLong speculated about Scarlechek's first administrative assistant, Janet Watson.

Lou's a shark, she thought. *A roaming scavenger, who's hungry and ruthless, and repeatedly biting people. It's all right,* she thought. *Ride the wave, surfer girl.*

"Adel Blair, please," she said to the telephone receptionist.

"Ms. Blair's office," she heard.

"Is Ms. Blair in? I'm calling for Lou Scarlechek."

"One moment."

"Hello," Marta heard. The voice was forthright and unpretentious.

Suddenly, Marta sensed a whoosh from behind and shivered. At once, the Great White had whizzed by her so fast her skirt tail flapped in the breeze.

"Ms. Blair, I'm calling for Lou Scarlechek at Western Town and, I'm sorry … but he's just stepped out of the office. Will you hold for him, please?" DeLong became embarrassed at the all-too-frequent moments like this, abhorring the appearance of incompetence. Scarlechek had commanded her to get Adel Blair on the phone, she rushed to do it, and then he jetted out of his office without explanation. She wondered what correlation intelligence had to ADHD.

Adel's voice was amused. "Yes, I'll hold," she said.

"Mr. Scarlechek wants to speak to you about giving a seminar out here about EEO concepts. Do you do that?"

"Yes, quite frequently. Is there any subject in particular?"

DeLong had no idea, but something came over her and she couldn't resist. "Sexual harassment," she uttered. "Is that within your forte?" DeLong smiled, stricken by the irony of the notion. *Lou Scarlechek requesting a seminar on sexual harassment—that's rich.*

"Yes, I do that often," Adel said. "In fact—"

"Oh, excuse me, Ms. Blair. Here's Lou now."

He blew past her and back into his office without explanation or apology.

"Okay," Adel said.

Scarlechek came on the phone, a little out of breath. "Adel Blair?"

"Yes, hello."

"Hello, I'm Lou Scarlechek," he said. "I'm the Executive Vice President of the Legal Department and the General Counsel for Western Town here in Orlando." His words were set heavy, seeking to impress.

"Nice to meet you over the phone."

"Very nice to meet you," Scarlechek said, switching his tone from "impress" to "charm." "I've heard that you are *the* expert on

Title VII issues; and we'd love for you to come give us a seminar on racial discrimination in the workplace."

"Racial discrimination? Your secretary said … hmm-m."

"Yes, racial discrimination," Scarlechek said. *No one will accuse me of being insensitive,* he thought.

"Any particular subject, or just a broad overview?"

"A broad overview would be best. Assume we don't know anything about it. Your audience will be the lawyers in my department. I hold bi-weekly update meetings with them, but every month or two we do a special meeting at a different place on property. We'd like to plan on doing this one with you in late January at The Southwesterner Steakhouse, in a private meeting room. You've heard of it?"

"Yes, I have."

"And, of course, you'll join us for dinner. Then you speak, and cocktails afterward," he said.

"Sounds lovely."

"My assistant, Marta, will contact you with the particulars in a week. Oh! And, of course, we'll expect to be billed your hourly rate for preparation and participation. What is it, by the way?"

"Two hundred an hour."

"Fine," Scarlechek said, squelching his normal instinct to quibble. "I may call you again soon, to talk about your presentation."

Adel was excited as they ended the conversation. Being paid to speak was highly unusual. Business groups could hold auditions for lawyers hoping to get a chance to show prospective clients how smart they were.

But his secretary, she thought. *Boy, was she off base.*

CHAPTER 20

It was early January and Tom Peckinpah relished the sight of Colorado snow piled high on the slopes as he drove through Vail to his WTOC meeting.

Thank God for El Niño, he thought, as he marveled at the fresh powder he'd just skied.

The meeting was still underway when he arrived. He'd taken a break while the others continued through the afternoon. He surveyed the plush conference room and saw his boys were all still there. It reminded him of his college football team, the guys all working hard to make him look good.

It was a Saturday evening and they were finishing up two days of business discussions. Ashtrays, remnants of refreshments, PowerPoint printouts, and crumpled papers covered the mahogany conference table, and charts and graphs bearing violent slashes and cryptic red markings decorated the room. The men propped their outstretched legs in various configurations on the table and chairs, while Cuban cigar smoke lingered in the air.

WTOC—the Western Town Operating Committee—was Peckinpah's brainchild. The members now congregated at the Carlisle Convention Center next to the corporate chalets at Vail to discuss major operational and directional issues. They met monthly, usually at headquarters in Phoenix, but occasionally elsewhere, depending on Peckinpah's preference. Expense was never a concern—those in the boys' club were entitled. At this gathering, Peckinpah had been particularly invigorated because of his passion for traversing the slopes.

He felt the warmth of power when he thought of what they'd

accomplished for him while he'd been skiing. The all-male group consisted of the ten executive vice presidents of the company, most of them hand-picked by him. He loved this committee. It'd been deliberately structured to resemble a football team—eleven members with himself and Waverly as the coaches.

He sauntered over to the window while the boys continued their talks.

Peckinpah stared intently at the snowfall, his hands on his hips and his legs spread, reveling in his station in life, as though he were the "Fortunate Son" in the Creedence song. Despite well-off parents and the best of everything throughout his life, an innate competitiveness and drive had spurred his ambitions, resulting in tremendous success in school, football, and business. He remembered how he'd met Donald Town's daughter, Janis, at the University of Arizona where he had thrilled the crowd as a Heisman-winning quarterback. Football and Janis had helped get him here, no doubt, but that didn't matter. *Using connections is fine,* he'd always thought, *so long as one uses them well.*

He picked out his image in the glass. He was a large, handsome man with wide shoulders, massive legs, short blond hair, and sky-blue eyes. The women had always fallen for his Aryan looks. Even Janis had been attracted to him immediately. She was a raving blonde beauty who could've had anyone she chose—the homecoming queen when Peckinpah was captain of the football team. She was smart as well as friendly and nice, and her popularity was real because she was real. After they met, she practically threw herself at his feet to the amazement of everyone in school.

He remembered the radical irreverence he'd had in his youth as a football star. Wild feelings of supremacy would overwhelm him. After all, he was admired by thousands. He could do whatever he wished and sometimes, when celebrating with buddies, he did. He felt that way now.

Through Janis, whom he married right out of college, he'd become a father and a responsible family man, quelling his reckless diversions. For the most part, anyway. She had tempered him in the same way water cooled a hot blade.

Scarlechek eyeballed the CEO from his reclining chair, studying the man on top of his world who stared out the window. After the Lake Eola regatta, Scarlechek had ordered and read everything that could be discovered about the man.

Peckinpah hadn't immediately gone to work at Western Town. It was two injury-laden years in the NFL that forced him into the business world. Peckinpah worked his way up to the position of president and then CEO of The Becklace Company, a publishing and multimedia conglomerate. It took him only fifteen years, becoming highly visible among the autocracy of corporate America. He was handsome, hard driving, and socially accepted on high levels, with many ties going back to his preppy youth.

Peckinpah long anticipated Donald Town's retirement when he grew too old to continue as Western Town's CEO—it'd be natural for him to bring in his son-in-law as his replacement. They genuinely liked each other, and Peckinpah had all the right training and attributes. When Donald Town retired, the Board of Directors ultimately offered Peckinpah the position, but he didn't come easy. It took three months of intense negotiations and his father-in-law's intervention before he finally signed a complex, but favorable contract chock-full of benefits, stock options, and incentive bonuses tied to the company's success.

Peckinpah became a national business icon when, five years after the opening of the Orlando Western Town Resort, the company's stock split three to one. He reported personal earnings of sixty million dollars to the SEC and IRS for that year. Every news and business rag in the country scrambled to plaster his face on their covers.

Scarlechek first met Peckinpah after Landis hired Scarlechek's firm for the Vancouver transaction. Peckinpah breezed in with his administrative assistant, received a better-be-quick briefing, blessed the deal, and breezed out to Whistler-Blackcomb to ski. Scarlechek envied Peckinpah then, pondering how wonderful it must be to have people rushing about to please you. These people worked hours and hours, weeks and months to give Peckinpah a five-minute update. They lived to receive ten seconds of his praise, all the while contributing to his tens of millions.

Now Scarlechek was part of Peckinpah's team of executives, but the man barely noticed him. In deference to Landis, Scarlechek was one of a few that Peckinpah had allowed to be hired, instead of handpicking someone himself.

Peckinpah turned and glanced at Waverly sitting at the head of the table. He smiled as Waverly continued to ramrod the meeting through the end of the lengthy agenda.

He's like my college center, Peckinpah thought, as he took his seat at the head of the table . *He makes things happen at my command, and protects me with undying loyalty.*

Catching Waverly's eye, he gave him a simple wrap-it-up twirl of his finger.

"Listen up!" Waverly snapped. "Look guys, it's been two days. We're almost done. Let's stay focused. Next on the agenda is Benjamin. What have you got, Mike?"

"Only the 'Glass Ceiling'," Mike Benjamin said.

"Christ, not that crap again," someone close to Scarlechek murmured. Scarlechek grimaced with empathy, forgetting for the moment that this was a matter of legal concern.

Western Town was a typically white-male dominated organization, and with good reason, thought the white-males. Further down the chain of command, the company employed twenty senior vice presidents, none of which were female. Out of forty vice presidents, a few females graced the guild, and there were a handful of female directors out of one hundred. Yet, females made up approximately fifty percent of the company's overworked and underpaid managers. Unseen was the barrier keeping the "softer side" to where they could be taken advantage of most.

The figures were roughly the same for male minorities through the ranks, except that there was one senior vice president of Mexican descent—Raul Martinez. He had risen through the ranks as one of the original employees of Western Town in Phoenix. When he was twelve, he'd been hired to play a Mexican boy in one of the original shows, and soon became a favorite of Donald Town. Through hard work, patience and tolerance, and the guiding hand of Donald Town, Martinez bootstrapped himself to the position of Senior Vice

President of Theme Park Operations. Even still, he never was able to crack into the good-ole-boys club, the Operating Committee.

"We've got to make some decisions about this," Benjamin continued. "Tiyona Morgan is pressing me hard. She says we may be targeted by the Department of Labor."

"What decisions?" Waverly asked impatiently. This issue had been discussed many times, but no one ever paid any attention.

"Well—"

"Tell me about this 'Glass Ceiling' again," Peckinpah interrupted. "I've forgotten what we discussed last month."

"It's Senator Simons from Iowa and the Women's Bureau of the Department of Labor. The Woman's Bureau maintains that since the enactment of the discrimination laws in the sixties, corporate America has let women and minorities flood the workplace but has kept them in lower level positions. They claim we've … I mean, corporate America … has erected subtle barriers that prevent women and minorities from rising too high in the ranks. Hence the term, 'Glass Ceiling.' You can't see it, but it's there. Simons conducted Senate hearings to study the phenomena. It's been described as 'second generation job discrimination.'"

"Hell, they've been let into the job market, they can't want to control it too," the same man who commented earlier lamented, not catching his own ironic timing.

"A fair chance to participate would be the point, don't you?" Peckinpah said to the man, who cowered and offered no response.

Let 'em pay their dues like I did, he thought.

"So anyway," Peckinpah continued, "what's this got to do with us?"

"Well, Tiyona believes we may be targeted by a Department of Labor investigation. She thinks the DOL views us as a prime example. She also thinks that organizations like NOW and the NAACP may be looking for a plaintiff or two in a few different companies, to file class action lawsuits."

Scarlechek suddenly snapped to, realizing the discussion could flow his way.

"Tiyona has been making recommendations in memos for some time now about what needs to be done," Benjamin went on. "She says we need to adopt written policies, distribute them, hold seminars, and start promoting women and minorities into higher management levels."

"How do you hold seminars on promoting people?" someone asked.

"It's not just about promoting people. The seminars would cover the whole gamut of discrimination issues. Erasure of prejudice, getting rid of harassment, you know, all those things to try to make the workplace more fair and less ... well ... hostile."

"At what cost?" Peckinpah asked.

"I really don't know," Benjamin said sheepishly. He knew what was coming.

Peckinpah shot Waverly a look.

"God Damn it!" Waverly yelled. "You know better than to come here expecting decisions without all the facts! How can you make a recommendation, and we decide anything, without all the fuckin' facts?"

"I'm sorry," Benjamin said, embarrassed. "But one thing might be in order now—promoting Tiyona as a symbolic gesture. I'd like permission."

"We won't do that only because she's a woman and she's black," Waverly said. "What the hell kind of an example would that set? You know we've restricted the appointment of new directors—we have too many already and they cost too much fuckin' money." The restriction was an unwritten policy that had resulted in the company's high number of women managers. These women hoped to be promoted to a director position, but never received it.

"Besides, I've told you, you don't have all the facts, so we're moving on ... to something pleasant, I might add—movies. Last subject, guys. Let's go. John, tell us about *Chief Joseph*."

"It grossed almost twenty-five million dollars domestic in its opening week!" John Martinson, the Executive Vice President in charge of Productions, boasted. *Chief Joseph* was the Company's recently released Western about the plight of the Nez Perce Indians in Idaho and Montana, and their famous chief. After a long, cold chase with many courageous battles against the ubiquitous white man,

Chief Joseph had finally given up and said, "From where the sun now stands, I will fight no more forever."

"Marvelous!" said Peckinpah. "And the projections?"

"It'll continue," Martinson said.

"Productions is going to save profitability, Tom," the Finance executive said. "With our prior hits and now *Chief Joseph's* pace, the Studio will hit its record year and better. This will far outweigh the theme park downturn in this damned recession, and overall performance will stay even. We're going to make it through this recession well."

"Outstanding, gentlemen!" Peckinpah slammed his fist on the table. "That's what I like to hear! And with the marketing strategies we discussed earlier, we'll end up with growth this fiscal year. Excellent! My board of directors will be very pleased."

Peckinpah couldn't contain his delight. The forty-two-year-old leader was guiding his company through the recession like no other CEO in America. Satisfaction pulsed through his veins as he thought of the financial rewards under his contract. Knowing that he'd spend the next day on the slopes contributed to his euphoria. He felt like celebrating.

Waverly terminated the meeting and Peckinpah gloated as he grasped Waverly's hand. Looking about, he observed his jovial troops doing the same. They stood in small groups and congratulated each other.

"Anyone want to join me in the Chair Lift?" he asked loudly. It was the lounge downstairs in the convention center.

Scarlechek perked up and wondered what opportunity this might present.

CHAPTER 21

Peckinpah felt gratified as he listened to the accolades from three of his lieutenants and Scarlechek at the Chair Lift Lounge table. *This is what life's all about,* he thought.

It was two hours, some hors d'oeuvres, and four dry, vodka martinis later. He couldn't help eyeing a gorgeous blonde sitting alone at the bar while he joked around with the guys. He felt warmed by the woman's subtle but unmistakable glances in his direction. Only he had a straight-on view from their table, so he leaned back in his chair and took in the sight of her crossed leg bouncing like she was on speed.

"Tom," one man said. "You've led the company better than Donald could've dreamed."

"He must be proud," another said.

"Janis, too," a third said.

Peckinpah didn't understand why he suddenly felt annoyed.

Scarlechek had sat back and let the others do the talking. The fourth martini barely affected him, and he drank and watched like a running back looking for an opening through the line. The hole appeared when the others left for their chalets.

Now I've got his royal ear, Scarlechek thought.

"Tom, can I talk to you for a moment about business?" he asked, anxious to see how he might be able to take advantage of this night.

Peckinpah consented, but was soon distracted when the blonde paid her bill and got up to leave. She walked toward Peckinpah and Scarlechek with intent to kill. Her sparkly, bright green mini-dress, halted a full ten inches above her knees, and glistened with seduction as she flung her fur over one shoulder. Her smooth, long legs were without hose, and her spiked heels declared to the room that she was ready to party.

Scarlechek, unaware of Peckinpah's distraction, rattled on about his budget needs until Peckinpah turned his head away to follow the blonde's movements. Scarlechek looked in the same direction then, and the pair ogled the smiling femme fatale as she slithered by.

"Excuse me, Lou, I've gotta go," said Peckinpah, with no trace of compunction for cutting Scarlechek off. He got up quickly and tossed a big bill down on the table.

"I'll follow you out," Scarlechek said, not seeming to mind as he hastily grabbed his briefcase.

As they scrambled after her, both men watched the brilliant green movement of the vamp's bottom, swaying toward the elevator as though beckoning them to follow. It was a masterful gamble on her part—a "hooker"—through and through. A hyper person, she'd grown tired of waiting, tired of looking; she believed with the confidence of a symbolic logician that if she got up, Peckinpah would follow.

As they rushed to join her in the elevator, she giggled, delighted that her ploy had worked. *I'm the bait, I'm the hook, line, and sinker, and I'm the fisherman,* she thought. *Now, I'll just reel 'em in.*

Scarlechek was so excited that he caught his shoe in the gap between the elevator and the building floor. It caused him to stumble into the hooker's chest and knock her back against the elevator wall.

"Oomph!" she uttered derisively, as she inflated her chest cavity with air and wriggled her bosom in his face.

"Oh, I'm so sorry," Scarlechek said, feeling like a clumsy schoolboy.

Peckinpah sneered at Scarlechek. But his attention to Scarlechek didn't last—he was too drunk to care. Feeling too good, too powerful, too irreverent, he directed his attention back to the hooker.

"What's your pleasure, gentlemen?" she hummed as the elevator descended.

"You, of course," Peckinpah said, trying to decide if he should ask whether she was a cop, hoping at the same time to appear suave.

"You're too well-dressed to be cops, aren't you?" she asked them both, first broaching the touchy subject.

"Absolutely."

"Good. Are you going somewhere?"

"My chalet, up the mountain. Will you join me?"

"Oh, I'd love to," her voice vibrated with mockery.

Scarlechek grinned, feeling like a squeaky third-wheel.

"You know, gentlemen, I'm very expensive," she said. She was confident as she moved to Peckinpah and nestled her enticing hip against his upper thigh, pulling him to her by the lapel. She simultaneously reached for Scarlechek's crotch and fondled him.

The elevator bottomed out at the parking garage, and their hearts jumped to their throats. The door opened and she stepped out. "Where's your car? We'll talk there."

"Let's go, baby," Peckinpah said, still with a nagging sensation that Scarlechek should be gone.

Scarlechek hung on and the trio climbed into Peckinpah's Lexus. They motored out the garage and up the narrow road toward the chalet.

On the way, the hooker set her price. One night would cost a thousand dollars apiece, which intuition told her they'd pay. She required half right then, and Scarlechek forked it over after Peckinpah's instructional nod.

Scarlechek asked her name and she said, "Whatever you want it to be, darlin'." Her demeanor changed momentarily, and she said, "Oh, one thing. You have to take me to the early shuttle flight to Denver at six in the morning. I'm flying back to New York."

"No problem," Peckinpah said. He'd always been an early riser anyway.

"Fine," she purred, and leaned over the console to caress Peckinpah's groin.

Not wanting to be left out, Scarlechek reached over the front seat and groped her breast through the tight dress.

Back at the chalet, they giggled and fondled their way inside, and she pulled them both to the fireplace. The fire had been started as usual by the night maid. The hooker wrestled the tube dress off to

91

reveal her shapely, naked body, which she warmed by the flames. The green spiked heels stayed on, and she swayed temptingly to imagined music in front of the fire.

She gestured to Peckinpah. "You first, baby."

"Wait! Come with me," Peckinpah said. "Let's do some lines!"

"Sounds great, baby," she replied, and Peckinpah led her to the bathroom upstairs, as she jiggled along in her heels.

Scarlechek lurked behind, delighted at the entire situation. Only he knew why.

CHAPTER 22

In the bathroom, Peckinpah opened a small leather kit he pulled from the corner of a cupboard under a black marble countertop. He opened a one-gram vial and gently poured the fine white powder onto a small mirror. Chopping the powder with a razor blade, he created the lines while the alluring hooker drooled. He pulled out three small, sterling silver straws, and ordered Scarlechek downstairs to fix three whiskeys.

The hooker and Peckinpah inhaled the cocaine with gusto, leaving a line for Scarlechek. Snorting like swine, they couldn't hold back any longer. Even the naked prostitute was hot. The cocaine hadn't been metabolized, but it was the idea of it all that appealed to her—the rebelliousness. She undid Peckinpah's pants, pulling a deep knee-bend as she tugged them and his shorts to the floor, rising back only as high as his penis. Shifting to a kneeling position, she took it into her mouth.

A few moments later, Scarlechek appeared with three drinks and something tucked away in his pocket that he'd retrieved from his briefcase—a small, flashless Japanese camera. He'd long ago developed a habit of carrying it with him, and it had served him well in the past.

Peckinpah moaned with pleasure, his eyes closed, knees bent, his back resting against the wall, his pelvis thrusting at her head. Her back was to Scarlechek as he peered quickly around the entrance to the bathroom. Scarlechek's giddiness was gone, replaced by calculated determination. He silently put the drinks down, pulled the camera out, and snapped three shots. In addition to the sexual activity, he made sure to capture the vial, the mirror and straws, and the last line of cocaine in the frames.

Scarlechek returned the camera to his pocket and put two of the whiskeys in plain view on the floor, under the bathroom doorway, as he saw Peckinpah's body begin to shudder and his legs falter. He smiled to himself, took the third whiskey downstairs, and took a satisfying pull.

Peckinpah and the hooker grabbed the drinks after Peckinpah recovered his composure, which didn't take long as the cocaine began taking effect. They raced each other down the hall into the bedroom and onto the luxurious bed, leaving the door open—their bodies catty-corner, heads toward the bed's foot.

The cocaine made Peckinpah feel stronger, more virile than ever. Like animals in heat, they began to screw.

Slowly and quietly Scarlechek returned upstairs and walked to the bedroom entrance. He again readied his camera, and then clicked off three more shots of the modulating couple copulating on the bed.

Almost as satisfied as Peckinpah for the moment, Scarlechek returned downstairs and locked the camera in his briefcase. Flopping down on the couch, he savored his whiskey, contemplating the possibilities of things to come.

CHAPTER 23

A few hours later, Tom Peckinpah and the high-class whore stumbled downstairs and nudged Scarlechek.

"Lou, wake up, I'm taking her to the airport," Peckinpah said, his voice bright, as though he'd showered after a ten-hour sleep. "I'll drop you at your chalet."

The CEO and his lady friend had been high on cocaine, talking about sex, philosophy, and then sex again. They'd done it one more time with Peckinpah's perpetual erection stimulated by the cocaine.

Who needs the little blue pill, Peckinpah had thought. *I'll take white powder every time.*

She likewise was fully awake and had realized she needed to hustle to catch her plane. "Come on, man, we got to go," she said to Peckinpah nervously.

"Calm down," Peckinpah said. "We've got plenty of time."

"I'll keep you company to the airport," Scarlechek mumbled thickly, half asleep and groggy from the alcohol, but having no intention of letting anything slip by.

It was still dark as the group got into the Lexus, and Peckinpah drove down the winding road. He tried to focus on the bends and turns in the road but his heightened senses seemed to whirl around the curves long before the car. The hooker didn't notice—being too spaced-out herself. Her mind was already in New York; and her heart began beating fast in anticipation.

Scarlechek reclined in the back seat and tried to sleep—about as successfully as a kid on Christmas Eve. With his eyes closed, he felt sneakier, like when driving home with his parents from grandma's.

Peckinpah was driving too fast. As he maneuvered the car, the cocaine toyed with his synapses and paranoia flooded his brain. Thinking he should be small-talking the attractive woman, he blurted out, "I travel to New York a lot, and I'd like your number."

"Sorry man, I don't work that way," she snapped.

He shot her a surprised look, as she continued to speak rapidly.

"I go where I please ... to the best places ... pick my John ... deal in cash—lots of it. I don't leave phone numbers. I don't even have a phone. I don't stay put long enough. I need anonymity, and I'll leave you guessing as to why. If we ever see each other again, it'll be your luck. Tell you what, I'll take *your* card and call *you*, next time I fly here."

She thinks I'm a fool, he thought. "Oh, no, I don't think so," he replied, wondering why she needed to be so secretive. *She must be in trouble with the law, not unusual for a woman in her profession.*

"See?" she said, analogizing her need for complete control to his.

Peckinpah's distraction increased as they talked. The winding, slippery mountain path seemed to be streaming at him from all directions and he endeavored to dismiss all extraneous thought. Focusing too hard and to little avail, the thought never occurred to him to slow down. The more he tried to force himself to react normally, the more reality escaped him and the more he bungled his movements.

As the car rounded a steep and sharp curve, gravity caused it to accelerate. He didn't see the icy patch in a dip in the road. Just as the rear tires hit it, he crammed his heavy foot on the brake pedal. Slamming the brakes caused them to lock up, and the car lost traction on the ice. As it began to spin out, Peckinpah felt like an astronaut, immersed in weightlessness for an eerie eternity. Finally reacting, he overturned the wheel into the direction of the spin, and the road was too icy to regain traction.

"Watch out!" the hooker cried. Her eyes opened wide at the sight of the cliff on the left side of the terrace. The car spun clockwise for another moment that seemed to last forever, and the spinning mass careened further to the right, away from the cliff and into a snow bank. They had twisted a full three hundred and sixty degrees and then some, before the car came to a complete stop.

Scarlechek's head popped up, as did the pulses of Peckinpah and the hooker. She turned ghostly pale.

"What happened?" Scarlechek asked.

"Oh, my God!" Peckinpah blurted, staring straight into the whiteness that shrouded the windshield.

After a moment, he peered over at the hooker, who sat slumped in her seat. His eyes widened when she began convulsing, and Peckinpah lunged to hold her and make her stop. But the tremors continued, and in the next instant, Peckinpah saw her eyes rolling back.

Oh my God, he thought, not knowing what to do.

"Lou, help me!"

Peckinpah stared at her in disbelief, confused. Scarlechek did too.

A second later, she stopped convulsing and her eyes became fixed and glassy. "She's passed out!"

The hooker's face began to turn blue. Peckinpah leapt out of the car, and rushing around to her side, he yanked open the door. Grabbing her and pulling her limp body out, he laid her on the icy roadside.

Check for a pulse, he told himself. *She needs CPR.* Frantically trying to remember his never-used training from long ago, he placed his left hand under her chin and tilted her head back. He pinched her nose and began to breathe into her mouth—the same mouth from which he'd so passionately sucked face earlier. Only this time, she didn't respond. He continued blowing air into her mouth, completely forgetting about chest pumps while the frigid air consumed her, turning her body a bluish-gray.

"Oh, my God! Lou! Help me!" His voice was even more urgent. *His Omnipotence* was suddenly reduced to utter panic. "She's dying!" he cried to Scarlechek, who'd finally stumbled out of the car.

Unfortunately, saving a person's life was something about which Lou Scarlechek never had the slightest interest in learning.

Peckinpah continued his efforts in vain, but it was obvious they were useless. She lay dead on the side of the road. The CEO began wailing in despair. His face, white with shock, was accentuated by the icy-blue cold. He stared at the dead hooker in disbelief.

Scarlechek, on the other hand, took on a new calm. He studied the situation.

The whore's reaction was induced by the cocaine—a heart arrhythmia, he speculated. He'd read about at least one basketball player suffering the same death on the court. *This is far better than I could have ever dreamed! I have proof of the cause of death, I didn't participate, I have the film. I have this man!*

"Tom!" said Scarlechek. "Come on, snap out of it! Help me get her into the trunk, quick, before someone comes!" Scarlechek's motivation wasn't to protect Peckinpah. He intended to protect his secret and its value on the marketplace—a value that had escalated exponentially with the hooker's death.

He ran around the car and popped open the trunk. Then he hurried back to the body, noticing then how his shocked boss looked at him so incredulously, like a helpless child seeking relief from anyone.

Peckinpah's eyes were fixed as he helped lift the body into the trunk. Afterward, he plopped down into the passenger seat.

Scarlechek observed Peckinpah's lifeless stare. *This is rich!*

Scarlechek pulled the car back away from the bank and drove back up the hill to the chalet. It was early on Sunday morning so the road was quiet.

Peckinpah asked, "What am I going to do?"

"Well, you're not going skiing today, Tom," Scarlechek said with new confidence in his voice, a tone he'd never used with Peckinpah before. It was the sound of ownership. "We're heading back to your chalet now to clean up some messes, and then try to get some rest. When Cookie comes to go over your faxes and e-mails this morning, I want you to send her away. Tell her to go back to Phoenix. You and I are going to take a drive into the high and lonesome this afternoon."

"Tom," Scarlechek said after a long silence. "We can't let this get out. We've got to protect you for the good of the company." His insincerity would have been obvious to anyone else, but it wasn't apparent to Peckinpah, who was too consumed by shock compounded by de-escalation from the cocaine. Instead, Peckinpah felt grateful for Scarlechek's strength.

By the time they reached the chalet, dawn was breaking. Scarlechek watched Peckinpah dispose of the remaining cocaine and paraphernalia like a robot, Scarlechek knowing better than to touch the evidence himself. Then they both lay down to rest—Peckinpah in the bedroom and Scarlechek on the couch downstairs.

Scarlechek smiled as he closed his eyes.

CHAPTER 24

The telephone ring startled Lou Scarlechek out of his sleep. It was ten o'clock in the morning.

"Hel … lo," he managed to spit out.

"Hello, who's this?" the caller asked, surprised to hear an unfamiliar voice.

Scarlechek recognized Cookie Albertson on the line, Peckinpah's administrative assistant. She traveled with him often and, regardless of where they were, each morning she gathered his memos, letters, e-mails, and faxes for review, taking dictation of his responses or composing them herself. Cookie handled everything for Peckinpah; she was the universal key to gaining access to any of his filtered attention, functioning as a feminazi gatekeeper.

She was the same Cookie Albertson who'd once been Adel Blair's legal secretary, and who had been lured away by the prospect of a higher-paying position at Western Town. John Waverly hired her as his administrative assistant in Orlando because his assistant back in Phoenix refused to travel. Cookie was stationed in Orlando full time. As a result, she often had little to do whenever Waverly worked out of his Phoenix office. It wasn't long, however, before Peckinpah recognized her competence. His assistant had quit because she had grown tired of the constant traveling. Usurping Cookie was another one of the perks of being the boss.

"Cookie," Scarlechek said. "This is Lou. Tom's asleep. We had a rough night."

"Oh," she said, her tone judgmental.

"He told me that if you called and he wasn't up, to tell you he didn't want to deal with anything today and that you should fly back to Phoenix."

"Oh-h?" Her voice was sharper, with an element of surprise. She'd come to know Peckinpah as a man of boundless energy who, regardless of the night before was always ready for business, even on days when he was going to play, like this one. "E-mails and faxes first," was his rule. She'd often known him to stay awake all night and then insist upon going over e-mails and faxes the next morning, while she had urged him instead to sleep. The situation was very odd to Cookie, and she knew one thing—she didn't like or trust Lou Scarlechek.

"I need to speak to him."

Scarlechek's mercury skyrocketed. Her curt, insistent tone irritated him. It often seemed the administrative assistants of his superiors had more power than he, running interference for their bosses.

How beautiful, he realized. This time, the roles were reversed. Scarlechek was the filter, and his revenge was both gratifying and amusing.

"Lou," Cookie repeated, "I need to speak to Tom. Please put him on."

The more she pushed, the more he refused to comply, just as was done to him many times in the past. It would have been so easy to assert his new authority over Peckinpah by having him tell Cookie to go away. But he enjoyed doing it himself. Little did he know that his childishness could ultimately prove to be a mistake.

"I'm sorry, Cookie, he asked not to be disturbed, and he specifically said not even by you."

"Hmm-m. Well, I'm coming to see him anyway. I'll be there shortly."

She hung up before Scarlechek could respond.

No problem, he thought. *I just won't let her in.*

Cookie was staying in the chalet adjacent to Peckinpah's, as was their custom on such trips. Within minutes she was there, unlocking the door with her own key. She barged in with printed e-mails and faxes in hand.

Scarlechek glared at her in disbelief as she marched past him to the stairs.

"Good morning," she said tersely.

Instinct made him turn on the charm, but it only fueled her distrust.

"Hi, Cookie ... uh, well, as long as you're here, Tom's upstairs," Scarlechek said as she mounted the steps. She and Peckinpah were that close, and she had done this many times. Ignoring Scarlechek, she climbed upward.

What she found was frightening.

CHAPTER 25

A grown man, symbolizing America's corporate power, in the fetal position?

Cookie couldn't believe it. Yet, there he was in underpants and t-shirt lying on his side, uncovered and shivering on the bed, with knees drawn to his chest. She studied his eyes, which were strangely wide-open and fixed. His dirty, disheveled hair stuck out in spikes. His colorless skin was accentuated by his unshaven dark stubble. He looked like living death.

"Tom! Tom, what have you done to yourself?" Her voice was husky with concern. She knew he could be wild, but she'd never seen him like this.

Scarlechek, who had followed Cookie's footsteps, overheard and thought, *Don't blow it, dumb shit!*

"Oh … hey, Cook," Peckinpah muttered weakly.

"Tom, what happened? Are you okay?"

"Well, I had kind of a rough night. I just need some rest … I'll be all right."

Scarlechek watched and listened at the doorway.

"Listen, Cook, I don't have the energy to do anything today. Why don't you catch the twelve-thirty shuttle and head back to Phoenix … I'll see you Monday."

Scarlechek sighed in relief.

"No," Cookie said. "I'll stay and take care of you. You obviously need help." She stared over her shoulder at Scarlechek.

"No, no, it's all right, head on back. Lou already told me he'd stay. Why don't you go on back and see Dan?"

She thought about it. Her boyfriend often complained about her schedule.

"Dan'll get over it," she said. "I want to stay and ski, if you won't let me take care of you. I'll head back tonight."

"Okay … thanks, Cook. I'll be all right."

"Okay," she said, concern still heavy in her voice. "I'll see you later."

"Bye, Cookie," Scarlechek said as she walked by. "We'll watch the NFL or something, and relax. I'll take care of him."

"Um hmm," she said uneasily. *I'll check back later*, she thought.

．．．．

It was late afternoon when Scarlechek roused Peckinpah for the daunting task ahead of them. In the Lexus-turned-hearse, Scarlechek drove as they ascended the mountain range up well-groomed country roads that were minimally traveled.

Peckinpah moved without emotion, like a zombie. Some part of him knew he couldn't do what he should do. That was the part that shut him down.

The timing is perfect, Scarlechek thought. A storm system that would bring fresh snowfall was heading in from the west and due to unload the next morning. His kept his eyes peeled for a secluded spot with exposed ground, knowing they had to bury her in the frozen earth. A grave in the snow would melt away during the spring thaw. He had packed a pick, shovel, flashlight, and two pair of snowshoes, which he'd retrieved from the chalet garage. It thrilled him to think that they were going to get away with this.

Shortly before the sun disappeared behind a distant slope, Scarlechek found a secluded location off a side-road. There was exposed ground under a large rock ledge, leeward of the prevailing winter winds over the hillside, and surrounded by thick tree lines. Although the precipice was visible from the road, Scarlechek thought they could bury her behind the trees without being seen. When Peckinpah wasn't looking, he snapped a quick photograph of the makeshift graveyard.

They waited until dusk before starting their cold, repugnant task. The frozen ground and the need to camouflage the site slowed their efforts so that three long hours had elapsed before they finally hiked in their snowshoes back to the car. The next morning's expected snowfall from the new storm would completely cover their tracks.

Peckinpah, still in his own Twilight Zone, was useless, so Scarlechek drove them back to the chalet. Scarlechek wore a smug expression as he calculated when to inform his unsuspecting prey of his peril.

Not now, he thought. *I'll wait until I decide exactly what I want.* He glanced again at Peckinpah, the great CEO. *You're not on top of the world anymore, are you, asshole?*

· · · ·

After a half day of skiing, Cookie Albertson returned to Peckinpah's chalet at four-thirty to find no one there.

Maybe he got better and went skiing, she thought. *That's more like him. But I can't believe he would've been up to it. I've never seen him like he was today.*

She'd already made arrangements to be taken to the shuttle flight and return to Phoenix, so with some reluctance she decided to go forward with those plans.

On the plane, she struggled with her novel, for her mind kept drifting back to the unusual events of the weekend.

CHAPTER 26

It was Monday morning, and Scarlechek sat on the Boeing flying from Denver to Orlando. Two things were foremost on his mind: film and sex. After all, he hadn't had any of the latter in five days. But what he'd gotten was even better. He planned to drop off the film at a certain photography shop on his way to the office, where he knew his prized film would be developed and printed with discreet and special care.

After I get to the office, he thought. *I'll go over things with Marta, send her home, and then buzz little miss DeeDee.*

He rubbed his hands together briskly causing the man across the aisle to look at him strangely.

"What?" Scarlechek said in a challenging tone to the man, who looked back to his magazine.

I'll call first to make sure she stays, Scarlechek thought.

He felt more than justified. Last week, he'd fulfilled his end of the bargain with DeeDee. He had hired a new attorney, Peter Spalling, and assigned her to him with a promotion as he had promised.

I'll find out how it's going tonight, he thought, feeling warm. *It's good that I care so much for my people.*

Peckinpah will be all right, Scarlechek reasoned. *After all, it wasn't really his fault the whore had an arrhythmia. She didn't have to take the cocaine. Besides, he has too much at stake. He won't blow it.*

His thoughts alternated between DeeDee and Peckinpah as the jet engines droned on, fancying the ease with which he now controlled them both. Of course, Peckinpah didn't know it yet. He thought of the Wicked Witch of the West: *All in due time, my pretty*

... *all in due time.* Scarlechek felt a quenching sensation and his pendulum swung upward. It peaked as his mind turned to Adel Blair. The thought of Adel Blair overwhelmed him with an inexplicable emptiness, a hunger he couldn't begin to understand.

. . . .

It was three-thirty in the afternoon when he arrived at the office and instructed Marta DeLong to bring his pile of faxes, memos, e-mail, and snail mail. They went through the pile for an hour. He responded by handwritten note, e-mail, phone call, dictated note or letter, each calculated response designed to put the monkey on someone else's back.

I'm such a good manager, he thought.

It takes real talent to deflect blame and responsibility so thoroughly, DeLong thought. *Ride the wave, surfer girl. Ride the wave.*

With at least another hour to go, Scarlechek said, "Let's take a break."

DeLong put down her pad and pen, walked behind Scarlechek's chair and began massaging his shoulders. A knock at the door cut short DeLong's rubbing. She moved back to the front of Scarlechek's desk.

"Come in," Scarlechek said.

It was the new attorney, Peter Spalling, with a puppy dog look on his youthful face.

"I just accepted process from a process server, Lou! Here's the complaint ... filed in federal district court."

Christ, what a rookie, Scarlechek thought. *Big deal.*

God, DeLong thought. *A Labrador with the newspaper.*

He's new, Scarlechek thought. *He's excited and wants to impress me.* "Let me see it," he said.

Spalling volunteered, "The company's been sued for sexual harassment!"

CHAPTER 27

Oh, shit!

Scarlechek's palms began to sweat. *DeeDee! My God! Not again! Shit! ... Shit! Shit! Shit!*

As his blood pressure rose, anxiety and panic invaded his mind and body. He raced through choreography of his act for the underling and DeLong, already conceptualizing the strategy of his defense. He hadn't thought DeeDee had the guts.

How did she do it so quickly? Scarlechek wondered. *Aren't there procedures for this sort of thing?*

DeLong experienced her own unease as her pulse quickened. For some time, she'd suspected someone watching her and Scarlechek, perhaps one of the other secretaries who'd also wanted the job. She worried that someone, somehow, had discovered how she obtained it, and a sense of guilt washed over her.

I cheated, she thought. *And worse ... I got caught. Papa always said it ain't cheatin' if you don't get caught.* Her face grew more pale than usual, and she experienced resignation to an unknown doom as she waited for Scarlechek to receive the complaint from Spalling and read the condemning declarations.

"There are also common law counts for sexual assault and battery, invasion of privacy, defamation, and negligence," Spalling continued, overjoyed to be reporting to his new boss. "And the plaintiff has demanded a jury trial and is asking for punitive damages." He didn't realize the untold consternation he was causing Scarlechek and Marta DeLong, each for differing reasons.

DeLong sat down, hard.

Scarlechek reeled with dismay. He reached out and took the complaint from Spalling.

How could that fuckin' little bitch have done that? We had a deal! She got her promotion! That little whore! ... Denial ... credible denial. She'll never be able to prove it. She's jealous that she didn't get Marta's job, that's all. I'll tell 'em she threw herself at me and she's the woman scorned, the jilted lover ... no wait! Woman! The jilted woman. Got to watch what I say here. Shit, I can't get fuckin' caught again!

He drew a long breath, and looked down at the complaint in his quivering paw. He read the style of the case on the federal summons: *Elizabeth G. Sorenson, Plaintiff v. Western Town Production Company of Florida, Inc., et al., Defendants.*

His shoulders collapsed in relief.

It wasn't DeeDee!

DeLong didn't understand the look on Scarlechek's face. She waited, wondering if she'd have to give up her new perks, or worse.

Spalling didn't have a clue about anything, let alone something as disjointed as what was transpiring among them.

"Who the hell is Elizabeth G. Sorenson?" Scarlechek asked roughly, trying to act as though nothing had happened.

"Apparently, she worked in the Facilities Division at the waste-water treatment plant," Spalling replied. "She says the work environment there was offensive, pardon the pun, and hostile," he added, thinking he was showing a sign of cleverness.

DeLong couldn't believe her ears. She composed herself, now amused. *Papa would still be proud.*

"She's alleged that the male workers at the plant hung offensive magazine pictures," Spalling continued, "and constantly made sexual comments and innuendos, so much so that she had to quit. There are also allegations of one or two incidents of inappropriate touching."

"Oh, for Christ's sake, is that all?" Scarlechek asked, annoyed at being startled by such a trivial matter.

DeLong was overcome by an impulse to laugh. She wondered what Scarlechek might have feared, her thoughts turning to DeeDee Lane.

Scarlechek glared at her, and then buzzed John Laughlin on the intercom.

"John?"

"Yes," Laughlin answered. John Laughlin was a vice president in the Legal Department. He was a large man with a massive frame. Quiet, sensitive, and intelligent, he'd been passed over in the search for someone to fill the position that had ultimately been awarded to Scarlechek. Laughlin's fault was honesty, a character flaw that prevented his advancement in the corporate world.

"John, can you come in here please?" Scarlechek asked with the easy charm reserved especially for the man over whom he had climbed, all the while purporting to be Laughlin's best friend.

"Sure. I'll be right there." Laughlin's voice was resigned.

When he arrived, Scarlechek fired, "John, the company's been sued for sexual harassment. Who's the best in town on that?" He already knew the answer, but now the stakes were higher than a mere seminar. The company could lose and blame could be assessed. As the newcomer, Scarlechek wanted to be able to say he relied on Laughlin's judgment if the case went bad. Laughlin had no knowledge of Scarlechek's seminar plans.

Laughlin had been with the company for nineteen years and had run the Legal Department for the past five. Having been courted by most leading Orlando law firms wanting Western Town's legal work, he knew all of them and had hired many.

"That would be David McKerrin's firm," he replied. "McKerrin, Smith and O'Donnell. There's a woman there ... her name's Adel Blair ... she's prominent in the field."

"She's not even a named partner?" Scarlechek asked, coolly continuing his charade even in front of DeLong, so confident was he that she'd remain discreet.

DeLong smiled derisively.

"I don't even know that she is a partner," Laughlin answered. "McKerrin is the senior partner. He's a well-known trial attorney in the area, and has the reputation of a seasoned warhorse."

"Then get me an appointment with McKerrin. Ask him to bring this Blair woman, although, I must say, I'm a little unnerved by that,"

Scarlechek said, enjoying his false foundation. Internally, he wallowed in jubilation at how conveniently this was all working out.

DeLong continued to smile, amazed at the mastery of her boss.

Laughlin didn't know why, but he sensed that if the case was handled poorly, he'd be blamed.

Spalling was disappointed the case shifted from his hands to Laughlin's. He'd hoped for an opportunity to show his worth. But there was no way Scarlechek would let Spalling, DeeDee's boss, oversee a harassment case.

DeLong wondered about Adel Blair as everyone was breaking up. But suddenly, she saw that look on the boss's face.

"Wait!" he barked. "Let's call Yates!" Scarlechek knew the wastewater treatment plant was in Sandy Yates' division, and he said it like a juvenile with a "neato" idea for a Friday night. Stay here," he commanded, ensuring witnesses to the conversation. "Get him, Marta."

As DeLong retreated to her office and made the call, Scarlechek and Spalling filled Laughlin in on the case. The intercom buzzed and DeLong's sardonic voice announced that Yates was on line two.

Scarlechek pushed his speakerphone button. "Sandy?"

"Hello, Lou." He was annoyed that Scarlechek had wanted to talk to him, but had made him wait on the line.

"Sandy, we've got a problem that concerns your area."

"Oh?" The laconic voice grew concerned.

"A woman named Sorenson has sued the company for sexual harassment. She worked at your wastewater treatment plant and claims that she was sexually mistreated. She's asking for reinstatement, injunctive relief, back pay, front pay, damages, and punitive damages." Scarlechek laid the heavy foundation like a concrete truck relinquishing its load down a slippery chute.

"What does she say we did wrong?" Yates asked.

"Well, she says your guys hung pornographic pictures and constantly made offensive remarks, and that there were even some touching incidents. I'll fax you a copy of the complaint. We just received it today."

"Please do."

"We're looking at hiring a local firm—one that John Laughlin has suggested—that specializes in this kind of thing. I'm sorry, but I just don't know the local attorneys yet. We're setting up a meeting with them. Do you want to attend?"

Scarlechek was playing three-dimensional corporate dodge ball. First was blame avoidance—besides setting up Laughlin's suggestion, he wanted his "client" in on the decision. Second, he was setting Yates up with the opprobrious allegations, laying groundwork to deflect responsibility just in case, or rather, when he'd later recommend that the company pay a settlement, all in order to avoid risk of being wrong about the outcome, a risk he was theoretically supposed to take.

"Yes, I'll send someone," Yates said, fully aware of Scarlechek's game. Yates was *not* one to shirk responsibility. "Minus the touching allegations, is what she complains of against the law?"

"Well, that's a complex question, full of legal nuances," Scarlechek said, knowing that his reply could apply to any case. *Baffle him with bullshit,* he thought, as he glanced at his audience, Laughlin, Spalling, and DeLong. "It depends on a lot of intangible factors: intent, her provocative actions, the judge. But the bottom line is: it can be. If she can prove her case, we may have to pay a settlement. There may be publicity; and the federal government could also come down on against us and adversely affect our bid on government contracts."

Scarlechek breathed deeply, having said a mouthful without saying anything.

"Well, that's not a crucial point for the company," Yates replied, referring to the government contracts. The company only occasionally bid on vacation and convention contracts for branches of the armed services. "Listen, I've got to go into a meeting. Let me know when you've scheduled the meeting with the attorney. In the meantime I'll talk to my people."

"Sure," Scarlechek said, "See you later, my friend."

Yates didn't consider Scarlechek to be a friend. And although Scarlechek was supposed to be *his* lawyer, he trusted the man no more than he trusted a seventeen-year-old boy to babysit his teenage daughter.

CHAPTER 28

DeeDee Lane felt numb as she headed to Scarlechek's office. She walked in stiffly and sat down on his couch, speaking only when necessary. She waited listlessly without conscious acknowledgment of his demands. She existed, but felt no life or vitality, like a dormant rosebush in winter.

He checked her over while he finished dictating a memo.

Her black suit hung from her; the skirt, safety-pinned around her waist from weight loss, flapped against her legs. Even her skin sagged, as though life itself was being sucked out of her from the inside like a grape in the sun. Depression had played havoc on her appetite and sleeping habits. She no longer slept in her bed. Instead, she collapsed into her couch every evening and watched old movies until she lost herself in the realm of the unthinking. Each morning, she struggled to get off the couch long enough to shower and dress for work. It took all the will power she could muster. Getting to work on time was no longer a priority, and she began calling in sick, staying late only when Scarlechek notified her in advance, as he had this day.

Scarlechek came over to the couch and seemed to be panting.

Wondering how he could enjoy it, DeeDee endured his slobbering motions as always, as she deadened herself like a pliable cadaver or an inflatable doll. She offered nothing, yet he never seemed to notice, or care.

He's clueless as to the art of love making, she thought, *because he's clueless about beauty.* Realizing that he must've never *truly* experienced beautiful sex, relishing that he couldn't take *that* from her, she wished he knew what he was missing. Disappointment shrouded her when she realized that he just didn't understand, and that he never would.

He's an animal driven by basic drives, she thought. *Instant gratification is the only thing that matters to him. No wonder he carries two phones.*

DeeDee rose to dress when it was over, impatient to get away. Usually, he just wanted her gone, as well. But uncharacteristically, Scarlechek spoke to her this time.

"DeeDee, I'm very glad about our little arrangement," he said. "It's so convenient. I'm glad you came to your senses, and I'm sure you must be happy about it, too." It was a statement, but he seemed to be fishing for a response. DeeDee didn't bite. She buttoned her blouse as she stared out the broad window and into the blackened night. The view matched her mood.

"You know, it'll mean even more for you in the future, too. Besides just your job with Peter, I mean. There'll be bonuses and perhaps new positions. You'll be treated very well. You'll see. You're so much smarter than ... others. You'll get your way out of life, and, let me tell you, that's what it's all about—getting your way. Women who get mad and try lawsuits always lose. No one ever believes them. Especially when it's consensual, like a deal, like it is between you and me. The courts enforce deals between people, and the woman *always* comes out looking bad, just like in rape cases. You could never sue. No attorney would even take your case. I'm glad you're above all that, and you enjoy it too."

DeeDee smirked at the blackness outside, saying nothing. *This is unusual for him,* she thought. *He seems almost ... frightened. The new lawsuit Peter mentioned this afternoon ... Hmm-m. It was a sexual harassment case.*

Scarlechek had risen and was suddenly behind her. He slipped his arms around her waist. She stiffened, but the urge to laugh was replaced by a new realization as he began to squeeze.

He's right. No one would ever believe me. I've taken the deal. It's my own doing.

It hadn't occurred to her that she had legal rights, but now that he'd raised the possibility, she knew he was right. She accepted his words blindly, not comprehending that she was being led astray by naiveté. It was natural for her to trust people, no matter how undeserving they were. She extracted herself from his arms and walked to the door.

"Good night, DeeDee," he said. His fear had subsided and he mocked her, confirming his power over her as she left.

She heard resigned words leave her mouth, "Good night."

CHAPTER 29

Tom Peckinpah sludged into his office Wednesday, the first day he could muster the gumption. He remembered the flight back. He'd traveled to the Denver airport on Monday with Scarlechek, Scarlechek vowing secrecy and urging Peckinpah to the same. Then he had taken the flight to Phoenix alone, wearing shades on the plane and being quite aloof to anyone who recognized him.

He had told Cookie upon his arrival, "No business—I want to be left alone for a couple of days." He explained to Janis that he didn't feel right and had caught a cold from skiing.

Monday night in bed, he had rolled over and embraced Janis at four in the morning.

"Feeling better?" Janis had said, wondering if he wanted sex.

"Not really," he replied. "I just need to hold you."

The next day over the phone, Janis told Cookie, "I don't know what's wrong with him. I've never seen him like this."

"I know, it's strange," Cookie replied. "I've never seen him unwilling to go over his communications."

"Did anything happen in Colorado?"

"Not that I know of," Cookie said, not lying, but not telling the whole truth either. She and Janis were friends, but loyalty to her boss overrode that.

"Tom, what happened?" she asked, pleading for his confidence.

"Forget it, Cookie," he said. "Let's get back to work." However, he knew she wouldn't forget it, and neither could he.

The cold facts confronted him every moment, and he recited them in his mind like reading a rap sheet.

I engaged in illegal solicitation and sex. I used an illegal substance. I drove while high on the stuff, and my recklessness caused another person's death. And then we buried her. We just drove up into the mountains and buried her in the hard, frozen ground. We wiped a life from the face of the earth as though it never existed.

He thought about her skin—the flesh he had so enjoyed touching was now engulfed by frozen earth. He thought about the worms that would crawl through her body after the thaw. He imagined a hyper-driven decay before his very eyes, and saw human tissue peeling away from her angry skull. He saw her tattered green dress collapsing onto bones, and the bones screaming at him in sheer terror. *Her skeleton hates me,* he thought. *It wants revenge. It'll come up out of the ground to get me!*

He shivered.

What's going to happen? What if I'm found out? I'll lose it all. I'll be disgraced. They can't find out! Lou's right. It's for the good of the company.

CHAPTER 30

Adel Blair and Dave McKerrin drove west on Interstate 4 to the tourist sector of greater Orlando. They were both excited in their own way, as they headed to an appointment with John Laughlin to discuss defending Western Town in a new sexual harassment case. Dave guided his ancient cream-colored Mercedes, a car he should've given up long ago. They were silent as they traveled, comfortable in the realm of their own thoughts.

The interstate meandered through a lightly wooded area, and Adel noticed a Western Town billboard to her right, set back among native brush. She studied the image of a happy cowboy being bucked by a snorting Brahma bull. He held on with a gloved hand wrapped in the bull rope, while an attractive female, dressed as though she'd just walked off the set of "Oklahoma," looked on and waved a lace hanky. The cowboy swung his battered Stetson in the air with a mechanically operated arm that protruded above the billboard. The arm summoned tourists to Western Town, reminiscent of the drowned Ahab lashed to Moby Dick with harpoon rope, beckoning to his crew as he went down.

Adel smiled at the billboard, thinking for a moment that its stereotypical images should bother her and wondering why they didn't. *That'd upset most feminists,* she mused, also wondering why she didn't think of herself as one.

Adel recalled her conversation with Marta DeLong about the seminar. *How strange,* she thought. *Was there something prophetic in that? Out of the blue I'm called to give a seminar at Western Town, the secretary says sexual harassment but the boss says racial discrimination, and then the company's sued for sexual harassment. The coincidence is interesting.*

The pair silently reveled at the good fortune to have the opportunity to represent Western Town, a highly visible company. Being able to say they represented such a company would enhance their firm's prestige. They were also thrilled because the case could lead to others—perhaps personal injury defense, which was a frequent, mechanized, source of bread-and-butter fees; or construction litigation, each case potentially a mega-case with mega-fees.

The recessionary forces creeping into Orlando were hitting lawyers hard. Firms had been scrapping for clients for some time, and McKerrin, Smith & O'Donnell was no exception. They'd been struggling even more than before—the partners had missed several paychecks, and the loan officers circled like buzzards.

Adel imagined Michael's derisive smile. *Another big corporation,* he'd say, chiding her for not fighting for "the little people." She was too pleased to dwell too long on such issues, however, happy instead that this prestigious client had sought her out and that she, like in rowing, could pull hard to help her floundering firm.

On cue, Dave asked, "Have you heard from my no-good nephew lately?"

"No, I haven't," she said, not disclosing that she had broken their last date in order to work late. It wasn't that she didn't enjoy Michael's company. To the contrary, she feared becoming enamored with him and allowing any feelings for him to interfere with her schedule. Wanting him was evidence of her weakness, so she denied the indulgence. Every time they started dating, she ended up closing the door again. After Mulvaney's, Michael hadn't even called.

"Don't you miss him?" McKerrin probed.

"Is that any of your business?"

"Yes, it is," he asserted. "I have a vested interest in both of you. So answer the question or I'll hold you in contempt."

"Yes, I miss him, Your Honor! I confess!" she blurted out, although only half-joking.

"Adel, you should cut yourself some slack. People are allowed to relax a little … to fall in love … you know? You need to do that …

uh, right after this case, that is."

She smirked at his blatant inconsistency. There was always another big case, always the need for one hundred and ten percent of her. He wanted her to relax, but then again, he didn't.

"Michael has his own agenda. I have mine. He's building quite a reputation prosecuting white-collar crime."

"Yes, he is."

"How appropriate for him, you know?"

"Yeah, he does have a bleeding heart. By prosecuting big corporations and corrupt officers, he's crusading for the masses. And he's getting good at it."

A strange ambivalence overcame Dave and his thoughts shifted back and forth. He wanted nothing more than for Michael and Adel to get together and stay together. They were perfect for each other. Yet, he feared losing Adel. Not in the personal way: their bond was too strong, and they'd be family to each other. He feared losing her from his firm.

But for her loyalty to me, he thought, *she would form a plaintiff's firm with Michael. That's when I'd lose her ... but it'd be worth it... Cast aside your selfishness, old man, and think about what's good for them. She needs guidance, what with no father an' all. She's blinded by her dedication to me ... and by her damned goals. She's so out of balance—just physical and mental, no emotional.*

They pulled into the parking lot and went into the building that housed Western Town's offices. By the time they reached the lobby elevators, Dave had resolved to do what he could to get Michael and Adel back together and keep them there.

Michael's right, it is too late for me. I'll be retiring soon anyway.

The elevator hummed as it climbed. When the door opened, a young towheaded woman rushed to get in, almost running into Dave and Adel.

"Oh, excuse me!" the woman said as she stepped back to allow them to pass.

"Quite all right," Dave replied, as he motioned to Adel to exit, holding the sliding door.

Adel smiled at the woman as she passed. Dave followed, and the woman finally entered and made her descent.

"Cute girl," Dave said as they walked away.

"Yeah, but there was something, I don't know, *sad* about her," Adel replied. When I smiled, she ... oh, never mind ... here we are."

Adel and Dave entered the Legal Department, where a matronly woman in a flowing royal blue dress sat at the receptionist desk. She had short, white hair and an attractive, friendly face, the kind that must've been ravishing in her youth.

"May I help you?" she asked.

"Yes," Dave said. "We're here to see John Laughlin and Louis Scarlechek. I'm David McKerrin and this is Adel Blair. I believe we are expected."

"Oh, hello. Won't you take a seat?" The receptionist gestured to the chairs, but not before sneaking a quick look at Adel. *Wow*, she thought.

"I'll let Mr. Laughlin know you're here." She buzzed Laughlin's secretary, and Dave accepted her offer of a cup of Starbuck's.

As the elderly belle was rounding her desk on her way to the kitchen, a sudden commotion materialized down the hall. Adel and Dave could see a man walking toward them, speaking too loudly, it seemed, for the circumstances. He was followed closely by a woman with a secretarial pad and pen, who was followed by a young man with a legal pad and pen, who was in turn followed by another woman with a legal pad and pen. They'd all just left a meeting room, and the man's entourage hung on his every word and scribbled furiously as it trailed. Adel and Dave listened to him ranting about some urgent memo to Phoenix.

It's obvious he doesn't care who hears him, Adel thought. *Unless it's that he wants everyone to hear.* She wondered whether this first impression would be important.

As the entire parade was nearing the reception desk, the man stopped abruptly, causing his followers to crash into each other like club cars piling up in a train wreck. He turned and barked orders while his followers gathered themselves. The man pivoted like the turret of a Sherman tank and pointed with his right arm, firing commands.

"Peter, redraft it like we said, and bring it to me in ten minutes!

This is urgent! Carol, call Larson and get the figures to Peter ASAP! Marta, set up a conference call in a half hour. You know the players."

Flipping his dark hair back, he pivoted again to another person, whom Adel surmised was a secretary, and whose desk was catty-corner to the reception desk. The man's gun-barrel arm pointed once again.

KaPow! "Jody, get me Peckinpah, now! Tell Cookie it's urgent!"

Then, he turned to the receptionist, as though to accentuate that he was in total control and that he was the center of the microcosm.

"Mary, fetch me another coffee!" he commanded the receptionist.

Adel surmised that his tone and the word "fetch" clearly irritated the former beauty queen. She watched the receptionist render a mock salute, then roll her eyes heavenward for Dave and Adel to see as she made haste for the kitchen.

Adel thought she picked up intent in the man's eyes to deliver an order to her, but it was apparently only a fleeting notion.

The domineering man was Lou Scarlechek, of course. Scarlechek noted Dave and Adel's presence, though he didn't acknowledge them. He flipped his dangling hair to the side and swaggered into his office. His entourage scurried after him like lab rats in a maze.

Dave raised his eyebrows and gave a snort. Adel smiled back.

Soon after, the receptionist returned and looked plaintively at Dave and Adel.

"Phew!" she said. "It *gets* like this!"

CHAPTER 31

John Laughlin peered furtively outside his office, wondering whether it was safe to come out. He caught sight of Dave looking at him, and he drew back in embarrassment. *I'm a corporate vice president, for God's sake.* Laughlin straightened his frame and walked out.

"Well, you've just seen the boss," he said to Dave after introductions. "Let me see if he's ready to meet."

Laughlin returned shortly, looking shame faced. Scarlechek needed "another ten minutes" he explained, saying, "I'm sorry, he says there's an emergency in Phoenix."

"Hey, no problem," Dave said. "These things happen."

Laughlin invited Dave and Adel into his office where they engaged in small talk for another twenty minutes. Finally, DeLong buzzed in with, "Lou is ready for you now."

The introductions went smoothly, somewhat restoring Laughlin's sense of dignity. Dave and Adel sat on Scarlechek's couch and Laughlin and Scarlechek sat in the side chairs.

Scarlechek poured on the charm while speaking of alma maters, disarming Dave, but Scarlechek became distracted. Adel's beauty mesmerized him, and lust enveloped him as he took her in with his eyes. Images of Adel on the awards stand crowded his mind. In due time, he would possess this woman. He need only play out his cards.

"Well, Ms. Blair," Scarlechek said, "I call you for a seminar on race discrimination, and then we get sued for sex. I understand you have quite a reputation in the field."

His double entendre surprised even Laughlin, who fidgeted in his chair.

Adel smiled, and assumed Scarlechek couldn't have meant it the way it came out.

Dave's face darkened as he took in the comment.

Scarlechek's gazed steadily at Adel. "Are you good?" he asked. His voice was blunt and challenging.

Adel didn't change her air.

"Yes, I'm good," she replied, acting as though the remark referred only to her abilities in court.

Dave's expression changed to full-blown anger after Adel's response, and he began to rise from his seat.

"Well, I'd like to experience … uh … see that," Scarlechek said, continuing the affront. He started to say something further, but DeLong interrupted by opening the office door and announcing a conference call.

"Oh, please excuse me for a moment," he said. "This is very important."

"No problem," Adel said.

Dave eased back down, following his associate's lead.

Laughlin's eyes narrowed as he thought about the seminar that Scarlechek mentioned. *He led me to think he didn't know her,* he thought.

Just then, another knock came at the door, and DeLong escorted a newcomer into the office, a black female carrying a file.

The woman smiled at Laughlin and they exchanged pleasantries while Scarlechek continued his ravings on the phone.

"Hello, Ti." There was warmth in Laughlin's voice.

"John, how are you?" the woman asked. "Sandy sent me. My apologies for being late, but I can see my tardiness hasn't made any difference." She glanced at Scarlechek.

Tiyona Morgan was the Manager of Equal Employment Opportunity in the Personnel Division at Western Town in Orlando. There was no director above her, and although she functioned in that capacity, she wasn't given the title, the pay, or the perks. She had been in her position for five years and was highly regarded in the company. As yet, she hadn't received the promotion for which many thought she was a shoe-in.

Tiyona was a slender but shapely, with long legs and hips that dwarfed her torso. She wore her hair short, curly and meticulously coifed. Her large lips outlined a wide mouth, revealing large teeth that contrasted starkly with her ebony skin. Her nose was flat and broad, and her eyes were large teardrops, accentuated by streamlined brows and long, curly lashes.

Adel instantly took a liking to Tiyona. *She's obviously athletic,* she thought. This was true. As a youth, Tiyona had been a basketball and track star at Evans High School in Orlando. On athletic scholarship she attended the University of Central Florida where she majored in psychology and minored in business, graduating with honors.

Thereafter, she took a job as an hourly tour guide at Western Town and worked her way up to a supervisory position. She openly expressed her desire to transfer to Personnel so that she could work in the equal employment opportunity field. Tiyona kept abreast of EEO concepts and law, and joined several related organizations. The company recognized the perfect opportunity and made her manager of the new EEO Department within the Personnel Division. With a staff of five, she studied the company's equal employment policies, recommended changes, and insured compliance. She was told that she would be responsible for interacting with the company directors and vice presidents to assure their department's compliance with policies, and she was directed to attend functions and join all related organizations in order to demonstrate Western Town's dedication to equal opportunity.

"Why can't we promote her?" Mike Benjamin had asked Waverly after the Operating Committee meeting in Vail.

"Why should we?" Waverly had replied. "Come on, I'm tired of talking about this."

Although Tiyona took her appointment very seriously, she soon realized that many in the company did not. A crusader at heart, she was fervent about the cause of equal opportunity. In her mind, equal opportunity was necessarily linked to affirmative action, but never to the point of doling out opportunity without link to merit.

She believed strongly in the merit of her race—and her gender. Yet, all too often, she'd seen in personal double dose, the damaging effects of stereotyping and other forms of discrimination. She'd studied it in college. Now, she was paid to do something about it, as though the company had handed her a loaded gun, and she was pointing it directly at management. But they'd only given her blanks.

Her superiors stifled her efforts with responses like: "Now Ti, let's be reasonable, we can't do that," or "Ti, we can't put these requirements in our contracts—they're already too onerous," or "Ti, his promotion is up to his manager and director, not you."

But Tiyona was a fighter. She took her causes to whomever was necessary. She never succumbed to pressures from her superiors and always forced a "yes" or a "no." To many, she was a corporate pain, a token manager who didn't know her place. Sometimes higher-ups considered eliminating her position, but the idea was always dismissed. She probably had the most job security of anyone in the company because it had certain appearances to keep up. This she knew. She had worked hard and had become too visible in the EEO community, including active membership in the National Women's League and regular correspondence with the Women's Bureau of the United States Department of Labor.

"How's Ray?" Laughlin asked.

She reported to the Vice President of Personnel, Ray Johnson. Johnson in turn reported to the Senior Vice President of Personnel, Steve Smyth, who in turn reported to Mike Benjamin the Executive Vice President on Peckinpah's operating committee. They were all white males who knew some things, but not enough, about EEO. For the most part, they left Tiyona to fight her own battles, and gave only minimal support when they could, or when it was politically correct.

"Oh, you know Ray," she said. "I'm never quite sure what he's doing." Tiyona was straightforward. There was never a question about her agenda. Because of this, she had the respect of many, including Sandy Yates, who had sent her as his representative to the meeting even though she was not in his division. Though she was not a lawyer, he knew she understood the sexual harassment laws and would give him an honest assessment. Yates would accept her advice.

Scarlechek's conference call finally ended, and the group looked to him expectantly.

"You're here for Sandy, I take it," Scarlechek said to Tiyona.

"Yes, he asked me to look into it. If there is to be a corporate representative on the case, he wants me."

"Have you met everyone?" Scarlechek said, ignoring her comment. "No."

Throughout the introductions, Adel was impressed by the composure and charisma of Tiyona Morgan. She was black and a woman, yet there she was in a high-powered corporate meeting, with everyone guessing as to what her comments on the situation might be. There as the confidant of the Executive Vice President of Facilities, in part to keep check on the Executive Vice President of Legal, she was to be Yates's eyes and ears, judge and jury. Did his people do wrong, would be his question to her. If Tiyona were not convinced of Sorenson's case, the company would be in a strong position, Yates had reasoned. She was the measure—for him, the corporate conscience. Her attitude confirmed from the start, "I'm here to judge. I'll listen. I'll report. I'll analyze and consider everything that's said. I'll decide. I'll recommend." Yet she was only a manager. Adel couldn't help being drawn to her.

The discussion centered first on the firm's experience. Adel's expertise in the Title VII field soon became clear. Dave put on no airs, and instead, relied on Adel's skills to impress Scarlechek. Scarlechek was coy. But Tiyona and Laughlin marveled at the impact of a defense team of Adel and Tiyona. Scarlechek let them advocate the outcome he secretly desired.

The discussion then shifted to the merits of the case and what was necessary to analyze it, for a response to Sorenson's complaint was due the following week.

"I know her lawyer," Adel said. "I'm confident I can get him to agree to an extension of two weeks or even a month."

"What if he doesn't agree?" Tiyona asked.

"We could file a defensive motion that would delay the proceedings," Scarlechek said, "and give him extra work to boot."

"Well," Adel said, "we shouldn't do things solely for those reasons, but I know I can work it out. I recommend we conduct interviews of the employees at the wastewater treatment plant, and a review of Sorenson's personnel file. Can you get that for me?"

"Yes," Laughlin said.

"I have an in-house dossier on her for you," Tiyona said. "It's a collection of information from informal interviews. Security did it when she filed her EEOC charge."

"Oh, good, that will help," Adel continued. "We'll serve a formal request for production of documents and written interrogatories under the procedural rules. Then, Sorenson's and other depositions will need to be taken. After that, having theoretically gathered all the facts, we can give our analysis and recommendation on whether to settle or proceed to trial."

"John, you monitor and collaborate with Adel and Tiyona, and report to me," Scarlechek said. "I'll counsel Sandy. Tiyona, I'm sure you'll be reporting independently to Sandy, but we should work together."

"What do you think of her complaint?" Tiyona asked Adel.

"Well, it's a 'hostile environment' case, which means she alleges that the company knew or should've known of the offensive conduct and it failed to do anything to stop it. The factual issues will include whether the events actually took place, and in the fashion alleged, including whether the alleged sexually harassing conduct was 'unwelcome' by Sorenson. Another issue is whether the company took 'prompt remedial action' to correct the problems. By law, the company could be absolved if it did. Another question is whether a 'reasonable person' would be offended by the conduct, so much so that the work environment could be considered 'hostile.' There's a technical legal issue of whether the test should be a reasonable person test or a reasonable woman test."

"The 'reasonable person' test has been the traditional test of the offensiveness of the conduct," Adel explained to the group, "of course, having been borrowed from the law of negligence. You know how ingrained that concept is. But some recent cases have recognized that what a man might consider reasonable might be entirely different from what a woman might think is reasonable. To put it plainly, to allow a man's thoughts to be the standard of offensiveness to a woman is akin to allowing the fox to guard the chicken coop. So use of the 'reasonable woman' standard is becoming a strong trend."

"Does that mean that only women can be on the jury?" Scarlechek asked, frightened of the prospect.

"No, although some women's groups advocate that," Adel said. Tiyona nodded in agreement.

"So men, under the new standard, remain in judgment of whether a 'reasonable woman' should be offended," Scarlechek said, pleased that men still had some control.

"Yes. That's the case, and I don't see it changing anytime soon," Adel said.

Thank God, Scarlechek thought.

"It's similar to how drug companies and researchers make conclusions about the effects of pills and supplements on women by studying their effects on men, you know," Tiyona said, with a smirk.

"But there's another major legal issue that could affect this case," Adel said. "Congress just passed a new amendment to the Civil Rights Act. It amends Title VII to give complainants like Sorenson additional rights. It allows for pain and suffering, the right to a jury trial—which they didn't have before, and even punitive damages."

A hush fell over the room at the dreaded "P" word.

Adel said, "Sorenson's lawyer is obviously aware of the new law because in the complaint he's asked for all the new remedies. He's taking the position, not surprisingly, that the new act applies to his case. But it's an unsettled issue. The alleged events happened before the law was enacted. She filed her complaint after. So the question is whether the new act applies retroactively to pre-act conduct. Congress has been heavily criticized by the courts for having 'punted' on this issue. The legislature purposefully didn't answer the question because the president vetoed the prior retroactive version. So to get the new edition past the president's veto pen, the boys on the hill left it to the courts to decide the question. It worked—the law was enacted. But so far there have been almost fifty decisions in the federal district courts coming down on differing sides of the issue of retroactivity, and the circuit courts of appeal have split also. One circuit court decision—the one from the Circuit for Washington, D.C.—was decided by then D.C. Circuit Judge, now Supreme Court Justice Clarence Thomas. His decision indicated the new act should *not* be applied retroactively. Of course, you're all aware of Anita Hill's testimony and his problems in his Supreme Court Justice appointment hearings."

"Well, that was obviously the correct decision," Scarlechek said, thinking out loud, but catching himself as Tiyona grimaced. "For him, anyway," he added with a laugh.

No one else in the room laughed with him.

Adel said, "We'll obviously want to maintain that the new act is not retroactive and, therefore, doesn't apply to Sorenson's case, thereby limiting the company's exposure to the new remedies and a jury trial. Sorenson's lawyer will argue the opposite, and in our circuit there is precedent that supports his argument—a couple of decisions from the Eleventh Circuit and one or two out of the district courts. They may eventually be overruled, but we just can't tell. In effect, some sixty thousand charges of discrimination, and hundreds and hundreds of pending cases, have all been placed in a stage of judicial limbo."

"Well, I guess we should thank the President," Scarlechek said. "Otherwise, the act would've certainly been made retroactive by Congress."

"I guess it depends on your point of view," Tiyona said, who had followed the issue as it had developed and was a proponent of retroactive application.

"And surely yours is for the benefit of the company, Tiyona," Scarlechek said.

"Surely," Tiyona retorted, focusing square upon Scarlechek's eyes.

Adel took Tiyona's comments to mean that the company would be better off acknowledging broader civil rights for its workers, and act accordingly—an "enlightened self-interest" point of view. Tiyona's meaning had gone right over Scarlechek's head, but Adel didn't allow herself to agree with Tiyona because agreement would make advocating the company's position more difficult.

Nonetheless, Adel couldn't help thinking that Tiyona's views made sense: if corporations broke the law, the policy of the law—that people should be treated fairly—would be better served by allowing full remedies for the victims. It was because of high-powered corporate America lobbyists that the president's administration reacted against retroactivity—a flank attack while the main lines battled at the Glass Ceiling.

Corporations themselves would be better served, Adel thought. *Treat people fairly and they'll treat you fairly. Give a little and you'll get more. My God, I'm thinking like Michael.*

The discussion turned to fees. Adel's standard hourly rate was two hundred dollars. Laughlin found it odd that Scarlechek didn't attempt to negotiate a lower rate.

Scarlechek had one last question. "Ti, as Sandy's representative here, do you feel we should hire this firm on the case?" He already knew the answer, but Scarlechek wanted Tiyona's statement for the record.

"Well Lou, I thought that was supposed to be your decision, but yes, I do." Tiyona's answer was straightforward and to the point— each of them.

She turned to Adel and Dave. "Ms. Blair, would you and Mr. McKerrin like to come see the plant? I can show you around, let you meet some of the people. It might be important. I also have this for you to read," she added, raising her file.

"Yes, I would," Adel said, turning to Dave.

"Adel, I can't," Dave said. "I've got another meeting, and I think we all know, you don't need me."

"Well, I can drive you back to Orlando on my way home," Tiyona said to Adel.

"Thanks," Adel said.

Tiyona and Adel were the last to leave Scarlechek's office. Just as Tiyona exited with Adel close behind, Scarlechek grabbed Adel's arm. At first his touch was forceful, but it softened, as if to show how gentle he could be.

Adel stood there, waiting.

He slid his hand to her waist, where it lingered as he spoke, "I'll call you next week to talk about our seminar. Perhaps we can do it over a quick dinner. My schedule is very hectic. Would you mind?"

"No. Just give me a call," Adel said, thinking things were going well.

CHAPTER 32

"That fuckin' bitch! She sued me? Fo' what?" Red Wade spoke in a throbbing cadence and muffled southern tone, as though his mouth was stuffed with cotton. It *was* stuffed with Redman, and he spat dark juice onto the asphalt in the parking lot. Tiyona and Adel had caught up with Wade, the treatment plant superintendent, just as he was leaving for the day.

For being a redneck asshole, Adel thought without the slightest change of expression.

Tiyona studied Adel, searching for a reaction to his rage. She'd suspected they'd find men like Wade at the plant. It was why she'd suggested they come here first. Adel's features gave no hint of her true thoughts, but Tiyona suspected that Adel had already sized him up and was calculating how he would fit into their analysis.

"Fo' what?" Wade reiterated. At six feet two inches tall, and two hundred thirty pounds, the man was nicknamed for his ruddy complexion and reddish blond hair, as well as his favorite chaw. His head was huge, with a high forehead over thick, protruding bone on his brow. Considered a man's man, he was big, ugly and mean.

Tiyona turned to Wade and said, "For sexual harassment." *Of course,* she thought.

"Sex'l h'rassment! She was a fuckin' ho', fo' Christ's sake! What da hell is sex'l h'rassment?"

A whore? Adel realized Wade's question wasn't as ignorant as it seemed; it was rhetorical, his implication being that a prostitute couldn't be protected. "You're serious?" she asked.

"Co'se Ah am. She turned tricks on da Trail." The "Trail" was

State Road 441—also known as the Orange Blossom Trail—that ran through Orlando's west side and was renowned for the darker side of life.

"How do you know?"

"B'lieve me, Ah kno'." He spat saliva and tobacco juice again.

"How?" Adel's voice hardened. "How do you know?"

"Me an' sum' da boys seen her. 'Co'se, dat was long time 'go."

"How long ago?"

"Eight years, Ah'd say," he replied, rubbing his chin. "So how da hell kin she sue me?"

"Anybody can sue anyone at any time, for anything," Adel said. "The question is whether they'll win."

She measured the man. He seemed placated by her response although her answer wasn't designed for that. Maybe he was just puzzled.

"She says that you allowed obscene pictures to be hung in the plant and that you even hung some. She says she complained a lot about sexual conduct and you didn't do anything. She claims there were some very inappropriate things done, and if it's true, she may have a valid right to sue you, Rick Osgood, and this Martyn Evans."

"Rick 'n' Mahty too, huh?" Rick Osgood was an operator on the first shift, and Martyn Evans was the plant manager.

"*And* the company," said Tiyona.

"Fo' Christ's sake. What a crock o' shit."

"Listen, you shouldn't worry about this now. I'm your lawyer. The company has hired me to defend you and the others, along with the company. I'll be talking to you a lot. Right now we want to see the plant."

Adel soon realized that the wastewater treatment plant constituted the dregs of the company in more ways than one. It reeked of human waste that festered and gave life to bugs. The bugs, Wade explained, fed on themselves and the slimy, dark brown substance known as sludge. Sludge was moved through the plant with consistent drudgery, like ancient slaves making brick from straw and mud.

The plant was class A, and with the work of only thirteen employees in three shifts, it moved twenty million gallons of raw sewage daily from all over Western Town. The influent moved first to the primary settling tank, where the bigger solids settled out. From there, it traveled into aeration bays, where oxygen percolated through, and microorganisms—the bugs—were introduced to lower the biochemical oxygen demand, or BOD.

"BOD's da way we measure da p'lutants in da water," Wade explained. "Da bugs ..."

"What are the bugs, exactly?" Adel asked.

"Wayell, little missy, 'cept, yo' ain't so little, er ya?" He sized Adel up and down. "Anyways, yo' got yo'r bacteria, yo'r viruses ... an' uh ... an' algae, co'se. Anyways, dey eats da bad stuff. C'mere, Ah'll sho y'all."

He moved them over to a big tank. Adel and Tiyona watched brown liquid move through a tube and into the clarifier tank.

"Here da sludge an' bugs settle out. Chlo'ine's added, an' da clear water flo's ovah da top o' da weirs an' back inta da water system. Da sludge's sucked out an' transpo'ted to da digester where da bugs eat it all gone, an' den dey eat each other. If'n dere's any escess, we move it back to da start, o' to drying beds where it dries into a nahce crusty, dick cake, jus' lahke Momma used ta make. 'Ceptin' yo' don't eat it. Wayell, yo' kin if'n yo' want to, but Ah don' recommend it."

He laughed at the thought.

"Da cake's compressed fo' fertilizer," he said.

Wade explained that the plant personnel included him as Superintendent; three Chief Operators, one for each shift, and each "class A" licensed; four other Operators; two maintenance men; an electrician; and two laborers. The plant operated in three shifts—seven to three, three to eleven, and eleven to seven. All employees worked the first shift, except for a Chief Operator and an Operator for each of the second and third shifts. There was little to do during these latter shifts except monitor the systems, add chlorine, and answer the occasional phone call. Employees often studied or watched television, whatever passed the time.

"We operate day in an' day out," Wade explained, "twenty-fo' hours a day."

The plant was nothing more than a giant filter, much like a human liver—saturated with reddish-brown nasty stuff. Adel wondered whether the plant reflected the moral fiber of Western Town itself, encrusted with dried stereotypes and caked-on attitudes.

Wade, who was ready for a break, basked in his good fortune. Escorting two pretty damn good-lookin' women (even if one of them was a "niggrah") was special, and he decided to entertain them with his sense of humor.

"Hey, y'all heerd da one 'bout da tall 'ho lady dat walked inta da bar?" Not waiting for an answer, he continued, "Yo' see, she's wearin' dis sleeveless dress, an' ah … an' she walks in an' raises her arm and points, an' looks all 'round, showing everyone her hairy-ass armpit an' says, 'Who'll buy a lady a drink?' An' dis blind-staggerin' drunk guy at da bar yells, 'Give da ballerina a drink.' An' da bartender says, 'Fine, but why yo' call her a ballerina?' An' da drunk says, 'Anyone who can lift her leg dat high, got to be a ballerina!'"

The redneck smirked, eager for acknowledgment from the ladies of his brilliant wit.

Adel changed the subject. "What more do you know about Sorenson?" she said.

Damn, dis bitch is cold, Wade thought. "Not much, 'cept what she done 'roun' here."

"Tell us about that," Adel said.

"Liza done started here as a "class B" Operator, workin' on da dird shift. Her Chief Operator was Andy … Andy Collela."

"Adel," Tiyona said. "I've got a work-up on all this. Why don't we let him go, and we'll go into the office so you can check it out? Then we'll be on the same page and we can talk a little more about how we want to proceed."

"Oh, that's fine," Adel said. "I guess you're off the hook for now, Mr. Wade."

"Wayell, good," Wade said. "Ah felt lahke a big ole bass Ah caught me once. Heh heh. Das a little joke dere, missy. Tell yo' what, yo' give me a call, an' Ah'll lern ya everthin' yo' need to know."

He winked at Adel.

"An yo' kin come, too, dere, little niggrah girl. Ah ain't no bigot.

An' Ah got mo' dan 'nuff to go 'roun.' Y'all'll find out what a *real* man's lahke."

Tiyona's blood began to boil and she began to lunge at Wade, but Adel held her back.

"Thanks, but no thanks, Mr. Wade," Adel said. "Ah don' think yo' little ole heart could stand it."

Wade opened his overstuffed mouth and spat, and then started to answer.

Adel interrupted with a forceful voice. "Where's the office, Mr. Wade?"

· · · ·

Inside, Tiyona remained livid. She tossed the Sorenson file onto the table.

"I'm sorry, Adel, I've got to take a walk and cool off. I'll let you read all this stuff, and be back in a half hour or so."

"Fine," Adel said. "Look, Tiyona, it's none of my business and I've just met you, but don't let a man like that get under your skin."

"Easy for you to say."

"No, it's not. It takes practice. … Listen, before you go, how'd you get all this info?"

"We've got some wanna-be private dicks in Security. They interviewed some people and put it together for us."

Tiyona left and Adel dug into the file. She found a few photos of Liza Sorenson, which Adel examined closely. Liza was of medium height with long brown hair and a shapely physique. She wore no makeup, but had a naturally pretty face. She looked like a tomboy who could be attractive if she wanted, but who appeared not to care.

Adel began to read the profiles of the plant employees.

Andy Collela was a single man, thirty-five years old, who took morning classes at the University of Central Florida after finishing the night shift at the plant. He did most of his studying on shift, and after class, he'd return to his mobile home to sleep. He was apparently content with his secluded, philosophical niche in the world, and Liza got along well with him.

Also a student at the same university, but majoring in psychology, Liza had found stability after a tumultuous first twenty-five years. Her mother died of leukemia when Liza was only eleven, and her father, an ironworker, taught her all about men of his caliber. The roughneck coerced her and made her his house-slave. He abused her sexually on a regular basis. She was sixteen when she ran away to Orlando. No one followed.

Rough, Adel thought. *I couldn't have handled that. Everything good that I had, this girl had the opposite.*

Liza had indeed turned to the street as Red Wade had reported. She had turned tricks on the Trail for a year and a half, seeing and doing it all: drugs, prostitution, other crimes. But one night, she escaped when a "john" offered to put her up and find her a job waiting tables. He was an unrefined man, but he had a streak of kindness for Liza.

Liza worked as a waitress for a year, and then took a job as a custodial worker at Western Town in the Maintenance Department of the Facilities Division. While working there, she heard about the easier fare of the second and third shift treatment plant operators, about their opportunities to study on the job. Although it didn't matter one iota to anyone in the world but her, she became determined to lift herself up and out, to learn, and to create a respectable life for herself.

Admirable, Adel thought.

Liza took a vocational course at Orlando Community College about wastewater treatment plants, and eventually transferred to the plant as a trainee. A year later, she'd earned her license. The only shift she wanted was the one she was assigned, the third, so she could study and continue taking courses.

Liza worked the third shift with Andy Collela for two uneventful years until Chuck Sullivan, an operator from the first shift, requested Liza's shift so *he* could study; he'd also decided to return to school. Chief Operator Bo Thompson, responsible for scheduling shifts, gave Sullivan the third shift and transferred Liza to first shift starting the next semester.

The male operators and Red Wade were all buddies, except for

Andy Collela who was viewed as odd. Red Wade, Bo Thompson, Rick Osgood, and Tommy Spikes (the second shift Chief Operator) were especially tight. They often hunted or play golfed, and sometimes, they'd include the two maintenance men, John Townsend and Barry Nielson. They even joked around with the two laborers, Manny Quintana and Mike Carmichael, but there was a natural pecking order that they wanted to preserve. The electrician, Jerry Morgan, and the only other woman in the plant, Christine Meyer, a second shift operator, distanced themselves from the boys club.

Liza accepted the idea of a new shift. She was ready for a change and could take some of her courses in the evening. Meanwhile, her interest in psychology grew fervent. This was natural, considering how she'd been treated in her youth, and she became a liberal feminist. By the time she started working the first shift, she'd learned about Title VII and sexual harassment.

Liza knew that the first and second shift men read and posted pictures from magazines like *Penthouse, Club*, and *Hustler* around the plant where Liza could see them. She'd taken them down every so often with Andy Collela's help, but new pictures would soon appear. In reaction, the men wrote epithets on the office blackboard and warnings against removal of the pictures. Liza always erased the message, and continued removing the pictures depending upon her mood.

When she was transferred to the first shift, she decided to change the practice. The first incident set the stage for the upcoming battles.

Tommy Spikes had picked up a *Club* the previous afternoon and cut out the picture of two blonds performing cunnilingus on each other. He'd liked the scene so much that he tacked it to the pin-up board next to the blackboard; the men paused to idolize the photo each time they passed. When Liza saw the photo the next morning, it particularly offended and embarrassed her. In her former occupation, she'd been paid to do what the picture depicted on at least three different occasions, as Johnny-handed johns looked on.

Bo Thompson saw Liza take the picture down, and told her to put it back up. "That's Tommy's," he said, spitting on the ground. "You can't do that."

139

An argument ensued, until Red Wade arrived and commanded her to pin Tommy's picture back up.

"Dat's Tommy's. Yo' hav' no raght to take dat down. If yo' don't lahke it, don't look at it!" Red yelled, puffing out his throat like a lizard. Liza protested, saying she shouldn't have to avoid the bulletin board where worker's compensation and other legal notices were also posted, including one about the EEOC.

Red said, "Look sistah, dis is Boys' Town. Yo' chose a man's profession. If'n yo' don't lahke it, get out!"

Liza took her complaint to Marty Evans. He patronized her, acting as though she'd overreacted, but agreed to take a look.

"Look Red, that's a sexual act," Evans said when he saw the picture. "We don't need to post that up. Let's keep the pornography down."

So the picture came down, but the battle lines were drawn. News of the incident spread through the plant. Within a week, three more pictures appeared, all nude women in sexually suggestive poses, but no "acts."

In another week, Liza came in to find taped to her locker, a picture of two naked women, one white and one black. The white woman was lying back using a dildo, and the black woman was hunched over the white woman from the side in a pose suggesting she was licking the white woman's breast. Below the picture, someone had taped a large dildo to Liza's locker.

Liza marched the items to Marty Evans. Although he was upset at the prank, he was angrier that the boys could force him to have to take action. But none of the men took responsibility and he sent Liza away with heartfelt regret. After all, he couldn't punish everyone. All he could say to her was, "Look, just try not to provoke them."

Christine Meyer entreated Liza to refrain from complaining. A homely woman, she'd worked at the plant for ten years. Her appearance didn't seem to matter and, at times, the men had directed crude, hostile acts and comments at her. She kept her mouth shut once she discovered that, every time she complained, the situation only worsened. The same pattern was happening with Liza.

Adel paused in her reading and pondered. *If this is true, this place is horrible,* she thought. *But still, was she really a prostitute? Is she still, and is this all a set-up?* Adel read on.

After work one afternoon, Red Wade, Bo Thompson, and Rick Osgood sat at a grungy tavern in a rural community near Western Town. They reminisced about their encounters with hookers (an expense they occasionally shared). That's when Osgood realized where he'd seen Liza before. Once, years ago, the three of them hired two hookers to give a show before each was serviced. Liza was one of the nightwalkers.

The next day was hell for Liza. She denied the truth, but Red Wade said, "Ah kin see it in yo' eyes, yo'r lahin'." From then on, in their eyes, she was nothing more than a hooker.

Osgood propositioned her, half in jest. She complained to Red Wade, calling Osgood's behavior sexual harassment. She realized her mistake as soon as she spoke the words.

On another occasion, someone posted a centerfold of a naked brunette spanking herself. Liza happened to walk by and notice the men crowded around the centerfold like chimpanzees around a banana bunch. Osgood chided her about her past and asked her to strike the same pose as the centerfold. Liza ignored him, which only egged him on. He offered to spank her himself, and did. Liza reeled, trying to fight back, but Christine Meyer restrained her and got her out of there.

A month later, Mike Carmichael, the laborer, drew a picture on the blackboard of a nude woman that revealed the woman's privates, with two mounds between her legs. He drew a square around her vagina, and wrote "USDA Grade A Choice." The men laughed, while Christine Meyer and Liza said nothing. Two days later, Rick Osgood added "L.S." to the caption. Liza, in tears, gathered her things and went home.

The following Monday, Liza paid Marty Evans a visit.

"Listen, whether you were or weren't doesn't matter, Liza. I'll talk to the men and tell them that the propositions, if they happened, had better damn well stop. But you know you're in a man's world on this job, Liza. The company didn't ask you to work at the plant, for God's sake. Boys will be boys, and you're just gonna have to live with the pictures or go somewhere else. I draw the line at pictures of sexual acts, and I'll tell 'em. Hell, I've told 'em. That's pornography in my book. Other than that, the boys have always posted pictures around here. What you see is everywhere, even on television. You don't have to look at them—just look the other God damn way."

Evans did as he promised, and talked to the men and laid down the rules. But the pictures proliferated. Sexual remarks increased. Christine Meyer chastised Liza. Liza asked for a change back to the third shift. Denied. She began looking for a new job. Later, she filed an official charge of discrimination, but the charge sat buried on the desk of a beleaguered EEOC investigator.

· · · ·

"Well, what do you think?" Tiyona asked during their drive back to downtown Orlando.

"I think you've got your work cut out for you."

"I heard that."

"Mr. Wade will be a problem witness. We'll have to work with him a great deal. But I think we should run another background check on Sorenson with a real private detective, this time. If we can prove she's a prostitute, I doubt her lawyer will let the case go to trial."

"What about if she was a prostitute, but quit?" Tiyona asked. Tiyona, on the other hand, had been with the company too long.

"Hmm-m. Interesting. I don't know about that."

"Well, have your secretary let me know the interview dates and times. " Tiyona said. "Listen, why don't I see you in any women's organizations around town?"

"Oh, I don't know." Adel didn't want to offend Tiyona by expressing her lack of interest.

"How 'bout coming with me some time? There's the Orlando chapter of the Women's League, or the Women in Business Group. Just if you want to, you know."

"Yeah, sure. That'd be fine," Adel said halfheartedly.

Tiyona didn't care, deciding she'd seize the opening. There was something about Adel that she liked.

CHAPTER 33

Adel placed her call the next morning.

"Hello, Steve, how are you?"

"Fine, Adel. And you?" he asked, his Latin accent perceptible.

"Just fine." Their exchange was restrained, in the same way dogs display their teeth before lunging at each other's throats.

Liza Sorenson's lawyer was Esteban Gonzalez, a Miami transplant of Cuban descent. A trial lawyer to the core, Gonzalez was a practitioner of fifteen years. He craved the excitement of trial, its preparation, the guessing and second-guessing, and the thrill of predicting the unpredictable. Trials brought his six-foot-two-inch frame to life. Working the judge, even the bailiff and the clerk, appealed to him, and he strived to gain their confidence, because it mattered.

Then there was the jury—the ultimate challenge for a trial lawyer. There was nothing greater than the power and control he experienced in front of a jury. The men of the jury envied Gonzalez's prowess and the women admired his wit, charm and intelligence while resting their eyes on his sleek, Latin body. He was full of himself.

Gonzalez and Adel often battled each other in court. They respected but didn't like each other, probably because they were alike in their competitiveness. They had settled several cases between them, with no one the clear winner, but of the two cases that went to trial, each won one. Adel had prevailed in the most recent one, but Gonzalez had filed an appeal on his client's behalf that was still pending.

"Well, what can I do for you?" Gonzalez asked.

"You've sued one of my clients, Western Town—"

"Oh! Adel, congratulations! That's a very good client for you."

"Thank you. Western Town engaged my services yesterday and its response to your complaint is due Monday. Would you grant a small extension to investigate the matter before we respond? Perhaps … thirty days."

"Thirty days!"

"Of course, I can file a simple motion or two."

Her threat was clear. Sorenson had filed her complaint without issuance by the Equal Employment Opportunity Commission of a "right to sue" letter, a required precondition to suit. While Sorenson probably had a legal excuse—the overworked EEOC had sat on the case—Adel could file a motion to dismiss the complaint and test the issue. She could also file a motion to strike the Title VII requests for future compensatory damages, punitive damages, and for a jury trial, by arguing that the new civil rights amendment did not apply to pre-act conduct. If she filed either or both motions, Gonzalez would have to prepare a memorandum of law. Adel would reply, and by the time the judge got around to reading their filings, thirty days would be long past.

"All right, I'll give you thirty days, provided you agree to answer and not file any motions." He really didn't mind too much, having expected a request anyway, just for a shorter period. Having the case on a contingency fee arrangement, so that he would only be compensated if and when his client recovered, he was averse to doing extra work in the meantime. His goal was to get to mediation or trial quickly and easily.

"Agreed," Adel replied. Her motions might be unsuccessful anyway, and she preferred to raise them as affirmative defenses and make a technical motion before trial. By then, a favorable decision might have come down on the applicability of the new act.

"You'll do the confirming letter?" he asked.

"Yes. We'll be sending out a request for production and interrogatories shortly. After that, I suppose we can get together on depositions. Thanks so much for suing my client." The gratitude was a polite, half-jocular cliché among lawyers.

"Well, tell your client thanks for their evil ways," he said. "You've got to change. Tell them Carlos Santana did a song."

"Hmm, well, we'll see about that."

CHAPTER 34

Three days later, Adel was traveling down Interstate 4 for her first interviews, when her cell phone rang.

"Adel, hello. This is Lou Scarlechek."

"Oh, hello. How are you?" she asked, wanting to be charming.

"Fine, thank you." The note of enthusiasm in her voice pleased him. "Listen, I know you're busy today ... you've got interviews, correct? And my schedule is as ridiculous as always." He just couldn't help himself. It was fun letting people know how busy he was, and saying it made it so. "So, how 'bout this evening, would you be good enough to meet me for a quick cocktail and dinner at seven? I can't get away before then, but I want to speak to you about the seminar and find out what you learn today."

"Sure, that'd be fine. Where?"

"At the Ranchero Hotel in the La Cocina restaurant," he replied. The southwestern style hotel was part of the Western Town Resort. "See you there?"

"Yes."

CHAPTER 35

Adel soon arrived at the wastewater treatment plant on Western Town property. Pulling her car into the parking lot, she looked around and took in the native forest surrounding the plant. Over the tree line, she could just see the tips of the taller attractions, including the rails of the Tombstone Tornado roller coaster. A tram carrying dozens of riders twisted and turned, rose and fell, while the riders screamed in both terror and delight. Farther off, the famous full-scale replica of Fort Apache sat on a hill.

The plant grounds, with its massive pipelines, drying fields and numerous tanks gave off a distinctive stench. Adel mulled how visitors might react to this side of Western Town. What would these visitors think if they knew what happened behind the scenes?

Tiyona appeared from the opposite end of the parking lot.

"Interesting contrast, isn't it?" said Tiyona.

"Yes." Adel noted Tiyona's perceptiveness.

"Well, shall we open Pandora's box?" Tiyona gestured toward the concrete block office building to the right of the plant. Adel smiled as they walked toward its front door marked, "Facilities Administration."

Their first interview was with Bo Thompson. He denied almost everything that Liza claimed. Although he did admit that a few pictures of naked woman had been hung, but none by him. He didn't know who had hung them or that Liza had been offended. He also denied hiring Liza as a hooker.

Adel studied him. He acted as though she and Tiyona were the police and he'd committed a crime. He answered their questions, but volunteered no additional information or any help in understanding the case. Adel tried to explain that she was on his and the company's side, but it didn't matter. He was convinced his evasiveness was helping him and the company, thinking if he kept the truth from the company lawyer, it could never be exposed.

"He's lying," Tiyona said afterward.

"I know," Adel replied. "He'll make a bad impression on a jury. Gonzalez will chew him up and spit him out on the witness stand."

Their interview with Rick Osgood went off better. Osgood told them everything and admitted all. He contradicted Thompson when he admitted that he, Thompson, and Wade had, indeed, once hired Liza as whore. He described what Liza had done to the other hooker and to them.

"The dildo?" Osgood said, as he laughed. "Yeah, I did that. I taped the picture of the women and the dildo to Liza's locker. Then I propositioned Liza. It was funny. But get this—she rejected me only after we couldn't agree on the price. She's expensive, man! Wanted two bills … Yeah, I added 'L.S.' to Carmichael's drawing, but only 'cause Liza demanded an outrageous price for sex. No one charges that much. … Yeah, I slapped Liza's butt. But she didn't mind. It was all a big joke."

It was unfortunate, but Adel knew that Osgood would make a believable witness—believably bad for the company. But his story about Sorenson negotiating a price for sex was intriguing. If the jury believed his version of the story, it could cause tremendous damage to Sorenson's case, especially once the jury found out about her history.

Red Wade was Red Wade. He cursed and spat dark, disgusting stuff into a plastic Coke bottle.

"Gimme a fuckin' break! Da world's a messed up place if'n we protects a little bitch-ho' lahke her. Sho' all dese things happened. Dere ain't no hidin' 'em. It don' make no nevermind to no one. Y'all put me in front a dat judge an' jury. Ah'll set 'em straight. Ah'll bet the women'll ask me out 'fo it's ovah."

At the end of his interview, Wade looked at Adel and said, "So ah, C'mone now. Y'all reconsidered mah proposition? Ah tol' y'all, y'all'll get to be wiff a real man."

Adel glared at him. "We're afraid, Mr. Wade—"

"Ahh, y'all doesn't have ta be."

"… of what we'd contract."

Wade scratched his head. Adel and Tiyona left and drove to the nearest employee cafeteria for a late lunch before their meeting with Tommy Spikes at the start of his second shift.

· · · ·

"Well, how do you like Western Town?" Tiyona asked Adel, after they sat down with their lunch trays, her tone overflowing with sarcasm.

"'Boys' Town adequately describes this place," Adel replied, mimicking the dossier's record of a conversation between Sorenson and Red Wade. She was having a difficult time remaining clinical.

"Adel, I see this kind of thing all the time. I've tried to counter it with policies, programs, and seminars, but I'm not taken seriously or even truly allowed to do my job. They won't give me the power I need to enforce my programs because they view me as an interference. The result is this 'wastewater treatment plant' mentality. It's not confined to the plant, but extends throughout the company, even in the upper echelons. It's not as blatant, but it's there. And anytime anyone ever cries harassment or discrimination, the response is that the complainant is just using that as a weapon to get ahead. It's in mainstream views too. Why, there was even a famous novel suggesting that once … remember? Crichton, perhaps. On top of that …," Tiyona said, as she paused to labor over her thoughts. "Adel, I'm not sure that I should be the corporate rep in this case. I don't know that I can support the cause. If they take my deposition, the company'll be in big trouble."

"Why?"

"Have you heard of the Glass Ceiling?"

Adel was familiar with the term, but said, "Tell me about it."

"Well, it's a phenomenon that's been studied by the Women's Bureau of the Federal Department of Labor. It's a term coined to refer to the artificial barriers within corporations that keep women and minorities down. It prevents them from rising too high through the corporate ranks. It's like the white males' answer to Title VII. Title VII was enacted in '64, saying you have to hire women and minorities. Well, corporate America did, but while the numbers of women and minorities entering corporate America increased, we've been kept down. For the most part, we're hired only so high, or allowed to climb the ladder only so much. You see?"

"Yes."

"Well, that's the case in this company. Look at me … I interact with vice presidents and directors, but I'm only a manager. Why? And the things I try to implement are not given full support. Why? Part of it is because I'm only a manager. I don't have the power. But part of it is for other reasons. There's at least a discriminatory effect, intentional or not, to keep us down. I was told to study this in the company and keep statistics. Sometimes I think they've forgotten they asked me to do this."

She paused and studied Adel, then continued, undaunted by Adel's inscrutable expression.

"Adel, with some it may be intentional, I don't know. But in my opinion, there's a disparate impact class action case lurking within the company, which upholds tacit, unstated policies that follow stereotypes. There's a belief that a woman is innately unable to project a credible image of authority to successfully interact on a high level. Or, that a black man isn't intelligent enough to deal with high-powered corporate politics. There are so many examples I can think of. I think the evil emanates from the very top."

"Also, anything in the company involving mentoring, grooming, and cronyism excludes females and minorities. Even the golf courses … well, 'birds of a feather' … you know. There's no written policy on all this, but it happens. Probably quite naturally, but minorities and women get shafted. You see? We're still not being treated fairly."

"Yes, I understand," Adel said, taken aback.

"Look, I'm sorry to unload on you like this. But if this case goes further, I may not be right for corporate rep. I'll talk to Sandy Yates about it. He'll probably want me to stay in it for my initial assessment, anyway."

"Speaking of which …," Adel interrupted, trying to get back to the case. She'd been feeling rather uncomfortable. After all, this was her new, prized client Tiyona was talking about. Tiyona could actually be lead plaintiff in the theoretical class action she'd mentioned. Adel changed the subject, but found little solace. "Our witnesses, so far, aren't so good. Thompson won't be strong or believable. Red Wade will be believable, but what he says hurts us. Plus, the jury will react negatively to his personality. And Osgood's even worse than Wade. He seems truthful, but he's a snake. The only thing that may help us is his story about negotiating her price with Liza on his solicitation for sex. Of course, she'll deny that, and there are no witnesses. After I depose her, I'll have to try to predict which of them will be more believable."

"I wonder what Spikes will add this afternoon," Tiyona said.

"We'll see."

"Um hmm. By the way, one of my women's groups meets this evening. Go with me?"

"I can't, Ti," Adel said. She was thankful she had an excuse, but hoped it didn't show. "Lou Scarlechek asked me to meet him at a restaurant to report on the case and to discuss a racial discrimination seminar he wants me to give to his department." She gathered some comfort by adding that bit of information, thinking it would be perceived by Tiyona as good news.

"Oh-h," Tiyona exhaled, ignoring what Adel thought would be upbeat. "What about Laughlin, will he be there?"

"Apparently not."

"Uh oh … watch out."

"What do you mean?" Adel asked.

"You're a big girl. I'll let you find out for yourself."

CHAPTER 36

Adel's high heels tapped against the hard tile floor of the La Cocina restaurant at the Ranchero Hotel, her tailored suit showing off long, shapely lines with each step. Heads turned and conversations buzzed in the room over the festive music of Mariachis in the background. She smelled the aroma of freshly baked tortillas, and stopped to allow a waiter to scurry past her with a plate of enchiladas smothered with green chilies.

It's been a long day, Adel thought. *But I have to be charming a while longer. This is a great opportunity. Still, I'd rather be home on the erg.*

Scarlechek was already waiting for her, and he rose as Adel took a seat.

"Good evening," Scarlechek said, grinning, dressed in a charcoal Armani. Removing the coat revealed ever-present suspenders and starched white shirt.

"Hello," Adel replied, noticing the monogrammed initials on his shirt cuffs. She didn't know why she had such an aversion to that typical, ostentatious badge. *Maybe his cleaner requires them,* she mused.

"Thank you so much for joining me. I only have about an hour break before I need to be back in the office, but this allows me to kill two birds with one stone—eating, while getting a report from you. But first ... I strongly recommend the margaritas here. They are excellent," he said, as the waiter arrived at the table. "Shall I order two?"

"Yes, I could use one right about now."

After they listened to the waiter's recitation of the night's specials, Scarlechek ordered their drinks. The Mariachis were moving and playing about the room. When the waiter returned, Scarlechek said to Adel, "You know, often when I come here, I have the chef make up a special sampler platter for dinner. It's excellent. Would you like to try it?"

"That sounds fine. I love Mexican food."

"Well, I didn't until I came to work for Western Town. But I had to learn to like it, fast. I'm from New York, you know, Wall Street."

He said to the Mexican waiter, "You know the drill, Manuel." Turning back to her, he inquired, "So tell me, how did it go today?"

"Well, if it weren't for the fact that Sorenson is allegedly a prostitute, or at least used to be, I'd recommend settling right now."

"What? She's a prostitute?"

"That's what our witnesses say. Or at least she used to be."

"Really? That's amazing. So, if it weren't for that, you'd recommend settling now. Why?"

"Our witnesses are horrible. They're either evasive or so chauvinistic that they'll come across poorly to the jury, assuming the judge allows a jury trial. Besides, three of them admit the things that happened."

"But are hanging pictures and making comments illegal?"

"They can be, under certain circumstances."

"Whom did you interview today?"

"Tommy Spikes, Bo Thompson, Rick Osgood and Red Wade, the superintendent. I'm not impressed with any of them, I must tell you. I'd be afraid to put them on the stand."

"Why does her being a prostitute or not make any difference?"

"Well, it doesn't, from a technical legal point of view. But it's relevant to the issues of unwelcomeness and credibility. If the jury knows about her prostitution background, they may disregard her testimony completely. Or, they may find that the conduct, which at least three of our guys admit, was welcome, not unwelcome."

"And, I take it, 'unwelcomeness' is a key element to a plaintiff's case in a matter like this?"

"Yeah, it's one of the most frequently litigated issues in the field.

153

And like in a rape case, the victim's conduct becomes an issue. You know, did the woman invite sexual remarks with her attire or, did she engage in flirtation, or implicitly invite the harassment. There are no per se rules of what is or is not harassing, except for quid pro quo, really. It's all in the eyes of the beholder. What's unwelcome and what's not. ... Then if it's not pure quid pro quo, even though it's unwelcome, it has to rise to the level of creating a hostile or offensive working environment. Here, the jury is supposed to determine the position of a reasonable person or a reasonable woman, depending on the jurisdiction."

"Why the two different standards, again? I know we talked about this some," he added, remembering their first meeting.

"Well, the field is still relatively young, and case law is evolving. Some courts have borrowed from tort law and simply utilized the reasonable person standard. Others have tried to become more sensitive to the woman's point of view, and have used the reasonable woman test. But believe it or not, some feminists are against that. They say it's patronizing, and there should simply be per se rules of violation. You offer a woman a position in exchange for sexual favors, for example, you get hit with liability automatically, regardless of how women view the conduct. The reasoning is that some women don't know what's good for them."

Scarlechek shivered. He'd done just that many times, and had something similar on his mind with her. "And what's your position on the issue?" he asked, disguising his discomfort.

"Does that matter?" she said. Then she remembered she wasn't with Dave McKerrin, and hoped she hadn't offended him.

"Of course it does," he said with conviction. He could've become defensive, but chose offense. "If I'm going to hire you for cases, I want to know where you stand politically, on that and many issues." Scarlechek directed the conversation to where he really wanted it to go, hinting he'd hire her more. "We need to get to know each other, don't you agree?" Hanging out tried and true bait, he attempted to pique her interest.

"Well, I'm not a radical feminist, if that's what you're asking." She ducked the question, not realizing why it was important. "I don't believe we should have per se liability, except to the extent we already have under quid pro quo analysis. I agree with the reasonable woman standard when it's the woman being harassed. If her feelings are going to be judged, they shouldn't be compared to a man's."

The margaritas arrived just in time, and Adel relaxed while dinner was served. She could hear the grilled onions sizzling on hot platters, and smell the red chili ranchero sauce on an enticing sampling of beef rancheros, taquitos, quesadillas, tostadas and enchiladas. Somehow, the hot Mexican food was soothing. Adel's natural introversion was challenged around most people, she'd rather be working out, or thinking through how to win a case. But this man ...

After the waiter left, Scarlechek continued his pursuit. "Now," he said, "You didn't answer my last question. Don't you think that I, as the executive vice president of the legal department, owe it to the company to get to know the attorneys we hire?"

"Certainly."

"Good, because I'm impressed with you, Adel. I want to give you a lot more of our work, even in other areas. But I need to get to know you a little better. So ... I thank you for joining me tonight. Will you join me like this occasionally?"

There it was—the surfacing malignancy—like an insect emerging from a cocoon. Sensing the need to take it slowly, he decided against anything too forward, but laid the groundwork instead. His intent wasn't illegal because the company didn't employ Adel. Nonetheless, it was incipient harassment. Here she was: a beautiful, intelligent Title VII expert, an attorney reporting to him about sexual harassment, and he had the balls to harass her while she was talking about it! He smiled.

Scarlechek's words startled Adel, and she grew wary. This wasn't the way clients usually approached her about more work. *But he's not coming on to me,* she concluded, swayed by the possibility that additional work from him would help her firm tremendously. *He just operates a little different because he's so busy.*

"Well sure, whenever it's convenient," was all she could think to say. Her awkwardness was apparent, but she dismissed the feeling that perhaps Scarlechek enjoyed her discomfort.

"Good. You know, Adel, I believe I can help your career a great deal. I'm going places in this company. I have political connections that continue to grow, and I want to help you because I believe in you."

She looked at him quizzically. "I have no desire to be political."

"Oh, but you should! With your looks and intelligence, there's no telling how far you can go!"

"Sorry. Not me. I don't like politics or politicians."

Scarlechek was irritated that his point—how much he could do for her—had taken on a negative path. He'd wrongly assumed she'd want as much power as she could get.

"No politics. Got it," he said, smiling. "Well, I still have confidence in you as a lawyer and want to help your career. I think I can." He smiled again.

Why? We barely know each other, she thought but said nothing.

"Good things happen to good people," he added as though reading her mind. "If you know what I mean."

They continued their meal in silence for a few moments. Then, Scarlechek asked how she kept in such great shape, deciding not to let on about seeing her at the Mayor's Cup Regatta. She explained about rowing and her rowing club. Telling her that he was quite a boating enthusiast, he wanted to know all the details—where they practiced, where they kept their boats, and more.

Finally, the conversation turned to the race discrimination seminar she was to give at Western Town. They agreed to postpone it for two or three months because of the timing of the Sorenson case. Now that his web was being spun around Adel, he couldn't care less.

He motioned to the waiter. "Well, I've got to get back now. Shall we?"

"Yes. Thank you very much for dinner."

As they walked out of the restaurant, Scarlechek noticed heads turning and gawking at Adel. He flipped back his hair and smiled proudly, for now, relishing the pleasure of being seen with her. *Let people stare. Let them wonder—they think she's mine.*

Just as they reached the corner leading to the hotel lobby and turned, Scarlechek was flushed by different emotions as he beheld the view. His cocky expression turned sheepish in an instant. One would've thought he'd come upon his wife, wondering about the business necessity of taking such a beautiful young woman to dinner.

But it wasn't his wife.

CHAPTER 37

The coincidence was poetic justice—DeeDee Lane's parents were in town, and she was showing them around.

It wasn't shame the vice president of the legal department felt. It was more akin to what a child felt getting caught with his hand in the cookie jar, regret that he'd been caught. It was awkward to him, because he was beginning the same business with Adel that he currently had going with DeeDee, and here they were together. Even Scarlechek had some sick sense of scruples.

There was no avoiding the encounter. All eyes had met and Adel smiled at DeeDee, whom she recognized from the elevator. It'd be ungracious not to acknowledge each other, though both DeeDee and Scarlechek would've preferred it. Scarlechek recovered his composure and led the introductions, turning on the charisma.

"DeeDee, now, why aren't you working?" he quipped, trying to make light of the situation.

"Hello Lou," she said coldly. She introduced her parents and Scarlechek introduced Adel, explaining that Adel was a lawyer representing the company on a case. DeeDee eyed them skeptically.

Small talk ensued and Scarlechek carried it off behind a crocodile smile. *My God, I deserve an Oscar,* he thought. *I've just introduced Adel to DeeDee and DeeDee's parents! I can do* anything *and get away with it. It's not what's said, it's* who *says it.*

DeeDee's shame was only exceeded by her hatred of Scarlechek, never feeling it so intensely until now. It was the shock of confronting this man, who represented evil in her eyes, in the presence of her parents—who personified good. It was blasphemy.

This man's a thief, she thought. *He's robbed me of my innocence. He's placed me in an impossible position and forced me to choose wrongly.* In a moment of clarity in the presence of her parents, she realized she could do it no longer.

Scarlechek bid adieu after offering the Lanes complimentary theme park passes and dinner reservations. DeeDee's parents were captivated and impressed. Their little girl *must* be doing well to have such an extraordinary man doting over them. She must be well worth her salt to the company.

Adel watched the interaction, and remembered the solemn look on DeeDee's face at the elevator. She recognized a similar look now. *She's cute, but there's something sad about her,* Adel thought, wondering about the story behind the young secretary.

CHAPTER 38

"Photos of nude women have been hung by the men since dirt around here," Marty Evans explained to Adel the next day, using an expression that referred to the beginnings of Western Town. "Boys will be boys," he added in a trite, shameless apology. The fifty-four-year-old plant manager explained that the pictures were not pornography—they depicted nothing more than what's depicted on television daily, at the movies, on billboards, and elsewhere in society. Liza Sorenson was hypersensitive or lying.

"I have never allowed pictures of sexual acts," he said.

"Would you have allowed Sorenson or Christine Meyer to hang a photograph of a nude man?" Tiyona asked.

"Hell no," he declared. "That'd be completely offensive to the men in the plant. They'd feel gay if they even glanced at it. Society doesn't focus on males the same as it does females."

Adel lingered on his comment. She figured it was true in some distorted way, and wondered what caused the phenomenon. But she found herself disagreeing that it made a difference, and she felt a twinge of impatience and anger. She looked at Tiyona, who showed similar feelings on her face.

"Whenever the boys were out of line," he said, "I straightened them out, *pronto*. Sorenson brought most of the problems upon herself by simply taking the job."

Like the notion in the law of "coming to a nuisance," Adel thought. *An attractive nuisance.*

"She chose a man's job. It's her fault," he reasoned. "She caused her own problems by her constant whining," he added. "Hell, she's probably claiming this just to get ahead."

Adel remembered her conversation with Tiyona in the cafeteria.

"The Chrichton novel," Tiyona muttered.

"Next she'll be after my job," Evans said.

"Do you know anything about Sorenson being a prostitute?" Adel asked.

"I have no knowledge of that. However," he added, his face turning red, "if she was, I want to know about it. I have no sympathy for her under those circumstances. Sounds like she's been just setting us up. We should've fired her skinny ass."

"Why don't I ever see you at any of my seminars?" Tiyona asked, marveling at his insensitivity.

"I don't need any seminars to tell me what I already know. I know we have policies against sexual discrimination, and I know that sexual harassment is part of that. But there's been no sexual harassment here—we haven't had any bosses demanding sex from the women in this plant!"

CHAPTER 39

That Andy Collela didn't want to talk to Adel and Tiyona was plain to see. It wasn't annoyance, or evasiveness like Bo Thompson's. It wasn't that he was a redneck and considered the whole thing a waste of time. Adel could see that he was gentlemanly, educated, and articulate in a shy, straightforward manner. Something else was causing his reticence.

"I don't want to hurt her," he told them. "I have strong feelings for Liza."

"How could you hurt her by telling the truth?" Tiyona asked.

"I just have a feeling that what I'd say will hurt her."

Adel didn't want to threaten the man or tell him his boss could require him to talk. "But Mr. Collela, you might as well talk to us now," she emphasized. "It's inevitable that you'll be deposed in this case, most likely by Liza's own attorney. He'll subpoena you, and you'll be compelled to speak. I'll be there and will ask the same questions I want to ask now. If the truth is damaging to Liza, and you're going to have to tell it one way or another, you may save her a lot of unnecessary aggravation by telling me now. It may help the case settle early."

"All right," he said, after some thought. "Go ahead."

Adel jumped straight to the point. "Okay, what is it that you know, that you believe will hurt Liza?"

He drew a deep breath, surprised by the woman's directness.

"Well …," he said. "Liza and I were lovers … in a way, anyway."

Tiyona and Adel looked at each other incredulously, stunned by this news.

"How could that—" Tiyona started to ask.

"It was how it began," he said. "One night on third shift, in the wee hours of the morning, I was lounging back, studying sociology, of all things. Liza was at the pin-up board reading job notices, or so I thought. We had no relationship other than just friendly ... working together, you know. She came over to me and stood beside my chair. 'Andy,' she said. I looked up, but she didn't say anything. She just had this strange look on her face. Then, she started unbuttoning her blouse ... and she took it off. She had no bra. She took off her shoes, pants, and underwear. How much detail do you want?"

"Please, tell us everything," Adel said, remaining clinical.

Tiyona was beside herself. "Uh huh!" she added.

"Well, next she undid my pants and gave me ... oral sex. It was the sexiest thing I'd ever experienced in my life. After that we had intercourse on the floor." He paused, recollecting for a moment. "Later, when I asked her why she did it, she said, 'I'm sorry, Andy, I saw those stupid pictures on the board, and I'm afraid I just got horny.' She told me she had always liked me. And then she said, 'Nothing messy or emotional ... we both have our own lives ... let's just do it every now and then.' She said it was 'so convenient.'"

"Wow!" Tiyona said.

"Had you ever said or done anything to—"

"Never," he interrupted Adel. "I just work and study. I'm pretty boring, I suppose. It was a big surprise. She said it was the pictures."

"When was that?"

"About a year after she started."

"How often would you do it?"

"It varied. It was totally up to her to dictate the pace. It became as frequent as once a week for a while, then once every two weeks to a month, depending on her. I didn't push her, although I admit I began letting her know when I needed it. Funny thing, I'd been celibate a long time, but I never needed it so much as when I was having sex with her."

"She never made you pay?"

"Oh, no!" The thought took him by surprise.

"Did you know, or ever hear, that she negotiated money for sex with others at the plant?"

"No. That would surprise me."

"Why?"

"She didn't like the other men here … at all."

"Did you know she used to be a prostitute?"

"Yes."

"How did you know?"

"She told me one night."

"Did she say she quit?"

"Yes, she had quit a long time ago. She was trying to better herself. She wanted to become a psychologist. Liza regretted her past and wanted to get away from it."

"Do you know how she reacted to the pictures and pranks around here?"

"Well, like I said, sometimes the pictures made her horny, but other times they made her upset. Like most of us, she's a little inconsistent. I saw her erase messages on the blackboard and take pictures down. I saw it get worse after she complained. I heard about the things they did to her on first shift."

"From whom?"

"From her, and Tommy Spikes."

"What did Spikes say?"

"Well, he told me that Osgood hung the dildo and picture on her locker. And he told me that Osgood changed Carmichael's little drawing and put Liza's initials on it. He also said that Osgood propositioned her."

"How did he know all that?"

"He interfaces with the first shift guys. They're leaving as he comes on. They told him, I guess."

"Is there anything else you can tell us?"

"Just that she really loves sex. At the same time, I know she really hated their behavior."

CHAPTER 40

It was five o'clock in the morning when Adel placed her foot on the footboard of her black, *Fluidesign* racing shell. She felt its twenty-seven foot long, carbon-fiber hull sink down in the water as its ten-inch beam wobbled. Feeling the boat's buoyancy beneath her, she tested her balance by bouncing the boat on the water with her right leg, keeping her left foot on the wooden dock. Then, with her weight over the keel of the boat and with her grip on the two oar handles low to the gunnels, she bent over the boat and gave a strong shove off the craggy edge of the dock.

The water lapped against the side as the craft moved quickly away from the dock. Balancing precariously on the unstable craft, with her portside oar serving as an out-rigger on the water, she eased down onto the sliding seat. She drew the starboard oar through the oar-lock and placed the oar-blade against the dock, using it to shove farther away. After taking a couple of lazy backing-strokes, she stopped to tie her feet into the shoes on the foot stretcher.

The moon was full and bright, and offered surreal company at the lonely morning hour. Its light glimmered off the slight chop on the lake. Adel could see seagulls resting on the water in the near distance, driven inland by a storm. She looked across the calm, dark vastness of the Central Floridian tarn, and felt at home.

She began her warm up drills alone in the sultry morning. Heat lightning crackled in the distance and added flickering illumination to the sky, revealing a solitary white ibis on the shore.

She rowed, first with her hands and arms only, keeping her back straight but angled back for good finishing posture. Her hands gripped the oar handles and rotated around a small oval, as she engaged a "pick drill"—picking off small strokes, alternating first on the square blade (with the plane of the oar-blade perpendicular to the plane of the water or "on the square"), and then on the feather (with the plane of the blade parallel to the plane of the water).

As in all water sports, with more speed, the water becomes harder and easier upon which to balance. Thus, the drill was so difficult—because it generated little speed. But it was necessary for proper technique, training a rower for posture, balance, and quickness of the hands in squaring and feathering the oars around the turn at the finish of the rowing stroke. She concentrated, keeping her boat balanced though going so slow, for a full two hundred meters.

She added her back to the stroke when, as her hands pushed down and away, she pivoted her lower back forward while extending her arms to full reach and rotated her fingers, causing the oar blades to "square up" to the water for the catch. Un-weighting her hands, the handles rose, causing the oar to pivot on the fulcrum—the rigger—and the blades to enter and "catch" the water. Pulling first with the back, then shoulders, and then her arms, she sent the boat forward with greater velocity. Rowing with her body and arms in this fashion for another two hundred meters, she felt sore muscles in her lower back stretching into painless comfort.

She took it to half-slide on the sliding seat, doing everything as before, but making sure she obtained proper body angle forward, and that her hands crossed her knees before contracting her hamstrings to pull her posterior forward on the sliding seat. Pushing first with her legs on the drive, she then engaged her back, shoulders, and arms. The craft increased in velocity again, and she rowed like this for yet another two hundred meters, still stretching and warming her body.

Finally she was ready to take the stroke to full slide and, after the next finish, she pushed her hands down and away and pivoted her body forward. She contracted her hamstrings after her hands crossed her knees, and glided slowly and surely all the way forward on the sliding seat, as the shell ran out from under her until her body became fully compressed with her knees to her chest and her arms reaching out. Her hands un-weighted the oar handles, catching another blade-full of water at full reach. Pushing again with her legs, and then pulling with her strong back, shoulders and finally her arms, the boat accelerated again, though she was only rowing at quarter power.

She continued in this fashion, rowing at an easy twenty strokes per minute. The seagulls scattered and made shrill noises as Adel propelled the sleek craft through the spot where they had been resting. The boat generated speed quickly, but it was she, repeatedly reaching full compression and dropping her oar-blades quickly and smoothly into the cool water, that was the engine—the constant, driving force.

As she faced the boat's stern, moving steadily through her strokes on the sliding seat, the boat lunged forward with every pull of her oars through the water. With each soundless stroke, the boat would jump forward; then, speed would wane as she moved up the slide preparing for the next catch, the vectors rendering force in opposite directions—her boat moving forward, her body moving to the stern. But the effect was undetectable because she was so fluid—the smoothness one develops after millions of practice strokes. Perfectly balanced and set, she and the boat glided as one through the water.

The boat developed its own momentum, cutting the water faster and faster until she could hear the earmark of efficiency—bubbles streaming under the boat's hull. Other than the sound of the gurgling, the boat's wake left the only evidence that the calm of the morning had been disturbed. That was part of the perfection of it: the boat, doing without being noticed, and she, doing without disturbing the boat. Just doing—calmly, silently, forcefully, forward … unnoticed and seeking no notice … undisturbed and disturbing nothing.

Adel felt lucky to know what it was like to row. The smoothness, the balance, the self-induced speed, the grace. The euphoria of mastery, of making something so very difficult, look and feel so easy, so perfect. These were the addicting points of rowing.

Glancing over her shoulder as she glided past, she could see a man and a woman in a fishing boat watching her. She was near enough to see the admiration in their faces. Intuition told her they were imagining being her; imagining what it might be like to create such beauty with their own bodies, imagining what it was like to row.

She had trained hard that week, and this morning was her "rest workout." She set out for a long, steady-state row, four full laps around Lake Fairview in northwest Orlando where her rowing club maintained a boathouse. It would take one hour. Repetition, balance, and relaxation were her goals. After awhile, Adel's strokes worked on her like a mantra, lulling her into a rhythmic trance of stroking and breathing. Under this spell, she allowed her mind to wander as she pulled stroke after stroke.

While she rowed, she revisited Marty Evans's words from the day before: "Society doesn't focus on males the same way as it does females."

It's a simple idea that's obviously true, she thought. *But is it so obvious? Do people realize it? How is it different? And why? Why is it that for decades, even centuries, women's sexuality is often displayed while men's, in general, is not?* She thought of how in the movies, and practically everywhere in society for that matter, the man's body would rarely be exposed, and certainly never his private parts. But women's were, throughout modern history. She remembered the famous painting, *The Picnic*, from the eighteen hundreds by a French artist. She had seen it in a college art course. The two men in the painting are fully clothed, as though they just came from a downtown business sector of Paris for a relaxing lunch. But the two women accompanying them are completely naked. *Obviously, a man's fantasy,* she concluded.

She thought maybe something very old and primal, going back to prehistoric man, could only explain the disparity. *Maybe it's about power and control. The image of a cave man dragging a cave woman by the hair translated through the ages into all forms of exploitation of women in society.*

Adel recalled cartoons from her youth of cave men clubbing cave women. They depicted the cavewoman as submissive, even groggily *happy* to have been clubbed and dragged off.

What does the fact that I was shown such scenes in my youth say about society? What role did history play? Does it relate to the simple fact that prehistoric men were bigger and stronger than women and, therefore, exercised their power and control whenever and however they pleased?

But the exercise of power and control are merely symptoms of something more basic—it's selfishness, a characteristic that has transcended the ages. Modern man is not so evolved, despite all the sophistication of the modern age. Men in general, at least in the United States, are changing. Title VII's mere existence attests to that. But perhaps the rudimentary causes are so ingrained, so fundamental, that rising above them is a difficult and prolonged process. Rising above one's selfishness is, after all, the act of ascending from the one thing that defines us, that makes us each an individual.

Adel wondered about blame. *Is the situation the fault of men alone? Or, do women share in the fault? How long and why have women submitted to the will of men?* She realized that perhaps she was part to blame, because she had done nothing about the problem. *Other women don't even recognize a problem—they believe they* should *be dominated. They* want *to be dominated.*

Tiyona. She doesn't want to be dominated. She is how we should be, Adel realized: *fighting for fairness and equality.*

She wondered about solutions. *Education is the only real solution. Education not only in the schools, but everywhere: in the homes, the churches, the business places, government, in the law—everywhere. People must raise the social consciousness of those around them, even in a Sartrian sea of absurdity. People must use educational tools, including the law. After all, the law is about justice. It's our best chance, given our evolving circumstances. Justice is about fundamental fairness, regardless of sex, race, color, national origin, religion, age, marital status or handicap. And to be true, it must also be regardless of other categories of unfair discrimination, sexual preference included.*

Adel marveled at the wisdom, simplicity, and correctness of the time-honored Golden Rule. *Treat others as you'd have them treat you. Don't judge the lifestyle of others. Don't interfere with what they want to do.*

But people interfere all the time. One person doesn't like another's lifestyle, so he tries to outlaw it. One person wants something he has no right to, so he takes it ... with force, if necessary. It happens on all levels:

person-to-person, city-to-city, county-to-county, state-to-state, and country-to-country. It's primal, driven by greed and selfishness. It's desire and force combined, without mind. It exists, still today.

Adel thought of Michael and her heart warmed with emotion, even as she rowed. *He fights for people. Like Tiyona, he fights for the underdogs. He fights against the misuse of the power of big corporations. In their own way, Tiyona and Michael each fight for fairness, for the Golden Rule. What do I do?*

She thought about her relationship with Michael, or the lack thereof. *Why?* she wondered. *Why won't I allow it? He's wonderful—handsome, athletic, intelligent—and he cares so much.*

She knew she was lucky.

But then her mind turned to other kinds of men: Lou Scarlechek. *Strange man,* she thought. *Why would anyone be so ostentatious?*

The thought lingered as Adel shrugged her shoulders, telling herself it was time to bring the boat in. She increased the speed and force of her strokes and sprinted the final meters to the dock.

CHAPTER 41

"Tom?"

"Hello, Lou," Peckinpah replied, making no attempt to disguise his displeasure of receiving the call at home on a Sunday morning. During the past few weeks Peckinpah's emotional state had steadily declined into a deep depression. It deepened every time he had anything to do with Lou Scarlechek. He despised everything about the man, and transferred his guilt onto Scarlechek. He felt sick on hearing Scarlechek's voice, and felt grateful his wife and daughter had gone to church.

The two hadn't talked about Vail, at least not openly. But Scarlechek had dropped subtle hints about "the problem" whenever they were out of earshot of others. Scarlechek had recently informed Peckinpah they'd "have to talk about the problem soon."

The time was now. John Waverly, the company president, was retiring. No formal announcement had been made yet, but through office rumors, Scarlechek had learned that the board of directors had asked Peckinpah to begin an unofficial search for candidates.

Scarlechek would've preferred to talk with Peckinpah in person, rather than by phone. He could feel more confident that there were no listeners, and that he wasn't being taped. But there wasn't time. He didn't know where Peckinpah was in the process, or when Waverly would announce. The time to exert his leverage was now.

"Tom, are you alone?"

"Yes," Peckinpah replied, annoyed but used to this from Scarlechek. It was comical at times, as though a spy lurked around every corner or had tapped the lines.

"This conversation isn't being recorded?"

"No," Peckinpah said impatiently.

"Are you sure? Tom, what I have to say is very important. No one can hear. It's regarding the Colorado trip." Scarlechek had worded this statement carefully. Peckinpah would know what he meant, but an eavesdropper could believe he was talking of an upcoming trip.

"No, Lou, the call is not being recorded, and there is no one here. Tell me what's on your mind." At the mention of Colorado, his mood changed to concern.

"Tom, forgive me, but I'll be blunt. I've heard Waverly is about to step down. ... I want the position."

Amused, and without realizing what was about to hit him, Peckinpah was deliberately vague. "Well, Lou, those are just rumors. Even if it were true, we couldn't let anything like that get out. The SEC, you know—"

"You're right, Tom, I do know," Scarlechek interrupted, his voice sarcastic and authoritative. "I don't want to play cat and mouse here. The position is coming open, and I want it. You're going to give it to me."

"And just why would I do that?" Peckinpah asked.

"Because, Tom, of what I know. Tom ... I have pictures."

There was a long pause. Peckinpah was stunned. Images flashed in his head of the hooker and her roadside death. He envisioned the rock ledge surrounded by trees, and remembered his pain as he buried her. He saw the bones, clawing up out of the ground again. *He has pictures!*

"I'm overnighting copies to you—privileged and confidential of course—for your eyes only. Make sure that nosey Cookie doesn't open the package. But I want you to see what I have, in addition to what I know. Now, need I repeat myself?"

Peckinpah was shocked, and couldn't speak. He was being black-mailed! *Options. Options!* He couldn't see that he had any. He felt trapped, and suddenly his wife's image popped into his head, then his daughter's. A montage of his career flashed before him. Disgrace would be his lot in life—he never dreamed it—unless, of course, he gave in to Scarlechek.

Why? was all he could think. It was the first of a hundred questions, but they all led back to one. *Why was I so stupid?*

"Lou," he said finally "You know I can't guarantee what you want." It was the truth—he had influence, but no one person had absolute control over the board.

"Look Tom, I want the position. I'd better be your guy—pushed by you. If you do that, I'll get the position. I'd better ... for your sake. And of course, I'll want my contractual terms. For appearances, I want less than you—but not by much. We'll talk more about all that later. Now, I trust I've made myself clear."

Peckinpah moaned, not believing this was happening.

"And Tom, I suggest you immediately destroy the pictures. I have the digital files saved, of course. We want to protect our little secret. Got it?"

"Uh huh," Peckinpah said, as he shuddered.

"Now, tell me about the timing," Scarlechek demanded, as though he was conducting a corporate meeting about a new project.

"It's up to me," Peckinpah said meekly. "Waverly is just waiting on me. I'll need to caucus the board members. I'll need ... a month."

"Fine. Don't make it too quick, but don't take too long, either. Tom, I have a source on the board. So, I'll know. You understand?"

"Yes, Lou."

"Good. For now, Tom, have a nice day." He threw it out sarcastically and hung up.

The words stung Peckinpah.

"That fuckin' son of a bitch," he uttered. "Have a nice day?"

CHAPTER 42

Ace Rider rose to leave Adel's office. *He's such an atypical private investigator,* Adel thought. *A has-been rebel, a surfer, of all things, trying to eke out a living in a conformist world.* He was mean, streetwise, and unafraid of stretching the law to get his information, and he was good at what he did. She was glad she hadn't allowed Rider to go too far on this job. She had ordered him only to place Sorenson under surveillance, and to deliver a report on her background.

His report had been positive. Sorenson had indeed been a part of the Orange Blossom Trail nightlife. Rider had located two witnesses. One was a bar owner who witnessed much of the street and its patrons. Another was a cop who'd arrested Sorenson at least three times, warning her countless others.

However, Sorenson was never prosecuted or convicted. Hanging arrest without conviction over a person's head was not favored in the law. But with the testimony of Osgood, Wade, and Thompson, and the testimony of Collela, she believed she could paint an ugly picture of Liza Sorenson. Adel might have a shot at winning the case.

And there was a new issue that had occurred to Adel. A First Amendment issue. The First Amendment protected freedom of speech, a liberty about as fundamentally ingrained in Americans as breathing. *Posting pictures is a form of political or even artistic speech,* she reasoned. *Making sexual comments is clearly speech. Posting pictures of nude women and making sexual comments can't be judicially condemned because they're constitutionally protected free speech.* She'd argue that the judiciary can't force rules and regulations on private corporations to abridge free speech. There was supporting case law in different settings.

It was a brilliant idea that she was compelled to raise, an ACLU argument to protect a big corporation. How ironic. Dave McKerrin would be proud. Adel Blair to the corporate rescue once again. Michael would admire her imagination but abhor the use. Tiyona Morgan would surely object to the notion that men had a constitutional right to hang nude pictures and make offensive comments to women, like whites claiming a constitutional right to harass blacks.

Adel owed Gonzalez a call. He wanted to discuss a joint case management order to present to the judge. Its purpose was to establish a trial time, and a schedule for discovery, the formal procedures through which attorneys and their clients can learn about their opponents' information. She decided to disclose her facts and test Sorenson's resolve.

"Steve," she said, "I really don't think you want to take this case to trial."

"And why not?"

"Your client is a prostitute," she said. "You'll have a severe problem on the 'welcomeness' issue, and with credibility. The jury won't believe her."

"My client *was* a prostitute, that's true. But that was a long time ago. She's now a young woman lifting herself from her past. She was making it, until your client robbed her."

The lawyers were at their finest, testing each other, showing some of their cards, and revealing what they'd argue to the jury. It was free discovery; a competitive but mutual game that allowed lawyers to analyze the other's case and to better predict the outcome.

"Yes, well," Adel responded, "I have a witness who'll testify that she still likes to negotiate dollars for sex. I even have her ex-lover who'll say that the pictures made her horny, and that she'd attack him on the job in the wee hours of the third shift."

"And just who is that?"

"Andy Collela, of course. Your client didn't tell you?"

"Of course she told me—but she just worked with him." Gonzalez was lying. He was taken aback and trying to cover.

Adel pushed on. "Well, he claims something different, and he's believable, not like the other rednecks I've got. Collela has no axe to grind and, in fact, he likes her. He's quiet, handsome, a normal

175

student. The jury will relate to him and his stories, especially once they learn of her past. He's ethical, and he'll tell the truth. I suggest you ask Liza what that is. And I'll be raising another issue—the First Amendment. It'll be a legal issue that could go to the Supreme Court. The case could last forever. You should give us a realistic demand and see if we can settle this one."

"Uh hmm." Gonzalez tried to sound unalarmed. "Listen, Adel, I'd love to continue this, but I've got to go. So we're agreed on the case management order, then?"

"Yes."

"Good, I'll send it to the judge and ask for it to be signed."

They hung up and Adel leaned back in her chair. She'd landed a powerful blow. But her thoughts turned to Red Wade, Rick Osgood and Martyn Evans, and she realized that her rabbit punch was for the boys' club.

She felt a moment of remorse before she dismissed the thought. *Hey, I'm just doing my job.*

CHAPTER 43

Boy, someone doesn't *want me looking at this,* Cookie Albertson thought. She had signed for the overnight delivery package addressed to her boss. It was stamped "privileged and confidential" and "for your eyes only" all over. She didn't open it, but she sure wanted to. This package was different from the norm. It was from Lou Scarlechek. Instead of placing it on Peckinpah's chair as usual, she kept the package at her desk to take directly to her boss when he returned.

When Tom Peckinpah walked in later, he was relieved to see no delivery on his chair. He'd been dreading it all morning, and had been distracted through his meeting. Perhaps the whole problem would just go away, he hoped. He sat down and rummaged through his pile of faxes and memos.

Cookie entered his office with the parcel. "This arrived this morning. It's from Lou."

Peckinpah could barely hide his despair. "I'll look at it in a moment. Please close my door on your way out." She wanted to ask, but decided not to and left, closing his door. He seemed unwilling to talk. Peckinpah rose and walked to his door and locked it. Cookie heard the clicking of the mechanism and mused, *now why's he doing that?*

Peckinpah sat back down and opened the delivery. There they were. Seven color photographs—three of him and the hooker in the bathroom, three of them on the bed, and one of the burial site.

"My God," he muttered, tears welling up as he studied the bathroom shots. In the picture, he faced the camera, and stood in sexual ecstasy as the hooker knelt in front of his pelvis. Her right foot, covered by a bright green stiletto heel, was raised from the floor. Her pointed toe drew the eye to the cocaine on the counter.

The pictures of them on the bed were just as incriminating. His profile was unmistakable. Her face was turned to the camera—her eyes closed, her open mouth jutted forward with a look of pleasure.

Last was the picture of the disposal site—a shot from the Lexus on the road that looked up to the rock ledge. He recognized his image in the foreground. He was holding the shovel. Waves of despair hit him, as he slumped down into his chair.

Go to the authorities, he thought. *But how can I? I'll lose it all. It'd ruin me. I can't have a Chappaquiddick hanging over me, even if I manage to fool the investigators. But how could I do that? The pictures and Scarlechek's testimony would bar that. Scarlechek would lie to make me look even worse,* he speculated. *If I don't give him what he wants . . .*

His thoughts turned to the woman. At times he didn't feel too sorry for her—this part was easier and easier to rationalize. She was after all, nothing but a hardened hooker and she knew what she was doing. No one forced her to do anything. But he still agonized. He'd been grossly negligent, violating the law, not to mention his wife's trust. At last count, he'd committed at least five crimes: solicitation, possession and use, criminal negligence—driving while high— and illegal interment. He didn't know it, but he could even be charged with the legal fiction of felony murder, because the hooker died during the perpetration of his crimes.

Peckinpah felt hopeless. He was like a small animal huddled in a dark and muddy hole as a storm passed, quaking with each thunderous clap of lightning. He knew he had no choice but to give into Scarlechek's demands. It was a sunken, shriveled feeling he experienced. He'd been omnipotent, but now he had no power. It'd been robbed by his own hubris. Scarlechek's move was but the follow-through of a foregone conclusion.

His self-esteem had been encased in a crystalline shrine his entire life, but ever since Vail, it had escaped him. He was perpetually moody, grouchy, and cross. Other times he needed unending praise, craving reassurance that his life was of the highest order, and that it wasn't a lie. But he still possessed ethical consciousness, and that part of him knew he was living a lie.

Thoroughly despondent, Peckinpah couldn't work. He put the pictures back in the overnight package and into his top desk drawer. He thought about leaving it unlocked, hoping to be discovered, like a death wish. But a contrary instinct prevailed, and he locked the drawer. He practically stormed out of his office.

"Tom? Where are you going?" Cookie inquired.

"I've just got to get the hell out of here for a while. I'll call in later."

She saw his face was deeply troubled. "What's wrong?"

He scowled at her. "Cookie, I've just got to be alone right now. I need some space. Cancel everything. I'll be all right tomorrow."

"But Tom, your e-mails and faxes—we need to respond. And you're meeting with Mr. Lookson today ..." Bartholomew Lookson was an important member of the board of directors.

"Cancel it, dammit! I'm out of here!"

Cookie sat there shocked, gazing after him in a daze. "My God, what's wrong with him?"

She reflected upon the morning. There was nothing earth shattering in his pile of communiqués. There were important matters, but nothing that would upset him. She couldn't recall ever seeing him like that. Then she remembered Scarlechek's overnight delivery. She'd given it to Tom and he had locked the door behind her. He had never done that before. Her thoughts soon landed on Scarlechek.

What a snake.

CHAPTER 44

Cookie Albertson waited until lunch, when the offices were mostly vacant. She was nervous, but she entered Peckinpah's office, closed the door, and locked it. Her eyes scoured the room, but she didn't see the package.

He didn't leave with it … it must be in his desk, she thought. She tugged on the top drawer, finding it locked. She returned to her desk and retrieved her own set of keys, which Peckinpah had long forgotten she had.

She again closed and locked his office door and moved to the desk. Turning the key, she opened the desk drawer and located the package. She opened the parcel and discovered the pictures.

"Oh my God!" she said. *This must've been what happened that night in Vail.*

Cookie noticed the date in the lower left corner of each photo and remembered the strange events of that trip, and how her boss had behaved. She thought to check her calendar to crosscheck the date on the pictures with the dates of the trip, but in her heart she already knew they'd match.

As she studied them, her uneasiness and disappointment grew. She knew her boss could be wild on occasion; however, she'd never seen signs of infidelity … or drug abuse. But there it was, laid out before her.

Scarlechek had been in the chalet, and that was unusual. Peckinpah didn't like Scarlechek at all, and certainly not well enough to hang out with him. He didn't want to do his work *that* day either. *What did that man do to Tom?* she wondered.

180

The last photograph puzzled her. In the picture, Tom was walking away with, of all things, a shovel. She thought it was Tom; at least it looked like his parka.

Cookie carefully replaced the photographs just as she had found them in the desk drawer. She locked it, and took a late lunch away from the office, contemplating this disturbing information.

CHAPTER 45

Tom Peckinpah headed west on Interstate 10 at seventy miles per hour. He was thinking, driving to nowhere for that purpose.

His meditations roamed directionless, as though their confines were as boundless as the terrain surrounding the roadway. He considered telling his wife, but she'd be mortified. The disgrace and the shame confronted him as clearly as the road signs. He reflected upon his eleven-year-old daughter. She was old enough to comprehend what he'd done. He thought of his mother and the grief he'd visit upon her.

He gazed upon the dull and barren desert. For the first time ever, he contemplated suicide. Taking his own life offered both an honorific escape and justice served for the hooker's death.

But then his thoughts veered from suicidal despair to the prospect of selling Scarlechek to the board of directors. *Seth Worman would be no problem*, he thought. He knew Worman and Scarlechek had old business ties and seemed to be friends. Bartholomew Lookson would be the biggest hurdle. Lookson was a billionaire who owned a major block of Western Town stock; he called a lot of shots. He was sharp and tough, and no doubt had his own thoughts on the man for the job.

Lookson doesn't know Scarlechek. That's a plus, Peckinpah thought, managing a smirk. *I've got to preserve my image.*

Peckinpah drove on, thinking about how to work it, as he realized there was no choice but to give in to Scarlechek. He didn't foresee there might be future demands. He didn't know that giving in to extortion once does not ensure an enforceable release. He didn't think that it only emboldens the extortionist, empowering him to return to the well again and again.

Peckinpah pulled off the interstate, and turned his car around to head back to the office.

CHAPTER 46

DeeDee Lane woke from her sleep after a long, fitful night. She showered, mulling over the subjects of her bedridden wrestling match.

To be confronted by Lou Scarlechek in front of her parents, and to have him disarm them, and worse, to have her parents like him, was revolting. It was a fraud. She had struggled with her predicament much through the night, and found herself forced to choose.

The warm water felt good, and the clean, faint smell of chlorine bolstered her. *The time has come to make a stand,* she thought. *I must live up to standards that are moral and honest and true, regardless of my pride. Forget my pride ... for my parents, and more importantly, myself. They might doubt my abilities to make it on my own, but eventually they'll understand. They'll believe in me more. I can do it. Even if it means sacrificing my dream job—I'll not let that bastard abuse me anymore!*

Her spirit felt cleansed and strong in the shower; sensational in her reborn freedom, a victim to be no more. Resolved—her soul wouldn't be subjected to rape any longer. Fresh, clear determination washed over her with exhilaration as the water streamed down her body. She realized with clarity that she was at another pivotal point in her young life. Never again would she succumb to what amounted to nothing less than extortion.

CHAPTER 47

"We are not concerned about your witnesses," Steve Gonzalez notified Adel. "We will have no trouble painting them as they are: redneck, chauvinistic pigs needing to be taught a lesson. Collela will not hurt us either, because he'll explain that what they shared was a form of God-given beauty between man and woman. We have confidence in the jury."

He was glad they weren't eye to eye. Bluffing would be much more difficult because, in truth, he was worried about going in front of a jury.

"We're also unconcerned about the First Amendment issue," he continued. "The Constitution doesn't protect pornography. And, I'd love to go all the way to the Supreme Court as much as you. But only because you've raised the settlement specter; if you'd like to seriously talk at this early juncture, we'd be willing to meet. It could save a lot of headaches for all—publicity and the like. For purposes of settlement, our initial demand is two million dollars. We won't bargain further without a good faith offer from you."

Um hum, Adel thought. "I'll let you know if my client wants to meet," she replied, unimpressed by Gonzalez's rant. Despite his posturing, Adel knew he wanted to settle because he wouldn't want the case before a jury.

Sorenson hadn't told him of her past as a prostitute when he initially demanded a jury under the new Civil Rights Act. He had scolded her for not disclosing her skeletons right off and chastised Sorenson yet again for neglecting to inform him of her relationship with Collela.

Adel reported the development to John Laughlin and Tiyona Morgan.

"There can be no offer without Lou's approval," Laughlin said. "I'll confirm, but he'll surely want a written report and recommendations, and he'll want a meeting with the three of us and Sandy. Let's pick some dates, and I'll set it up."

Adel immediately went to work on her analysis, as did Tiyona.

CHAPTER 48

Sandy Yates was the last to arrive at Scarlechek's office for the meeting. Adel, Tiyona and John Laughlin sat patiently. Adel noticed that Yates was tall and trim, and obviously in good shape. He was wearing a light tan suit with brown shoes and belt, and his short, medium brown hair was graying around the temples. His green eyes flashed about the room.

Lou Scarlechek was at his desk, ranting into the phone about something "very important." He'd received a call from a forensic accountant, a consultant on one of the company's large construction cases. The accountant had been sent with the company's lawyers to review documents of the plaintiff—a subcontractor claiming six million dollars in extra costs on the construction of a new Western Town hotel.

The accountant, a former FBI agent really into the spy scene, had hypothesized that the subcontractor was secretly linked to organized crime. He was telling Scarlechek that he had set booby traps in his hotel room that led him to believe his things had been searched, confirming his theory that organized crime was involved. Scarlechek was eating it up, and loved the guy.

After about five minutes, Yates rolled his eyes, annoyed that Scarlechek still hadn't gotten off the phone.

Suddenly the group heard Scarlechek sharply inquire, "Are you on a cell phone? … Then don't use that term!" His voice was terse. The accountant had relayed something further about "organized crime." "You never can tell who may be listening on these things. Make up a code … yes, OC … yes, that'll do. … Yes, well," he said loudly, "if OC is involved, yes, that could happen. ... Uh huh, but OC wouldn't launder funds in that fashion would they? ... And do you think OC could avoid the IRS like that? ... I see."

By this time, everyone in the room also saw, let alone anyone who might have been tapping the call, all having figured out that the code word "OC" stood for organized crime. Laughlin chuckled, as did the rest of the group.

At last, Scarlechek hung up and released a heavy sigh, as though he were carrying the weight of the free world on his shoulders.

"Sorry, but that was extremely important," Scarlechek said, thinking he was impressing Adel and Yates as he pulled up a chair.

"Now, fill me in on the Sorenson case in twenty-five words or less," he said flippantly, as though Yates, a man of equally high stature in the company, wasn't even there, and as though it was possible to do. In fact, he said it in such a fashion, glancing around the room at each of them, that it wasn't even clear to whom he was directing the command. It was obvious he hadn't read Adel's or Tiyona's reports—the reports that he had demanded.

Laughlin smirked at Scarlechek's command. He'd seen it given many times, always designed to convey how terribly busy Scarlechek was. But with Scarlechek's tendency to interrupt with questions designed to display his intelligence, Laughlin had never seen the command fulfilled.

Adel spoke up as instructed, thinking it was her job.

"Well," she said, "the company should settle. But for no more than a half million." She closed her mouth, having accomplished the assignment.

A dozen or so words to spare, she thought.

Scarlechek looked at her, dumbfounded. He would've trashed her with a tirade of epithets were she not the latest object of his desire. Her eyes reported back: *you get what you ask for.*

Laughlin instantly broke out in a horselaugh. "Hmm," he said, counting on his fingers. "Thirteen words. Not bad."

Yates dismissed the humorous moment, desiring to get to the point and end the annoying meeting. He *had* read the reports and wanted a few answers.

"Ms. Blair," he said, raising his copy of Adel's memorandum. "Are our witnesses really so bad?"

Adel's report was thorough, detailed, and technical. It covered the law and all defenses to each of Sorenson's claims, including the legal issues about the applicability of the new civil rights act and the First Amendment. Because of new precedent in the Eleventh Circuit, she assumed a jury trial would be allowed, and that compensatory and punitive damages were a real potential. Her report summarized witness interviews, and forecasted the potential appearance and testimony each witness would make to the jury. She reminded the reader that when you deal with people—including judges, juries and witnesses—nothing is certain, and everything is gray. "Imagine the most surprised that you could ever be," she had written, "and you have imagined what could happen in this case."

Essentially, with the exception of Collela, Adel predicted that the jury would believe anything bad about the company's employees against whom Gonzalez offered any evidence. However, she also predicted that the jury would believe Collela.

The defense of "prompt remedial action" was a loser. The company didn't take *any* remedial action to correct the problems. Martyn Evans only made sure that sexual acts were not depicted. He neither reprimanded the boys, nor required their attendance at "the black bitch's" seminars. He didn't stop the offensive incidents. His argument was "boys will be boys," and that the pictures were nothing out of sorts with social context—nothing worse than what was seen everyday, everywhere. Adel predicted that Gonzalez would argue that Evans's attitude showed reckless disregard for Sorenson's rights, which would trigger a right to punitive damages.

Adel concluded that the case came down to whether the jury would believe that an ex-prostitute, who initiated and encouraged progressive sex in the workplace with one of her fellow employees, could, at the same time be sexually harassed by a bunch of redneck chauvinists. She couldn't say either side had better than a fifty-fifty chance at winning. It depended on the individual jurors and whether they would consider Sorenson to be undeserving of redress, or whether they'd feel sympathy and understanding of her plight. It depended on whether they'd react so negatively to the employees' behavior and the lack of direction from management that they'd send Corporate America a message. The bottom line: the case ultimately turned on the background and personality of each juror and their individual social consciousness which were complete unknowns. The case literally could be won or lost in jury selection.

The potential exposure was haunting and Adel had no choice but to recommend settlement.

Her analysis next addressed the issue of "how much?" After considering attorney fees, costs, back pay, interest, front pay, and the possible punitive damages, she calculated Sorenson's case to be worth as much as a half million dollars. She considered that the company could be hit for punitive damages not only on the Title VII claim under the new Act, but also on the counts of intentional invasion of privacy and defamation. These counts were serious exposures. The "boys" had told everyone that Liza was a prostitute, constituting an invasion of privacy, and also proclaimed that she still was, constituting defamation. There was strong risk of a runaway jury. Because of the blatant chauvinism, the potential desire to punish was a festering sore that couldn't be ignored.

Accordingly, Adel had recommended in writing that the company settle with Sorenson for up to the value of a half million dollars, suggesting that anything over was paying too much at this point. Adel suggested the possibility of working out a "structured settlement" with Sorenson, that is, a settlement that would cost the company a relatively low amount, but with the time value of money, could net Sorenson much more.

Adel reflected on Yates's question: are our witnesses really so bad?

Are you kidding? she thought. "Yes, they are," she said. "Except Collela, they're the worst I've ever seen. In my opinion, the jury will be inflamed by them."

"And why is that?" Scarlechek asked, trying to break in and lead the conversation, to recover from having been made a fool.

"Because they are such rednecks. They are bigoted, and they can't disguise it. Gonzalez will bring it out. They still don't think they did anything wrong, especially because she's a former prostitute."

"But can the company be liable just because they hung some pictures and drew a silly drawing?" Yates asked. This was the question he had asked Scarlechek long ago, to which he didn't receive an answer.

"Well, that's not all they did, but yes, it can," Adel said. "The law is emerging on this point, but there is precedent now to the effect that merely hanging pictures can be sexual harassment if it creates a hostile or offensive work environment, and if the employer doesn't take prompt remedial action."

"So, if a woman sees a sexual picture hung in her work environment, and it offends her, and she complains but the company does nothing about it, we can be liable?" Yates asked.

"Yes, provided a reasonable woman in the eyes of the jury would agree. In other words, a hypersensitive woman can't recover. It depends upon what the jury thinks is reasonable and what's not. Maybe Ti and I are jaded because we're women, but in my opinion the jury will agree that a reasonable, modern woman would be offended by what the wastewater treatment plant employees admit they did."

She paused. "But the confusing aspect of this case," she continued, "is the 'welcomeness' issue. She's an ex-prostitute who, according to Collela, actually became aroused by the pictures and seduced him. Then, she carried on a love affair with him at the workplace that she dictated. The question is whether the jury will buy the notion that such a woman can at the same time be sexually harassed by the other male employees. I can't predict the outcome of that with any greater factor than fifty-fifty. I use that factor when I see an issue as a toss-up."

"Yes, but if we have a fifty percent chance of winning and the exposure is a half million, why should we settle at that amount?" Yates asked. In other words, why don't we settle at fifty percent of the exposure—two hundred and fifty thousand?"

"That logic assumes the other side buys our methodology. But it doesn't. Unfortunately, I'm just one lawyer and I'm telling you the way I see and predict the case. But it's all guesswork. Gonzalez sees it much differently. He'll not agree that we should just ignore the state law claims of gross negligence and battery, the way I have. He'll see the exposure as much greater than I. I'm telling you what amount I think you have a fifty percent chance of losing. However, if you lose, all that could be visited upon you and possibly more."

Yates stroked his chin thoughtfully.

Adel could tell her words weighed in heavily. *Dave always said prediction is the bane of every lawyer,* she thought. *It really can't be done with any real degree of certainty. We try, because clients want it.*

She continued, "I'd offer one hundred thousand initially, then go up in small increments; and when you're asked to go more, when it's at the deal-break stage, then offer your maximum, but offer it to be paid over time. That way, for example, you don't spend five hundred thousand, but they get five hundred thousand."

"Yes, we can buy Sorenson an annuity that will net her the five hundred thousand, but we spend much less," Laughlin said. "Our insurance and accounting personnel can help us here."

"Well Sandy, what do you think?" Scarlechek asked.

"Well, you're always telling me that you're my lawyer. What do *you* think?"

"Hey, it's going to be charged against your budget. You'll need to decide. Based on what I've heard here today, I'd try to settle if it were my decision."

"Ti?" Yates asked.

"Sandy, you know how I feel."

Tiyona Morgan's report had taken the form of a brief memorandum to Yates. She had sent copies to Adel, Laughlin, and Scarlechek. Although she focused on the case in a different, non-legalistic fashion, her conclusions about the company's employees were consistent with Adel's. She simply stated, "I believe the company will lose," and zoomed in on the potential for damaging negative publicity. "We are supposed to be a wholesome place for family entertainment," she had written. "This case can have a very negative impact on that image and the desire of tourists to visit us, even if we win." Tiyona had suggested consulting the Marketing Department on the matter. Her report closed by focusing on the injunctive relief Sorenson was seeking. "We need to enact and enforce meaningful policies and procedures to prevent this sort of thing. If we don't settle, we will potentially lose control over this important change. Instead, it will be dictated to us by a federal judge."

"Try to settle," she continued. "If you do, it can avoid a lot of negativity and distraction, and eliminate greater exposure. It'll be much better for the company."

"Sure," Yates complained. "My department's budget takes a major hit for the sake of the company, because of a company-wide problem. It's easy for you people in Legal and Personnel to talk of the good of the company. You're just charged out as an expense to the other divisions. I've got to account for my budget."

Yates paused. His eyes traveled about the room. "Ms. Blair, make the offer of one hundred thousand. Tell this Gonzalez that we wanted to make a serious offer, but that you don't see that there is much more movement. Please let us know the reaction and response right away."

"All right."

"Ti, I don't care what the rest of the company does. I want you to set up mandatory seminars on sexual and racial harassment. I'll send out a memo to my vice presidents and directors requiring attendance by everyone. I'll deal personally with my wastewater rednecks. I don't want this happening again."

"I'll begin immediately, Sandy. How soon will the memo be out?"

"Tomorrow."

"Please copy me on the memo, Sandy, to make it an attorney-client privileged and confidential memo," Laughlin interjected. "That way it can't be subject to production in the litigation. Correct, Adel?"

"Correct. It could potentially be disastrous to the litigation otherwise, depending on what you say in the memo."

"Should I run it by you first?" Yates asked Adel.

"I'd appreciate it."

"Very good. Well, thank you very much ladies and gentlemen—I guess!"

Yates stood, the others following his lead.

As Adel began packing her briefcase, Scarlechek leaned over and asked her to stay. After the others had walked out into the lobby, he said, "Adel, you did a very fine job. Thank you very much. I'm very impressed. And, may I say ... you are so very beautiful."

"Thank you," Adel said, struck by the incongruity of his last remark.

"I've decided I have another case for you. It's a commercial litigation case. Can you handle it?"

"Yes, of course! That's great! Thank you very much."

"Well it's not a huge case. I want to get to know you a little better before I send you one of those."

"I understand."

"We're going to be the plaintiff, so there's no immediate hurry. Perhaps we can meet for dinner in a week or two to discuss it?"

"That'd be fine. Just let me know."

CHAPTER 49

Adel caught the elevator door and stepped in to join Tiyona.

"Wow! I barely caught up to you," Adel said, as the door shut behind her. She noticed someone else in the elevator, too. It was DeeDee Lane.

"Oh. Hello," Adel said.

"Hi!" DeeDee said. She looked at Adel eagerly.

"We met in the Ranchero Hotel ... and at this elevator once."

"Yes. Good to see you again."

"Thanks. Good to see you." Adel noticed DeeDee's upbeat demeanor, which was quite different from the forlorn appearance she'd seen before.

"I was beginning to wonder if you'd been trapped in Scarlechek's lair," Tiyona said to Adel.

DeeDee's face suddenly changed, the strange look returning.

"Oh, no man could trap me," Adel said, not realizing the impact of her words.

DeeDee looked down at her feet.

"Well, good," Tiyona laughed. "Listen, Adel, I'm on my way to a Women's League meeting now. Want to come?"

"Yeah, I'd love to," Adel replied, surprised at the coincidence. She'd decided to become more involved in women's groups. She sensed DeeDee gazing at them. "Ti, can anyone come?" Adel asked, gesturing toward DeeDee.

"Sure. Come along DeeDee."

"Really?" DeeDee inquired.

"Let's go."

The trio stopped for a simple dinner allowing Adel and DeeDee to become acquainted. They discussed the Sorenson case and the issues it presented for womanhood.

"So what made you decide to come tonight, Adel?" Tiyona asked.

"Oh, I don't know exactly. I think that you inspire me, Ti. And this case too. Maybe Liza Sorenson isn't the model of womanhood, but there's something about her. Something is gnawing at me, making me want to do something. I'm always for the underdog." *At least, I used to be,* she thought. "It just seems like women, and minorities, are the true underdogs in the corporate world. I want to do something. I can fight, so I want to."

DeeDee gazed at Adel with admiration.

"You know, Sorenson's lawyer spoke to our group once," Tiyona said.

"Really?" Adel said.

"Yes. About harassment. He was very effective as a speaker. Very entertaining. And half the women in the group fell in love with him."

"Oh, he's a charmer," Adel said. "You should see him in court. He's very good. If we go to trial, he'll tear our witnesses up."

"But I've checked on you, Adel. I've heard the same about you."

Adel took a sip of her wine.

This woman is so good, thought DeeDee. *She's smart, beautiful, and tough. She commands respect. Lou would have no chance doing to her what he's done to me. This is what womanhood should be. This is what I want to be.* Knowing she'd never be physically like Adel didn't matter, her physical limitations being what they were. Adel became DeeDee's ideal woman that night, reinforcing DeeDee's resolution to fight back against Scarlechek's demands.

At the Women's League meeting, there was an engaging discussion led by a local psychologist on women in the workplace. Adel watched DeeDee, noticing the determination in her face.

· · · ·

When Adel finally returned home that evening, she noticed there was a message on her machine. Her heart raced when she heard Michael's voice. To her surprise and joy, he was asking her to dinner on Friday. Glad that he was still interested, she lay back in her bed and stared at the phone.

Is it too late to call?

CHAPTER 50

"Steve, the company wants to make a serious offer, but we don't want you or Ms. Sorenson getting any false hopes on how high we might go," Adel said. "Do you understand?"

"Adel, my dear, I know I'm Cuban, but you may assume that I'm of average intelligence and understand the English language."

"Good," she replied, acting as though this was news.

"How much?" Gonzalez asked, sounding irritated.

"We offer one hundred thousand, but that's basically it."

Gonzalez gave the obligatory response, "I'll pass it along, but my client will reject it." Later, he called Adel back and said, "Because Western Town has moved one hundred thousand, we will move one hundred thousand. Our counter is one million nine hundred thousand dollars." Then Adel gave the obligatory speech.

They avoided the trap of arguing about the law and the merits, knowing they'd convince each other of nothing, at least nothing that either of them would admit. Back and forth they called, until smaller and smaller increments of movement made it clear they were polarized. Big surprise, they had quite different goals on where the case should settle.

When Gonzalez moved down to one million five hundred thousand, and Adel moved up to only one hundred and fifty, Gonzalez grew frustrated and declared he'd negotiate no more: her last movement was so small, it wasn't in good faith and didn't warrant a response. Adel suggested hiring a mediator. Gonzalez agreed.

Mediation was not a process in which the parties offered evidence or testimony. Instead, the mediator met with the parties, explained the procedure, heard minimal opening presentations, and then, through private caucusing with the parties and their lawyers in separate rooms, attempted to bring the parties together to settlement. The mediator, often a practicing lawyer or retired judge, hammered on each side in secluded rooms, striving to convince each to give a little more or receive a little less. At some point, evidentiary matters and legal arguments became irrelevant. It was just, "how much more will you pay" and "how much less will you take." As one mediator often puts it, "the deal is his client."

Gonzalez and Adel agreed to schedule the mediation immediately. They exchanged names and selected three mediators acceptable to both. The first one was available.

Thomas Wolfe was a seasoned trial attorney who, in his forty years of practice, had undergone every kind of battle an attorney could imagine. He had a ruddy complexion on a round head, piercing blue eyes and aged, back-flowing white hair. If there was ever a man that looked like God, Adel thought, Wolfe was it. His low-pitched, booming voice confirmed the impression.

Once they scheduled the mediation, Gonzalez insisted on obtaining a formal court order requiring attendance by the parties, specifically requesting someone with ultimate authority to bind Western Town at the bargaining table. That someone had to be Yates, it being his budget.

Because Yates had to attend, Scarlechek decided it was important for him to attend. "I'm not letting you go into the lion's den alone, my friend," he told the executive vice president as if he were Yates's only ally.

"Thanks," Yates replied without any comfort in his tone.

In all, Sorenson and Gonzalez, Yates, Scarlechek, Tiyona, and Adel would attend the mediation with Wolfe. They agreed to meet at a conference room at Western Town's corporate office building, just downstairs from Scarlechek's office, the mediation to take place on Friday.

CHAPTER 51

Tom Peckinpah and Cookie Albertson each read on the plane to Orlando. Peckinpah perused a series of two-page memos on everything from the proposed new stock option plan to construction delays on the latest themed ride being constructed in Orlando—the Geronimo Ghost Dance. The ride brought its riders high into a rising wigwam, where they witnessed the performance of a ghost dance until suddenly the natives disappeared and the wigwam opened to a soaring vista overlooking the park. It then dropped, causing the palefaces to turn ghostly white and swallow their hearts. The author of that memo wrote, "Universal has one. We have to out-do them."

Cookie returned to her Grisham novel and wondered if everyone in the world really had a southern accent.

Peckinpah thought about his meetings in Orlando on Friday. They included a rescheduled meeting with Bartholomew Lookson. He would talk to the financial mogul about his choice for company president—Louis Scarlechek. Lookson lived in Miami, and would travel north. *How can I sell this to Bart?* he wondered. *It'll depend on what Bart wants from me. But given the financials the shareholders have seen, I still have the clout.*

Peckinpah hadn't yet informed Cookie about his decision to push Scarlechek, deciding it'd be easier to tell her after he met with Lookson. *I'll let Cookie believe this is Lookson's idea,* he thought. *She won't believe it from me. Janis wouldn't believe it either.*

Cookie flipped the pages of her novel, skipping over paragraphs and paragraphs of what she thought was needless description. She was unable to concentrate. Images of Vail nagged her and she debated whether to ask her boss for the story behind the pictures.

But she didn't.

CHAPTER 52

Friday, March 6, was a big day in the bowels of Western Town. Peckinpah would be conducting meetings in the executive suites on the sixth floor of the corporate office building, across the open atrium space from Scarlechek's office on the same floor. The Sorenson mediation was to take place one floor below in the main conference room, breaking off into smaller rooms.

It was also a special day for DeeDee Lane. She felt excited as she marched down the hall to her office. She was helping oversee the last day of a massive document production in another multi-million dollar construction case in which the company was embroiled. The way she understood it, Western Town had fired the contractor when it refused to accept blame for delays on the Geronimo Ghost Dance attraction. The contractor insisted on extra payment for necessary upgrades ordered because the ride wasn't as thrilling as Universal's, and the tightly budgeted Western Town project managers refused, looking for a scapegoat. The contractor sued, and the company was producing an entire room full of boxed construction plans and specifications, contracts, correspondence, log sheets, diaries, memos and notes, to the contractor's attorneys, two of whom were down from Atlanta. The production and review process had taken two days already, and would probably take the lawyers into the evening in order that they could finish and go home for the weekend. DeeDee knew she'd be there late, but that was okay now.

Scarlechek had asked Adel to meet with him, Yates, Tiyona, and Laughlin at eight in the morning to discuss the mediation prior to its start at nine.

It was seven fifty-six when Adel saw Cookie Albertson sprint across the atrium to catch the elevator in which Adel was standing. Cookie entered and was surprised to discover her old boss.

"Adel Blair!" Cookie exhaled, out of breath, and delighted to see her friend.

"Hello, Cookie," Adel smiled, stepping forward to embrace Cookie. "It's so good to see you!"

"Thanks, it's good to see you too."

"What are you doing here?" Cookie asked as she looked down at Adel's carrying caddy, loaded with her bomb bag and briefcase.

"I represent your company. We have mediation today."

"Oh, wow! What kind of case?"

"Sexual harassment."

"Ooh. I'm sorry to hear the company's involved in that."

"Well, it hasn't been found guilty yet."

"Not with you on the case. ... Listen, when can we get together? I'd love to visit for awhile."

"Well, not tonight. I have a date." Adel knew Cookie would be pleased to hear that, having always fussed at Adel for working and rowing too much.

"Oh! Anyone I know?"

"Michael." Adel was proud.

"Still?"

"It's been off and on over the years."

"That's great, Adel. You know how I feel about him. Keep it *on* for a while. Listen, I'm going to be in town through all next week. Can we do it sometime next week?"

"Yeah, that'd be great. I'll call you Monday," Adel said as the elevator reached the sixth floor.

They exited and spoke briefly in the lobby overlooking the atrium.

"Where are you going to be?" Cookie asked.

"Well, I have a meeting in Lou Scarlechek's office now. Then I guess we'll be in the conference room downstairs."

Cookie frowned. "Oh well, have fun." Her expression was sarcastic. "I'll be over here in the executive suites. Maybe, I'll see you. If not, be sure to call next week."

"I will!"

CHAPTER 53

Adel Blair struggled with the number Thomas Wolfe requested as a counteroffer in the Western Town private caucus room—seven hundred and fifty thousand dollars. It was far more than she thought the case was worth. More importantly, she realized that with the polarity of the parties between seven hundred fifty thousand to one million, two-fifty, the pressure would be immense to settle in between at one million dollars. She explained this to Tiyona, Yates, and Scarlechek. It had been a long day, and the group was tired.

Wolfe had been at his finest as a mediator, and the deal truly was his client. The mediation had dragged on all day long, and he had pushed and hounded each party. He had tirelessly cajoled movement like a coach extracting performance from exhausted athletes. With his forceful demeanor, the parties found it difficult to say no to him. When they did, he hammered at the weaknesses of their case in the separate rooms. To Scarlechek and Yates, he asked how they thought the jury might react to the unabashed chauvinism of the wastewater treatment plant employees. To Sorenson and Gonzalez, he pounded on Sorenson's past and how that might inflame the jury against her.

It was nearly five o'clock when conflict developed between Wolfe and Adel. Wolfe wanted the company to go to seven hundred and fifty thousand dollars, when they had already offered the top dollar Adel recommended—a half million. Wolfe wanted more in order to get Gonzalez off the one million two fifty mark. If he could do this, he figured the case would settle.

"It's too much," Adel said, annoyed. "You're handing this woman a windfall."

But Wolfe said in his booming low voice, "You know, lawsuits are like train wrecks. You're traveling down the tracks at runaway speed. Suddenly, you crash to a dead stop. Where the debris and body parts will land, you just don't know. Now, Ms. Blair here is an exceptional lawyer with a sterling reputation. But I'm telling you, you can lose this much and more, very easily. I'd want to avoid the negative impact of that at all cost if I were you. Maybe your boss knows little of this case now, but what will he think and who will he blame if there are nationwide headlines that Western Town is guilty of sexual harassment?"

Scarlechek was way ahead of Wolfe. "Sandy, I agree with Mr. Wolfe here. It's your budget, so of course it's your decision. But as I've said all day, I'm concerned about the risk of an inflamed jury."

That squarely placed all blame on Yates if he chose to follow Adel's counsel. It wasn't that he mistrusted Adel. It really had nothing to do with that. Like in most big companies, blame avoidance was the name of the game in the upper echelons. Scarlechek had so neatly placed it all on Yates. Knowing exactly what was going on, Yates had no choice.

"Well, because Lou says we should settle, offer the seven fifty," Yates said. "Tiyona, you agree?"

"Yes, we need to settle."

Adel was amazed. At this point there was nothing left for her to say or do. A new dynamic had materialized, and she might as well have been invisible.

Wolfe recognized the unstated forces and sensed the case would soon settle. It took him only another half hour to obtain agreement at a cool one million. He wrote up the agreement and the parties signed. Sorenson and Gonzalez rejoiced. Scarlechek congratulated them and Yates, telling Yates he'd made a good decision. They all thanked Wolfe who had served his client—the deal—well.

Adel sulked in disbelief: the company had settled for twice as much as what she recommended. It was like the old game of "chicken," only in reverse. Instead of each player seeing who would "chicken out" first, Scarlechek and Yates did the opposite, pulling their necks in so fast in order to avoid having them cut off, she was surprised their heads weren't spinning. The "reverse chicken" phenomenon caused the company to cave in and Gonzalez got exactly what he wanted—what he thought the case was worth.

Adel thought about Sorenson and the wastewater treatment plant, and the attitudes of the rednecks there. She realized that she admired the plaintiff. The young woman had won. She stood up for herself in the face of the dark side of corporate power, and she'd won. Things would change at the plant; Adel sensed Yates was serious about that. Things had already changed—and the men there couldn't get away with it any longer. Adel remembered the Women's League seminar she attended with Tiyona a few nights back. Then she thought of the work of Michael McKerrin.

Maybe this settlement was a good thing.

CHAPTER 54

"Let's go to dinner and celebrate," Scarlechek said, after the group returned to his office and was joined by Laughlin.

"No, thanks," Yates replied. *There's a crude expression for taking it up the butt,* he thought. "I don't feel too much like celebrating."

"Adel?" Scarlechek asked.

"Okay."

"Count me in," Laughlin added. He couldn't resist hearing the details on how and why the company settled for one million dollars. That amused him, especially because he'd predicted to others in the department that the company would cave when he learned Scarlechek was going to be in on the mediation.

Tiyona accepted for a more practical reason—she was hungry.

Adel accepted because Scarlechek was her client who promised additional work for the firm. She also needed to understand the rationale behind what had happened. She wondered whether there was a lack of confidence in her. She thought to call Michael and cancel their date, but elected instead to ask him to come a little later.

The four of them dined and Scarlechek raised his wine glass.

"To Sandy's decision!" he said. "It was the right thing to do for that young woman. I would hate to see what would've happened to her at trial, so all in all, this was better. Adel, you would have made her regret that she'd ever brought the suit, if you had her on the witness stand. I just know it."

This made Adel feel better, for a moment. *It was the right thing to do, but we would've won?* she thought. *Is that what he's saying?*

"Let's talk about something different," Scarlechek suggested.

"Tell me more about your rowing club, Adel. Are there any big races coming up?"

"Masters Nationals in the late summer."

"I'm an avid boater, I think I told you. Is anyone allowed to row?"

"Yes, certainly."

"I want you to teach me to row sometime. If I meet you at your Lake Fairview boathouse will you teach me?"

"Of course I will." To herself, she doubted that Lou Scarlechek would ever see the parts of a rowing shell.

"How do you find the time?" he asked.

"Well, it's difficult, but I make time. Often, I'm at the boathouse alone, working out early in the morning or late at night."

"Interesting," Scarlechek said, imagining catching her late at night in a dark boathouse in her skintight rowing clothes.

Why can't I have her tonight?

Dinner ended, and Tiyona and Laughlin left for home. As Scarlechek took care of the check, he said, "Adel, Landis chewed my butt yesterday when I told him that commercial case I mentioned to you hasn't been filed yet. Will you come with me to my office to get the file?"

"Sure. No problem," she responded, finally satisfied there wasn't a lack of confidence in her.

"I can tell you about it, too. It'll only take a few minutes," he assured her as they left. "That is, provided Arizona doesn't catch me on the damn phone."

. . . .

When they arrived at the corporate office building, it was about eight o'clock, and it seemed all personnel in the Legal Department had gone home. Even Marta DeLong had called it a night. A shroud of darkness surrounded the glass-walled building and obscurity infiltrated the interior of the structure through the skylight windows. Across the atrium from the Legal Department, Adel made out two office suites with lights on and, hearing the hum of a vacuum cleaner, guessed that only the cleaning lady graced the halls.

She'd worn her conservative olive green suit for the mediation, and her hair had been up until dinner when she had excused herself to let it down. Her curly waves flowed fully, and no matter how she turned they delicately framed her golden-brown skin and her enchanting, cat-like eyes taking on the shade of her suit. She was alluring. She'd removed her tailored suit coat, revealing a thin, light gold-pastel blouse that was clingy, hinting at the marvelous form underneath.

Adel and Scarlechek walked the sixth floor hall to the Legal Department offices, her suit coat nonchalantly slung over her shoulder. With her long, loping strides, she looked more like she belonged on a runway than in court.

Scarlechek spoke incessantly while they walked, streaming charm like a faucet of warm syrup. Adel half-listened, reminding herself: *he's a client, pay attention.* But she could hardly wait for her rendezvous with Michael at her apartment.

They entered the Legal Department and Scarlechek flipped on the foyer light.

"Oh, my word!" He grimaced, shielding his eyes with his hand. "I'm sorry, Adel, bright lights make my head hurt sometimes. My doctor tells me it's something called 'chronic keratitis.' I'll be all right in my office. I have a dimmer."

They walked to his door. He opened it and turned on his office lights, immediately dimming them very low. He motioned to Adel, saying, "Have a seat. I'll get the file." He pointed to the couch and shut the door behind him.

Adel was taken by the charm of Western Town at night. From the sixth floor the view was spectacular, and the lights sparkled with active beauty. She didn't sit, instead walking to the window to admire the view, her thoughts straying again to Michael.

From his desk, Scarlechek also admired the view. Her figure was silhouetted against the window, and he imagined the lines of her body underneath her skirt.

His pulse began to rise. He remembered how men and women alike had gawked at her at the La Cocina. Tonight had been the same. He lifted a file from his desk and walked to her.

"Beautiful, isn't it?" he asked as he touched the small of her back with his hand.

"Yes," she said softly, snapping out of her pining for Michael.

"Well, here's the file. We can discuss it briefly and then ..." He paused, suggesting an unspoken alternative. "Let's sit down," he said, motioning to the couch. Like a master, he let her move first so he could control their proximity.

She sat down on the right side of the couch. Setting the file on the coffee table in front of them and opening it, he sat with merely a foot between them. He pointed to a photograph of a piece of heavy mechanical machinery in the file and said, "Now, this is the problem ... Oh, I'm sorry ... the lights. Here."

He scooted to be just next to her on the couch as he lifted the file to their bodies, as if to be able to see it better. Their upper thighs touched.

Adel's expression changed. She turned sharply and saw his face, and that's when she realized what he was doing. The thought was so alien to her; and she, preoccupied with Michael and excited about Western Town as a new client, hadn't seen it coming.

Scarlechek sensed he'd been discovered. Suddenly, the file was quite irrelevant, and he smiled as he put it down.

He placed his arm on the back of the couch behind her, turning his body to stare her in the eyes. He began to speak, as he moved his hand to her thigh.

"Adel, I want you to understand how much work I intend to send you," he said.

"In exchange for sex?" Her voice was cold.

"You catch on quickly," he said, mocking her. His hand began massaging her thigh.

"Apparently, not quickly enough." She stared down at his hand and then looked up at him.

It was unadulterated contempt he saw in her face. Though it was unsaid, it stung him.

She rose and started toward the chair where she'd left her coat. He stood quickly and followed. As she turned to the door, he spoke.

"Adel, wait! You're turning your back on an incredible amount of work," he said as he scurried after her. She stopped to listen without facing him, her back to his face. He approached and put his hands on her waist.

The work, she thought. *The firm. Dave's retirement.* She hesitated and Scarlechek sensed it.

"It could be approximately three hundred fifty to five hundred thousand a year on various matters," he said as his hands moved forward and up, and his body moved close to hers. "Or, it'll be nothing."

She hesitated again. It encouraged him and his hands kept moving, slowly. They reached her breasts.

In an instant, Adel was shocked and angry. Without thinking, she rocked her body weight forward onto her right leg, bending her knee and pivoting forward at the hip, simultaneously contracting her left hamstring with all her possible might, jamming her left heel up and backward into his groin. She hit the mark square, and the lift of her leg drove the blow home—the same powerful leg drive that propelled so many rowing strokes.

Scarlechek screamed in pain as his eyes widened with surprise. He doubled over with the ache beginning in his testicles and emanating through all of his lower organs. His arms involuntarily contracted to his belly as his knees bent and drew together.

His horrified face looked up, still grimacing at Adel as she reeled about, cocking her right arm and clenching her fist. Her left leg stepped into her ensuing blow.

Scarlechek saw nothing but her knuckles as they rushed closer and closer with the mighty velocity of a pile driver. It came so fast, yet the moment seemed so prolonged, it was as though every second clung to its fleeting existence. With a fist like Thor's hammer, she caught him square on the left jaw.

In an instant he was on his butt, traumatized and dazed. The pain in his lower abdomen momentarily merged with disorientation; returning, it was accompanied by a new and throbbing misery in his aching jaw.

"Not in this lifetime!" he heard a female voice shout. The words seemed surreal, booming in from everywhere around him, echoing in the room and his mind.

Adel Blair left.

CHAPTER 55

By the time Adel reached the first floor she was trembling. She managed to reach her car and begin her drive home, all the while trying to calm herself. It was her instinctual rage that was most astonishing. She wondered from where it came, as she noticed the throbbing in her right hand.

I can't believe the nerve of that jerk, she thought. She formed a thought she hadn't realized until now: *I hate Western Town. Anything that can be called discrimination, this company has it to offer—state-of-the-art harassment.*

The thought crossed her mind that she'd led him on, accusing herself just as she had accused many female plaintiffs in the past. Her own argument would be that she'd received just what she deserved for going to his office after dinner with wine, at eight o'clock at night. But her actions were consistent with the actions of a person trying to appease the desires of a new client, with honest hopes of securing more work. At the same time, she knew that if she'd been a man, no one would have questioned her judgment. Realizing she acted properly, she wondered how many of her past opponents had also. How many of those that she'd flattened.

Now, she might be sued for assault and battery. *But he battered me,* she thought, knowing that if a lawsuit resulted it would be *her* actions on trial. She imagined Scarlechek's attorney making final argument to a jury:

Ladies and gentlemen of the jury, take one long look at this woman. Look at her actions. Look at her dress and the way she carries herself. Was Lou Scarlechek incorrect in his assumptions that she wanted sex with him? I think your experience in life will tell you otherwise.

But maybe Scarlechek won't sue. Maybe he couldn't stand it if people knew he was beaten up by a woman. He'll vent his anger in other ways. Certainly, we'll never get any more work from Western Town.

She thought of Dave McKerrin and what the three hundred fifty to five hundred thousand dollars a year could've meant to him and the firm. She loved Dave and wanted him to be able to retire comfortably. *He's such a good man and he's worked so hard. I'll have to tell him about this first thing in the morning. No ... better on Monday morning,* she thought, predicting how he'd react—he'd want to kill Scarlechek. *I'll be able to keep him calm in his office.*

But Adel understood she should tell *someone.* The lawyer in her knew she wouldn't be credible to a jury if she didn't tell someone that night. And then her tired mind finally broke down—she *wanted* to tell someone. She *needed* to tell someone. She needed someone now. Tears accumulated in her eyes and she thought of Michael. She needed Michael. The thought occurred to her to pull off the road to collect herself, but she didn't. She wanted more than ever to be home so she pressed on.

She took momentary solace in what she'd done to the man. *That bastard got exactly what he deserved, whether a jury'll believe me or not.*

She marveled again at her rage, and how instantaneously her reactions materialized when summoned. Wondering from where they derived, she was amazed at the power of her blows. It was pure instinct. It was the internal energy of her body unleashed and uninhibited ... something primal, something not many people have a chance to experience. It was beautiful in a way ... thoughtlessly tapping the inner self. It occurred to her how sad it was to discover something like that during such an ugly episode, thinking she'd much prefer to have discovered it in a rowing race.

By the time Adel reached her apartment complex and walked to the stairwell toward her apartment, she was exhausted. Looking upward immediately bolstered her downtrodden spirits—at the top of the stairs sat Michael McKerrin, wearing baggy shorts and an old "Washington Crew" t-shirt. His long, muscular arms were draped over his knees and his angular hands dangled about a bottle of Cabernet. He was forty-five minutes early.

He had wanted to be early, sitting Indian style in exactly the spot he was ... waiting for her. He lifted his head and smiled, his blue eyes and black hair glistening in the stairwell light.

Adel flew up the two flights like a tigress attacking her prey. But, for once, she wasn't on the attack—Adel Blair was crying. By the time she reached the top, he'd risen, and she dropped her briefcase and flung herself onto him, practically knocking him over as her arms wrapped over his broad shoulders, and their bodies collided.

Seeing her eyes and hearing her sobs, he embraced her and held her close. Never had he seen this emotion out of this strong woman. *Something's terribly wrong,* he thought.

Later, inside the apartment, he listened as she related the story, and they talked through every event and angle over several glasses of wine.

"Michael," she whispered later, as they embraced on the couch.

"Yes?"

"Don't tell Dave. Let me handle it. I don't want his blood pressure spiking over the likes of Lou Scarlechek. I'll handle it Monday."

"Sure. Don't worry."

She gazed into his eyes and found refuge in his lips and arms, until the entwined pair found sleep together.

CHAPTER 56

Lou Scarlechek hadn't been knocked unconscious by Adel's blows. But he'd doubled over on his side, moaning in misery. The blow to his jaw had knocked it numb and he rubbed it, only to clutch his aching belly. He pressed inward, trying to suppress the growing pain, and stayed in this position for a long moment. The executive vice president of the Legal Department of one of the most exciting companies in the country was sprawled on the floor of his office, beaten up by a woman.

As the pain in his lower abdomen began to subside, the numbness in his jaw began to wear off and it began to throb and match the rhythm of his heartbeat. It felt as though Adel's fist was still pounding on his bone.

Goddamn! he thought. He pulled himself up and hobbled to his couch. Sitting tenderly with elbows on his knees, he buried his head into his hands and massaged his jaw. His tongue gingerly explored his mouth for loose teeth.

"That fuckin' bitch stiffed me!"

Regaining his strength, he stood up and began to pace. Like a caged animal at the zoo, he prowled back and forth within the confines of his office. His thoughts centered on Adel and how he'd exact his revenge.

I'll sue, he thought. But this didn't sit well. There was publicity and notoriety in that tactic.

I'll ruin her! I'll blackball her, he thought. *Yes! I have the power. I'll use that. I'll talk to her clients. I'll be President of Western Town soon. If they want to do business with us, they won't deal with her or her firm. And the ones that don't deal with us, I'll get to them somehow, too ... through the politicians that we'll buy. She'll* never *represent Western Town or any major company again!*

But somehow, he wasn't satisfied ... it wasn't enough. What she'd done to him was fundamental, and he wanted to respond in kind. She had challenged his manhood down to his very soul, having committed the highest abomination to his self-esteem by forcefully saying "no." Momma didn't do that. No one did that.

Her images now stung him, over and over, and he paced faster and faster, gesturing wildly with his arms. The gestures turned into lunging punches into the air; and he uttered obscenities at her with his gnarled mouth. "Must have her! Will get her!" viciously erupted from his soul.

Scarlechek's frenzied state was suddenly interrupted when he heard a sound outside his office. He violently pulled the door open and searched for the source. A young woman farther down the hall was carrying a box of documents into her office.

It was DeeDee Lane.

DeeDee! The document production! Yes! She was the salve for his wounds. It wasn't a conscious thought; it was instinctual, like that of a jackal on the hunt. He stalked her down the hall.

Reaching her office door, he said with a snarl, "DeeDee, get your pad ... I need a letter done now!" His voice was low and threatening, indicating that there was no compromise.

DeeDee lurched around to face him. "What letter?" she said defiantly.

"To Peckinpah. Now come on. I need you now!" In his fervor he'd forgotten that Peckinpah was in town, but DeeDee didn't know, and it hardly mattered.

"Lou, I'm not going to do it anymore!"

"DeeDee, just get your damn pad! This is urgent!"

But *everything* was urgent to him. She didn't believe him any more than the villagers believed the boy who cried wolf. It was typical for him to ask anyone to do his work. Anybody to do his bidding ... any female body, that is. Although DeeDee was angry and skeptical, she was also too trusting. A different person would have refused to walk down the hall.

"No sex!" she uttered, snatching up a pad and pen, too flustered to notice his heavy breathing.

DeeDee entered his den and brightened his office lights with the dimmer switch, and sat down in front of his desk with her pad and pen.

He followed her in, but stopped at the switch. Deliberately dimming the lights, he reached to close the door. As he began to swing it shut, DeeDee rose. "Lou! No!" she blurted and started to leave. The door slammed in front of her, and Scarlechek grabbed her arms with both hands to prevent her departure.

"Don't give me that 'no' crap!" His voice was ugly and violent. He now imagined he was speaking to Adel.

"Lou, I said no! Now let me go!"

"Sorry, bitch! Get over here!" Still grasping her arms, he jerked her sideways toward the couch. She stumbled, but he didn't let her go. Holding her up, he forced her closer to the couch, overpowering her with his strength.

"No!" she screamed as Scarlechek threw her down on the sofa. Collapsing his body on top of hers, he grabbed her arms again. She screamed—mindless, rasps at the top of her lungs.

She flailed her arms, but he was too quick and strong. He pinned her arms over her head and held her wrists together. His left hand tightened and pushed down hard to keep her wrists over her head. With his right hand, he snatched her blouse at the neckline and pulled. DeeDee felt the blouse dig into the back of her neck. He yanked harder, and her torso rose off the couch and her head fell back while the top buttons on her blouse popped off.

DeeDee tried to knee Scarlechek in the groin, but he anticipated and blocked her move. It allowed him to position his leg between hers in order to open her.

Grunting, he yanked again with all his might. The bottom button under her skirt didn't give, but her blouse was now out of his way, dangling to the side of the couch. Grasping her bra between the cups, he shoved it up to her neck and knocked her chin. The push successfully revealed her jiggling breasts. He molested them with his right hand while he slobbered over her. But his left arm tired and DeeDee, sensing his fatigue, tried to wrestle her wrists free. So he reinforced his left arm with his right, grabbing her wrists with his right hand and shifting weight between the two equally, instantly relieving his left triceps.

With both hands now over his head, he shifted his body and moved his head down to her right breast and sank his teeth into her nipple. DeeDee screamed in agony. Each time she wriggled about, trying to free her nipple, he bit deeper and that made it worse, so she settled back in pain.

Scarlechek's mind was in overdrive. It was Adel Blair he was assaulting. It was Adel Blair from whom he was exacting his revenge. It was Adel Blair over whom he was asserting his power and control. The control focused him, and his mind processed it, storing it below … in his penis. Despite the nature of his actions, he filled with blood and grew erect.

Scarlechek relinquished his suction on her nipple and undid his trousers, and then extracted himself. He pulled up her skirt to get at her panties. DeeDee's intermittent screams continued with each new development, including this one. Every aspect of her body was tiring from the fight, from the lactic acid filling her arms, to the pain in her wrists from his grip, to the emerging desire in her mind to resign. Redness appeared around her wrists bordered by a yellowish-white where he clamped down tight. Her right nipple was numb and trickling blood.

Scarlechek discovered her pantyhose, and tried to pull them down. But DeeDee still had enough strength to contract her lower muscles, making it difficult. He tried ripping them, but he wasn't strong enough, so he reached into his right pocket and pulled out his Swiss Army knife attached to his keys.

She screamed in desperation one last time, as he moved to open up the blade and flash it before her eyes.

"Let me pull them off," he said. "Or else …" When he saw resignation in her face, he lifted himself off of her and yanked her pantyhose and panties down, still threatening her with the blade.

As he stood over her like a prehistoric savage, she sobbed in anticipation of what was to come. She could see the frenzy in his eyes as he wielded the knife. "Don't resist," she heard him say in a threatening voice, as he flopped back down upon her.

DeeDee didn't resist. She had only one thought—*persevere*—as he separated her legs and penetrated her. *Endure*, she thought as he began his sporadic, jerky movements. *Survive*. Amid the grotesqueness, the loathsomeness of the scene, something strong and beautiful emanated from DeeDee Lane.

"What the hell is going on in here?" It was a different voice shouting—strong and commanding. DeeDee Lane jerked her head and saw a large man through her tears. She recognized him. It was the CEO of the company, Tom Peckinpah. He'd been working in one of the offices across the atrium and had just come out of the restroom when he'd heard DeeDee's scream.

Peckinpah stood by the door Scarlechek had neglected to lock. He took in the dangling blouse, the knife in Scarlechek's hand, the cruel expression on Scarlechek's face, and the tears of anguish on DeeDee's as she pleaded with him.

"Help me! He's raping me!"

Scarlechek had been entranced, and about to reach orgasm. But his movements abruptly stopped. It was too late; she'd spoken *those words*. They jolted him, and the feelings subsided, unfulfilled.

"Tom, leave us to our games in privacy," Scarlechek said, the best he could do under the circumstances.

"This is no game, I'm being raped! He's still in me. Get out of me!"

"This doesn't look like a game to me, Lou! Get off of her, now!"

Scarlechek feigned annoyance as he complied. "Tom, you don't understand. This little vixen and I have been doing it for months. She likes these rough games. She's playing with you now. Come on DeeDee, snap out of it." As he dismounted and put himself back in place, DeeDee scrambled to cover herself, pulling her skirt and bra down and wrapping her damaged blouse around her.

"That's a lie!" She pointed at Scarlechek. "He raped me!"

Peckinpah could see her anger—it was growing in intensity as she dressed. He believed her.

"DeeDee, get off it!" said Scarlechek, acting incensed.

"I'm calling the police," Peckinpah declared.

"Tom, I wouldn't do that if I were you," Scarlechek said. He peered at Peckinpah with a threatening expression. Peckinpah stared back hard at Scarlechek, and then let his eyes fall to the floor.

"I repeat … we've been doing it for months. Just ask her,"

"Is that true?" Peckinpah asked DeeDee tentatively, struggling as he remembered his own predicament.

The anger on her face changed when she realized that her story wouldn't be believed. It *was* true, they had been doing it for months. As soon as she admitted Scarlechek's allegation, it would be unbelievable that he was raping her now. She felt embarrassed—the shame of having to admit the horrible, humiliating fact. Her hesitation betrayed her.

"Is that true?" Peckinpah reiterated, suddenly grateful for an excuse to believe Scarlechek.

"Yes! That's true! But not voluntarily! … I can see it's hopeless to be believed around here." DeeDee couldn't get out of there fast enough. Still grasping her unbuttoned blouse to her body, she fled, never wanting to step foot in Western Town again.

CHAPTER 57

"You son of a bitch!" Peckinpah hissed at Scarlechek after DeeDee had gone. He trusted his eyes and knew that DeeDee hadn't lied. It was poetic justice that Scarlechek, who'd witnessed Peckinpah's debauchery, and was blackmailing him for it, had now been caught in this despicable diversion. *Now we're even,* Peckinpah thought. *Now, I can escape your clutches!*

"Fuck you, Tom! I own you! I don't give a damn what you've seen, or what you think!" Scarlechek fired back. "But I do give a damn what you'll say. She may sue or prosecute. The story is this: there was no knife, and you walked in on us making love. She was so embarrassed at being caught, she left. The conversation we had didn't take place. You only scolded us for our lack of discretion, and she left. Got it?"

Peckinpah grimaced, slowly moving his head from side to side. He let Scarlechek see the hatred on his face. It wasn't akin to conscious thought that poised him, ready to assault the man. It was instinct. Every muscle in his large body yearned to beat the shit out of Lou Scarlechek. It'd be so easy; he could feel it, and his fists clenched at his sides. His body leaned forward in angry anticipation, ready to pounce, his footballer nature fully aroused. Tensing his legs, he took a quick step forward. But then, something chained him to that spot.

They *weren't* even. Peckinpah couldn't escape. In a chess match confrontation of pawns, one has to be willing to lose the pawn. But Peckinpah wasn't willing; it guarded his king, and he had way too much to lose.

"Got it?" Scarlechek reiterated, the trepidation in him starting to build. "That's the story, Tom, or the problem comes out—every sordid detail."

Peckinpah's face went blank. His muscle fibers lost their explosiveness as though his strength had been blown from him by a sudden wind. He couldn't bring himself to say, yeah, I got it, but he looked down at his feet in acquiescence.

Seeing Peckinpah's eyes, Scarlechek's fear subsided.

In one last desperate attempt at defiance, Peckinpah said, "If there's a lawsuit or prosecution, you can forget about the job."

"We'll cross that bridge when we get to it," Scarlechek said, knowing he'd won. Instantly, his mind raced, carrying Peckinpah's thought to logical conclusion. "For now, I need some money. I want one million dollars made available to me. I'm going to buy the little bitch's silence. Yours or the company's, Tom, I don't care. But I want it available on Monday."

Another wave of shock hit Peckinpah. It wasn't the money ... that would be easy for him. It was the sudden, certain realization that he'd *always* be under Scarlechek's control that shook him, and that there was no enforceable release from extortion. It was check and checkmate. Game over.

"Fucker," Peckinpah muttered, resigning himself to Scarlechek's power. His spirit was broken. Mr. Corporate America, the once mighty and powerful, felt deflated to the point of despair.

"Now, get out. I've got to call my lawyer," Scarlechek commanded. "Remember! Stick to the story!"

CHAPTER 58

DeeDee Lane considered the ease with which she could
steer her automobile into a concrete utility pole. A mere flick of her
wrists at eighty miles per hour, and it could all be over. She undid
her seatbelt. *The tranquility,* she thought. *Endless, safe, blissful sleep
... heaven.* Increasing her speed, she visualized her head and chest
rebounding off her windshield and steering wheel, killing her upon
impact. *Killing.*

Her focus shifted to an idea completely alien to her—something
she never thought she'd contemplate—*murder.* She conjured up a
scenario, the steps she'd take. She visualized his body hogtied, and
with a sharp knife she cut his bleeding penis right off! The thought
sustained her as she drove home.

Her vengeful trance was interrupted by an overwhelming desire
to be clean. She screeched into her parking space and bolted upstairs
to her apartment. Inside, she ran to her bathroom, tore off her clothing, and jumped into the shower.

Clean ... must be clean! she thought as she washed. Scrubbing
frantically, she couldn't decontaminate quickly enough, all the while
throbbing from the internal violation. She scrubbed and scrubbed
until she broke down, collapsing onto the hard, tiled floor of the
shower. She wept and wailed, and her chest began heaving forth
uncontrollable, tremoring sobs. Suicidal emotions invaded her once
again, and she couldn't stand the despair. Escape.

Her spirit floated outside her body. Looking down, she saw herself as she was—a heap of human misery slumped on the shower tile.
Anger emerged, bringing her back down, and engulfed her like the

steam from the shower. DeeDee thought again of murder. It came down to a simple choice—her life, or his. She raised her head in the vapor and swore to kill him. She stepped out of the shower to dry off and set about the task, marveling at her thoughts, amazed that she was capable of such intense rage. The sweet little girl from Iowa was so ultimately pissed-off.

But then, DeeDee wiped away the steam on the mirror with her towel. She studied her image, until she realized she wouldn't do it. She wouldn't be a common criminal, lowering herself to Scarlechek's level.

"If you don't respect yourself, no one else will," she remembered the words of the psychologist at the Women's League seminar. "It's so complex, yet so simple," the speaker had said. "You gain self-respect from knowing who you are and liking what you see. You are what you do. You must do, to define yourself. You must try—always try, no matter what."

"No matter what!" DeeDee repeated aloud, memorizing her naked body in the mirror.

DeeDee suddenly envisioned a woman overlooking a majestic precipice. She stood tall and proud in the face of a strong wind, her hair blowing back. Zooming in, DeeDee saw that the stalwart female was Adel Blair. But at once the vision changed, and the woman became DeeDee herself!

Her vision injected power and resolve into her body. She had lived with despair for too long, and enough was enough. Scarlechek had been raping her all along, she thought, and she was now at the breaking point where she could either retreat into chronic unhappiness or fight back.

DeeDee Lane chose life that night. Alone, completely despondent, and in utter despair, she willed her spirit upward and onward. The rape had only been the culmination of what had been happening all along, sexual harassment being nothing but a rape of the soul. The physical rape of her body was the final manifestation—the final taking. If she could survive the rape of her soul, she could survive the rape of her body. After the La Cocina meeting, she'd made a strong decision. Now she decided she wouldn't let Scarlechek's recent actions diminish her determination. She wouldn't let his force overcome hers and she'd live the vision.

Don't give up, she thought to herself. "Don't give up," she said aloud, and repeated it over and over again, the sound of her voice echoing in the bathroom.

There she stood on the cold floor, her naked body bruised and battered, tears mixing with remnants of shower water on her cheeks, her eye makeup running and her wet hair disheveled. She was a thing of true beauty.

The living thing stepped out of the bathroom, still dripping wet, picked up her phone and dialed information for the home phone number of the attorney she heard about from Adel and Tiyona— Steve Gonzalez.

CHAPTER 59

"DeeDee Lane?"

"Yes," came the raspy voice, barely audible over the phone.

"I know it's late, I apologize. My name is Richard Golumbo. I'm an attorney and I represent Mr. Scarlechek. Please don't hang up! He has an offer to make."

"There's nothing that he has that can be offered to me."

"No, please! Don't hang up. He has plenty to offer you. He's truly remorseful and wants to make amends. Just hear me out, please."

She hesitated. "I'm listening." Her voice was cold.

"Not on the phone. I want to come over, immediately."

"All right," she said without disclosing that Steve Gonzalez was already on his way. *Won't he be surprised,* she thought. She gave Golumbo directions and hung up.

Scarlechek had called his attorney, Richard S. Golumbo, as soon as Peckinpah had left his office. Golumbo was a competent lawyer of questionable ethics. In the past, on personal matters, Scarlechek had hired Golumbo with great success, and Golumbo had been rewarded handsomely. He hadn't minded the late call.

Golumbo was a man who could relate to Scarlechek on an unusual level, realizing that most things Scarlechek told him were lies. With a wry smile, Golumbo was quick to discern and admire the reasons for his client's fabrications. Like a chess fan who lauds a master, Golumbo appreciated Scarlechek's slick moves.

Scarlechek told Golumbo that he'd been having an affair with a secretary in his department. Golumbo smiled, thinking, *here we go again.* Scarlechek told Golumbo that the secretary had been setting him up because now she was going to claim rape, and was possibly going to the police straight away. He anticipated she was going to sue for sexual harassment, sexual battery, and other torts. Golumbo continued smiling. Scarlechek added that he had a witness—the company CEO—who would testify he walked in on them making love, not rape.

An important fact, seemingly dispositive, Golumbo thought.

But then Scarlechek told Golumbo he would have no less than one million dollars by Monday to settle with the girl. He wanted Golumbo to contact DeeDee ASAP and negotiate an agreement.

Golumbo's smile widened. He asked, "If you didn't do it, and have a solid witness, why do you pay a million bucks?" The question was rhetorical, and the answer seemed obvious to Golumbo.

"Shut up and listen, asshole," Scarlechek snapped. "If you get her to settle for less than a million, up to the first one hundred thousand dollars saved is yours. But it has to be done immediately—I mean now, tonight. Is that clear?"

Golumbo's oversized Adam's apple moved up and down in his gullet and his expression turned serious. Scarlechek had his attention now. *A hundred thousand for a night's work!*

Without hesitation, he asked for DeeDee's address and phone number.

CHAPTER 60

Esteban Gonzalez listened intently to DeeDee Lane. He was shocked to hear it was Lou Scarlechek. The very man with whom he'd just spent the entire day mediating a sexual harassment case was the harasser! But somehow it fit, and his curiosity had been piqued enough to make the late house call.

It was nearly eleven o'clock when Golumbo arrived at DeeDee's apartment. He was astonished to find Gonzalez already there. "Well, she's sure acted quickly to hire you, almost as though it was planned," Golumbo drawled.

"We'll have none of that!" Gonzalez snapped in his heavy Cuban accent. "My client has been through an ordeal tonight. If you cannot behave in a civilized fashion, I must ask you to leave. Now, you told her you have an offer. We will listen."

"I don't know how much you know, so first I'll tell you what I know," Golumbo said. "We have a witness—the company CEO, no less—who says he'll testify they were just making love." He said it proudly.

"I know all about Mr. Peckinpah," Gonzalez said ... though he didn't. "That helps the charge of rape only. Mr. Scarlechek's problem is far worse. And we will see if Mr. Scarlechek wants to put his CEO through a deposition. State your offer. I'm tired and growing bored."

"We'll pay five hundred thousand dollars next week, in exchange for a complete release of Mr. Scarlechek and the company, an agreement not to prosecute criminally, and a strict confidentiality clause. If you agree, we'll write it up and sign the agreement right here and now."

"And what about my client's job?"

"She can keep it, that is, if she wants it."

"What guarantee does she have that Scarlechek won't do this again, or sexually harass her again? And, what guarantee does she have against him later retaliating in some manner, seeking revenge against her somehow, like failing to give her a better position, or a bonus, or—"

"Steve ... no," DeeDee interjected. Her voice was tired, but determined. "I don't want to do this. He'll be free to just go on doing it to others. Everybody just turns their heads. Maybe he pays a little money, but the bastard just goes on doing whatever he wants. It's not right!"

Gonzalez turned to Golumbo. "Will you give us a moment to discuss this?"

"Of course."

"DeeDee, where can we go?"

"Back to my bedroom."

They entered her bedroom and closed the door.

"DeeDee, listen. I just got this case. I don't know you. I don't know the facts, other than what you've said. I don't know what the witnesses will say, except he claims the CEO of a prominent company will testify against you. But the man is offering a half million dollars in exchange for nothing but silence ... just after it happened!"

His expression grew contemplative as he spoke.

"Doesn't quite make sense, does it?" he continued. "I'll bet we can get more, here, tonight. It can set you up for life, if you're wise, and you can put this mess all behind you."

"Can I? I'd have to look at him and know I didn't do anything about him. I'd be just like all the others. You've heard the fable about the emperor's new clothes? Well, maybe I'm supposed to be the one who says the bastard's wearing no clothes!"

"But DeeDee, they have a strong witness, and I promise you this: it will be *your* actions that are on trial in the court and in the media. There will be publicity, nastiness, lies, and more lies. Your humiliation will be broadcast throughout Central Florida, and probably become national news. You'll have to give your deposition and trial

229

testimony, and the cross-examination will challenge your soul."

Gonzalez paused, looking her in the eye.

Her gaze drifted to his shoes and she took a deep breath, and then looked back up at him. "I know," she said, nodding with resolve.

"All right," Gonzalez shrugged. "I'll be proud to take your case. We'll discuss my fee arrangement later."

They walked back to DeeDee's living room.

"No deal," Gonzalez said to Golumbo arrogantly.

"Well, I'm not going to bid against myself. Make me a counteroffer. Let's get it done," Golumbo said, as if this were a matter of course.

"Perhaps you didn't hear me," Gonzalez said. "I said no deal."

Golumbo's head snapped back in surprise. *There's always a deal,* he thought. "She won't even negotiate?"

"Your quickness betrays your intelligence." Gonzalez insulted Golumbo with the hope that he would leave.

But Golumbo wouldn't leave. Even though it was anathema for a lawyer to ever bargain against himself, he said, "Seven hundred and fifty thousand."

"No deal." Gonzalez said again, exhibiting impatience.

Golumbo stepped back, swallowed hard, and made one last offer. "One million dollars," he said, realizing he'd just given away his bonus. He knew he had to exhaust the authority he'd been given, even if it meant the appearance of desperation.

Gonzalez's faltered and looked at DeeDee long enough to measure her resolve. She shook her head no. He turned back to Golumbo and said, "Mr. Golumbo, I've grown weary of watching you wallow and grovel. Now, I must ask you to leave. We are going to bring your man down."

CHAPTER 61

"Sheriff's Department. You're being recorded," the voice said.

"I want to report a rape," Steve Gonzalez said. "I'm the victim's attorney."

"Where, sir?" The first concern was always jurisdiction.

"In the corporate offices at Western Town."

"Where's the victim now?"

"Here with me, at her apartment. The address is ..."

A marked unit was dispatched with haste. DeeDee sat in her living room and tried to relax, while Gonzalez made coffee in her kitchen. She couldn't believe this was happening to her—the homecoming queen and the missing darling of her hometown in Iowa. She thought of her parents, and flushed with shame, but her thoughts turned to Scarlechek, and she enjoyed the image of him being arrested.

Deputy Karen Edwards listened to Gonzalez relay his client's story, and observed the signs on DeeDee of mental and physical trauma.

Gonzalez was forthright, disclosing the prior sexual conduct between Scarlechek and DeeDee, and about Peckinpah. He explained Peckinpah's identity and Edwards acknowledged knowing about him from the papers. Telling Deputy Edwards about Golumbo's earlier visit, Gonzalez relayed that Peckinpah would say it was not rape.

Gonzalez said, "We are only trying to be up front with you, Deputy Edwards. Golumbo wouldn't have told us about Peckinpah unless he was confident of Peckinpah's testimony. But such testimony would be untrue. My client was raped tonight, and we want to swear out the complaint. We are serious, and we will follow through with the prosecution. We will be filing a civil lawsuit also."

"Do we know where Mr. Peckinpah is?"

"I'm told he usually stays in the Ranchero Hotel presidential suite when he's in town," DeeDee said, hoping for Scarlechek's arrest.

"Give me a few minutes, please," Deputy Edwards said as she got up and walked out to call the duty detective on her shoulder-radio, her leather squeaking as she moved. She could see that DeeDee had suffered trauma, and the immediate settlement offer certainly suggested something to her story. But because Peckinpah had interrupted Scarlechek, there would be no semen. On top of that, Scarlechek and Peckinpah were high-powered executives with Western Town, which actively supported the Sheriff's Department. Edwards needed advice, and consent.

After ten minutes, Edwards returned. "The duty detective isn't available, but I've called a technician and a rape counselor. They'll be here shortly. I want to take your statement, and then I'm going to try to get Mr. Peckinpah's and Mr. Scarlechek's. After that, assuming they say what you've predicted, I probably won't be making an arrest." She said it heavily, looking DeeDee square in the eyes.

"I believe you, Ms. Lane, but it's not my decision. I'll turn all the statements in to the assistant state attorney I work with and let her decide whether or not to issue a warrant for Mr. Scarlechek's arrest."

"But why would Mr. Golumbo come over tonight and offer one million dollars for my client's silence?" Gonzalez protested, though he knew he was treading on thin ice. Offers of settlement are inadmissible in court to prove liability, the policy being to encourage the settlement of disputes.

"I don't know," Deputy Edwards replied. "It does seem strange. But we can't go forward on just that."

"I understand," Gonzalez said. Seeing that she was disappointed, he put his arm around DeeDee.

"I'm concerned that the assistant state attorney may kick this up to her boss, and given who these people are, and what they'll supposedly say, he may shelve it. It seems as though your remedy may only be in the civil courts," Deputy Edwards said to DeeDee. "Unless something changes, or something new develops," she added.

DeeDee's disenchantment was manifest, but she couldn't let Edwards's news thwart her determination. If she was to live up to the vision she'd seen, she knew she must endure the tough road ahead.

CHAPTER 62

At the Ranchero Hotel, Deputy Edwards disturbed Tom
Peckinpah's already sleepless night.

"No, I didn't see any signs of force," Peckinpah told her, as his
anxiety rose to new heights. "They appeared to be making love. I
scolded them. She was embarrassed and left."

Edwards wrote Peckinpah's statement based on his claims; and
he signed it and returned to his room and a fitful night.

Edwards's next stop was Scarlechek's house—a large
Mediterranean-style house in a gated lakefront community. Marsha
Scarlechek, flabbergasted to find a sheriff's deputy at her door, only
grew more confused when she discovered the nature of the investigation. Scarlechek, in turn, admitted to his wife that he had had an
affair. It was that or admit to raping DeeDee.

"You have the right to remain silent," Deputy Edwards said to
Scarlechek. "Anything you say may—"

"Are you arresting me?" Scarlechek demanded to know.

"No," Deputy Edwards said, resisting the impulse to say, "Not
now." She continued, "But you're the accused, and I'm here for a
statement. I have to do this."

"I'm an attorney, for Christ's sake."

"All the more reason," she replied, and finished giving Scarlechek
the Miranda warning.

"Now, sir, you want to tell me what happened?"

"We were ... making love," Scarlechek said. Feigning sheepish-
ness was easy for him, and he held his head down.

"Oh shit, Lou!" Marsha said. "Can't you keep it in your pants
for five minutes."

"Ma'am, please," Deputy Edwards said. "I need to take his statement. You and he can sort things out later." Deputy Edwards had the impression that Marsha was not as disappointed as she should have been. It almost seemed that she didn't care, except that the deputy's visit was disturbing her sleep.

"Well, God damn it! I have needs too, you know. I'm tired of this shit! I have a very busy day tomorrow. The girls and I are going shopping! Why don't you come back tomorrow when I'm gone, so I don't have to hear all these sordid details?"

"Marsha, calm down," Scarlechek said, surprised by her assertiveness. "I'm really sorry, honey. Why don't you just go back to bed? I can handle the officer."

"Well, sure, Mr. Sex Addiction, I'll go back to bed. But you better damn well have my account replenished in the morning!"

"I will ... I'm sorry, Marsha," Scarlechek said, knowing the money would placate her. "But honey, it's not my fault ... I promise. This little girl in the department threw herself at me. She's been after me since I got there," he said. "She seduced me, and now she's set me up for personal gain."

"All right, that's enough!" Deputy Edwards said. "Ma'am, I'll have to ask you to go inside ... now! I want to take Mr. Scarlechek's statement alone."

"I'm so sorry, honey," Scarlechek said. "I'm so embarrassed. I never meant to cheat on you, I promise ... I promise!" he shouted after her as she scurried into the house in a huff.

• • • •

Back at the station, after taking Scarlechek's statement, Edwards filled out her report and a request for arrest-warrant form. She placed the papers in the box for delivery to the State Attorney's office on Monday morning, realizing that with two upstanding witnesses contradicting DeeDee's story, she probably wouldn't be making any arrest.

CHAPTER 63

It was approximately six fifteen Saturday morning when Michael McKerrin opened his right eye. His left eye seemed to be frozen shut, compressed against the side of Adel's neck. He was on his side, wedged between Adel and the couch back. His right arm was draped across Adel's lean torso, and his large hand dangled off her side. At that moment he wasn't sure he even had a left arm.

He tried lifting his head, and the pain in his neck told him to go slow. His left eye finally cracked open, as he suddenly became all too aware of his left arm. Sharp twinges shot through his neck and disappeared into the now half-dead appendage. The tingles grew worse, beginning to buzz as he raised himself up to a sitting position with his legs over Adel's. He rotated his left shoulder several times, shaking his arm, as he looked at Adel. She was stirring.

"Good morning," Michael said, as he leaned over and kissed her cheek.

She smiled, her face flushed.

They roused, gradually reaching sufficient presence of mind to make ready to set out for their morning's task.

. . . .

The rowing club building on Lake Fairview was like any boat-house worth its salt—overcrowded. It was a rudimentary structure that had been there almost thirty years, brimming with tools, spare riggers, and rowers' junk. It was eighty feet long, sixty feet wide, and divided into three bays—the "fours" bay to the left as one came in the

236

main entrance, housing several four-person rowing boats on racks; the "eights" bay in the center of the house, filled with no less than ten eight-person boats; and the narrow "singles" bay to the right, packed with singles and doubles. The wooden boat racks on each side defined the bays, except that on the far right side in the singles bay, oar-racks along the wall held the oars. Several of the club's rowers, Adel included, used handcuffs to secure their personal sculling oars to the oar-racks, to prevent others from pilfering oars without permission. Boats were stored upside down on the racks with their riggers—the hard, metal fulcrums for the rowing levers, that is, the oars—dangerously protruding outward.

Pine trees and one giant live oak surrounded the building, which had an electronic roll-up door leading into the main and biggest bay—the eights bay—but it was far from sealed. Rusty nails had taken their toll, and leaks could be found in countless spots in the tin roof. There were no soffits—deliberately so, in order that the building, which lacked air-conditioning, would be bearable in the hot, humid, Florida summers that lasted from May to October. Various creatures found their way into the building: bugs, snakes, squirrels, and even rats, until the latest wild creature invaded—wild cats … boathouse cats.

Welcome but feral, one didn't try to pick up a boathouse cat. They were lean and mean, and one scratch would stay infected for weeks, even with antibiotics. They'd hide, sleep, have babies and wail, especially at night when a new tom entered the neighborhood. Experienced club members never placed a hand or foot in any dark recess amongst the clutter of the boathouse because it could be infested with young cats; and at night, training alone, the cats startled even the bravest rowers. But it was when they jumped out of the ancient live oak onto the tin roof that they frightened rowers the most—causing an unexpected thunk and then a crumpling sound from the sheet metal. Falling pinecones made the sound too, but the rowers could tell when it was a cat.

Adel and Michael were eager to breathe in the air and take in the morning sun reflecting off the water. Lifting their boats out one at a time, they dodged the metal riggers and oar-locks of the many doubles and singles on the racks, and navigated the narrow confines of the singles bay. For a moment, Michael looked down as he carried his thirty-one pound Hudson at his waist, to make sure he didn't step on an oar that a careless rower had left in the way. Instinctively realizing his eyes had been averted too long as he moved forward, he glanced back up just in the nick of time to move his head to the side, and avoid a protruding boat rigger. Experienced rowers never looked down too long in a boathouse, at least not after learning the hard way by being clobbered a time or two.

After successfully navigating the boathouse, they each put in on opposite sides of the slimy dock. The knuckles on Adel's right hand throbbed in the damp morning air as she grasped her oars and shoved off the dock. Images of her roundhouse connecting with Scarlechek's jaw tormented her, but she repeatedly dismissed them—they were unworthy of conscious thought.

Adel looked over at Michael, grateful that he was with her. He could scull fairly well, though in college he'd been purely a "sweeps" rower, where each rower has only one, larger oar. In the masters' circles, Michael still enjoyed rowing sweeps, in eights, more than anything. Adel, on the other hand, had focused on single sculling for the last five years. She'd become a repeat national champion in her age group the previous summer, and her technique in a single shell, which was nearly flawless, was her advantage. Michael's advantage was his size and strength; it gave him length and power in each stroke. Adel was tall for a woman, but Michael was six foot five, and just as muscular and lean as Adel. Michael in his Hudson, Adel in her rigger-in-back *Fluidesign*, considering all, the two were good racing matches for each other.

After a three thousand-meter warm-up, Michael looked over at her. She was checking her Speedcoach, an electronic device that measured performance. "So what's your pleasure today, babe?"

"Well, I've been kicking so much male butt, I think I want some more."

"One thousand-meter pieces?" The distance was the length of a standard short course race for masters' rowers. It took about four minutes, depending on the size of the boat and the rowers.

"Four of them. We'll see who wins the most."

The first two pieces were close, with Adel winning both by half a length. Michael won the third, by a closer margin, and then they came to the last—the piece that tried a rower's soul. It was the all-out, gut-wrenching piece that tied a rower's muscles into square knots, un-doable only with an ice pick. That was the thing about rowing: no matter how much one trained to be in shape, giving full measure on every stroke during a piece always took one to the lactic-acid-filled brink of complete exhaustion, like hitting the wall in a running marathon. Rowers know it's going to come, but they do it anyway.

They sculled their shells about one last time for the start, but Michael pulled forward another foot, thinking Adel had positioned herself to take a slight head start.

"Why are you taking a lead off?" Adel asked. "Do you think you need it?"

"It's you who took the lead off," Michael said. "You're the one who's afraid."

"Yeah, right," she said. "You're cheating. It's okay. It won't matter."

Michael laughed, and Adel smiled at him. But it was time to be serious, so they reset their Speedcoaches and contracted their hamstrings to bring themselves up to three-quarter slide. While oxygenating their lungs with loud bursts of breath, they squared their blades and readied their bodies.

"Ready all ... row!" Adel commanded, and their blades jumped to life, thrusting their boats forward. Looking from the side across their bows, Adel was quicker and smoother, her bow streaming forward, pulling away from his with a faster stroke rate just as she'd done at the Mayor's Cup Regatta. She stroked at forty-two strokes per minute. He stroked at thirty-seven.

But Michael hung on, so she built only a half-boat lead. She settled her rate to a thirty-five for the body of the piece; he, to a thirty-two. Summoning all his power, his puddles—the turbulent eddies created and left by each oar-blade as they rushed through the water—increased in size and intensity. But so did the pain in his rippling thighs.

Welcome, pain, he thought. *Have a nice visit in my thighs … you'll be there for a while. To the end. Stroke! for smoothness,* he thought. *Stroke! for length. Stroke! to feel the pain. Stroke! to accept the pain. Stroke! to move through her.*

And he did. By the halfway mark, the small, white ball on the bow of his boat lurched ahead for the first time. *Ten! to pull away,* he thought. He pounded each catch of the water, his legs now throbbing. But he was moving on her, and he built a half-boat-length lead heading into the sprint to the finish.

Jack it up! Adel thought, unwilling to concede the race. Mentally tough, hurting all through her limbs, she increased her rate to a thirty-eight to increase her boat speed. She summoned the untapped power she'd discovered against Scarlechek. Envisioning his face, something primal kicked in—an instinctual drive—which she suddenly had no mental capability to shut off until the finish. Her raging heart commanded, *Fight him! Until you die!*

Take it up! Michael thought desperately. *She's coming!* But it was too late—she'd pulled back even. *Hands!* he thought, his chest heaving and sucking air like never before. His throbbing legs filled with lactic acid.

Last Ten! Adel thought, grunting violently. *Up again!* she commanded her soul.

Last Ten! Michael thought. *Faster hands!*

The bow balls on their boats alternated leads with each one of their alternating strokes every time one of them drove their blades through the water. His! Then hers! His! Then hers! Each sprinted fiercely, striving without thinking, their legs bursting with pain. Pure, perfect effort; they were each beyond the pain—having ascended into the ethereal purity of the race. They were in the zone.

Last stroke!

Adel drove it through first, beating Michael by six inches. It was too close for either of them to tell, but a female club member had been watching from a dock and pronounced Adel's victory.

Michael paid tribute to the "Unknown Rower" and vomited over the side of his boat. That was the ultimate for rowers—to know you had pulled so hard that it made you puke. Knowing you had nothing left to give was like a medal of honor. It was what Adel had achieved at the Mayor's Cup.

After recovering, Michael said, "Give me a break, Annie's biased! She's a girl! Of course she's going to say you won!"

"Sour grapes," Adel said. "You need to open a winery and process that fruit."

"Ahh, its just that *Fluidesign* of yours."

"That's part of being a complete rower, Michael, knowing what equipment to buy."

Though they each knew the results really didn't matter, they continued their banter. To give in now would be like giving in during the race.

Both knew the truth despite their teasing. It was a thing of beauty—their workout together. Man against woman, woman against man. No cheating, but each with their individual strengths. Fairness. It didn't matter who won. Although they competed hard, Adel knew they had really worked together. *We each gave our all, each striving for ourselves, yet pushing each other.* They had touched the divine, in themselves and each other. Stuff of life was rowing.

"Hey!" Michael said. "You alive over there? What are you, dreaming you're a man or something?"

Adel laughed as she rowed to the boathouse. "Why should I want to do that?"

Michael kept his mouth shut as he followed her in. They put up their boats and went to breakfast at an old diner down the road, the usual hangout for rowers after weekend morning practices.

Michael and Adel joined friends at a large table in the back. They teased Michael for losing to Adel three out of four times.

"Let's see any one of you guys do any better! Come on, right now!" said Michael. The challenge quickly silenced his tormentors, and the conversation turned to movies, politics, and current events.

"Hey," Annie Jakes said. "Did you guys see the news about that doctor in town that was accused of rape, got out on bail, and then murdered the victim?"

The group attacked the criminal system for this atrocity.

"Let's see any of you come up with a better system," Michael said.

"Man, a prosecutor defending this?" one of the rowers said.

"Michael's a bleeding-heart liberal," Adel said, smiling at him. They laughed and relaxed.

The conversation flowed, but Michael, who'd turned somber, spoke to Adel under his breath, "Do you want to prosecute Mr. Scarlechek?"

"No," she whispered. "He got what was coming to him."

CHAPTER 64

On the other side of town, Steve Gonzalez entered the law library for a day of intense legal research. His goal was to file suit against Western Town and Scarlechek on Monday, and serve the lawsuit the same day. But there was a problem: Title VII required the filing of an administrative charge of discrimination and the issuance of a "Right to Sue" letter before a lawsuit, a process that usually took at least six months. The idea was to allow the EEOC, or its state equivalent, time to administratively solve the problem. But Gonzalez didn't want to wait. He could smell the sensation and drama of his new case, and he wanted to send a prompt, forceful message.

Gonzalez's home and office phones rang incessantly that day, but to no avail. Golumbo's *and* Scarlechek's phone calls went unanswered. When they became frustrated and desperate, they tried to reach DeeDee directly, although it was a violation of ethical rules to contact her when Gonzalez represented her. The "thou shalt not go around thy fellow lawyer" rule was ostensibly designed for protection of clients, but wasn't without collateral benefits to lawyers. To say the least, it was an inconvenient regulation in this case, so they ignored it.

"Stop calling me!" DeeDee said to Golumbo through her phone. Golumbo had called one more time from his office with Scarlechek in the background egging him on like a third base coach.

"But young lady, please listen to me. I would like—"

"No, I told you, talk to Mr. Gonzalez. I don't want to talk to you. I will not answer this phone again! Now, leave me alone!"

She hung up on Golumbo with a slam.

"One more time!" Scarlechek commanded.

Golumbo grimaced and dialed again. DeeDee heard the phone ring again and couldn't believe it. She tromped over to her wall jack and jerked out the cord.

There, that'll do it.

She went over to stay at her friend's, finding seclusion and a sympathetic ear. The woman was Kate Winslow, and she owned an old home on a small lake.

DeeDee called to inform Gonzalez where she was, so he could reach her for questions and signatures. They'd reached contractual terms between them and she had given him the go-ahead. She knew he'd be working on the case all weekend and wanted to act promptly on Monday. DeeDee also knew she wouldn't be going back to work at Western Town for a long time, if ever.

Golumbo finally reached Gonzalez at home that night and offered a higher settlement, Scarlechek having thrown in some dough of his own.

"No deal," Gonzalez responded and unplugged his own phones.

CHAPTER 65

The following morning, Scarlechek called Peckinpah.

"Do what you'd normally do when the company has a legal problem involving you ... call Landis," Scarlechek instructed. "We can't ignore your involvement. You've got to do what you normally would—bring in your lieutenants. Make Landis aware of our story. It'll look suspicious if you don't. Tell him to call Golumbo and that you want a settlement reached right away in order to keep it all quiet. Tell him you don't want any negative publicity for the company and that you don't want to waste your precious time being a witness. Make sure that he knows that I'm being considered to replace Waverly and to keep it under lid."

That'll get to Landis, Scarlechek thought. "Got it, Tom? Now here are the money-wiring instructions ..."

Peckinpah called Landis at his Phoenix home. The general counsel was skeptical, but thought better than to question. When he contacted Scarlechek he wanted to chew his ass, but he couldn't. According to Peckinpah, the man might end up as his new boss.

"What can I do to help?" Landis asked.

"Keep it totally secret," Scarlechek said. "No one can know but me, Peckinpah, and you. That way, if settlement is reached before suit is filed, the damage will be kept to a minimum."

• • • •

At eight o'clock Monday morning, Gonzalez's secretary printed the final version of the complaint. Gonzalez checked it over, signed it, and charged out the door to file it himself, filing fee check in hand. As he left, he could hear his receptionist on the phone, "I'm sorry, we don't know where he is."

At eight-thirty, when the deputy clerk opened her doors for business, Gonzalez was first in line. He filed the complaint with a sense of excitement, and had the clerk sign the summonses. His client's allegations were now public record.

There's no turning back now, he thought.

He called his process server to come pick up the documents for service.

CHAPTER 66

At ten o'clock, swamped Assistant State Attorney Ann Gentry reached the third stack of paperwork on her desk with the aid of her third cup of coffee. She saw they were from Karen Edwards, a deputy for whom she had a great deal of respect. She glanced at the request for warrant and flipped over to Edward's report, reading it and the statements with heightened interest.

Wow, she thought. *Western Town.*

Gentry was a young, ambitious prosecutor in the Sex Crimes Unit, but she was no fool. She immediately took the papers to her boss, Heath Robero, the Chief Assistant State Attorney for her unit. Together they decided to take the matter to the Managing Assistant State Attorney, Marlon Marbury, the chief aid to the State Attorney for the circuit himself.

"Shelve it," Marbury ordered, just as Deputy Edwards had predicted. "There's sure to be a civil suit with tons of pub. The boss'll be best served by staying out of this mess. You two been reading the papers about the basketball player? Why would we want to get into a fuckin' fiasco like that? Come on, start thinking, will ya'?" Like any good administrative right hand man, Marbury protected his boss. He knew the people involved in the report were too powerful, and the case was too weak. "We'll monitor it, and file a criminal charge later if something changes. I'll inform the boss."

For now, DeeDee's charges remained a civil case only.

CHAPTER 67

The Legal Department was relatively quiet that Monday. By one o'clock, Lou Scarlechek still hadn't arrived at work. With visible bruises on his jaw, he remained in Golumbo's office, while they strategized and continued their attempts to contact Gonzalez or DeeDee. They were unaware that Gonzalez had already filed the civil suit.

No one at Legal, not even Marta DeLong, knew Lou Scarlechek's whereabouts. Only DeLong cared. No one knew DeeDee Lane's whereabouts either. Many asked about her; and Peter Spalling grew concerned.

Mary, the receptionist, summoned John Laughlin to receive service of new process. It was part of the daily drudgery of the Legal Department. He lumbered out to the lobby. The company was sued almost daily for one reason or another, with about ninety percent of the cases going nowhere.

The process server was an attractive woman, used by many plaintiffs' lawyers for serving unsuspecting males. She handed Laughlin a package. He sighed and signed for the legal papers.

Laughlin noticed that the package was thicker than usual. *Probably a construction case,* he thought. But when he saw the summons, he took a double take.

Apoplexy galvanized his face, and his eyes shrieked, "*Oh my God!*" without him saying a word.

Mary, equally unimpressed by being served with process for the company, noticed Laughlin's face and realized something was terribly wrong. "John? Are you all right?"

Laughlin's mouth was paralyzed. He couldn't even turn the first page to read the complaint. All he could do was fixate on the summons, the style of which read:

DEEDEE T. LANE, individually,
Plaintiff,
vs.
WESTERN TOWN PRODUCTION
COMPANY OF FLORIDA, INC., a
Florida corporation, and
LOUIS VICTOR SCARLECHEK,
individually,
Defendants.

_____/

Laughlin guessed what it had to be—*sexual harassment! DeeDee was suing the company and his boss for sexual harassment!* He flipped the pages over quickly to confirm.

Hmm-m, he thought, *I should keep this quiet.* His first reaction was to not respond to Mary, but something impish overcame him. *People will know ... it's public record. What a shame.* He finally answered dryly, "It's a lawsuit ... by DeeDee ... against the company, and Lou."

Mary's chin fell and instantly he knew he shouldn't have said anything. "Mary, keep this quiet. I've got to read it. Hold my calls."

Laughlin rushed to his office and digested the complaint like a hungry dog gulping down dinner. It contained six separate counts against Scarlechek, including sexual assault, battery, trespass, false imprisonment, intentional infliction of mental distress, and defamation. Contrary to Laughlin's initial prediction, it did not have a count for sexual harassment. Instead a set of "common allegations," common to each count, alleged all the facts of the sexual harassment DeeDee had suffered. But paragraph ten contained one very unusual allegation:

"The Plaintiff has filed a charge of discrimination and harassment with the Florida Commission on Human Relations and the Equal Employment Opportunity Commission on the same date as the filing of this Complaint. The Plaintiff is seeking an expedited 'Right to Sue' letter from those agencies and, upon receipt of such letter, the Plaintiff shall, and reserves the right to, file an Amended Complaint adding counts for sexual harassment, and to remove this case to Federal Court."

This was the result of Gonzalez's research over the weekend. Gonzalez couldn't wait, but legally, he couldn't proceed on sexual harassment grounds without the "Right to Sue" letter. So he made the harassment allegations anyway, without suing for Title VII relief, with that to come later. In the meantime, he sued for everything else.

Laughlin read and reread the allegations that Scarlechek had repeatedly demanded sex in exchange for favorable workplace terms and conditions, and that when DeeDee finally refused him, he raped her. Gonzalez sought to hold Western Town liable for Scarlechek's actions by alleging that he performed the intentional acts while acting within the course and scope of his employment. Though Laughlin hadn't witnessed any of it, he believed every word.

Finding himself enjoying the complaint more than a scintillating novel—because it was real—he laughed, realizing all his reservations about Lou Scarlechek had been justified.

He hypothesized that holding the company liable would be a tough proposition for DeeDee. No company would openly condone such actions. *We certainly didn't,* he thought. *The complaint could be frivolous, giving the company the right to recover attorney's fees under Florida law from DeeDee* and *Gonzalez … except for two scenarios.* He contemplated them; wanting them to be true … realizing that he *wanted* Scarlechek and the company to pay.

First, the torts complained of all took place under the guise of work-related performance—every time Scarlechek called DeeDee into his office. It was alleged that Scarlechek always needed her to take an urgent letter. Second, Laughlin observed that there was an additional count against the company, for the negligent hiring of Lou Scarlechek. Gonzalez had a lawyer's hunch that Scarlechek had done this kind of thing before, and the company either knew or should have known about his behavior. It was a gutsy move without any evidence. Laughlin wondered whether it was true, and realized it very well could be. He thought of Scarlechek's first administrative assistant, again wondering why she had left. He was at once happy and relieved that he didn't have anything to do with the hiring of Scarlechek. His superiors, who had passed him over, did it all. *This will show them,* he thought.

Company liability wouldn't be a problem when DeeDee was finally given her "Right to Sue" letter. Under Title VII and Florida's Human Rights Act, the employer was directly liable for quid pro quo harassment by a senior executive like Scarlechek. Until then, Laughlin knew Gonzalez would try to get, and keep, the company in the suit as best he could. Gonzalez wanted publicity. He wanted to intimidate Western Town with the threat of the biggest, ugliest verdict pasted all over the newspapers.

Given his experience in the Sorenson case, Laughlin realized that Gonzalez would have high monetary hopes. The complaint sought general and special damages for past and future mental and physical pain and suffering, loss of enjoyment of life, and psychological costs. Gonzalez had demanded ten million dollars in punitive damages!

Along with the summons and complaint, Gonzalez had served a special motion for expedited discovery and a notice of hearing on the motion for the following Friday.

My God! That's quick, thought Laughlin. *I've got to get someone on this right away.* He read the motion. Gonzalez hoped to take Peckinpah's and Scarlechek's depositions as soon as possible before their stories could become further refined and coordinated. The motion sought a court order allowing him to take the depositions immediately, regardless of the Florida rules of civil procedure that usually didn't allow discovery until forty-five days after service of a complaint. Circuit Judge Kenneth M. Zovich would hear the motion at ten o'clock on Friday.

Laughlin leaned back in his chair. It creaked as he lifted his feet onto his desk.

He knew he had to act quickly; the company needed a lawyer before Friday to prepare and gather facts. Laughlin also knew it was too late to avoid publicity. Newspapers had reporters on the courthouse beat that checked for new lawsuits daily, and this one was probably already sounding alarms all over Central Florida.

Laughlin normally notified Scarlechek of any lawsuit that could mean negative publicity. But this was different. He called Landis.

"What can I do for you, John?" Landis asked.

"We have a huge problem, Geoff. I'll come right to the point … Lou and the company are being sued for what amounts to sexual harassment. I just got served with the complaint."

"Oh Christ," Landis's voice trailed to the point of being barely audible. "Tell me about it." Laughlin complied, revealing the details.

"Does Lou know?" Landis asked.

"I don't think so … he's not here."

"Who do you hire in cases like this, down there?"

"A woman … Adel Blair is her name. She's good."

"Well, better get her on it right away. I want you to oversee the case and report directly to me, not at all to Lou, understand? I'll talk to Lou about it, and get back to you. Bad press tomorrow, huh?"

"Undoubtedly."

"Fax a copy to my private line. I'll call back later today. Hire the lawyer."

CHAPTER 68

"Well," **Laughlin said** to Adel Blair over the phone. "We need your services again ... but you won't believe why. I'm still shocked to even say it ... a little embarrassed, too. Are you sitting?"

"Yes."

"A secretary in our department has sued the company and our illustrious boss for sexual harassment."

"Lou?" she asked, already realizing the answer.

"Yeah. Lou."

"Who's the secretary?"

"DeeDee Lane."

There was a long pause. *Oh my gosh, the forlorn looks ... the Women's League seminar ... Lou Scarlechek.* "Oh my God." Although it was a big, new case, it wasn't excitement she felt. It was compassion for DeeDee, and ... anger.

"You know her?" Laughlin asked.

"A little. We've met. We went to a seminar together with Tiyona Morgan."

"That won't be a problem will it?" Laughlin asked.

Adel didn't know how to respond. *It's Scarlechek that's the problem! I can't represent him.* "I don't know yet," she replied. "What happened?"

"Well, the complaint alleges Scarlechek was harassing her for months—requiring sex—but get this! It says that just last Friday night, apparently after we all broke up from dinner, he raped her!"

"My God," she said with a gasp.

"Do you believe it? We settle a big harassment case ... Oh, and by the way, guess who represents DeeDee—Steve Gonzalez! We settle a big harassment case with him, Friday. Lou's involved. We all go to dinner. Then Lou rapes ... I mean ... allegedly rapes DeeDee, and Gonzalez sues us on Monday! It's incredible! How could anyone, let alone an executive vice president of a legal department of a major corporation, settle a sexual harassment suit for a million bucks, and then go out and rape someone?"

Adel listened, caught up in her thoughts. She knew her encounter with Lou fit in there too, and wondered how. *It's interesting that Laughlin isn't challenging the allegations as preposterous,* she thought. Concerned and confused, she remained quiet.

"Adel, you went to Lou's office with him after dinner, didn't you?"

"Yes." She said it flatly.

"It was to discuss a case he wanted to give you, wasn't it?"

"That's right."

"Well, you're his alibi, then."

"What time does Gonzalez say the rape occurred in the complaint?" Adel asked.

"He doesn't. He just says Friday night, March 6th."

"I left Lou's office around eight-twenty," Adel said, her voice grave, unsure of what to reveal to Laughlin.

"Well, we've got to find out the time of the alleged rape. We need you to do some interrogatories to DeeDee," Laughlin suggested, not knowing of the witness statements, the police report, or that his CEO was a witness. "If the time matches, he has an alibi, at least for that part of the case."

"And I become a witness," Adel said.

"Is that a problem?" Laughlin asked, assuming until now that Adel would handle the defense.

"Yes," she replied. She knew that there was a long ingrained distinction in American jurisprudence between the role of an attorney as trial advocate and a witness, a distinction the law long held very fundamental. It was never so bluntly put in the case law, but some lawyers, as advocates, are likely to say anything to win, while a witness is supposed to speak nothing but the truth.

"There's a prohibition against attorneys acting as advocate and witness in the same case," she said. "But the rules have been relaxed somewhat. I'll have to research it, if you want me on the case."

"I do. Go ahead."

"But John ...," she said. She realized her involvement must be disclosed. "There's something very disconcerting about all of this. I've been thinking about it as we've talked. I feel I must tell you before you hire me ... or, before I decide whether I even want this case, for that matter. I want your promise of complete confidentiality, unless we discuss and agree together who we'll tell in the future."

"Okay," he said. There was a note of caution in his expression.

"No, I'm sorry. I want more than just 'okay'. What I have to say is very personal and private, and ... condemning of Lou."

Laughlin's curiosity was rising like mercury, and, at this point, he craved dirt about Scarlechek more than a politician covets a crowd. "Adel, I give you my word."

"Good ... after dinner Friday, as you know, he took me back to his office. He was going to give me a new case. He complained of bright light and dimmed his office lights ... I think now, to prevent being seen from the outside. He approached me sexually, John. And, for a brief moment ... he touched my breasts. I kicked him in the groin and decked him ... then I left."

Laughlin's eyes lit up. *Unbelievable! Will this man ever cease to amaze?* Laughlin let out a tremendous belly laugh. The image of Scarlechek being clobbered by Adel was too much. Asking for more detail, he listened intently, chuckling and apologizing to Adel intermittently. "I'm sorry, Adel, I just can't help it," he said over and over.

Finally, Laughlin turned serious. "What would a man, who did what he did to you, be capable of doing after being beaten up by a woman?"

"You see how difficult it will be for me to advocate the company's position," she said. "I would be inclined to believe DeeDee. I know her. I don't think she's a liar, and I don't have great feelings about Mr. Scarlechek."

"Have you told anyone about this?"

"My boyfriend, Michael McKerrin. He's an Assistant State Attorney in the Economic Crimes Unit. He asked me if I wanted to prosecute for sexual battery. I told him no. I thought Lou got what he deserved."

Laughlin guffawed again, and apologized again.

"Well, Adel, as long as we're baring our souls ..." He chuckled a little more, but didn't apologize this time. "One time I came into the office to work on a holiday, and found the Legal Department opened. I looked around to commiserate with whoever was there. I went to Lou's office. I should've knocked, but I didn't ... something about the informality of working on a holiday. I opened the door. To my chagrin, I saw Lou and Marta naked, doing it on the floor. This wasn't too long after his first administrative assistant flew the coop. I don't think they saw me. If I'm called to testify," he added, "I'll have to tell the truth if asked."

"I think the company needs to settle this case," Adel said, not knowing that Scarlechek had been frantically trying to do just that all weekend.

"Well, first things first," Laughlin said. "I still want you on the case Adel. I think the company will do right with you on the case. Please research your conflict and I'll sign anything you need. You'll be reporting only to me. I'm reporting directly to Landis in Phoenix. He already knows about it and gave me authority to hire you. I'll fax you the complaint. But, Adel, I'll need to tell him about your incident with Lou. That may change things."

"John, I'll represent the company, if I can. But I won't represent Scarlechek. You'll have to get separate counsel for him."

"I understand. In this case, I think that's best anyway."

CHAPTER 69

Adel Blair sat stroking her chin after the call.

How can I represent the company in this case? I might be a witness. I don't even believe in the company's side. This must be what criminal defense lawyers feel. I've met DeeDee and I like her. How can I paint her as a liar, on top of my feelings about Scarlechek?

Laughlin knows all this, and he still wants me. The firm ... the recession. Dave hasn't taken a draw in six weeks. The firm is struggling and it needs this fee.

Dave had advised Adel to avoid partnership in the firm for a while—there was no real equity. She could buy in, "but for what?" were his words. To buy the privilege of becoming an unpaid employee? She knew the firm needed the cash from associates who bought in, but Dave knew it was a quick fix. He didn't want her in that position. Adel also knew the firm needed good, paying clients. She desperately wanted to help.

Adel's choice wasn't completely rational, but she dove into researching the lawyer-witness issue, guided by a subconscious desire to have the work despite loathing Scarlechek. Laughlin wanted her on the case, and that buoyed her. It seemed he had an agenda, too.

She found the relevant rule. It disallowed a lawyer to testify on behalf of a client, except in certain specified circumstances. The key phrase, "on behalf of a client," implied the possibility for a lawyer to testify where it was *not* on behalf of the client.

Adel recognized two issues from the rule that she couldn't resolve without more information. First, whether she would indeed be a witness "on behalf of the client," and thereby cause impermissible prejudice to DeeDee from a dual role as advocate and witness. This depended on whether she'd be Scarlechek's alibi, and at what time DeeDee would maintain the rape occurred.

Adel thought how bitingly ironic it'd be if she turned out to be Scarlechek's alibi. Her argument to the jury could be, *Mr. Scarlechek couldn't have raped DeeDee at the time, because he was busy sexually harassing me!*

This led her to the second issue: whether her testimony about her encounter with Scarlechek would create a conflict of interest. Assuming Scarlechek would lie about what had happened between them, her testimony wouldn't hurt the alibi because it didn't matter what they were doing, so long as they were together. But her testimony could contribute to establishing the pattern of Scarlechek's behavior, that Gonzalez would clearly want to establish. A jury would more likely believe DeeDee's testimony if the company's own lawyer testified to a similar incident. Exposure of what had happened to her would be against the company's best interests.

Adel turned to the conflict rule. A lawyer shall not represent a client if the lawyer's exercise of judgment may be limited by the lawyer's own interest, unless the lawyer reasonably believes the representation wouldn't be adversely affected and obtains client consent.

I will not lie, thought Adel. *If called as a witness and asked the right question, I will not perjure myself.* But she questioned whether that meant her representation of the client would be adversely affected. At long last, perhaps through jaded eyes, she concluded it would not. *Even if what happened between Scarlechek and me had happened to someone else, my analysis of the case would be the same,* she reasoned. *If those facts come out, and Laughlin's facts come out, then the company should settle, because the jury will probably conclude, "Where there's smoke, there's fire."*

Adel figured that if she explained the possible conflict in testimony to Laughlin and obtained his written consent, she could begin the representation. Later, if it appeared her testimony would be required, she and the company could revisit the issue. She decided to write to the ethics hotline of The Florida Bar to cover herself, subconsciously disallowing herself to think about any broader moral issue.

Adel faxed a letter to Laughlin setting forth all they'd discussed, what she'd learned from her research, and her analysis and conclusion. She included a place for Laughlin to sign and give his consent on behalf of the company. Her secretary embossed the letter and the fax cover sheet with a bold "PRIVILEGED AND CONFIDENTIAL" stamp. In the letter, Adel asked him to sign it and fax it back, so that she could begin work on the case.

Laughlin received the fax and sent it on to Landis. As much as he wanted to, Laughlin wasn't going to make this decision by himself. Laughlin discussed the "Adel incident" with Landis, who also told Laughlin of Peckinpah's involvement.

In the end, Laughlin convinced Landis to give the go-ahead to hire Adel. Both men secretly hoped that Scarlechek would be fried. Laughlin signed the fax, and sent it back to Adel.

She was hired.

CHAPTER 70

"Are you nuts!" yelled Dave McKerrin. They were in his office; and it was the first time that he'd ever yelled at Adel. Telling Dave what had happened with Scarlechek set him off like a firecracker. Relaying the subsequent story about DeeDee, and that she'd taken the case wasn't sitting well at all.

"But Dave, I called the ethics hotline, and they told me it was okay provided the company gave informed consent. I told Laughlin everything and they consented!"

"I don't care … that pompous ass; you oughta be suing him, not defending his company!"

"But Dave, you know we need the work, and Laughlin wants me on the case! I don't think he's too loyal to Lou. I think he believes that with me on the case they'll get a straight-shooter who'll tell them what and when to pay, and I think he and Landis want to blame Lou."

"Who the hell else would they blame?"

"I don't know, but it's all right. They know exactly what they're getting with me, and they want it."

"And you want to take this case? No, Adel, it just isn't right. I don't care what the hotline says. I want you to consider suing the man yourself."

"No, Dave, I'm not going to do that. I'm going to take this case." Her face was stern, letting him know just how resolute she was, but she could see that he was upset—not the reaction she'd hoped for.

Dave threw up his hands, knowing full well that she wouldn't give in unless he flat out forbade her to take the case, and he knew he couldn't do that.

"I don't approve," he said gruffly. "You'll do what you want to, no doubt. Now get out of here, I don't want to hear about it anymore."

CHAPTER 71

"Adel Blair! I don't want that fuckin' bitch on the case!" Scarlechek shouted. Landis had called him earlier and told him of the suit, and he and Golumbo had asked for a copy of the complaint. After speaking with Laughlin about the "Adel incident," Landis had called Scarlechek again.

"But wait … no … on second thought … it's okay," Scarlechek said, calming down. *How beautiful,* he thought. *It's perfect. That way she won't become a witness! Gonzalez will never think to depose the company's lawyer.*

"Look, Geoff, of course it's all untrue," he said cavalierly. His tone changed to one of authority when he spoke again. "Have you heard that I'm up for company president? This case is going to rake the company and me over the coals. It's *all* untrue, but we've got to settle! Damn it, though … DeeDee won't settle," he uttered, thinking aloud. "I want Adel and Rich to get Gonzalez to agree to an expedited trial so we can get this resolved. I'll have Rich call Adel to discuss it, but I want you to call Laughlin about it, and have him call Adel also. The sooner we get this all over with, the sooner the company and I can go on."

"By the way," he said. "Laughlin should tell Adel to keep her big fuckin' mouth shut."

They hung up. Landis and Scarlechek both tried to called Peckinpah, but Landis got through first.

"Tom, the company should distance itself from this. Forget Scarlechek as president. I can't imagine why he's being considered anyway. Things look very bad. We need to let him go. Even our own lawyer claims Lou harassed her. And Laughlin walked in on Lou and Marta DeLong. And I told you what happened with his first assistant."

"I'll think about it," Peckinpah said, although he immediately dismissed the idea.

Later, Scarlechek called Peckinpah:

"Tom, I want the presidency. You're going to get it for me. DeeDee's suit is a minor distraction. I've instructed everyone that we need to expedite it. Ninety-eight percent of all suits settle, and this one'll settle before trial, especially since we're going to make it known at every stage that we want to settle. The company is going to pay, and pay my fees to Golumbo. When we settle, I want my promotion. Got it?"

"I doubt the board will support this," Peckinpah said.

"You'd better try."

"What about my money?" said Peckinpah. He'd assumed he'd get it back since DeeDee hadn't settled.

"My bank has it," Scarlechek said. "What about it?"

CHAPTER 72

On Tuesday, the story covered the bottom half of the front page. The headline read:

Western Town Sued for Sexual Battery/Legal Exec Accused of Rape

The piece summarized Gonzalez's complaint, stating that Scarlechek and the company could not be reached for comment. The reporter quoted the more graphic aspects of the complaint and speculated at the length of time before trial. It also quoted Peckinpah's statements that DeeDee admitted having voluntary sex with Scarlechek, and that what he'd seen was not rape.

It was another sexual harassment scandal in the paper. Some readers skipped over it. Many didn't. Some questioned, "Why do they print this crap?" Others wondered why it continues to happen.

The reporter Nolé Reynolds, who broke the story, loved it. She knew it was big news and likely to go national over the AP and UPI wires. A frenzied media blitz could result, especially if it was a slow news day. Reynolds knew this could be her ticket to the big time, and she was not about to let the tale go. She decided to follow this court file and call the lawyers regularly.

Peckinpah read the paper in the privacy of his hotel suite. His heart sank when the article mentioned his statement. Excelling at everything, he had never needed to spin tales before. This had fostered the arrogance in him, but it was no more and he was frightened.

Alone on his unmade bed he stared at the paper, feeling the abysmal low of a man without a soul. With his mind wandering, he imagined that he was a pie-crusted statue of a man, with his insides eaten out, and that he would crumble away if anything touched him. He imagined his collapsing self, devoured by ravenous cockroaches from the inside; and after they ate the crust away, only his bones remained. Then, in his twisted mind, his naked bones became the screaming skeleton of the hooker, again rising out of the ground to terrorize him.

That morning, for the first time in his life, Thomas Armstrong Peckinpah made an emergency appointment with a local therapist.

CHAPTER 73

DeeDee Lane opened her blue eyes slowly Tuesday morning in the guest bedroom of Kate Winslow's modest home, overlooking a small lake. Kate had been a great help since Saturday, and a good friend. The two talked long and often over the weekend, and DeeDee appreciated Kate's support.

Enjoying the quaintness of the pale green room, DeeDee rolled on her side to face the bay window overlooking the picturesque lake. The water was smooth and glassy, and the green tree line across the tarn was reflected upon it, no less perfectly than in a mirror. It was serene. Just watching, DeeDee began to notice tiny circular eddies on the placid water where fish nibbled at water bugs.

She noticed a wood duck swimming into the scene, followed by eight small ducklings paddling as fast as they could go. They ducks appeared panicked, and at once DeeDee saw why: a large osprey circled closely above them. The powerful osprey was hungry, and the young ducklings would be easy prey for its sharp talons.

DeeDee watched in horror when the osprey tucked its wings to begin a graceful, albeit deadly, swoop. But just as the predator began its dive, a valiant mockingbird came from nowhere and assailed the far larger bird from the side. *Did the mockingbird have babies in the area too?* DeeDee wondered, as she became mesmerized. Every time the hungry raptor dove, the brave little mockingbird attacked, pecking at it ferociously. DeeDee observed the smooth, powerful flight of the osprey. It was certainly a faster top-in flier, but the plucky little mockingbird was quicker and ... relentless of heart.

In the meantime, the wood ducks paddled for their lives toward a thicket of cattails. Just as the bird of prey separated itself from the mockingbird by two powerful motions of his majestic wings and started its dive again, the mockingbird took several furied flaps and charged the creature one more time, allowing the wood ducks to reach the cover of the cattails. The drama was over, and the frustrated predator flapped back to its high perch, while the courageous mockingbird returned to her own nest.

As DeeDee contemplated what she'd just seen, Kate entered with the newspaper and a cup of coffee. "Well, you made the headlines this morning," she said. "Do you want to see? ... I'll leave you to it, I'm late for work. Will you be all right today?"

"Yes, Kate, I'll be fine. I'm feeling good."

"All right ... I'll call you later."

"Bye, Kate. Have a good day, and thanks again."

DeeDee picked up the steaming brew. Feeling its warmth going down, she lifted the newspaper and scanned the front page for the article. She read, discovering unexpected confirmation of her resolve. It was her statement ... the little girl from Iowa making a stand.

She had called her mother and father on Saturday, and they'd flown in the next day and were staying in a local hotel. She thought of them reading the same headlines and became embarrassed and ashamed. Despite her parents' assurances to the contrary, DeeDee believed that she'd failed in her quest. She'd come here from Iowa to find herself and make it on her own, and all she'd accomplished was to become the center of a sordid scandal. Though her parents were encouraging, she still couldn't help feeling depressed. It was redemption she needed now. The headlines helped, yet they didn't.

DeeDee read about Peckinpah's statement, and felt small and scared. *Who am I?*

She wondered who the company's lawyer would be, and fretted over what he'd do to her. Feeling like one of the ducklings fleeing the talons of the osprey, she prayed for help from a mockingbird and wondered who it might be.

Remembering her vision, she realized the die was set. She couldn't quit or cower, not now. It'd gone too far, and she owed it to everyone, especially herself. *I will see this through! It was he that brought this on me, not the other way around! And now, half the people who read this article will think it's my fault, and that I'm just some gold digger. Well I'm not! I just want to make it in this world, on my own!*

She called her lawyer.

CHAPTER 74

"Yes, I represent the company," Adel told Gonzalez. "Golumbo will continue representing Scarlechek," she added. "What's happening on the criminal side?"

"It ended up on Ann Gentry's desk," Gonzalez said. "I'm told that she took it up, but it was shelved pending our civil case."

"Do you have copies of the witness statements?"

"I do."

"Will you fax those to me, or make me go through discovery channels?"

"Adel, I wish to cooperate. But I need your agreement to expedited discovery, especially the depositions of Mr. Scarlechek and Mr. Peckinpah." He was following the principle of many lawyers—never give without getting something in return.

"I'll go you one better than that," Adel replied. "We'll agree to an expedited trial. My client wants this matter resolved quickly."

"Well, that's all well and good, but I'm bringing a Title VII claim and removing to Federal Court when I get my Right to Sue letter from the agencies. So if your offer is designed to ace us out of that, forget it."

"It's not, Steve. I've been thinking about it. We know that'll be coming. I believe that if we write a letter to the FCHR and the EEOC, agreeing to the immediate issuance of a Right to Sue letter, they'll do it. Then, we jointly remove the case to Federal Court, request a case management conference with the judge and ask for a fast tract to trial. What do you think? A plaintiff's lawyer never dreamed of such a deal."

"That's what I'm worried about."

"Don't. We're not trying to pull anything over on you," Adel reassured him. "My client just needs this case resolved quickly, on *all* of your client's claims. True, we're taking the EEOC and FCHR out of the picture, but you'll be seeking injunctive relief anyway, won't you?"

"Of course. This time, so far at least, it seems to be extremely important to DeeDee." They were referring to DeeDee's right to seek a court order requiring Western Town to adopt specially tailored policies to prevent harassment and discrimination in the future, and requiring Western Town to comply with them under court auspices, which was what the agencies typically went after when they were involved. Sorenson had sought similar relief but gave it up in the settlement.

Adel said, "My client is not hiding from that, or anything. We want to meet all the issues squarely—just quickly, if we can't settle, that is."

"All right, let's do it."

"That means no discovery motion on Friday, correct?"

"Well, when do you anticipate writing the commissions?" Gonzalez asked suspiciously.

"Today. In fact, I think we should meet today ... in your office. We should call the commissions, send off whatever they need, then sit down, and map out our course to trial, discovery and all."

"Agreed!" This was too good to be true for a plaintiff's lawyer—a defense lawyer making his job easy.

"Now, why can't we settle this case?" Adel asked.

"It's too soon. DeeDee is angry. Even more so after the newspaper article this morning. She wants her case aired against Scarlechek, and she wants the company to deal with him appropriately. She thinks, at the very least, he should be discharged. She wants her job back, but she certainly doesn't want to see him there. I don't blame her."

Adel couldn't blame DeeDee either. She wished she was representing DeeDee instead of the company. She thought of Michael. "I understand," is all she said. "What time Friday night did the alleged rape occur?"

"Nine o'clock. Why? There isn't some contrived alibi, is there?"

Adel sighed heavily, quickly grasping that she was not Scarlechek's alibi. "Steve," she said. "You know we wouldn't contrive anything. As to an alibi, I just don't know yet." She didn't want to reveal that there wasn't, not realizing that Gonzalez knew there wasn't. There couldn't be an alibi. The witness statements that Adel had yet to see from Peckinpah, Scarlechek, and DeeDee all precluded that. The issue was consensual sex or rape; and because of DeeDee's admission of having sex with Scarlechek several times, the broader matter of contention would be whether the consensual sex was unwelcome conduct or not. Can consensual sex between employer and employee be "unwelcome" and illegal under Title VII, supporting a claim for relief?

"Steve, how is DeeDee?" Adel asked. Her concern was genuine.

"She's doing just fine. The young lady has a lot of heart," Gonzalez answered. He detected something he'd never seen before in all their battles— softness in Adel—almost as though she believed his client. *Does her impenetrable armor have a soft spot after all?*

271

CHAPTER 75

Adel conferenced-in Golumbo and Laughlin, and reported the relative success of the discussion. She informed them of the proposed meeting that afternoon to call the two commissions and work out the expedited procedure. She told Golumbo he needed to be there, and relayed that DeeDee wouldn't settle unless the company discharged Scarlechek.

The three lawyers, Adel, Gonzalez, and Golumbo, met as planned.

"My client is incensed at the publicity you shamelessly sought out," Golumbo said to Gonzalez, who took in his comments indifferently. "You've defamed my client's good name! He will not settle now!" In truth, Scarlechek figured the damage was done and, if DeeDee wouldn't settle, with Peckinpah's testimony he could win the case anyway, keeping Peckinpah's million dollars for himself as a first installment.

"Spare me," Gonzalez said. He glanced at Adel. "Spare *us*."

"Let's get down to work, guys," Adel said.

Once Golumbo got over himself, what took place at the meeting was a rarity—the three lawyers cooperated. They called the agencies together on a conference call. Never had the commission investigators heard of such a request—expedited Right to Sue letters requested by all sides. The trio learned that agreement of the parties represented by a cover letter signed jointly by the three of them, which they drafted and sent, would prompt immediate issuance of the letters.

They worked through and established a schedule for discovery. Gonzalez gave up his demand for early depositions, figuring Scarlechek and Peckinpah would cement their stories by the time it could be accomplished anyway, if they hadn't done so already. However, a minor altercation arose.

"I want production of Scarlechek's personnel file," Gonzalez said. He wanted to flesh out a hunch.

"Why?" Adel asked.

"It's clearly relevant and discoverable," Gonzalez replied.

"It certainly is not!" Golumbo said.

"Oh-h," Gonzalez said. "What if there is evidence he's done this before? I want to know whether there are any documents relating to other claims of harassment against him. That's clearly relevant and calculated to lead to admissible evidence."

"Other claims aren't relevant, even if there are any," Golumbo said.

Adel remained silent.

"We won't agree to produce things that will lead a jury to an inference that because my client supposedly did it before, he did it again," Golumbo said. "That would be highly prejudicial."

Adel thought such an inference might be right on.

"We'll take the matter up before the judge," Gonzalez said, not backing down an inch.

Obtaining facsimiles of the Right to Sue letters from the agencies, Friday morning the lawyers drafted a stipulation for removal of the case to Federal court and Gonzalez penned his amended complaint, adding the Title VII and Chapter 760 state law claims and seeking all the benefits of the new civil rights act, which were compensatory damages, punitive damages, and a jury trial. The three lawyers met at Judge Zovich's chambers to inform him of the removal of the case from state to federal court. Zovich was happy to have one fewer case in his docket, and relieved to specifically avoid this case.

Gonzalez paid the recoverable filing fee in federal court and filed the removal papers. The clerk stamped in the case and disappeared into a back room for the process of assignment to a judge.

Gonzalez was momentarily taken aback when he learned the case drew Federal District Judge Elke A. Wozynski—purely luck-of-the-draw coincidence under the district's random system of assigning new cases. Gonzalez knew Judge Wozynski, and at once thought of her common Polish heritage with Scarlechek. On the other hand, Wozynski also shared gender with DeeDee. But he knew these characteristics wouldn't make a difference in her responsibilities. He knew Wozynski to be tough and impatient, yet a keenly intelligent judge, who was also known for fairness. Judges season in their career. She had some idiosyncrasies, but they could deal with those.

Gonzalez simultaneously filed the joint stipulation for a case management hearing, which governed the schedule to which the lawyers had agreed for discovery, motion practice and trial. It needed the judge's agreement, so he attached a proposed order for Wozynski to sign.

Gonzalez also filed his motion to compel production of the documents that Adel and Golumbo refused to produce.

Within one week, each attorney received an order setting the case management conference and a hearing on the motion to compel.

Thus, the stage was set: DeeDee wanted Scarlechek fired and Scarlechek wanted to be president of the company. Ironically, Peckinpah had been reduced to a mere pawn. Adel, too, was a foot soldier now, focused upon on her duty. As though in the Vietnam War, she wondered whether she was doing the right thing.

It was almost mid-March. The lavender flowers were beginning to wilt and drop off the Azalea bushes in Orlando. Pollen-laden stamen from the water oaks floated to the ground like slow rain, and collected so densely on the ground it could be gathered to stuff pillows. Bright green, new growth sprouted on the trees. The lawyers wanted to be done with the case by July when the thunderstorm-thatched summer would be squarely upon them. That was the time Waverly had picked to step down, and Lou Scarlechek wanted to step up. The parties wanted to do in four months what would normally take a year and a half.

CHAPTER 76

"Libby, send this communiqué to all offices nationwide," said Deputy Cayhall Johnson of the Witness Security Program in the U.S. Marshal Service. The Witness Security Program, or WITSEC, had been established by the Organized Crime Control Act of 1970. Basically, on advice from U.S. attorneys, the Attorney General decided who was eligible for the program, and since 1970, over seven thousand witnesses and nine thousand family members had been relocated and given new identities, as well as federal subsidies for living expenses. Johnson was the Witness Security Inspector for the Northern District of New York and was stationed at the regional office in Syracuse. He was a large, black man with a round, affable face.

"What is it?" Libby Butterfield asked without looking his way. The secretary was overworked, and continued to type.

"It's on Kelly Parker, one of my witnesses. She hasn't checked in to pick up her check for the second month in a row. Yesterday, I went to her apartment and the landlord says February and March rents are unpaid. Her stuff is still there, but no one has seen her."

"What case was she on?" Libby asked.

"Esperanza—you know, the Columbian drug lord that DEA nabbed in Miami. She was his stateside girlfriend. Knew too much ... turned government witness for immunity and protection."

"Why'd we let so much time go by?"

"Christ, woman, I can't do everything around here!" Johnson's face turned angry. "You know how busy last month was. She used to be a hooker, and she still likes to walk on the wild side. She's done this a few times before, and each time she was off doing her thing—usually out west. But this is the first time she's missed two months."

"Where, out west?"

"Colorado."

"Leave it there. I'll get it out this afternoon," Libby said. "I'll put in a special note about Colorado."

CHAPTER 77

"I'm really sorry, Adel," Cookie Albertson said. "I really wanted to get together tonight, but Tom's pulling me back to Phoenix. I told him I had plans, but he said we have to rush back this afternoon. That's the breaks of this job."

"When do you think you'll be back?" Adel asked, disappointed by the news.

"I'm not sure now. I guess that depends on you now, too, since Tom's a witness. I still can't believe all this stuff. He'll be deposed, right?"

"Yes. My office will be setting that up with you. I'll need to meet with him in advance, of course."

"Then we'll find some time to get together, I'm sure of it. It'll be so nice … and such a relief. Tom's driving me crazy. He's so moody these days." She said this flippantly, and laughed.

"Why?"

"I don't know," Cookie answered, though she had the Vail pictures in mind. "All I know is that he's just not himself. He's mopey, depressed, and downright cross sometimes. I've never seen him like this before. Something's bothering him." An urge rushed over her to disclose he had seen a therapist yesterday, but she thought better of it.

CHAPTER 78

"Mehhmp! Mehhmp!" The buzzer shocked everyone in the courtroom—it was the signal that the judge would be entering through the door from her chambers, strategically situated behind her broad and stately bench.

"All rise," the bailiff blurted out. The clerk, the court reporter, Adel, Golumbo, and Gonzalez stood, sitting again after the judge took her place and the bailiff commanded, "Be seated." The mahogany bench swallowed Judge Wozynski's body. But when she peered over the edge of the bench with her half-rimmed reading glasses and fired questions and orders at cowering attorneys, one realized she was in full control.

"Well," the judge said. "We seem to have an interesting case here this morning. I've read the amended complaint, the joint stipulation, the motion to compel, and its accompanying memorandum of law. Normally, the magistrate rules on discovery motions. But because of your desire for an expedited procedure, I thought I'd take care of it this morning. I trust there's no problem with that." Her voice was sharp.

"No, Your Honor." The three lawyers sprang to their feet and replied together. You didn't address a federal judge without standing, unless you were given specific permission or were fond of jail cells.

"I applaud the fresh approach you have taken to resolve this case. I can hold the trial in July, it so happens. I just had a three-week antitrust case settle, and that leaves my calendar open during late June and early July. Other small matters have filled June already. We'll begin picking a jury—time certain—on Wednesday, July 1, at nine-thirty."

"But be advised, I assess contempt fines—ten dollars per minute for lawyers who keep me and my jurors waiting. Don't be late. Now, is there anything else we need to discuss about procedure or trial? I assume, for example, that the defense will forego early motion practice directed to the pleadings?"

"That's correct, Your Honor," said Golumbo who stood first to assert himself and show that he was "the man." "We will have several technical, legal defenses and the company will have even more, but we have agreed to raise them all in our answers, and not by way of motion, in order to move the case more quickly along to trial. Ms. Blair and I will bring the technical defenses up by a pretrial motion for partial summary judgment or judgment on the pleadings, or by directed verdict motion."

"All right. Mr. Gonzalez, I assume you're prepared to accept the potential consequences of being trapped by your own pleadings. There will most likely be no amendments allowed in this fast-tract case."

"Yes, ma'am. We have confidence in our pleadings as stated," Gonzalez replied.

"So be it. Now, about the motion to compel ... this is about documents related to any past charges of harassment against Mr. Scarlechek. ... Hmm-m. Mr. Golumbo, are we actually fighting over something that exists?"

It was a simple question, one that Golumbo didn't want to answer. But the judge was right to the point. He had no choice.

"Well ... yes, Your Honor, we are," he admitted.

Gonzalez smiled. His hunch was right. Like most other sexual harassers, Scarlechek had done it before.

Adel sat motionless, concealing her sudden shame.

Scarlechek and Golumbo would've preferred to lie about it, but too many people knew. Landis knew and he'd told Laughlin, who'd recently told Adel. The victim was Scarlechek's first administrative assistant, Janet Watson, who fled the company shortly after Scarlechek had been hired.

Watson was a free-spirited, naturally beautiful woman—a baby boomer who grew up in Southern California. When Scarlechek was hired, he immediately tested Watson, using his tried and true modus operandi. She bolted, physically and mentally, determining she didn't need that job. As an afterthought, she contacted a lawyer friend of hers, who contacted his friend, Geoff Landis. Landis negotiated a quick settlement agreement. They signed, and Scarlechek paid fifty thousand dollars. The confidentiality agreement, which was part of the settlement, was tight, so initially, only Watson, her lawyer, Landis, and Scarlechek knew of the accusation. Janet Watson trekked off to Montana to work on a ranch, and Scarlechek began his search for a replacement, finding Marta DeLong.

"Hmm-m," Judge Wozynski pondered aloud.

Golumbo took this opportunity to interject. "Your Honor, we've prepared a supplemental memorandum of law in opposition to Mr. Gonzalez's motion." He walked to the bench with a thick set of papers.

Adel cringed, and looked over to see Gonzalez smiling.

"The undisclosed documents," Golumbo continued, "that Mr. Gonzalez is seeking are irrelevant and may be highly prejudicial to the defendants ..." Golumbo laid his left elbow on the judge's bench as though sidling up to the bar at his favorite watering hole, and started to hand the memorandum to the judge.

Adel shut her eyes and hunched her shoulders. She should've told Golumbo, but the thought had never occurred to her that he wouldn't know. The clerk and court reporter mimicked Adel.

Bam! The judge's gavel came down hard, as her face grew red and fierce.

"Don't you ever touch my bench without permission!" the judge yelled. "The next time you do that, you'll be scoopin' flies off concrete in jail! And don't approach the bench without permission either!"

Golumbo stumbled as he tried to utter an apology and slink away. Looking rueful, like a cowering canine after having been scolded, he snuck back into his seat.

Some judges were like that—there was something sacred about their bench. Wise lawyers didn't touch one unless they knew—it was part of the "practice" of law, one practiced until embarrassing mistakes were eliminated.

Just as abruptly, the judge returned to her temperate, firm demeanor. "Now, Mr. Golumbo," she said. "Do you have something you wish to hand to the bailiff to file with the Court?"

"Ye ... yes, ma'am," Golumbo muttered.

The bailiff walked over, took the memorandum, and handed it to the judge. The judge read through her half-moon spectacles, while the lawyers sat quietly. Finally, the judge peered over the top of her glasses, and focused on Gonzalez.

"Well, Mr. Gonzalez, what of it? Does one incident a negligent entrustment case make?"

Standing and buttoning his coat, Gonzalez said, "Your Honor, we do not know if there was only one incident, and we don't know the nature of the incident or incidents. The documents relating to whatever happened are relevant or, at the very least, reasonably calculated to lead to the discovery of admissible evidence. As you know, that standard defines the scope of permissible discovery. We want to know about the incident or incidents, and to identify the witnesses involved so we can speak to them. It's relevant to our negligent entrustment case and our ability to prove a pattern and practice of wrongful behavior, and that the company knew of the behavior. If they did, they were negligent in entrusting this man with his position ... his power."

"Ms. Blair, would you like to be heard?"

"Yes, Your Honor," Adel said, standing up. "Your Honor, there is no pattern or practice alleged in the amended complaint—only specific incidents." Adel had trouble with her own argument. Although the pattern was not alleged, she knew there *was* a pattern: first Watson, then Marta DeLong, then DeeDee, and then herself. Each with differing results, but Lou Scarlechek remained the common element.

"I would submit," she continued, "that one incident does *not* a negligent entrustment case make."

"Kind of like the old free first bite rule on dog bite cases?" the judge asked. She was setting Adel up by referring to the old law, before enactment of strict liability dog-bite statutes, in which dogs owners were allowed the first bite "free," before they could be sued for negligence. Likening sexual harassment to a dog bite was amusing to the judge.

"Well, no, Your Honor, because this would allegedly be the second bite."

"Precisely!" the judge interjected, slamming her gavel down again.

"The motion to compel production is granted. You'll have one week to produce the documents. No fees are awarded because of the stipulated nature of this procedure. Is there anything else we need to discuss today?"

"No, Your Honor," both Gonzalez and Adel responded. Golumbo was still too shaken.

"Mr. Golumbo?" The judge demanded his response.

"N … No, Your Honor," he managed to spit out.

"Very well. Good day."

"All rise," the bailiff barked on cue.

As Adel stood, she felt dog-bitten by the judge. At least she hadn't been gashed open like Golumbo. Deep down, she knew the judge's ruling was correct. That part of her was disgusted that it was her job to try to keep the information away from Gonzalez.

CHAPTER 79

Steve Gonzalez stopped by Assistant State Attorney Ann Gentry's office after the hearing.

Gonzalez knew Gentry fairly well, having once represented her father in a civil dispute between him and a business partner, while Gentry was in law school. Her father had asked Gonzalez to keep her informed, so that she could interpret the "legalese" for him.

"Trial in four months!" Gentry kidded Gonzalez. "That's fast for you civil sloths. Sure you can handle it?"

"Just be ready with your dictator when it's done, Ms. Speedy Trial," Gonzalez replied. "We'll want a criminal charge brought against Scarlechek right after we win."

Don't forget about this one, was what he'd actually come to tell her.

"Don't worry. We'll be watching."

CHAPTER 80

Butte, Montana, was damp and muddy from the early melting snow, and very cold, especially to a Cuban boy hailing from the perpetual sauna of South Florida. Gonzalez zipped his ski parka up to his neck as he left the Range Rover dealership. He climbed into the four-wheel-drive rental vehicle, and though he was in a place where a Range Rover could be truly necessary, he couldn't help feeling like a yuppie. At least his secretary didn't set him up with a Hummer.

Following the sales person's directions, he headed east toward Wheeler Ranch. When he finally drove up to the majestic ranch house, Gonzalez was reminded of the Ponderosa in the Bonanza television series. He stood in front of a two-story structure, built out of giant logs cut from indigenous trees. The mammoth chimney wafted smoke into the damp and gloomy air. A woman walked out onto the massive front porch. She was clad in worn jeans, cowboy boots, and a blue flannel shirt rolled at the cuffs over a thermal undershirt.

Her green eyes sparkled as she checked him up and down. Gonzalez felt silly in his white Reeboks.

The woman was Janet Watson. She was living with the rancher, Joe Wheeler, and had been for the last five months. Wheeler was out with his ranch hands, mending fence.

She and Gonzalez greeted one another and she invited him into the warmth of the log foyer. He watched her move, and understood how Scarlechek had been attracted to her. Everything about her depicted unadulterated health, wholesomeness, and beauty. Her long, brown hair was thick and curly, pulled away from her face; random strands floated over her shoulders. Her high cheekbones and her clear skin, save scattered sunspots, enhanced her good looks.

As he took in the rustic interior, Gonzalez was struck by the vast differences in lifestyles one could find within the United States. It was decorated in early American wood—everywhere—nothing but wood. Watson offered him coffee poured from a tin pot. They sat by the glowing fireplace on furniture fashioned from pine, and began to talk.

Gonzalez and Watson had already discussed her settlement agreement with Scarlechek and Western Town over the phone before Gonzalez decided to fly out to see her. Along with her personnel file, it was the settlement document that Judge Wozynski had compelled the company and Scarlechek to produce. The agreement contained a confidentiality clause requiring her to remain silent about the matter, but the clause contained an exception: it wasn't a violation for her to testify pursuant to a court-issued subpoena. Gonzalez told her he'd bring a witness subpoena to serve on her for the trial in July. But, he warned that talking to him was not, strictly speaking, testimony.

"So what are they going to do, sue me?" was her savvy response. "I doubt it. All I have is what's left of my settlement and they'd never find that, even if they won such a silly lawsuit. I'd much rather know that I've helped Scarlechek get exactly what he deserves."

With that answer, Watson relayed to Gonzalez her story as the first Western Town administrative assistant to Lou Scarlechek.

"At first I wanted to please Lou. I assumed he was competent and intelligent, and someone I could respect. How else could he get to that position? I looked forward to being around him every day. But his personality changed my attitude, real quick."

"What do you mean?"

"Well, he was too loud, unnecessarily demanding, showy, you know, ostentatious. He had to have control over people, had to have all the attention. And then, he started flirting with me—more than just the usual stuff. I began to sense that he had a purpose. He complimented me … unnecessarily, I thought. I was just doing my job. He talked about bonuses and the power he had. That's what did it. The more he did that, the more I wondered about him. I began thinking he wasn't what he should be."

"Then, a week or so after he started, he asked me to stay late one evening. He called me into his office to take a letter. He had dimmed the lights, but I didn't think anything of it. Before he started working, he had me install the dimmer, because he told me he suffered from keratitis … you know, sensitivity to bright light. So I go in, and he's sitting on the couch, in the middle. He asked me to come over. I did. I sat down. But then he asked me to rub his back for a while before doing the letter. Like a dummy, I did. Then, he wanted to rub mine, and after a while he touched my breasts."

"The same old sneak attack," Gonzalez remarked. "How unoriginal." Watson hadn't heard the details of DeeDee's story, so her own story chillingly corroborated DeeDee's. This would clearly make Watson's testimony admissible in court, because it was evidence of a common method or plan. Evidence of one incident wasn't normally relevant to prove occurrence of a second. But the law allowed an exception for common method or plan, under the rationale that the commonality linked the incidents, corroborating whatever other evidence may exist.

"I couldn't believe it. I felt so violated. He had planned it all. And I felt so stupid. So, I just left. It was simple. Never went back. I'd been thinking about Montana for awhile, anyway."

"Then you called your lawyer?"

"Yeah, after awhile, I got angry and called him. He knew Geoff Landis. Scarlechek, the asshole, denied it all, but he paid me fifty thousand dollars to shut me up!" Her voice was bright. "What a … I'm sorry, my boyfriend has a special word for him."

"Ah, come on."

"Dickhead."

Gonzalez smiled and stifled his laugh. "Janet, your testimony will be very helpful to us, even crucial. We'll fly you to Orlando for the trial and pay your expenses. Will you come?"

"Of course," she said, smiling.

"But the lawyers from the other side will probably want to take your deposition once I list you as a witness. You can require them to come here or they can fly you to Orlando for that—it'll be your choice."

"I'll make them come here. Will Scarlechek come too?"

"He has a right to, but I doubt it. He'll let his lawyer handle it."

"Good. If he came here, my boyfriend would probably hog-tie his ass and have him dragged by a quarter horse ... You know I wouldn't want that!"

She smiled and Gonzalez laughed.

"Now," Gonzalez asked, "have you ever given a deposition before?"

"No."

"Okay, let's talk about that."

CHAPTER 81

"Tom, have you decided on those dates yet for your depo-prep and deposition?" Cookie Albertson asked her boss.

"Leave me alone, will you!" Peckinpah snapped. "Can't you see I'm thinking about something else?" The last things he wanted in his head were Orlando, Adel Blair, and especially Lou Scarlechek. He'd tried hard to block it all out, and resented anyone who forced it back in.

"Tom, what's wrong with you?" Cookie was annoyed and losing patience. "You're like this so often, these days."

"Nothing! You pick the dates, and just tell me where to be and when to be there. I don't care!"

He obviously does *care,* Cookie thought, and picked up the phone to call Adel's secretary. Once she'd scheduled the date, Cookie asked whether Adel would be available to meet for dinner after the deposition. Adel came on the line, and they agreed to a time and place.

"What's happening in the case?" Cookie asked.

"We have DeeDee's deposition in two weeks," Adel responded. "Then Tom's, and then Scarlechek's. Should be interesting."

"Yeah, should be."

CHAPTER 82

"DeeDee, don't volunteer anything!" Gonzalez said, mad at his effusive client. "And only answer the question, I told you!

They were in his conference room preparing for her deposition in two days. He had explained in detail how to give a deposition, and now they were going through her testimony with him. He was asking questions as though he were Golumbo or Adel. He'd asked a simple question about whether her father was in favor of her taking a job at Western Town, and she inexplicably went off on a tangent about her boyfriend, Dirk. The answer could clue their opponents to ask about Dirk, and then their sex life, and who knows what else.

"Oh, I'm sorry. You're right."

"That's precisely what I'm talking about. You *only* answer the question. If it is a 'yes or no' question, you answer 'yes or no,' or 'I don't know,' or 'don't recall.' If you add any more than that, you'll trigger something in your interrogator's mind to ask further questions and discover more information that could be helpful to them. It's a game, DeeDee, and you have to be mentally tough to play it. Remember, no matter what they say, they're there to trick and cajole you into saying things they can use against you. This is *not* a popularity contest, and it's *not* about being liked. This is your case, DeeDee. You have to be tough and strong."

"I'm sorry," she said. "I can do it. Let's try again."

"The only time I ever want you to volunteer anything, is if you can send in a zinger against Mr. Scarlechek or the company, okay? That's it. *Nada mas.* And if you can't stick to that, well, I'm liable to take that discretion from you. All right? Now, let's try again."

"Okay, I'm ready."

CHAPTER 83

"State your name for the record, please," Golumbo said two days later, as he commenced DeeDee's deposition. They were in Gonzalez's conference room where he had prepped her. The room was painted a deep golden color over textured walls, and there was mahogany trim around the windows, matching the conference table and door, and the place was filled with the trappings of a successful lawyer. At least in this familiar setting she was still on friendly soil. Gonzalez sat on her right, while Adel and Golumbo faced her across the table.

She was nervous. *Take your time,* she thought. *Only answer the question.*

"DeeDee T. Lane," she replied.

"And your father is a farmer?"

"Yes."

"Has quite a sense of humor, doesn't he?"

"I'm sorry?" DeeDee inquired.

"He named you DDT?"

"The 'T.' stands for 'Theresa,' the name of my father's mother. 'DeeDee' was my mom's mother's name. It just worked out that way. There was no humor intended."

"Your father didn't intentionally name you after a poison?"

"Objection! Move on, and be gentlemanly and professional about it, or we'll leave!" Gonzalez shouted at Golumbo. "This is not starting the deposition off well!" But Gonzalez knew the deposition would be like this. He had coached DeeDee for hours to stand up to this kind of treatment. He fired back to let the other side know that it wouldn't be easy or pleasant for them either, and he glared at Golumbo, causing Golumbo's eyes to cower. Then he glanced at Adel. Her gaze was unchanging, but it was not support for Golumbo that Gonzalez saw on her face.

DeeDee looked at Adel too. She had idolized Adel when they first became acquainted. She had admired Adel's strength of character, the command of respect, and she had wanted to emulate Adel. She wondered now how Adel could represent Western Town. *Maybe she needs the fees.*

It was DeeDee's strength that made her wonder these things. She was ready for this deposition and wasn't going to let Adel's presence rattle her. *How can Adel sit on the same side of the table as Lou Scarlechek's lawyer? Maybe I was wrong about her.*

It had been decided earlier that Golumbo, not Adel, would interrogate DeeDee. Scarlechek didn't feel comfortable with Adel doing the main work. Adel silently welcomed relief from this duty.

Golumbo backed down and moved on. He took DeeDee through a long series of background questions covering her entire life, all for the purposes of wearing her down and finding any possible dirt that he could. But it was to no avail. And DeeDee didn't show any weariness. "Did you ever do drugs?" "No." "Do you drink alcohol?" "No." "Have you ever been arrested?" "No." "Have you ever engaged in prostitution?" "Certainly not." "Have you ever been sued?" "No." "Have you ever seen a therapist?" "Not until after the rape."

Gonzalez allowed all the questions and answers because he wanted Golumbo and Adel to know exactly how clean his little homecoming queen was. He'd warned DeeDee that the questions would be insulting, but he trained her to answer them directly and without reaction. It would be a test of endurance, he had told her.

Finally, unsuccessful in finding anything worth exploring, Golumbo moved to the incidents with Lou Scarlechek.

"Tell me when you first met Lou Scarlechek," he said.

"It was when I transferred to Legal in September of last year."

"What were the circumstances?"

"I was transferred from Hotel Operations to Legal as a secretary. It had been a goal of mine, and eventually I wanted to become a legal secretary. It was what I studied in college. It was the reason I came to Western Town."

"Whom did you work for as a secretary?"

"I worked in the secretarial pool then, so ... no one in particular."

"And what happened precisely, when you first did work for Mr. Scarlechek?"

"Well, his administrative assistant had just left; that is, we had all heard that she'd quit. He came into the secretarial pool and looked us over. Then he asked me to come with him to a meeting room. He needed some work done."

"What did you think?"

"I was delighted."

"You were delighted," Golumbo repeated. His tone was cynical. "Did you think Mr. Scarlechek was handsome?"

"Mildly."

"What did the other girls in the pool say?"

"Well, they were happy for me, and wanted to hear all about it afterward."

"All about *what* afterward?"

"All about what I was to do for him."

"And what were you to do for him?"

"Letters mostly. Couple of phone calls. It was only one afternoon."

"Anything else that you wanted to do for him?" Golumbo asked sarcastically.

"No, only what he asked."

"Ah! You wanted to do what he asked?"

"Objection," Gonzalez said. "Your double entendres and innuendos are tedious. This question has been asked and answered, and you're not coming out and asking direct questions about what you mean, which is sex. You're trying to create a paper record of innuendo for the jury."

"Are you instructing her not to answer?"

"No. DeeDee, just be careful to specify when you're talking about sex and when you're not, for the record."

Golumbo, realizing what he'd get if he pursued the last question, left it. "All right, Ms. Lane, isn't it true that you told the girls in the secretarial pool that you thought Mr. Scarlechek was handsome?"

"Yes, but they disagreed."

"So you were sexually attracted to him, weren't you?"

"No, I wasn't."

"Well, how can you think he's handsome and not be sexually attracted to him?"

"I ... I was not sexually attracted to him. I just thought he was mildly handsome. ... Before I got to know him, anyway."

Gonzalez smiled. *She's catching on.*

"Well, doesn't *handsome* mean that he was pleasing to your eye ... at least initially?"

"Well, yes, I suppose so."

"And he's a man and you're a woman, correct?"

DeeDee looked at Gonzalez expecting an objection to the silly question. Gonzalez rolled his eyes, and glanced at Adel. *Are you really on their side?*

"Correct," DeeDee said.

"So as a man, he was pleasing to your eye?"

"Yes, initially!" DeeDee was getting angry now.

"At this time, when was the last time you had had sex?"

"Steve?" DeeDee asked, hoping she didn't have to answer.

"Yes, DeeDee," Gonzalez said in a soothing but firm voice. "We discussed this. Answer the question."

"It had been six months," DeeDee said after a pause.

"Why so long?"

"My boyfriend and I had broken up."

"Now ... you were never married, correct?"

"Correct."

"So you believe extramarital sex is okay, correct?"

"Yes, I suppose I do, under the right circumstances."

"And what are those?"

"When two people love each other—two responsible, mature adults."

"How often would you have sex with your boyfriend before you broke up?"

She glanced again at Gonzalez. He was resolute—she needed to answer. DeeDee glared at Adel, as if to say, "I can't believe you're a part of this. I can't believe you're letting me go through this." Adel looked away.

"Weekly," DeeDee answered, "sometimes more."

"Do you enjoy sex?"

"Yes, I do, under the right circumstances."

"Tell me about the first alleged harassment incident with Mr. Scarlechek?"

DeeDee went on to describe the incident. They took a break after she finished. When they resumed, Golumbo took DeeDee through the subsequent encounters, including the incident when she first succumbed and the most recent rape. Hours had passed, and DeeDee began showing signs of fatigue. Tears welled up in her eyes and trickled down her cheeks when she spoke about the rape. Golumbo peppered her with questions about her actions and intentions, implying she'd led Scarlechek on.

"Are you all right?" she was asked. It wasn't Gonzalez ... it was Adel. She handed DeeDee a tissue from across the table.

"Yes! I'm all right!" she said with a scowl. DeeDee wiped the tears away and looked Golumbo square in the eyes.

Golumbo tried to attack DeeDee's dressing habits after that, but to no avail. She had never dressed provocatively at work. "Not that it matters, Mr. Golumbo," she said, "but every day at work I dress the same way as I'm dressed now—in a conservative suit. I have never dressed otherwise at work. Are you provoked? If you are, it's *your* problem, not mine!"

Gonzalez began to worry. DeeDee's outbursts were driven by anger, and he needed her to stay calm. He didn't mind the tears, but he didn't want the anger. Perhaps it was time for another break.

Golumbo moved on. "So, aside from the alleged rape incident, where you allegedly said 'no' after many prior encounters ... aside from that incident, you consented to having sex with Mr. Scarlechek, correct?"

"Yes, but only because he would've fired me if I didn't."

"Oh come now, did you really believe that in this day and age?"

"Yes, he told me so!"

"Oh? What did he say exactly?"

"I told you already! He said I needed to grow up. That we were in the big time. And that he'd be real interested in my next review."

"Is that all?"

"That's enough! He implied that he'd fire me! I'd lose my job! I'd never be promoted!"

"That's what this is all about, isn't it? You gave him sex because you wanted a promotion, didn't you?"

"No! Ye ... No! He required it!"

"But you said you consented, correct?"

"Yes!"

"And you did want a promotion, didn't you?"

"Of course I did!"

"So it was voluntary on your part, correct?"

There was a pause.

"Correct, Ms. Lane? He didn't hold a gun to your head, did he?"

"He held a knife!"

"No, I said *aside* from the alleged rape ... in all the prior incidences, he didn't force you, did he?"

"No! He didn't!"

"So, it was voluntary, correct?"

"I suppose so," she said.

"So, it was not unwelcome conduct, was it?"

"Yes! It *was* unwelcome!"

"Well, how can it be unwelcome if it's something you voluntarily do? How can it be unwelcome if you consent?" Golumbo fired the questions at her.

"He made me do it! I never wanted to! He made me!"

She finally broke down, laying her head on the table and crying.

"All right, that's enough." Gonzalez said. "We're taking a break." He supported DeeDee as they walked out of the conference room.

Alone with his client, Gonzalez held her in his arms until she broke away. "I'm going to the restroom," she said, still sobbing. "I can do this. I'm all right."

DeeDee splashed cool water on her face. It felt good—refreshing. From behind her, Adel emerged from a stall and approached the sink next to DeeDee. The two didn't speak, although DeeDee glared at Adel's reflection in the mirror. Adel stared back expressionless.

A few minutes later, DeeDee and Gonzalez reentered the deposition room. Adel was reminded of Camus as she watched DeeDee resolutely take her chair. Like his *Sisyphus*, DeeDee was shrugging her shoulders and pushing the fallen rock back up the hill.

"When did you first learn of Title VII or the sexual discrimination laws?" Golumbo resumed.

"In college, I believe," DeeDee said, composed again.

"And what was your understanding of that law?"

"That people cannot be treated differently because of their race or sex, or even religion."

"Did you know what sexual harassment was?"

"No."

"Never heard the term?"

"I didn't say that."

"So you had heard of it?"

"Yes."

"So what was your understanding of what it was?"

"I don't know that I had an understanding. I never much thought about it."

"So how was it that you had already hired a lawyer and he was at your apartment so quickly the night of the alleged rape?" Golumbo asked, his question dripping with innuendo.

The answer was remarkably simple. "I called him."

"How did you know to call him? I mean, why didn't you call Ms. Blair here, or me, for that matter?"

"Believe me, I wouldn't call you," DeeDee said, pausing for effect. Gonzalez smiled.

Adel empathized with DeeDee as she watched her withstand the grilling. *She's standing her ground*, Adel thought. *She's strong—fragile, but strong. Strength from the powerful is one thing*, Adel thought, *but strength from the weak is far more admirable. When a weak person is strong, it's a greater feat. Equally so, when a strong person becomes weak, it's a greater tragedy.*

CHAPTER 84

Adel drove along the interstate toward Western Town's corporate offices, where she and Tom Peckinpah would prepare for his deposition. Her eyes were drawn to the billboard—the cowboy on the bull with the young lady looking on—that she'd seen so many times before.

Pecos Bill was still being bucked by the snorting Brahma, as he hung onto the bull rope and waved his battered Stetson, beckoning people to Western Town. His arm still reminded her of Ahab, calling to his crew to attack the monster. The billboard almost hypnotized her, and she resented that it could distract her so.

Her mind turned back to Tom Peckinpah. *I wonder how he'll do.*

Later, as she walked past the atrium and into Admin, she spied Cookie at the end of the hall. They embraced, happy to see each other once again.

"Listen," Cookie said, "Tom's ready for you now, so we don't have any time, but when can you get together?"

"How about tomorrow night?" Adel replied. "I'll have my secretary call you tomorrow and pick a restaurant and time. She can give you directions, if you need them."

"Sounds great. Come on, I'll show you in."

Adel entered Peckinpah's office, following Cookie. She was struck by the southwestern-styled opulence. Like Scarlechek's office across the atrium, this, too, was a corner office with two of its four walls made of glass windows overlooking another view of Western Town property. She observed a large man with his back to them, sitting behind his desk of petrified desert burl. He was speaking on the telephone on the matching credenza behind his chair, and overlooking the view through the window-wall behind his credenza.

He seemed to be surveying his kingdom while he spoke.

Cookie showed Adel to a chair in front of Peckinpah's desk but before Adel sat, she took a look around the room. Behind her, there was another seating area in front of a very large television encased in a burl wood entertainment center. On the left, there was a huge, bronze Remington statue of a cowboy, riding a bucking bronco and waiving his hat, not unlike the troublesome billboard. On the other side, there was another brass Remington, just as large, of an Indian riding a pony and shooting an arrow into a stumbling buffalo. On the walls were southwestern-style paintings, numerous civic awards, and photographs of Peckinpah with movie and radio stars, and from his football days. Several framed blowups of him on magazine covers completed the tangible homage to his success in life.

"He'll be right with you, Adel," Cookie said, as Peckinpah swung around.

While Adel waited for him to finish his phone conversation, she took note of his appearance. *Handsome,* she thought. *He should make a great impression on a jury.*

"Great," he said into the receiver. "Umm hmm ... yes. That'll do. All right ... bye."

"Well, hello there," he said, as he turned his attention to Adel. His accountant had just told him what the continued success of the movie *Chief Joseph* was going to mean to his personal finances under his contract.

"You must be Adel Blair. In fact, now that I see you, I remember seeing you before ... at a rowing race as I recall. You had just beaten the men. I didn't see the race, but ... how did you do that?"

"Well ... I just went a little bit faster that day."

"Yeah, but I saw those guys. They were no slouches. You must be at the top of your game to do that to them. I admire that."

"Well, thanks," Adel said. "It looks like you've been at the top of a few games, yourself," she added, as she gestured toward Peckinpah's awards.

"Yes, I've had my day. But tell me, what do we have to do today?"

"Well, we've got to prepare you for your deposition in the Lane case. I'll need to talk to you about how to give a deposition, and talk to you about the facts," she said. "Have you ever given a deposition before?"

"Oh yes, many times. One doesn't get to my position without going through a few lawsuits. I know all about it really ... only answer the question ... don't speculate ... if you don't know the answer, say you don't know ... all those things."

Hmm-m, Adel thought, *here we go again with another know-it-all client.* Experience caused her to distrust his assurances. "Well," she replied, "I really should go over—"

"No, seriously, I really don't want to do that. I don't have time, and I know all about it. Let's just get to the facts," Peckinpah said.

"Well ... okay." *Boy, I thought these corporate types listened to their lawyers. We'll see how well he can do,* she thought, but aloud she said, "What were you doing there that night?"

"Oh, come now," he said sternly. "What I was doing there makes no difference whatsoever. We'll just cover what I saw. That's all you really need to know."

Adel frowned. She had seen this type of attitude before. It usually meant that the client was holding something back. Many clients never understood that a lawyer needed to assimilate all facts, and even the smallest, undisclosed matter could make a huge difference in a case. Some clients, however, understood this all too well, and it was these clients that she distrusted most. Now, she had a choice—be insistent, or submit to his dictates. In this already strange case, she chose the latter, thinking perhaps to come back into it another way. "All right," she replied, "if that's your wish. Just tell me what you saw."

Peckinpah leaned back in his chair, satisfied that he'd imposed his will.

CHAPTER 85

"State your name for the record, please," Gonzalez asked two days later in deposition.

"Thomas A. Peckinpah."

"What's the 'A.' stand for?"

"Armstrong."

"Now sir, do you understand that you are under oath to tell the whole truth, and nothing but the truth, so help you God?"

"Yes, of course."

"And do you understand that any intentional deviation from that standard is a crime called 'perjury'?"

"Yes, yes. Let's get on with it." Peckinpah was impatient. He certainly didn't need a lecture about perjury from this Hispanic lawyer.

Coldly and methodically, Gonzalez guided Peckinpah through a standard opening line of questioning. Glaring straight in the eye at Peckinpah with each question, Gonzalez conveyed his belief that Peckinpah was a liar, and that he'd show Peckinpah no respect until he told the truth. Gonzalez intended to intimidate Peckinpah throughout, asking every surly question he could, all the while searching for any weakness. Last week, the Defendants poked and prodded at DeeDee; now, it was his turn to test the resolve of their key witness. Scarlechek was not the key, Gonzalez knew—it was Peckinpah. Outwardly, Gonzalez 's demeanor was mean and nasty; inwardly, he scrutinized Peckinpah.

Peckinpah was the vision of corporate correctness. He was neatly trimmed and manicured, and wore a double-breasted suit, folded hanky in the breast pocket, Italian shoes and finely patterned silk socks. But he heard his stomach gurgling like an eddy behind a river-rock, and hoped no one else did. The knowledge that he was about to perjure himself made him nervous as hell.

"Have you ever been convicted of a crime?" Gonzalez asked, implying he thought the answer would be affirmative, but actually anticipating the opposite.

Adel rolled her eyes. This was the CEO of one of the most famous corporations in the country. She knew Gonzalez had a right to ask the question, so she didn't object, but it was an intentional insult, designed to annoy Peckinpah. The lack of decorum angered Adel.

There followed an unexpectedly long hesitation, and Peckinpah gulped hard.

"Yes," said Peckinpah. Everyone in the room—Golumbo, Adel, Gonzalez, even the court reporter—looked up in shock. The key witness had a past! Gonzalez wanted to do a back flip, but strained not to show his glee.

"And what was your crime?" Gonzalez said with a snarl.

"Possession of marijuana."

"When were you convicted?"

"At the end of my senior year in high school."

"Did you serve time?"

"No, other than when I was initially arrested. They credited me with time served and suspended my sentence as part of a plea bargain. I was placed on parole."

"You plea-bargained to a conviction of possession—that indicates you committed a greater crime, doesn't it?" Gonzalez's suspicions were right on. No state attorney would convict a high school senior with Peckinpah's background and an otherwise clean record, unless there was something more serious. In actuality, Peckinpah had engaged in a small marijuana growing and distribution operation with a few of his football buddies.

"Objection! Don't answer that," Adel blurted out. Golumbo wasn't far behind. "That's irrelevant and immaterial and you have no right to treat a witness of Mr. Peckinpah's caliber this way!" Adel continued. Conviction of the specific crime, plea-bargained or not, was all that was admissible under the rules of evidence, and all he was entitled to ask about. It was ironic that Adel was so vehemently defending Peckinpah. But it was her nature.

"Are you instructing the witness not to answer?" Gonzalez asked, hoping to pin Adel down on the record.

Adel's tone was sardonic. "What part of 'Don't answer that', didn't you understand?"

Gonzalez smirked. "Certify the question," he commanded the court reporter coolly, implying he'd seek a court order compelling an answer later. But he knew he wouldn't. He already had enough.

This set the stage, and the deposition continued on with similar flare-ups and certified questions. The two dogs were fully engaged now. Adel was fighting, but it was like she had one hand tied behind her back: part of her believed she was fighting for the wrong side.

"All right sir, and when you walked in, it wasn't rape you witnessed?" Gonzalez eventually asked.

"No," Peckinpah answered. His voice was low and his eyes shifted away from Gonzalez's direction. Adel watched him closely.

"What brought you to that side of the office building in the first place?"

"I saw Legal's lights were on when I went out to the restroom, and I wanted to ask Lou a question, if he was there."

"What question?" Gonzalez inquired, entering territory Adel wasn't allowed to explore in depo-prep.

"I don't remember. Just something related to what I was doing."

"You don't remember? How could you not remember?"

"Asked and answered," Adel said. She had no idea how Peckinpah would answer.

"I don't remember," Peckinpah said, agitated.

"What had you been doing at the office?"

"Looking over a list."

"A list of what?" Gonzalez was relentless.

"I need a moment," Peckinpah said. He leaned over to Adel's ear and whispered, "Do I have to answer this? It's private company business—very sensitive."

"What was it?" Adel whispered back, annoyed that she hadn't previously been allowed to analyze this.

"A list of candidates for company president—our current president is stepping down in July. It's secret."

"Let's go outside," Adel said aloud. "We need a break." They abruptly walked out, knowing they didn't need permission and showing it. They turned right down a hall and found a secluded area to speak.

Gonzalez spoke sarcastically after they'd left. "Let the record reflect Mr. Peckinpah needs to confer with counsel and has left the room."

"Will disclosure of this affect the company's stock?" Adel asked Peckinpah.

"Probably not."

"What then?"

"It's just a secret," Peckinpah said, not knowing what to tell Adel.

"Well, 'it's just a secret' is not yet a recognized exception to the right to discovery in federal court. I'm afraid you'll have to answer absent some drastic effect on the company." She motioned him back into the depo room.

"Read back the last question please," Gonzalez instructed the court reporter. She complied, reading back, "A list of what?"

"It was a list of candidates," Peckinpah said, still hoping Gonzalez wouldn't dig further.

"For what?" Gonzalez demanded to know.

"For … for company president … Mr. Waverly is stepping down."

"Oh," Gonzalez said, as though a light bulb had just been switched on. It was why they called it "discovery." "When?"

"In July."

"Who is on the list?"

"Do I have to answer that?" Peckinpah said aloud to Adel.

"Yes, answer the question!" Adel snapped, still not understanding the big concern, and becoming more and more annoyed with her own client.

Peckinpah hesitated, and then sighed, "Mark Woodson, Sandy Yates, and … Lou Scarlechek."

Adel turned her head and gaped at Peckinpah. *Why the hell hadn't anyone told her this? Didn't they think I should know this?* Now the reason for the quick trial was obvious.

"Ah! So that's why the need for a quick trial," Gonzalez said, thinking out loud. "Strike that … that's not a question," he said to the court reporter, having all he needed, and wanting nothing else on the record on the point.

Adel was dumbfounded. *Lou Scarlechek as the president of Western Town? The assholes deserve whatever they get!*

"So, this was a secret, correct?" Gonzalez continued.

"Yes, it was," Peckinpah said.

"And no one at all knows?"

"That's correct."

"So, why then were you going to … let me see my notes here … 'ask Lou a question related to what you were doing'?"

"Uh … I uh … I just wanted to ask him something." Peckinpah's brow quivered. He fidgeted in his chair and felt his body temperature rise as he began to sweat.

"What?" Gonzalez said. He wouldn't let it go.

"I don't know … I just wanted to ask Lou about Sandy's employment agreement. I had been reading it. Lou didn't know, and wouldn't know from my question." Peckinpah's voice changed to relief. He had made this up quickly, and thought it sounded credible.

"What question did you have about Mr. Yates's employment agreement?" Again Gonzalez was relentless. Instinct told him that Peckinpah was lying and he was close to boxing him into a corner.

"Geez! … It was just something … about the confidentiality clause. I wanted to know how strong it was."

"And Mr. Scarlechek wouldn't want to know why you asked?"

"No. Not if I made it clear it was none of his business."

"And you were looking at the clause in relation to your considering Yates for President, correct?"

"Correct."

"You're certain of that?" Gonzalez asked.

"Yes. Yes." Peckinpah feigned impatience.

"Why?" Gonzalez mocked Peckinpah, challenging him to concoct a reason.

"Oh, for Christ's sake! ... Adel?" He glared at her, angry that she was allowing this to happen, not realizing she had little choice.

"Answer the question," Adel snapped, just as annoyed. "If you don't know or can't remember, say so!" He had professed to know all that in depo-prep.

"I can't remember!" Peckinpah blurted. He was angry at everyone.

Oh, what a tangled web we weave, Adel thought.

"All right, fine," Gonzalez said. "Tell me, do all your executive vice presidents have employment agreements like Mr. Yates?"

Peckinpah desperately wanted to answer something—anything—without having to lie. He didn't really know the answer, but his desire to regain his dignity compelled it. "Yes," he stated confidently.

"And a copy of these would be kept in their personnel files, correct?"

"Yes, of course."

When first we practice to deceive, Adel finished the poetic line to herself. She'd caught on to where Gonzalez was going. The next question was predictable.

"So one would be in Mr. Scarlechek's personnel file ... between him and the company, correct?"

"Objection!" Golumbo also caught on. He wanted to save Peckinpah, but he didn't know how.

"Grounds?" Gonzalez asked.

"Uh ... he doesn't know what's in there ... no foundation!" Golumbo stated.

"Fine. Now that one of your lawyers has told you how, you can answer the question, sir," Gonzalez said, staring back at Peckinpah.

"Ye ... yes, there would be," Peckinpah said with less confidence, given the direct hint from Golumbo, but feeling a need to stick to the storyline he'd concocted.

"Well ... madam court reporter, please mark this as Exhibit 2. ... Mr. Peckinpah, I'm handing you what has been marked as Exhibit 2 for your deposition." Peckinpah's witness statement had been introduced earlier as Exhibit 1. "It's a copy of Lou Scarlechek's personnel file that your attorney produced to me. You want to show me exactly *where* in that exhibit Mr. Scarlechek's employment agreement is?"

Peckinpah searched and searched, and finally said, "I can't find it in here." Of course, Gonzalez knew it *wasn't* in the file. There wasn't one.

"Can you explain that?"

"No."

Gonzalez glared at Peckinpah and then said, "Now, will you agree to produce a copy of Mr. Yates' employment agreement ... the one you were supposedly going to ask Mr. Scarlechek a question about on the evening in question?"

"Sure, we will," Peckinpah said quickly, wanting again to appear forthright and eager to verify his story.

"Objection!" Golumbo yelled. "We will not produce that. It's irrelevant and it's Mr. Yates's private business."

"Mr. Golumbo," Gonzalez said, "my understanding is that Ms. Blair here represents the company, not you. He said he'd produce it ... Ms. Blair?"

Gonzalez looked at her.

"We will produce it, if it exists ... subject to deleting private provisions you shouldn't be allowed to review," Adel said. She'd learn later that an employment agreement between Yates and the company never existed.

"All right, Mr. Peckinpah, let's go back to the rape. It wasn't really a scream that brought you to Lou's office?"

"No."

"And you didn't see a knife in his hand?"

"N ... No." Peckinpah's brow was quivering again. The word "perjury" kept flashing in his head like a neon sign.

"And DeeDee didn't yell out, 'Help me! He's raping me!'?"

"No!"

"As far as you were concerned, they were just making love, and you chastised them for doing so in the workplace?"

"That's correct."

"And then DeeDee left?"

"Yes, she did."

"Why?"

"I thought she was embarrassed at being caught."

"What did she say to make you think that?"

"She said 'Oh my gosh.' Then she dressed herself and left."

"Did you threaten to fire either her or Mr. Scarlechek?"

"No," Peckinpah scoffed.

"Then, why'd she leave?"

"Asked and answered," Adel objected. "Let's move on!"

"Isn't it true, sir, that DeeDee admitted to having sex with Mr. Scarlechek before?"

"Yes, that is true," Peckinpah said, relieved to be saying something truthful.

"Well, if she 'just left because she was embarrassed,' why would she have told you she had sex with him before?" Gonzalez knew what he'd get in response, but he was showing his hand, a little.

"I don't know why."

"Yeah. Well, how did it come up? What was first said?"

"Objection. Compound question. Which do you want him to answer?" Adel asked.

"The latter. What was first said when you walked in?"

"I said 'what the hell is going on here?' Then, DeeDee said 'Oh my gosh!' I think Lou said something like that, too. Then, she said she's had sex with him before, many times, and then she left."

"Seems a little weird, doesn't it?"

"Objection! Argumentative. Don't answer that," Adel barked.

Peckinpah just shrugged.

"Certify the question again," Gonzalez said to the court reporter.

The protracted deposition continued on for several more hours. Gonzalez didn't let up on Peckinpah, and hounded him relentlessly. Peckinpah's shoulders collapsed when he finally heard, "No more questions."

There was a brief cross-examination by Adel concerning Peckinpah's lack of real knowledge about the contents of Yates's personnel file. Adel asked little, to avoid opening up new avenues of inquiry for Gonzalez.

When the deposition ended, Gonzalez stood up and glared at Peckinpah, a caveat of what was to come. As he glowered, Gonzalez extended his hand to Peckinpah—again, another test. Peckinpah should have been charming. He was just there to help after all. But when he took Gonzalez's hand, he could barely squeeze, and his eyes wandered from Gonzalez's gaze.

Peckinpah slinked out of the room with barely a word to Adel.

CHAPTER 86

That evening, Tom Peckinpah sat across from Dr. Marian Brooks. It was no coincidence that he'd picked a woman. He first called her on March 10, after Dee Dee's lawsuit hit the news. He'd picked her name out at random from the phone book. Despite his mixed emotions before the first session, he'd soon disclosed everything to his new therapist.

She was only five feet one—but her face was warm and patient. Finding her to be compassionate and understanding, he yearned for her maternal demeanor. He looked at her, longing for comforting words and forgiveness even though she was younger, possessed far less social status, and was tiny in more ways than one by comparison to him.

Dr. Brooks listened as Peckinpah lamenting that he had lied again, this time perjuring himself in the deposition. She noted his self-contempt; and observed great despair. He'd been treated like a common person accused of lying, and worse, it was true.

"But how do you think you can rise out of your self-contempt?" Dr. Brooks asked.

"By telling the truth, I guess." This was the foregone conclusion of his visit.

"Is that why you came to see me again, to hear me tell you that?"

"Maybe. I don't know."

"And what do you think will happen if you do tell the truth?"

"Scarlechek will tell about Colorado."

"And what will happen then?"

"I'll lose everything."

"Will you? Will you lose your life?"

"No."

"Will you lose your wife?"

"I don't know … probably not. She'd be real angry … and hurt. But I think she'd stick by me."

"Will you lose your status and position?"

"Most assuredly. I'd be asked to resign by the board."

"Will you lose your wealth?"

"I have more than enough of that."

"Will you go to jail?"

"I don't know. It's hard to say. I can afford the very best criminal defense attorneys who could probably work out a deal. But what if there is some prosecutor looking to make a name? I've done so many crimes. I just don't know."

"Well, you need to know that, at least, don't you?"

"Yes."

"And you can get advice on that?"

"Yes, I have a personal lawyer."

"Don't you think you should talk to him?"

"Yes, I should. You're right."

"Do you trust him?"

"Yes. I'll call him right after I go back to Phoenix."

"Good. Now," she said, shifting gears, "if you lose your position with the company, but not your wife and not your freedom, how would you feel?"

"I'd be disgraced."

"Is that so bad?"

There was a long silence.

"Tom?"

"I don't … I can't answer."

"Do you mean, 'you won't answer'?"

There was another long silence.

"Are we dealing with ego here, Tom?"

Again, nothing.

"You're having trouble with these questions, aren't you, Tom?"

"Yes."

"Maybe you should think about them for awhile. Let's assume for the moment you won't lose your freedom and you won't lose your wife or wealth. Assume also that you can handle the loss of your status. How can you defuse what Scarlechek knows?"

"By disclosing it first," he said. "Resigning first. Having my lawyer handle Colorado first," he replied, thinking aloud.

"Tom, you need to think hard about whether you can let it all go, but in the meantime, what will you do?"

"I'll call my lawyer," he said, as he searched for approval in her motherly face.

CHAPTER 87

From Adel's vantage point that night, the Finnegan's Reef Restaurant was a barrage of sensation. Numerous, eclectic artifacts splattered all corners of the walls, walkways, and ceilings. A four-person racing shell even hung above the walkway adjacent to her booth. The menu too offered an abundance of delectable items.

These people don't know anything about rowing, Adel thought; but then she focused upon the name of the boat—the "Straightforward"— and was delighted to realize that it was the very same old wooden boat in which she had first rowed sweeps in high school. Seeing it took her back as though she was sitting in it now, in the middle of a race. Remembering her first race as a high school freshman, and the extreme pain in her forearms because she'd been rowing incorrectly, she recalled how her father had coached her then, correcting her form so her forearms wouldn't hurt the next time.

She suddenly missed her father. She needed him, now.

Cookie Albertson joined Adel in the booth. It was a happy time for them both—catching up on each other's lives. Adel left the stress of the day behind her and Cookie soon forgot about her dreary boss—something new they now had in common.

But eventually, the conversation turned back to Peckinpah. Relaying mutual concern for him, they each spoke in a reserved manner, neither willing to reveal too much. After awhile Cookie finally broke and said, "Adel, I have mixed emotions about telling you this. But Tom is a friend. ... I ... I believe he's in trouble. He's deeply troubled about something."

"What do you think it is?"

"I ... oh ... gosh, please don't take offense ... I guess I shouldn't tell. If it's what I think, it's very bad."

Adel wondered what Cookie suspected, and chose her words carefully. "Don't worry about it, Cook. Whenever you feel comfortable talking about it, just let me know."

"Thanks Adel. Let's talk about your training ... are you still erging at the boathouse late at night?"

"You know me ... I'll be there tonight, after we eat."

CHAPTER 88

The Lake Fairview boathouse was dreary late at night, so much so that Adel considered skipping her workout. From under the roll-up door, she gazed out to the deserted dock and lake. Just when she decided to leave, it started to rain hard and she knew she'd get caught in the downpour if she ran to her car. Instead, Adel changed into her rowing clothes toted in her sport bag and pulled out an erg for a workout.

The rain was loud against the tin roof, and it sounded as though she were in a freight car attached a long train. Adel flipped on the radio switch and turned up the volume. She glanced quickly over her shoulder at a sudden wail, and caught a boathouse cat scurry away into the shadows. Then she stretched before climbing onto her erg to row.

Starting slowly, feeling the pain in her lower back as the strokes on the erg loosened her muscles, her movements eventually became longer and more efficient. As she warmed up, her five-hundred-meter split time—automatically calculated by the erg's electronic monitor—became faster and faster, until it settled to where she wanted it to stay. Then, she just rowed, stroke after stroke, after stroke.

The Rolling Stones blared from on the radio, yanking her thoughts back to where she didn't want them—onto Western Town and its bevy of messed-up men. The song "19th Nervous Breakdown" began playing and Jagger's rhythmic lamentations turned her mind to Tom Peckinpah.

"Here it co-mes," Jagger sang, and Adel wondered what was going on with Peckinpah, and what Cookie knew. "Here it co-mes,"

Jagger repeated, a little higher, and she speculated as to how it might relate to the case. "Here it co-mes ... Here it co-mes," Jagger repeated twice more on the high notes, and Adel wondered whether and when she'd learn what it was. "Here comes your nineteenth nervous breakdown," Jagger warned.

"Oh ... who's to blame?" Jagger asked. "That girl's just insane," he complained, and Adel thought about DeeDee.

She's not to blame, Adel thought. *I'll bet Scarlechek raped her. I still can't believe I'm representing the company on this case ... but Laughlin wants me, and oddly, Scarlechek doesn't object. Why?*

CHAPTER 89

"I don't remember," Scarlechek said defiantly.

After another question from Gonzalez, "I don't recall," was his response.

It's too bad the court reporter can't depict arrogance, Gonzalez thought. Whenever he tried to pin Scarlechek down, Scarlechek responded with, "I don't know," or, "I don't remember," leaving all options open and enjoying it. It was just another mental game to the executive vice president of Legal, and he was good at it.

Scarlechek testified that DeeDee had instigated their "affair." She consented every time, and swore he'd been set up. Unabashed, he also testified that Watson had marked him as well. He joked, "Look behind me ... see the target on my back?"

Later, Scarlechek relayed to Gonzalez that during the night in question, Adel had returned to his office after dinner. He'd given her a new file, and she had left after discussing the matter. It never occurred to Gonzalez to ask additional questions about Adel. When Gonzalez asked what file it was, Scarlechek claimed attorney-client privilege, guessing correctly that Gonzalez would leave it alone. Gonzalez never thought to call Adel as a witness; he had no clue that DeeDee's rape was directly tied to Scarlechek's anger against Adel.

Gonzalez also never learned that Laughlin had seen Scarlechek and DeLong having sex, so it never occurred to him to depose Laughlin. Thus, two essential pieces of the puzzle to Scarlechek's pattern were overlooked, two key pieces that could ensure DeeDee's victory.

Adel looked down at her yellow pad for almost the entire deposition. *For Dave and the firm,* she kept thinking. *For Dave and the firm.*

During a break, while Gonzalez searched his files for an exhibit, she felt Scarlechek's eyes on her. She looked up at him, but immediately wished she hadn't when he winked at her. Anger scorched her soul, and it was all she could do not to walk out.

CHAPTER 90

Two weeks later, the lawyers were still in the midst of the deposition process. They traveled to Montana and the Wheeler ranch for Janet Watson's deposition.

Adel conducted the direct exam. By the end, she'd concluded that Watson would come across very well to the jury. She was pretty, smart, and witty. She easily withstood the double-teaming from Golumbo's follow-up questions, and handled Adel and Golumbo like a politician at a press conference. Truth empowered her.

Gonzalez didn't ask a single question; his witness had done so well on her own.

On the flight back to Orlando, Adel could see the Rockies to the south and west. She thought about Watson's story and the impact it would make on a jury. *I like her,* she thought. *She'll make an excellent witness, and her story about Scarlechek's harassment is so similar to DeeDee's—and mine—and then, she was paid off. The impact of that on the case will be like a slam dunk.* Gazing south toward Arizona, her thoughts turned to Tom Peckinpah. *He should be a fantastic witness, but he's not. He doesn't come across well at all. The conversation with Cookie ... what's wrong with him?*

· · · ·

Later in May, Gonzalez took Marta DeLong's deposition, seeking to discover corroborating events between her and Scarlechek. DeLong lied systematically, professing Scarlechek's high moral character, and that he'd never done anything to her like what DeeDee and Janet Watson claimed. She acted appalled at the allegations. She testified that Janet was known to be a radical Southern Californian with loose morals. That night, DeLong received a hand-delivered envelope containing a five-figure cash bonus.

CHAPTER 91

It was late June. The melting snow in the mountains of Colorado had turned most of the state muddy. Just west of Vail, the Flakey Run Development Company had begun site clearing for a new ski slope.

"Sam!" the bulldozer operator yelled at his obstinate dog. "Get out of the way!" He always brought Sam with him, and Sam knew better, but the dog was a tough, adventurous beagle with the keenest of noses. He smelled something that excited him tremendously.

"Brooo! Sniff, snort, sniff! Brooo!" Sam stubbornly stayed with the scent despite the menacing approach of his master's dozer.

"Damn it, dog!" the operator exclaimed, as he stopped his bulky machine and dismounted, letting it rumble in idle.

Walking toward the blade, he could see that Sam was digging in the overturned dirt by a pair of uprooted trees. Sam still growled and snorted, and sent dirt flying in every direction, until he suddenly began biting and tugging at something. His teeth were clenched tight, snarling as he pulled. The operator could see it ... emerging from under the dirt with each one of Sam's pulls ... but it was too heavy for the courageous dog. It was bright green.

A human body! Oh my God! the operator thought, as he ran closer and began helping Sam.

Fear swept over him, and he looked around to be sure he was alone. The stench reached his nose, and almost knocked him off his feet. He'd never come across a human corpse in his life, and he wanted to get Sam and bolt. *Call the cops from somewhere safe, and let them deal with this,* he thought. But he knew that this responsibility had befallen upon him.

Stoically, he began to hyperventilate in order to gather his strength and courage to help the dog, and then, a horrifying inspection. He tugged with all his might with his dog by his side, and the corpse broke free, splattering mud on them as they both sat back and looked at each other in surprise, and then studied their find.

The corpse had only just begun to deteriorate in the spring thaw. He could tell that at one point it had been a very attractive female. The chills rushed through him again, as he feared that she'd come to life, or that her ghost was behind him.

Gathering his wits, yet still compelled to glance over his shoulder, he made his way back to his radio and notified the authorities. Soon enough, a sheriff's deputy arrived, then a homicide inspector and a medical examiner, and later, a TV news van.

All the while, Sam wagged his tail proudly.

CHAPTER 92

Deputy U.S. Marshal, Kevin Ingersoll watched the Denver newscast that night. The reporter on the screen asked, "Who was this woman? How did she die? Who was involved?" Ingersoll remembered his stack of communiqués on missing persons and decided to review them in the morning.

. . . .

At work the next day, one bulletin from Witness Security in the Northern District of New York caught Ingersoll's attention: it was about a young woman who frequently visited Colorado. Ingersoll called the Syracuse office and requested fingerprint and orthodontic records of the subject—one Kelly Parker. An hour later, he was at the Eagle County sheriff's office talking to the homicide investigator, Paul Walters, who'd been assigned to investigate the death of the unknown woman. The two of them set up crosscheck procedures with the medical examiner and a technician. Not much later, they had identified the body—it was Kelly Parker from New York.

Ingersoll notified his captain, who notified Witness Security in Syracuse. As usual when a federal witness is compromised, the Witness Security officer contacted the FBI, this time through the field office in Denver.

"What did the death doctor say?" the captain asked.

"She died of a cocaine-induced heart arrhythmia," Ingersoll said.

"Well, I guess *you* get to figure out why she was buried illegally at a new ski slope. Witness Security suspects a drug cartel, because it was her testimony against them that put her in witness protection in the first place."

"The ski resort developer," Ingersoll said, "disclaims any knowledge of the situation, and there's no reason to believe otherwise."

"Well, get with the Bureau and see what those boys say," the captain said. "Cooperate, and report back to me."

Ingersoll called his longtime buddy, Denver Special Agent Steve Winkle of the FBI. Due to multiple state and federal implications, and because of her identity, they agreed that Winkle, Ingersoll, and Walters would conduct a joint investigation.

Because of the way Parker's corpse was clad, the team decided to sweep area bars for leads. Ingersoll hit a dead end, but when Agent Winkle came to the Chair Lift Lounge, he discovered that Mitchell Weeks, the bartender, and Lori Salvera, the waitress, both knew her.

"Have you ever seen this woman?" he asked, showing pictures obtained from Witness Security.

"Oh, yeah, that's Carrie," Weeks said. "Take a look, Lori, isn't that her?"

"Yeah, that's Carrie," Salvera said.

"Did you know her last name?"

"No, I didn't," Weeks said.

"Me neither," Salvera said.

"How did you know her?"

"We watched her operate all the time," Salvera said. "About once every couple months, or so, she'd appear, pick up a wealthy john and then leave with him. She'd usually have two or three drinks at the bar first, chatting it up with us. We knew what she was, but the boss didn't mind, and we liked her. The boss figured she was good for business."

"Yeah," Weeks said. "She was something. Really smart, you know, and she could reel in any fish she wanted, and knew it. I saw her move in on Tom Peckinpah once, you know, the CEO of Western Town. I never thought a guy like that would go for a girl like her, but I saw them leave together."

"Tom Peckinpah!"

"Yeah, Western Town has chalets up the road, and they come here often for meetings, and shit."

Winkle gave an understanding nod.

In the meantime, Walters got in touch again with Cayhall Johnson at Witness Security in New York, who explained all he knew about Parker. Her former boyfriend, drug lord Esperanza, had threatened her and made two attempts on her life before she had been secreted away.

"So why'd she go back to turnin' tricks?" Walters asked.

"Boredom with life is often an acute problem for protected witnesses," Johnson said. "And it hit this finicky little white chick particularly hard. I mean this girl was hyper. She yearned for excitement and found it in you Denver ski bums ... or so I've heard. She was always a little wild, and she liked men and ... sensual pleasures."

Winkle, Walters, and Ingersoll considered their evidence: a hooker dead from cocaine and a witness who saw her leave a bar with a high-powered corporate executive. It wasn't difficult to determine their next move.

"It doesn't matter how rich and powerful you are, does it boys?" Winkle asked the others.

With cynicism etched in their faces, Walters and Ingersoll nodded.

CHAPTER 93

On Monday, June 29, Agent Winkle and Deputy Ingersoll flew to Phoenix to pay a visit to Western Town headquarters. Respecting jurisdictional protocol, they picked up Phoenix-based FBI agent, Brian Karnes, who escorted them to Peckinpah's office.

When the trio arrived at Peckinpah's office, Cookie Albertson stopped them. She was curious, suspicious, protective, and intimidated, all balled up into one package. Winkle was a large man with very broad shoulders and looked like a linebacker stuffed into a business suit. Karnes was small and sinewy, but seasoned and tough-looking. Ingersoll looked like her neighbors' son, though stylishly dressed. She didn't know what to think about such men visiting her boss.

"I'm sorry officers, he's in a meeting," she told them.

"Do you know how long it'll last?" Winkle asked.

"No, you never do with these things. Can I help you?" she asked, hoping to learn why they were there.

"No, I'm afraid not. We'll wait for awhile," Winkle replied. They sat down and Cookie nervously continued her work. Under normal circumstances, she'd turn away unknown visitors, calling security to escort them out if need be—but not these guys.

Peckinpah's door swung open and there he was shaking hands with a business guest. Winkle, Ingersoll, and Karnes stood instantly, but waited until the guest left before identifying themselves to Peckinpah. The color drained from Peckinpah's face upon learning their identities. The thought occurred to him that he had been dumb for not following the course suggested in his session with

Dr. Brooks—calling his lawyer and disclosing the truth. Now, the ignored problem confronted him again, refusing to go away more defiantly than a migraine headache. There was no choice now but to show them into his office.

"We're investigating the death of one of our federal witnesses," Agent Winkle explained behind closed doors. "She was discovered buried in the mountains in a remote area west of Vail, Colorado. Do you know this woman?" he asked, showing Peckinpah Kelly Parker's headshot.

Peckinpah's heart raced, as though reliving the cocaine-high that the hooker and he had shared. His eyes were riveted to the photo, part shock that he'd been tracked down, part stalling for time. *Refuse to talk,* he told himself. *Call your lawyer,* he thought. *No, that's too obvious. It'll signal guilt. Why didn't I call him before?*

"How did she die?" Peckinpah heard himself ask coldly.

"Cocaine-induced," Kevin Ingersoll said. "You know—heart arrhythmia. So, you know her? You didn't answer."

"No. I don't. I'm sorry, officers, I can't help you," Peckinpah said, as he walked to the door to show them out.

The officers looked at each other, amused. They certainly weren't ready to leave.

"I'm sorry, Mr. Peckinpah, but this won't take too long," Winkle said, indicating with his eyes. "Take a seat." For an officer formerly a linebacker, stalking a former quarterback was instinctive.

Peckinpah returned to his desk.

"Do you like to ski?" Ingersoll asked, as he and Winkle also sat down in chairs in front of Peckinpah's desk. Karnes had already made himself comfortable on the couch and began to take notes.

"Yes, I do. What's that got to—"

"Ever been to Vail?"

"Yes, we have corporate chalets there."

"Near the Carlisle Convention Center?"

"Yes."

Ingersoll and Winkle took Peckinpah through a long series of cross-fired questions about the chalets, their location, his trips to Vail, and the last one in particular. What did he do during his last visit, who was he with, who arranged the travel plans, and more. Karnes kept writing and watching.

The three officers exchanged looks when they heard Peckinpah's last trip to Vail was in January—the approximate time of Parker's death according to the medical examiner. Peckinpah could've been the last person to see her alive.

"Ever drink at the Chair Lift Lounge?" Winkle asked.

They know, Peckinpah thought. "Yes," he heard himself answer.

"But you don't know this woman?" he asked with subtle incredulity.

"No! I told you!"

"You know Mitchell Weeks the bartender at the Chair Lift?"

"Mitch? Yes, I know Mitch."

"What do you think of him?"

"Mitch?" he replied. "Oh, he's a great guy—sharp as a tack. Shouldn't be bartending, you know?"

"Think he's honest?" Winkle asked, delighted that his witness had just been endorsed by the suspect. It wasn't so much a question as a hint.

Peckinpah suddenly felt stupid and trapped. Wondering what Weeks had said about him, he immediately thought to end the conference and demand to call his lawyer.

"Am I being accused of a crime?" Peckinpah asked. It was a question he had never dreamed he'd have to ask. *So it's come to this,* he thought.

"Not yet," Winkle said. The linebacker's tone was ominous. "Are you planning on going anywhere?" he asked, sensing it was time to leave. It was time for the prosecutors and the grand jury—time for the witness to have advice of counsel.

"To Orlando, tomorrow," Peckinpah growled.

"I suggest you cancel the trip."

"I can't," Peckinpah said, hoping they'd think he'd been subpoenaed. "I'm supposed to testify in federal court."

"What kind of case?"

"It's a civil case against the company and one of our lawyers, for sexual harassment."

"What's your involvement?"

"I walked in on them ... making love. I'm testifying as to what I saw, that's all."

"Wholesome company, this Western Town," Ingersoll said to Karnes.

"Makes me want to take my kids there," Karnes said.

"What's the case style and number?" Winkle asked.

"I don't know, but Cookie can tell you."

"Where will you be staying?"

"At the Ranchero Hotel," Peckinpah said. "I have nothing to hide," he added, then feeling stupid for saying it.

"All right sir, we'll be in touch," Winkle said, confident they'd be able to track the man's every move. They got Peckinpah's hotel information from Cookie and left.

Peckinpah closed his door after they'd gone, barely keeping Cookie at bay. His first realization was that his dream life was over. He staggered to his couch and fell to his knees before it, as though it was a church pew. Holding his hands to his face, he sighed as tears escaped from his eyes. Despite his visits with Dr. Brooks, he'd been clinging to the possibility of salvage. But his lies were directly threatened now, he knew. Trying to calm himself, he crawled up onto the couch and sat.

After much deliberation, he called his personal attorney, Charles Mix. Mix and he had been together through many battles, deals, and negotiations, and they were friends. He'd know what to do.

CHAPTER 94

Charles Mix immediately ordered his long-time client to his office. Once he heard the full story, Mix became distressed.

"Tom," he said. "You need a criminal defense attorney. And you need him now."

"Who do you suggest?"

"The best criminal defense attorney I know, Mohawk Jones."

They set up a meeting that evening at Jones's office.

• • • •

Later, Peckinpah checked Thomas Mohawk Jones over when they met. Contrary to what his name suggested, Jones didn't appear at all to be flamboyant. Instead, he was strait-laced and business-like.

Peckinpah had asked Mix about Jones.

"He's tall and lean," Mix had explained. "And an exceptional middle-aged athlete—a runner. His nickname came from his high school days, I've heard, as a cross-country runner. His teammates said he could run like an Indian brave across the arid southwest; and one day, he supposedly showed for a big race with a Mohawk haircut. The name stuck."

"Is he good?"

"He's the best. He has a reputation of studying all angles of every problem, rendering calculated confidence to his positions. Like a good athlete, he always out-prepares his opponents."

Jones showed Peckinpah and Mix into his office. "What can I do for you, Mr. Peckinpah?"

"Get me out of the mess I'm in."

Jones absorbed Peckinpah's story, grasping the multifarious nature of the predicament. There were four jurisdictions involved—Arizona, Colorado, Florida, and Federal—and numerous crimes—solicitation, possession and use of cocaine, criminal negligence, felony murder, illegal interment, obstruction of justice, and perjury.

"You have a full plate," Jones said. "And I'm very concerned about the lack of time. When are you testifying again?"

"The trial begins on Wednesday," Mix said. "And it looks as though Tom will be called to testify on Thursday."

"Today's Monday—that really only gives us tomorrow and Wednesday to see what we can accomplish."

Jones had read about Peckinpah in business magazines and the Phoenix newspaper. He felt sympathy for the beleaguered CEO before him, but that would have no effect on the price of his legal retainer. This was going to take his undivided attention for the rest of the week.

"Mr. Peckinpah," he said. "I think I can help you, but it's going to be expensive. I'll need to get on this immediately and devote all my time to it, until the deal is done."

"How expensive?" Peckinpah asked.

"I'll need an initial retainer of one hundred thousand dollars. I can't know how much it will cost until I do some calling around."

"No problem," Peckinpah said. He pulled out his checkbook, wrote out the check without hesitation and handed it to Jones. "But what can you do for me?"

"I'm going to contact the U.S. District Attorneys in Phoenix and Denver," Jones said, "and the State Attorneys in Phoenix, Vail and Orlando. I'll also contact the agents and deputies. Let's see ... yes, you've given me their cards. I'm hoping we can arrange to keep you out of jail. I think because of who you are, we might be able to negotiate a deal. We may be able to obtain immunity from prosecution for you under certain circumstances. But, there's no doubt, you'll have to tell the truth."

Jones's last statement crushed Peckinpah, who still hoped for some miraculous misdirection play. Reality set in like a heavy fog.

In exchange for immunities from prosecution he'd have to disclose his lies. It was exactly what the weary CEO had foreseen on his therapist's couch.

"Will you be able to protect me?" Peckinpah asked.

"I don't know. It depends upon the agendas of each official. Phoenix will leave you alone, I'm relatively sure. The Feds are mainly interested in what happened to their witness. You're not a cold, calculating criminal. However, when you're dealing with people, you never know. Someone may get bug-eyed at the prospect of bringing down the CEO of Western Town."

Jones pulled a book from a shelf and flipped through it. "Orlando … Orange County," he said. "Vail." More flipping. "Eagle County. My guess … the State Attorneys for Orange County and Eagle County will probably leave you alone in exchange for the truth. Orlando will most likely be far more interested in your testimony about the rape of DeeDee Lane. They might also want to go after Scarlechek's extortion against you. Eagle County might wash their hands of the whole thing once the state attorney understands it all and the other jurisdictions. I'll get to work immediately. I know some of the players and I'll be able to track the others down. You're flying to Orlando tomorrow?"

"Yes."

"What airline?"

"Delta."

"Fine. I should go. Can you put me up in one of your hotels?"

"Yes. My secretary will make the arrangements. Please be careful though. She doesn't know."

"I'll call you later tonight," Jones said.

"Call Charlie, will you? I'm tired of all this. Charlie, you tell me what I have to do and I'll do it."

Jones nodded, at once wary of his new client's apparent desire to avoid reality.

. . . .

Mohawk Jones called his old friend from law school and the Justice Department thereafter, Breeland Lamar, the U.S. District Attorney in Denver. Then he called the State Attorney for Eagle County, whom Lamar knew, and finally the D.A. in Phoenix whom Jones also knew. It was too late to call Orlando, and he had no contacts there.

After explaining the details, he achieved some success. He called Mix and explained that except for Orlando, he had elicited the rudimentary form of an unusual agreement. All at Peckinpah's expense, attorneys from the three offices would fly to Orlando to receive a "proffer"—a statement by Peckinpah with questioning to follow. The interview was to be given Wednesday in exchange for immunity from criminal prosecution.

"Will you be coming to Orlando?" Jones asked Mix.

"No," Mix said. "I can't. I'll call Tom and tell him he'll have to deal with you in Orlando. He can call me if he needs to."

Jones still needed to make contact with the State Attorney in Orlando, but that would have to wait until first thing the next morning, or when he arrived.

The wheels of justice are spinning fast, Jones thought. *Hopefully we won't fishtail and crash into the sidewall.*

CHAPTER 95

Tom Peckinpah was feeling his first sense of relief in months as he drove home that night.

It's going to work out, he thought. *Jones seems to know his stuff. Charley was right to take me to him.*

He drove on, pulling up to a stoplight. The family in the car next to his recognized him. He could tell they were excited when they pointed, and then waved. Peckinpah smiled and waved back, and as the light turned green, he pulled away. *People love me,* he thought.

He pulled onto the interstate and headed for home.

I might even be able to pull it off without anyone knowing. I don't have to tell Janis yet, or even the Board. Maybe Landis ... and he'll have to tell that female lawyer. But other than that, no one needs to know. We'll settle the suit. Require confidentiality. No press. But Vail—I've got to tell Jones and Charley that no press has to be part of the deal.

He pulled out his cell phone and called Mix.

"Yeah, Tom," Mix said.

"Charley, you've got to call Jones and tell him how important confidentiality is. He's got to be sure that everyone agrees—no press. And I want them all to sign confidentiality agreements. You know, like you guys are always insisting upon in our civil suits."

"Tom, it's highly improbable that civil servants are going to—"

"Don't give me that crap, Charley. I know how persuasive you can be."

Is Tom losing it? Mix wondered. "Tom, these guys are part of the government ... Jones didn't even suggest the improbability that he could—"

333

"Charley, I know you. You're just giving me that conservative lawyer crap so you can deliver better than you promise. That's all right. I'm turning off the freeway now, so I've gotta go. Just do it. I'll call you tomorrow from Orlando."

He flipped his phone shut.

Is this some twisted form of dementia? Mix wondered. *Boy, the rich and famous have one thing in common—hubris. I better call Mohawk.*

We can do this, Peckinpah thought. *I don't have to lose it all.*

Peckinpah pulled up to the stop sign before his turn into his gated compound. His closest neighbor, a basketball star with the Suns, drove by in his Rolls.

That pompous ass, Peckinpah thought.

He pushed the clicker for his gate and rolled into his eight-car garage. The thought occurred to him to tell Janis he was late because he had to meet a board member for cocktails. Walking out, he looked over the valley and sucked in the crisp air. *It's a beautiful night,* he thought. *I've still got it.*

The view made him forget everything. He forgot about the hooker. He forgot about his crimes. He put Mix and Jones and deals he didn't understand out of his mind. And ... he forgot about Scarlechek.

. . . .

The next morning, Cookie Albertson and Tom Peckinpah pre-boarded the monstrous 767, and sat in their first class seats while others paraded past to coach.

I should have the company buy a jet for these trips, Peckinpah thought, as a young woman passed and smiled at him. *But then I'd lose touch.*

Mohawk Jones boarded soon after and stood in front of the first class cabin. His eyes caught Peckinpah's. There was a moment of acknowledgment, before Peckinpah glanced down at his Wall Street Journal and pretended to read.

Interesting, Jones thought, as he brushed by and took his seat two rows back.

Peckinpah grew melancholic with Jones looking over his shoulder. Cookie noticed his mood change and her curiosity consumed her. She leaned over close to Peckinpah and whispered, "Tom, what's going on?" Her eyes were big and sincere, telling him she knew something was terribly wrong.

Peckinpah's sigh was heavy, seeming to admit the accuracy of her inquiry. *Tell her,* he thought. *She's got to know.* But he couldn't.

He glanced behind at Jones, who was busy typing on a laptop. He whispered to Cookie, "I don't know what you mean."

His insincerity was almost comic, and Cookie tried again.

"Tom, something happened in Colorado and I believe Lou is holding it over you. And this trial with DeeDee Lane, I'll bet he did it. And the FBI yesterday? Tom? Come on! What is going on?"

Peckinpah sighed again, resignation blanketing his face.

"Cookie ... I can't talk about it. I need you to respect that."

They looked into each other's eyes, and she saw the forlorn look of a boy in trouble.

"Please, Cookie. Please."

CHAPTER 96

"I'm sorry Dave, I can't. I've got to prepare for trial," Adel said. Dave McKerrin had just offered to take her to lunch. It was Tuesday and she was still preparing for DeeDee's trial less than twenty-four hours away.

"How do you think it'll go? Have a shot at winning?"

"It depends on Peckinpah, I believe. If he holds up, we have a good chance. Gonzalez will put on DeeDee, her therapist, and the company's personnel representative regarding a merit raise and benefits DeeDee would've received. He's also planning on calling Tiyona regarding the company's lack of meaningful policies to prevent harassment. We'll call Scarlechek, Marta DeLong, and Peckinpah. DeeDee will finish in rebuttal with Janet Watson. It'll be a swearing match—DeeDee's word against Scarlechek's and Peckinpah's, and Watson's word against DeLong's. We have a motion to keep Watson's testimony out, but we'll probably lose. Watson and DeLong may neutralize each other, and so may DeeDee and Scarlechek. I think it'll depend on how the jury reacts to Peckinpah. He'll be the tie-breaker."

"How do you think he'll do?"

"I'm not sure," Adel replied. "Normally, he has great presence— the aura of real corporate power. He's handsome, tall, and fit. The jurors are bound to have heard of him. Gonzalez will have to deal with that. He lends such credence to Scarlechek's side of the story— coupled with DeeDee's admissions of prior consensual sex—it'll be tough for them to prove sexual battery, and if the jury doesn't believe that, they might not believe the harassment either. They could believe DeLong over Watson ..."

Adel halted in mid-sentence. She wondered what her own testimony might add to the mix.

"Adel?" Dave asked.

"Sorry," she said. "I lost it there for a moment."

"You sure did. You faded out."

"Sorry ... there's something strange about Peckinpah," she continued. "He came across poorly in deposition. They were relatively minor points, but Gonzalez made him look like a liar, and he may do it again. Something's not right."

"What about settlement?"

"Well, the company was desperate to settle before the case hit the media, but they took that completely out of my hands. They offered DeeDee one and a half million dollars, and she didn't take it. Wouldn't even counter unless Scarlechek was fired. Then ... once the story broke, no more settlement talks."

"What's her program?"

"She wants Scarlechek fired or it's no deal. But Scarlechek is up for company president for some strange reason, so settlement was doomed to fail."

"How'll that pretentious ass, Scarlechek, do?"

"Oh, he's a master of the show. He'll do fine."

"Well, keep 'em all straight," Dave said in parting.

The words echoed in Adel's mind. It was a simple statement—a command imparting trust in her, confidence that she'd do the right thing, and make them do it too.

Keep 'em all straight. She relished that he would say that to her, though not liking the sound of it this time. It nagged her that she wasn't going in the right direction herself. Guilt crept into her mind, which she extinguished with a single focus—keeping the case meant helping Dave.

Adel rehearsed her opening and direct examinations. She reviewed the outlines of her cross-examinations of DeeDee's therapist and Janet Watson, but something deep and yet to materialize hounded her. Slapping herself to, she was relieved that Golumbo would cross-examine DeeDee.

Later, Adel's secretary buzzed her. "It's Cookie Albertson. She says it's important."

CHAPTER 97

"DeeDee, are you sure you want to do this?" Gonzalez asked. They were in his office, going over her testimony.

"Yes." Her voice was resolute.

"But why? I'll bet we can still get them to settle, and you could be a very rich, young woman. If we go through with this, there's a significant chance that you'll lose. It doesn't make sense to throw all that away." He was concerned about his client ... and about his fee. If they settled, he'd receive one third of a very large amount. They'd already been offered one and a half million dollars and he knew he could get that amount back on the table. Going to trial and losing, on the other hand, would net nothing but more work on appeals that may or may not succeed and, even then, they'd have to go through trial a second time.

"Steve, we've gone through this before. I may be small and insignificant in the grand scheme of things. But this is my chance to stand up for what's right—for womanhood, and even mankind when you think about it. I've thought this all through and my parents are with me. We know what the risks are—you've explained them so well at every stage. I want Scarlechek fired! If that happens, I'll settle. If it doesn't, we're going to trial! We may lose, but then again, we may not. I know that puts you in a tough spot, but you have a choice to make also."

Gonzalez gazed at her with brooding eyes. He'd never seen his client get so red in the face, and he knew the issue was closed. There would be no more discussion of settlement and, she was right, he was faced with the choice of continuing as her lawyer or not. Ultimately,

338

there was always that choice. But it had been made long ago, and he knew he'd see it through no matter what.

"All right," he said. "We won't discuss it anymore. Now, let's go over your potential cross examination."

CHAPTER 98

After landing in Orlando, Mohawk Jones reached the Orange County State Attorney, Don Remington, by phone.

"I remember being informed of this four or five months ago," Remington said. "We shelved the criminal charge against Mr. Scarlechek." *The case had bad politics written all over it,* he thought.

"That's right," Jones said.

"But now you want to deliver a proffer from Thomas Peckinpah?"

"Yes. As I said, I represent him, and we are working this out with several jurisdictions."

I never cease to be amazed at this job, Remington thought. *It doesn't matter whether you're wealthy or a pauper. What matters is what you do. Tom Peckinpah admitting to perjury and obstruction of justice, and that it really was a rape. That's something that would eliminate the political fallout for the boss.*

"Will you play?" Jones asked.

"Well, as much as I'd like to teach Mr. Peckinpah a lesson, rape is far more serious. And it really won't do much good for the county to prosecute him. He'll get his, anyway. We'll agree—complete immunity for Mr. Peckinpah. I'll tell my people. It'll be Heath Robero and Ann Gentry, I'll send them to the proffer."

"Good," Jones said. "I've prepared a proposed agreement on my laptop and I'll provide it to your people on Wednesday. They're simple terms."

"Very well, Mr. Jones. You've done a good job for your client."

CHAPTER 99

Cookie Albertson and Adel Blair met Tuesday evening at the same restaurant as before, and spoke softly in a quiet booth. The same four-person racing shell that hung over the walkway loomed in Adel's line of sight.

"Adel, I just can't handle it any more," Cookie said. "I've got to do something to help Tom. I'm meddling, I know, and I may mess something up. But I need to help him for his own good. If I tell you these things, will you handle it discreetly?"

"I can promise you that I'll try as hard as I can," Adel said. "But I really don't know what we're talking about, so it's difficult to say."

"That's good enough for me."

She told Adel all she knew about Colorado and the strange photographs Scarlechek had sent. She explained Peckinpah's dislike for Scarlechek, and her amazement that Scarlechek was being considered for president.

"Sounds like blackmail," Adel remarked, leaping to the impact it could make on the trial, especially if Gonzalez found out.

"You think? That's what I thought. I mean he's been so moody since the January trip ... a completely changed person. And he's seeing a therapist now, too. But, Adel, it gets worse ... on Monday, three FBI agents came to see him."

"What about?"

"I don't know. He wouldn't say. And he's got a meeting tomorrow that he won't tell me about. And tonight, he's turned off his cell and won't answer my calls."

"I've got to see him," Adel said. "But not tonight or tomorrow.

I've still got a lot more to do for the trial and Dee Dee's witnesses will consume all day tomorrow. Tell him, I must see him tomorrow night before his testimony on Thursday. Will you do that?"

"Okay."

"We'll get to the bottom of this. Cookie, don't tell anyone about any of this."

"I haven't—only you. Adel, I'm just so worried about him. It's all so strange."

CHAPTER 100

It was Wednesday, July 1, three days before Independence Day. Nolé Reynolds and other reporters had been waiting outside the main entry to the courtroom for statements from the attorneys and litigants, but to no avail—everyone had entered through the back door. Frustrated but determined, the reporters waited in wooden pews behind a gated partition. Three television camera crews waited in the hall outside.

Aside from the reporters, several other individuals lingered, and some could be overheard speaking about the price of Western Town stock on the market.

Adel, Tiyona Morgan, Golumbo, and Scarlechek sat at the mahogany table to the left, facing the Judge's bench. Adel gazed at the wooden jury box, the witness stand and court reporter/clerk station, below the massive bench where Judge Wozynski would sit. The contemporary décor made the room impersonal and cold, as did the gray fabric on the walls.

Adel looked at Tiyona. Tiyona had been chosen with some trepidation as the company representative for trial. She didn't know much about the case, but she knew she liked DeeDee and despised Scarlechek. Her presence before the jury was important for psychological effect; and Gonzalez was going to call her to the stand anyway. Adel realized that Tiyona felt like a turncoat, to be sitting across the aisle from DeeDee. Adel understood the feeling too well.

Adel spread her files, trial notebook, legal pads, and rules of evidence and procedure in front of her. Golumbo was engaging in similar pre-trial preparations, when Gonzalez and DeeDee arrived.

They took the table to the right. Adel stole quick glances at DeeDee, who appeared determined and grave as she took her seat. *She's ready,* Adel thought.

Having relived her deposition many times, DeeDee expected worse this day before the jury. It was written all over her face. She was dressed in black, and her suit contrasted with her towhead hair. Her resolve seemed more intense than ever—yet, she was nervous.

It was DeeDee's decision that was to be tested—her desire for Scarlechek to get the axe. Gonzalez had recommended settlement, and even admitted that to Adel on one occasion. But DeeDee remained firmly disinclined. Scarlechek was a snake that lay in wait in the grass, and DeeDee demanded her day in court. She required justice and she was there to collect. If she won, the company would be compelled to let Scarlechek go.

Was it to be her day?

Scarlechek wore a dark blue pinstripe suit over his monogrammed shirt and suspenders. A white silk hanky glistened from his breast pocket. It was fake, sewn in for appearance's sake. When he first arrived, he had walked over to the bailiff and the clerk, both males, with a crocodile smile and shook their hands as though they were his family.

"How are you gentlemen, this morning?" he had said.

"Well, fine, thank you," the clerk replied. "How are you, sir?"

The serious bailiff said nothing, wondering whether he might need to arrest someone to maintain decorum in this trial.

"Well, I tell you, I was almost run over on my way here by a tourist looking for the theme parks. I could just tell, you know?"

"Don't I," the clerk said.

Scarlechek looked down at the good-looking court reporter adjusting her machine.

"Hello, there," he said to her, smiling widely. "You look very nice today. Will you show me how that thing works? I've always wondered."

"I'm sorry, I don't really have time—"

"Oh, of course not," Scarlechek said. "I'd better go sit down and get out of the way."

When he sat, he leaned over and whispered to Adel, "After the trial, I want to get together with you and talk."

It hasn't occurred to him that he could lose, Adel realized.

"Mehhmp! Mehhmp!" the buzzer rang.

"All rise," the bailiff commanded, as the judge entered with her law books and legal pad. The drama was about to begin.

"Good morning, ladies and gentlemen," Judge Wozynski said. A chorus responded. The judge continued, "We are here today on a very serious matter—DeeDee T. Lane verses Western Town Production Company and Louis Victor Scarlechek, case number CIV 555 1991—a real-life problem among real people. I will expect everyone here to give this procedure the respect and dignity it deserves."

Which means, don't touch her precious bench, Golumbo thought.

"Now, are there any preliminary matters we must discuss before we bring in the venire?" the judge asked.

"Yes, Your Honor," Adel proclaimed as she stood, still disturbed by Scarlechek's earlier message. "The defense has filed a motion *in limine* to prevent the plaintiff from in any way mentioning anything in the presence of the jury about Janet Watson and what, if anything, happened between her and Mr. Scarlechek."

"Well, I've seen the motion and I'll hear argument, but of course you realize that your motion completely eliminates Ms. Watson as a witness," the judge stated.

"Yes, Your Honor," Adel replied. *That is the point,* she thought, knowing the judge wouldn't do it.

"Go ahead, then."

"Your Honor, we've filed a memorandum on the subject, giving argument and citing cases in detail—"

"I read it this morning," the judge interrupted.

"Well, our objection to such evidence is two-fold. It's not relevant, and even if it is relevant, it should be excluded because it will have the effect of being highly prejudicial. The jury will potentially infer from what Ms. Watson says, that what happened to DeeDee must be true because it happened before—"

"Well, Ms. Blair, it's interesting, the way you put that ... but let me stop you right there. The defense is not conceding that what Ms. Watson says is true. Is it?"

"No, Ma'am."

"So you're not relinquishing your right to cross examine her or put on your own evidence on the matter, correct?"

"That's correct, Your Honor."

"So the jury will simply weigh Ms. Watson's testimony against Mr. Scarlechek's, consider the cross examination, and decide whom they believe, correct?"

Adel knew she'd already lost. "Correct," she responded.

"So it's not really a question of prejudice—it's a question of relevance. I don't buy your argument that it's not relevant. Your argument is simply that what happened to Ms. Watson has no relation to what allegedly happened to Ms. Lane. Well, if true, I think it would. It would tend to prove the plaintiff's negligent entrustment case—the dog-bite, Ms. Blair, remember? And it would tend to prove the hostile atmosphere on the plaintiff's harassment case. It would tend to prove motive, plan, or intent under Rule 404(b). In fact, Mr. Gonzalez has cited precedent from the Eleventh Circuit right on point. Moreover, Ms. Blair, I'm aware of other case law holding that the harassment of other women is relevant to proving a hostile environment. I'm sorry, but your motion *in limine* is denied."

The judge stopped speaking, daring Adel and Golumbo to say anything further.

"Now, are there any other preliminary matters before we begin?" she asked.

"No, Your Honor—the plaintiff is ready," Gonzalez said, standing quickly.

"The defense is ready, Your Honor," Adel said.

She sat there resigned—knowing the judge's ruling was correct, knowing Watson's testimony was directly relevant, and knowing that her testimony, too, would be relevant.

"Bailiff, bring in the venire," Judge Wozynski commanded.

The bailiff exited a side door to the right, and when he returned, he held open the door and commanded all to rise for the potential jurors. Even the judge rose. Twenty-six people from various walks of life entered and sat down in the courtroom.

From a small podium in front of her bench, the judge smiled and bid them good morning. After introducing the parties and their lawyers, she explained the process, and the role they'd play.

"In Latin," the judge said, "*voir dire* means literally to see and to speak. The process is where the lawyers have the opportunity to question you, as members of the venire, in order to select a panel of fair and impartial jurors. I'm going to ask some basic questions to each of you, and then the lawyers will have their turns."

She conducted her initial questioning. Then it was Gonzalez's turn.

"Ladies and gentlemen, thank you so much for your time. Ms. Lane and I appreciate so much how busy you are and what an imposition it is to take time away from your busy schedules to come hear and resolve a dispute among strangers. However, people do have disputes, and this is our system; and, frankly, I think it's the best system. Because in our jury system, we rely on common sense—the common sense of people like you. I love *voir dire*, because it's our opportunity to get to know you." He paused and looked over the group.

"For example, how many of you here own Western Town stock?"

A preppy woman raised her hand. Gonzalez glanced at his chart of names. "Ah ... Ms. Robinson, you own Western Town stock?"

"Yes," she said. "I do."

"Well, Ma'am, do you think that you can decide this case based on the evidence presented despite your ownership of stock in the company?"

"Will this case cause the company to go under?" she asked, smiling.

Gonzalez laughed, as did most others in the room. "No, ma'am, I'm sure your investment is safe."

"Well, then, yes, I can," she said.

Later, Gonzalez turned to the discussion to the pre-eminence of the witnesses against DeeDee—the executive vice president of the legal department, and the CEO of the company.

"Does any one think you would ascribe more weight to the testimony of such witnesses simply because of their position or fame?" he asked.

The group glanced at each other, and no one responded affirmatively.

"My client is only a secretary," Gonzalez said. "Can you decide the case based on the evidence, regardless of the status or position of the witnesses?"

Most in the group nodded as expected.

Gonzalez picked out Mr. Smith, an elderly man who hadn't responded. "Mr. Smith, can you?"

"Yes," he said. "I can."

Gonzalez didn't like the body language, and made a note. Then he made a mistake.

"Ladies and Gentlemen," he said, "as you know, this is a sexual harassment case. My client, Ms. DeeDee Lane, claims that she was sexually harassed and battered—raped by Mr. Scarlechek—and that Mr. Scarlechek and Western Town are liable under the law. Now, as you can see, Western Town has two representatives at counsel table—both women," his voice lingered as he gestured to Adel and Tiyona. "Prominent women, I might add."

Adel and Golumbo both stifled impulses to object. This was improper *voir dire*. Gonzalez was not seeking information from the venire, he was advocating. But they didn't object, realizing at once how silly it would appear if they stood and objected to his statement that they were prominent.

Gonzalez continued. "Now, do you believe that you can decide this case based on the evidence, as opposed to what the lawyers say?" He changed the focus to "lawyers," including him, because he couldn't tell the venire to ignore only Adel. In so doing, he implied that Tiyona was a lawyer.

Adel stood and said with a hint of a smile, "Your Honor, I object—I want the jury to listen to me." The courtroom broke out in laughter, venting its tension. Gonzalez became embarrassed. He realized that all he could do was laugh at himself. "Excuse me, ladies and gentlemen," he said, smiling. "What I meant to ask was whether you can decide the case based on the evidence, regardless of the psychological effect of the presence of Ms. Blair and Ms. Morgan at the defense table. Can you?"

The members all nodded, still smiling but stealing glances at both women.

By the time Adel inquired of the panel after Golumbo's turn, the venire was primed to cling to her every word, a tendency compounded by her appearance. Gonzalez watched as Adel approached the jurors with her questions like a person cozying up to a warm fireplace. He realized then the breadth of his mistake. The defense had jumped to an early lead in the race.

After *voir dire*, the parties exercised peremptory challenges. Golumbo and Adel played the game well, eliminating just enough women but retaining a conservative young lady. They believed Gonzalez would want this woman off, and when it came to his last challenge they guessed he'd remove her. They guessed correctly, and welcomed the replacement, Mr. Smith. It worked beautifully, and Golumbo and Adel ended up with a favorable panel: seven men, five women, and a male alternate. The defense increased its lead.

"Congratulations," the judge said to the jury. "You've been selected to serve as jurors in this case. Now we come to the time in the trial when the lawyers are allowed to tell you what they think the evidence will show. Mr. Gonzalez?"

Gonzalez stood. "Yes, thank you, Your Honor," he said, returning to the podium. Gonzalez explained DeeDee's testimony and damages to the jury, then he paused. "Ladies and Gentlemen," he finally continued. "It's not only DeeDee Lane that Mr. Scarlechek has done this to. We will call Ms. Janet Watson, Mr. Scarlechek's former administrative assistant, and her testimony will show you that Mr. Scarlechek imposed the same unwelcome behavior on her, using the same method. We will prove to you that Mr. Scarlechek is an unrepentant, repeat harasser, and that he sexually harassed and raped DeeDee Lane."

Adel gave her opening statement for the defense. "There are no witnesses to the alleged harassment," she said. "The alleged rape *was* witnessed by the CEO of the company, no less, and he'll tell you it was *not* rape. He will testify that Ms. Lane admitted having consensual sexual relations with Mr. Scarlechek for months. As for Ms. Watson, the evidence will show that Mr. Scarlechek has a very different version of what happened, and there was never any lawsuit or judicial finding of the truth of those allegations. The current administrative assistant of Mr. Scarlechek, Marta DeLong, will testify that nothing of the sort ever happened to her."

What Adel stated next stung DeeDee deep inside. "Ladies and gentlemen of the jury," she said. "The evidence will show that DeeDee Lane and Mr. Scarlechek had consensual sex for some time … an affair. It's very easy, after the fact, to complain that it was all unwelcome, and that one session was a rape, for monetary gain. We believe the evidence will show this matter is all contrived."

It stung Adel as well.

CHAPTER 101

Gonzalez called his first witness, DeeDee Lane. She approached the witness box with apprehension, as she felt the jurors' scrutiny.

"DeeDee," Gonzalez said casually, wanting to personalize her to the jury. "Please state your name for the record."

"DeeDee Theresa Lane," she said. She was a bundle of nerves, and she was amazed that sound came out of her voice box.

"DeeDee, tell the jury about your long-time desire to become a legal secretary."

She explained how she'd visited Western Town with her parents when she was young, and it was then that she had decided she wanted to work there when she grew up.

"In school," she said. "I focused on secretarial course work and became proficient with computers and word processing."

"DeeDee," Gonzalez said. "Tell the jury about your break away from Iowa."

"I wanted to be my own person," she said. "That's all. I knew that I had to get away, and I had always wanted to work at Western Town, anyway. So I came with hopes of landing my dream job in Legal. When I got it, I couldn't wait to send news to my family and friends. I was making it on my own, away from them, and I hoped they'd be happy for me."

It was difficult for Adel to assess how DeeDee was coming across to the jury. She seemed bitter, tainted like a rose singed by the sun, and Adel thought it might put the jury off. But then DeeDee described Scarlechek's first approach, and Adel saw the jury grow mesmerized with DeeDee's explanation of Scarlechek's offers and threats, her dilemma and eventual submission.

Gonzalez focused on the issue of "unwelcomeness" after that. He asked, "Now, Ms. Lane, although you consented—in the sense that Mr. Scarlechek didn't rape you—did you let Mr. Scarlechek know his advances were unwelcome by you?"

"Yes, I did. The second time he called me to his office I told him 'No,' and that I didn't want it to happen. That's when he threatened me."

"What exactly did he say?"

"He told me I could kiss my job goodbye and that he'd be watching for my next review, implying that he'd fire me."

"So you consented?"

"Yes, I did."

"How did that make you feel?"

"Very small and insignificant, like a plaything."

"Did your feelings change?"

"Yes, I grew depressed. I hated myself for giving in to his demands. I despised him even more. I despised work. To me, it became a bastion of evil, where all my dreams were destroyed."

"Ms. Lane, at some point did you decide you would not allow Mr. Scarlechek any more sexual episodes?"

"Yes, I did."

"After how many times?"

"Six."

"Did you welcome or encourage any of those?"

"No."

"Did you let him know they were unwelcome?"

"Yes, but he forced me. If I made any attempt to stop him, he'd threaten me."

"To bring you back in line?"

"Objection, Your Honor, calls for speculation," Adel blurted, rising to her feet.

"Sustained," Judge Wozynski announced.

"Did Mr. Scarlechek ever tell you why he threatened you?" Gonzalez asked, approaching the question differently.

"Yes, he did."

"What did he say?"

"He told me I needed to learn the ways of the world, and that he wasn't used to having to do that much talking about it. Then, he threatened my job."

"What happened, Ms. Lane, which caused you to decide not to allow him to take sexual advantage of you any more, even though he threatened your job?"

"Well, in February my folks came from Iowa for a visit. I was showing them around when we ran into Mr. Scarlechek leaving a restaurant."

"Where was that?"

"At the La Cocina restaurant at the Ranchero Hotel."

"Was Mr. Scarlechek with anyone?"

"Yes ... Ms. Blair," she said. The jurors all looked to Adel, digesting this new information, synapses bursting with electrical activity.

"What happened?"

"Well, I felt so embarrassed and ashamed in front of my parents that later I decided I couldn't do that to them. I couldn't allow him to take advantage of me any longer. I decided—no more sex—even if it meant losing my job."

"What happened next?"

"Well, it'd been awhile since we had any contact. It was the day of the Sorenson case settlement—"

"Objection. Your Honor, no mention should be made of other cases that have nothing to do with this case," Adel said, hoping not to focus too much attention on the matter.

"Your Honor, it's just part of what happened that day—the day of the rape," Gonzalez said.

"Were you involved in that case, Ms. Lane?" the judge asked.

"No, Ma'am."

"Then let's explain what happened to you without any further mention of this other case, whatever it may be."

"Yes, Your Honor."

"Ladies and gentlemen, I'm instructing you to disregard any mention of this other case. We have no idea what it was about and it's not relevant. This is, after all, a legal department. They no doubt handle many cases."

Several of the jury members nodded while others glanced at one another. Adel cringed, realizing this was perfect for Gonzalez. The judge had instructed the jury to forget the purple cow—something no one forgets.

"Ms. Lane, what happened during your next contact with Mr. Scarlechek?" Gonzalez continued his direct.

"Well, it was Friday night, March 6. I was working late, aiding the production of documents ... May I say this? ... In a different case, a construction case." DeeDee cringed, expecting an objection, but it didn't come. There was an objection about mention of the Sorenson case, but none about the construction case. Gonzalez hoped the jury noticed and wondered why.

DeeDee continued, "The lawyers in that case were eager to return to their homes in Atlanta, so they wanted to stay late to look at all the documents we were producing and be done with it. So I had to stay with them. It was about eight forty when I packed up a box of documents and carried it back up to my office for safekeeping. That's when Mr. Scarlechek startled me. He ordered me to come to his office to take an urgent letter he had to fax to Mr. Peckinpah."

"But, Ms. Lane, wasn't Mr. Peckinpah in town?" Gonzalez interrupted, wanting to defuse this point from the cross-examination.

"Yes, he was. But I didn't know that then."

"Then what happened?"

"Well, I told Mr. Scarlechek that I wouldn't give him sex anymore. He immediately became very cross, and yelled at me to get my pad. He told me it was urgent. But everything is urgent to him—"

"Objection!" Golumbo said.

"Sustained. Ms. Lane, please try to avoid speculation about Mr. Scarlechek," the judge said.

"What happened next?" Gonzalez asked.

"Well, I got my steno pad and walked down the hall to his office. The lights were already dimmed, so I brightened them ... once again to let him know nothing was going to happen. Then I went in and sat in a chair in front of his desk because I didn't want to go anywhere near his couch. But he dimmed the lights, in spite of what I had said.

So I yelled 'No!' because then I knew for sure what he intended. I started to leave, but ..." She began to stagger her words, stuttering a bit. "He grabbed me ... and ... he threw me down on the couch ... and he raped me! He raped me!" she repeated, outstretching her arm and thrusting her finger at Scarlechek.

A hush fell over the courtroom as DeeDee wept. It was exactly the drama Gonzalez wanted. He turned to the women jurors and saw them leaning forward in their chairs with widened eyes.

"How did he do it?" Gonzalez asked.

"He ... he pinned my arms over me with his hand ... then ... he tore my blouse open and grabbed my bra. He shoved it up to my neck and grabbed my breasts. Then, he held my wrists with both hands, because I almost wriggled my hands free of his left hand. And then he bit my ... nipple ... very hard, and it began to bleed."

She was weeping again, sobbing intermittently. The jury was riveted and the women were horrified.

"Then, what happened?"

"He took himself out of his pants and pulled up my skirt. But I had on pantyhose, and he couldn't get them off."

"Why not?"

"I was able to contract my muscles in a way that he couldn't."

"You were resisting?"

"Yes, as best I could."

"So, what did he do?"

"He p-pulled out a ... pocket knife and threatened me with it. He told me to let him pull off my pantyhose."

"How did you feel then?"

"I was very scared seeing that knife. I screamed one last time. But I was so tired from fighting him. I remembered women's group discussions where they said not to resist, because you'll get hurt or worse yet, even killed. So I didn't—I couldn't any longer. The main thing was to stay alive."

"What happened next?"

"He pulled down my pantyhose and panties, and he penetrated me with his penis." She stated it coldly, almost as though she were not sitting at the witness stand, not even in the room. The jury watched, enthralled with her tale—men and women alike.

"Then what happened?"

"Well, all of a sudden, Mr. Peckinpah came in the office and asked what the hell was going on."

"Now, let's go back for a second," Gonzalez said. "Had you been screaming throughout?"

"Yes … until he pulled out the knife. When he did, I remember screaming one last time, as loud as I could, and then I knew to not scream or resist any longer."

"How did you know that?"

"I had heard it, you know, on Oprah or some show like that."

"All right, what happened next when Mr. Peckinpah came in?"

"Well, I yelled 'Help,' and 'He's raping me,' and then Mr. Scarlechek lied, and said we were playing games."

"Games? You mean like sexual games?" Gonzalez asked, wanting to make it clear to the jury.

"Yes."

"And what did you say?"

"I said it was no game, and that I wanted him out of me. I yelled in frustration, 'He's still in me!'"

"And what did Mr. Peckinpah say?"

"He said, 'Lou, this doesn't look like a game to me.' Then Mr. Scarlechek finally got off me, and told Mr. Peckinpah we had been having sex together for months. Then, Mr. Peckinpah said he was calling the police—it was like he believed me—"

"Objection! Move to strike!" Golumbo yelled.

"Granted. Ladies and gentlemen, you are instructed to ignore Ms. Lane's statements about what Mr. Peckinpah might have believed."

"How did he act?" Gonzalez said.

"He acted very mad at Mr. Scarlechek and said, 'I'm calling the police'."

"Then what happened?"

"Mr. Scarlechek said he wouldn't do that if he were Mr. Peckinpah. And then Mr. Peckinpah seemed to change. He turned on me. And he asked me if it was true that we had been having sex before."

"How did you feel then?"

"I got the distinct impression that no matter what I said, he wouldn't believe me. I admitted the truth about the prior incidents and I got out of there. I went home."

"What happened next?"

"I took a shower and just sat for awhile in my shower—crying and thinking. Finally, I got dressed and called you. I decided to fight this, and I knew that I should report the rape promptly. I wanted to take action before I changed my mind."

"How did you hear of me?"

"Objection. Relevancy." Adel said, knowing where Gonzalez was going.

"Mr. Gonzalez?" the judge asked, wondering why the question mattered.

"I'll withdraw the question, Your Honor," Gonzalez said. He had wanted to link the case to the Sorenson case once again.

"Ms. Lane, what happened next?" he asked.

"Mr. Golumbo called me that very night, and—"

"Objection, Your Honor ... Your Honor, may we approach the bench?" Golumbo asked, having learned his lesson well.

"Yes, you may," Judge Wozynski answered.

When the attorneys converged in front of the bench, Golumbo quietly said, "Your Honor, I was hired by Mr. Scarlechek that night and given instructions to settle the case at that time. I called Ms. Lane and then went over to her apartment and attempted to negotiate a settlement. All this should not be mentioned in front of the jury because settlement discussions are not admissible under the rules of evidence. It might lead to an impermissible inference of guilt just because of the settlement offers."

"Yes ... it might," Judge Wozynski said, enjoying a moment of sarcasm. "Is there another reason why testimony about Mr. Golumbo is relevant?" she asked Gonzalez.

"Your Honor, we are just trying to prove what happened that night," Gonzalez said, knowing he wouldn't get away with it.

"Mr. Gonzalez, you and the witness are instructed to avoid any discussion about Mr. Golumbo that night," the judge admonished.

"Thank you, Your Honor," Golumbo said.

Gonzalez next led DeeDee to talk about her emotional distress and damages.

At one point she burst into tears. "I felt like a cheap piece of meat! He made me feel insignificant! I hated myself and everyone else. I felt like I could die and no one would care. I felt that there was no beauty or goodness in the world and that there was no reason to live. This wasn't what I expected out of life, and I didn't want to go through another forty or fifty years of it. All because I wasn't allowed to pursue my own dream to work hard as a legal secretary and be rewarded accordingly. I just wanted to earn my right to feel good about myself. It was all stolen from me! ... Robbed!"

She began sobbing as a hush fell over the courtroom. It was an eloquent silence—thick, and pounding everyone's senses.

Judge Wozynski ordered a break for lunch.

CHAPTER 102

The proceeding reconvened two hours later for DeeDee's cross-examination.

Gentle at first, Golumbo focused on little details, seeking to lull DeeDee to sleep. He had realized that DeeDee had evoked a tremendous amount of sympathy and that any immediate attack wouldn't be well received. He waded through less consequential questions until the right time.

"Now, Ms. Lane," Golumbo said. "You mentioned on direct that you had six sexual encounters with Mr. Scarlechek before the alleged rape, correct?"

"Yes."

"And each of these times you engaged in full sexual intercourse, correct?"

"Yes."

"And you don't claim that any of these occasions constituted a rape, do you?" He fired the questions rapidly.

"No."

"So, therefore Ms. Lane, each of these occasions constituted sexual conduct between two consenting adults, correct?"

"Yes, I suppose so," DeeDee said, remembering her deposition.

"Thank you, Ms. Lane," Golumbo said, emphasizing to the jury how important that was. Then he held up the transcript of her deposition for everyone to see, and he looked at it. "And, Ms. Lane," he continued, "you believe that sexual conduct between two unmarried, responsible adults is okay, don't you?"

DeeDee thought about her former boyfriend, Dirk. His face appeared in her mind, but suddenly and inexplicably, his face turned into Scarlechek's. It was irreverent and nasty, and she was horrified. Her emotional defenses were weakening like the walls of a fort under bombardment.

"Ms. Lane?" she heard Golumbo's voice. Her hesitation looked bad.

"Yes, I do," she finally admitted, gathering herself. A few of the more conservative jurors shifted in their seats.

"Thank you, Ms. Lane. So, you believed that the six sexual episodes between you and Mr. Scarlechek were okay too, didn't you?"

"No, I didn't! He required it from me! That's not okay!"

"Well, you gave him what he wanted six times, didn't you?"

"Apparently so," she said, as tears began to flow.

"And you testified earlier that you let him know that these six occasions were unwelcome, correct?"

"Yes, I did."

"All right, on the second occasion of your having sex with him, what exactly did you say to him, to let him know it was unwelcome?"

DeeDee paused. The question shocked her. She realized that she hadn't said anything of the sort on the second occasion. Tired, emotional, and now she was suddenly scared.

"Ms. Lane, tell us!" Golumbo raised his voice. "We are waiting!"

DeeDee rolled her head back. She was so weary. Staring out the window, she couldn't believe this was happening.

"You can't tell us, can you Ms. Lane?" Golumbo hammered, knowing he was scoring.

Still she said nothing, wishing she wasn't there.

"And about the third occasion ... you can't tell us what you said to him to let him know it was unwelcome then, either, can you?"

Scarlechek leaned forward in his chair, relishing the moment.

Still DeeDee was silent.

"And the fourth occasion, Ms. Lane? The fifth and sixth occasions, Ms. Lane?"

The challenge, DeeDee heard a voice from deep within—meet the challenge. She turned to Scarlechek, who was almost drooling in his chair. She turned to Adel, and saw her again as a vision of strength, even though Adel opposed her. *Her eyes.* Adel was with her, rooting her on, silently with her. *Answer the question. There is an answer.*

"Mr. Golumbo," DeeDee said with refreshed power, "as I said before, Mr. Scarlechek required it. He told me the first time that I had to do it because it was the big time, with big time rules. He told me he expected it, and wasn't used to having to talk about it so much. He implied that he'd fire me if I didn't give in. That all happened during the first encounter. I told him 'no,' but he ignored it. Nothing he or I said, or didn't say, after that changed that. He required it. I didn't say anything later, because he would fire me if I did. He abused his power. There! Does that answer your question?"

Gonzalez smiled. Adel wanted to smile too, but suppressed it. Golumbo cowered, and some of the jurors sighed with relief. DeeDee had come through.

Golumbo tried to recover by changing the topic. He turned to the predictable slant and raised the "what did you expect" argument from hotel room rape cases. But there was a major difference and DeeDee remained strong-minded. She said, "Mr. Golumbo ... he was my boss. I went with him because he told me to! I refuse to take responsibility for being raped under those circumstances, or any other circumstances."

Golumbo pressed on, getting nowhere, until he eventually sat down.

Gonzalez proudly announced, "No redirect, Your Honor." His witness had done just fine.

CHAPTER 103

DeeDee bravely stood up for herself on one level of the court-house, while Peckinpah, the powerful CEO, defended himself just two floors below Judge Wozynski's courtroom. As DeeDee's cross-examination began, the parties gathered for Tom Peckinpah's proffer. In that room were Mohawk Jones and Peckinpah; Agent Winkle and Deputy Ingersoll; Assistant U.S. District Attorney, Alexa Montgomery from Denver; Assistant U.S. District Attorney Clint Matson from Phoenix; along with Deputy Edwards, Ann Gentry and Heath Robero.

Jones spoke first. "I want everyone in the room to state your name and where you're from, starting with you, please." He pointed to Deputy Edwards.

When complete, Jones spoke again, "Now, each one of you has received a letter agreement from me, agreeing to the ground rules for this discussion. I take it no one wants to rescind or change those, and we still have agreement. Anyone disagree?"

No one answered.

"Good. Now, my client has prepared a written statement, which I will now read on his behalf. After that we will answer further questions. I am passing out copies of the statement now. It's been signed and notarized."

Jones read the statement aloud. It disclosed the truth—all that happened with Kelly Parker in Vail, Scarlechek's subsequent extortion, and that Peckinpah believed the sexual encounter he had observed appeared to be rape, but Scarlechek had threatened to expose

Peckinpah, so he lied to Deputy Edwards and in deposition. The statement also admitted lies to Agent Winkle and Deputy Ingersoll.

Peckinpah fidgeted in his chair, overcome by anxiety, as Jones read the lengthy statement. As he looked around the room watching the various attorneys and officers, they suddenly appeared faceless. He felt ashamed like never before, and it frightened him to think that this was just the beginning. His family and friends still didn't know. The public still didn't know. To them all he was still a king. He was still the virile ex-football star and paragon of corporate America, idolized by millions—capable of no wrong.

He barely managed to answer the questions after the reading. As the afternoon dragged on he became more and more depressed, overcome by defeat. He was bitterly disappointed as he entered the realm of the dishonored and disrespected. His rich and famous life-style was being swept away like a wisp of wind through his hand.

The attendees were pleased as the proffer concluded by the end of the business day. They left for the evening, each with new direction, especially Ann Gentry and Heath Robero. Planning to discuss the matter first with Remington, they assumed criminal charges against Scarlechek would be their task the very next day.

Peckinpah struggled to drive himself back to the Ranchero Hotel. He lay down on his plush bed and stared at the elaborate ceiling. He thought about calling his wife, but couldn't bring himself to do it.

CHAPTER 104

That evening, Adel Blair still had not been informed of Peckinpah's revelations. She knocked on his door and entered his suite.

She confronted him with what she'd discussed with Cookie. "Tom, I'm worried that you're being blackmailed and, as a result, you lied in deposition," she said. "I think Scarlechek raped DeeDee that night, and I think you know it."

Her forceful words jolted him. He staggered.

"No. It's not true," Peckinpah said, his face covered with bored denial. "I don't know what you're talking about. Now, if you'll excuse me. I've got to go over some faxes. I'm too busy for this nonsense." He moved to the door to show her out.

Adel stared at him, studying his strange expression. He was looking through her as though she weren't even there, yet ordering her to leave. His gaze was fixed and his eyes were glassy. Adel sensed that something was dreadfully wrong as she walked to the door.

"Tom," she said before leaving, "if you lie on the stand tomorrow, I'll immediately move to withdraw."

Peckinpah stared at the closed door after she left. After thirty seconds, he sprang to life and began pacing about his room, agitated, his hands shaking violently. He fidgeted with his faxes and muttered about board meetings. Turning to his coffee table and flipping through business magazines, he noticed one cover photo showing him stepping off a helicopter.

"That's me!" He laughed, out of control.

Then, in an instant he was back to his faxes, the papers quivering in his tremulous hands.

"I have to go over my faxes," he said to no one.

CHAPTER 105

Adel needed the advice of her mentor, so she called Dave McKerrin and explained the situation, including Peckinpah's strange behavior.

"I know we have an ethical duty to our client," Adel said. "Western Town."

"Yes, but as officers of the court," Dave replied, "there's an overriding obligation to justice, and avoiding fraud on the court. We are prohibited from knowingly participating in the elicitation of false testimony."

"But there's the rub," Adel said. "I have no real proof that Peckinpah is lying, only a very strong suspicion." She didn't know that messages had been left with her secretary by Mohawk Jones throughout the afternoon.

"Dave, I'm so sorry about all this. I don't know how I let myself become involved in this."

"Adel, that's a question for another time," Dave said. "I think you've learned a valuable lesson. We have to focus on our legal ethics, now. There's little choice at this point. I think you'll just have to go tomorrow and be very watchful and careful. If something you know to be false comes out, ask for a recess and withdraw."

CHAPTER 106

On the second day of trial, Gonzalez rested DeeDee's case. The defense made a perfunctory motion to the judge to direct a verdict, arguing that DeeDee had not met her technical burdens. But Judge Wozynski quickly denied the motion, having no intention of taking the case from the jury.

The defense started their case with Louis Victor Scarlechek.

Scarlechek was stately in his double-breasted suit as he flipped his hair and walked to the witness stand.

"I do," he said, smiling as though it was a matter of course after the clerk administered the oath to tell the truth.

"I accept full responsibility for our affair," he testified later. "However, it happened at a vulnerable time for me."

"How so?" Golumbo asked.

"Well, unfortunately, my wife and I were considering separation at the time."

"Why?"

"I found out ..."

He paused, feigning embarrassment, his eyes downcast to his Italian shoes.

"Yes?" Golumbo said.

"My ... my wife had been having an affair ... with a young water ski instructor at the Ranchero Hotel."

He looked over to the jury, holding onto a serious demeanor, while enjoying that they were believing his lie.

"How did that make you feel?" Golumbo asked.

"I was crushed … shocked … betrayed. I had been working so hard for our future … and I found that she …"

He paused again. A slight quiver in his voice hinted at tears. He covered his eyes with his right hand—a practiced move. Then he changed direction.

"And DeeDee was so vibrant and interested in me. Not like my wife who wanted only … DeeDee wanted me—she made that clear. Every day she acted cute and flirtatious. And … the way she dressed."

Several of the jurors were nodding slightly, wanting him to fill in the blanks.

"Did you try to resist this seduction?" Golumbo asked, slipping in a leading question.

"Yes. I knew it wasn't right. But she was always there, always doting on me. And I was so forlorn over my wife—finally, I gave in."

"Did you ever do anything with Ms. Lane that was unwelcome by her?"

"Oh no, of course not. She invited it all … constantly, in fact. At one point she asked me to divorce my wife. She became rather persistent about it, too."

"Did you ever rape DeeDee Lane?" Golumbo asked.

Scarlechek laughed. "No," he said coolly, "we were making love, as we had done many times before. She admitted that yesterday. Just ask Tom Peckinpah, he'll tell you."

"Your Honor!" Gonzalez yelled, leaping to his feet.

"Ladies and gentlemen of the jury," Judge Wozynski said without hesitation. "I'm striking Mr. Scarlechek's last comment from the record. You are to pay no attention to Mr. Scarlechek's speculation about what Mr. Peckinpah may say."

Again, the purple cow, Adel thought, *this time for us. But what will* he *say?*

Smiling, Golumbo resumed. "Now, did you and Ms. Lane discuss anything regarding your relationship that night?"

"Yes. I told her we couldn't do it anymore. I told her my wife and I were trying to work it out."

"Was she upset?"

"Yes ... very. Actually more mad, than hurt, it seemed. But then she changed, and she asked me to make love to her one last time."

"Do you believe she's doing all this because you jilted her?" Golumbo asked. The pace of his delivery was fast, hoping to get away with it.

"Objection, Your Honor," Gonzalez blurted.

"Sustained!" Judge Wozynski said before Gonzalez even could state his grounds.

"Withdrawn," Golumbo said, having planted the idea. "No further questions."

On cross, Gonzalez couldn't crack Scarlechek's facade. *Trials are like football games,* Gonzalez thought. *When it was our turn to present evidence, it went well, like moving the ball down the field for a touchdown. But just because we scored, the game's not over. The other side has a chance to carry the ball, an opportunity to present its evidence. Scarlechek has moved the ball down the field and scored.*

Marta DeLong testified next for the defense, and she also lied, bringing the defense closer to victory. *The ease at which I can fool people is amazing,* DeLong thought as she stepped down from the stand. She was smug, and wondering how she'd spend the fat wad of green in the nice brown envelope she'd been given the night before.

The defense witnesses had been crisp, sharp, and apparently forthright. There was confusion on the faces of some of the jurors, and one of them even took a long, inquisitive stare at DeeDee. Adel was convinced that she'd been correct all along, and that Peckinpah was going to be the key. If he made a strong showing, it might be enough to overcome the final witness for DeeDee, Janet Watson. *But what will he say? And will it be the truth?*

Scarlechek senses it, too, Adel thought. *His charade swayed the jury, and it sickens me. Until today, I've never* wanted *to lose a trial in my career.*

As the judge spoke about the timing of the lunch break, Steve Gonzalez also thought about Mr. Peckinpah. Intending to sit right where he was through lunch and practice his approaches to the man, he knew his cross would be crucial. Possessing weapons from Peckinpah's deposition, it had to be done just right or it wouldn't come across well to the jury. Peckinpah would be no ordinary man in their eyes. This was the critical time for Gonzalez; he knew he had to shine.

DeeDee appeared to be listening to the judge, but she wasn't. Replaying her testimony, she was glad it was over. Pride welled up in her, and she caught herself breathing deeply. She didn't know what psychological affects this or that witness had on the jury. But, by God, she had told her story, in a forum where they cared. She felt catharsis.

But something nagged at her—Scarlechek was such a masterful liar. She thought also about Tom Peckinpah's status and suddenly felt diminished. How could she ever prevail over these men? Who would believe her? She felt an urge to pray, and found herself asking God for someone to rescue her, like the mockingbird that had saved the ducklings.

CHAPTER 107

Lunch was over, and it was time for Tom Peckinpah's testimony. It was to be the final thrust from the defense, the final sweeping punch from the rich and powerful, to snuff out the lowly and weak. Adel Blair was to extract the telling testimony with the EEO manager, Tiyona Morgan, at her table.

DeeDee sat quietly in her chair. Gonzalez shifted nervously, having lost all his earlier arrogance. At last, the bailiff escorted Peckinpah from the witness room. Adel stood ready at the podium.

Both Mohawk Jones and Dr. Brooks were in the gallery to observe, each unaware of the other's connection to Peckinpah. Ann Gentry also attended, to ensure that the proceedings went as agreed. Jones and Brooks were independently disturbed that Peckinpah had not communicated at all with them, and had, in essence, gone AWOL that morning. They each had called repeatedly, but Peckinpah had slipped away for an unannounced tour of Western Town—the king reviewing his kingdom, guided by a more-than-delighted theme park manager. Jones's inability to communicate with his client carried an unfortunate side effect—he never disclosed to Adel Blair that Peckinpah's testimony would be different from deposition, at very least the courteous thing to do. Although he had called Adel's office Wednesday afternoon, he stopped calling Thursday morning while he searched for his wayward client.

"State your name for the record, please," Adel commanded her witness.

"Thomas Armstrong Peckinpah."

"Where do you reside?"

"In Phoenix, Arizona."

"And how are you employed?"

"I am the Chief Executive Officer of Western Town Production Company, and have been for many years."

"Please tell the jury what your duties entail as Chief Executive Officer."

Peckinpah complied, and the jury was awed by him. It was like putting on a modern-day Walt Disney.

"Please tell the jury about your position's traveling requirements," Adel continued.

Peckinpah had logged over three hundred thousand miles in the last ten years, flying among Phoenix, L.A., Denver, Orlando, and other locations in the country and the world. The jury lapped this up, imagining the glamour of a corporate executive—rich, spoiled, and flying through life in first-class.

"Where were you on the night of March 6?" Adel asked.

"Orlando, at the corporate office building, working until about eight forty in the evening."

"And what happened at that time?"

"Well, I walked to the legal department."

"Did you observe anything unusual at the legal department?"

"Yes, I did. I walked into Lou Scarlechek's office and was surprised to find Lou and DeeDee Lane in a sexual position."

"What exactly did you see?" Adel asked.

"Well, I saw them making love," Peckinpah said like an innocent child.

Adel couldn't tell whether he was lying. The jury watched her—they had expected this answer and wanted desperately to hear more. Adel stared at her witness, who stared back expressionless.

Trepidation had arisen in two observers: Dr. Brooks and Mohawk Jones. Ann Gentry was confused and becoming angry. Jones had never seen such a situation in his entire career. He was unsure what to do, technically having no right to stand and address the court. But his client was on the stand in front of him, once again committing perjury, and this time before his very eyes. It was in direct violation of the agreements with the state and federal authorities he had arranged, contradicting his client's written statement and what had been disclosed just the day before. Jones too, like all attorneys, was an officer of the court.

"Was Mr. Scarlechek raping Ms. Lane?"

"Oh no," Peckinpah stated coolly.

Scarlechek smiled. DeeDee glared.

But from the gallery, a disturbance arose. Mohawk Jones jumped up and pushed his way through the gates. "Your Honor," Jones said, causing all eyes to focus on him. "Your Honor, I'm an attorney from Phoenix and I represent Mr. Peckinpah. May I approach the bench, Your Honor? It's extremely important."

"Stop right there, sir!" Judge Wozynski shouted. The bailiff was upon Jones with his handcuffs ready for use.

"Your Honor," said Jones quickly. "I beg your indulgence, and would ask that you remove the jury, immediately."

Ann Gentry stood up in the gallery and the judge recognized her. "Your Honor, I can confirm the necessity of this," she said.

"Bailiff, remove the jury!" Judge Wozynski commanded, angered, but deciding that the jury had better not hear whatever the man had to say. She didn't like surprises in her courtroom, especially those that could lead to mistrial. Scarlechek, for the first time, looked concerned.

Peckinpah stared ahead, closing out the developments from his mind. He muttered to himself, though no one could hear his words. Jones approached and stood beside Adel at the podium. She had no idea who he was or why he was there, except that he represented Peckinpah.

"Excuse me," Jones said to Adel, as he reached for the microphone and bent it his way. Apprehension pulsed through Scarlechek's veins, as beads of sweat formed on his forehead. Golumbo sat dumbfounded at the counsel table.

"Your Honor," Jones said, "my name is Thomas Mohawk Jones. I'm an attorney practicing in Phoenix, and I'm a member in good standing of the Arizona Bar. I represent Mr. Peckinpah. I need to speak to Mr. Peckinpah, right now. His testimony must be interrupted in the interest of justice."

"Well, Mr. Jones ... that is a very vague request! You certainly haven't interrupted the sanctity of this court for something about which you don't intend to tell me. Now, out with it!"

Jones gulped. "Your Honor, I have reason to believe that Mr. Peckinpah is not well mentally."

An immediate hush enveloped the room and everyone turned to Peckinpah on the witness stand. For the first time, they took note of his strange demeanor. Although his body was sitting there, he was not there. He stared straight in front of him muttering to himself, while his hands fidgeted.

Another voice interjected from the gallery.

"Your Honor, may I be permitted to speak to Mr. Jones?" It was Dr. Brooks. She stood and was walking through the gate to Jones. "I'm the witness's therapist. My name is Dr. Marian Brooks. I believe something is terribly wrong here."

The judge looked at Peckinpah, then back at Jones, Brooks, and Gentry. "Someone, please tell me what is going on!"

Jones hesitated—it wasn't an easy thing for a lawyer to confess that his client had just committed perjury, again. It violated one of the most fundamental fiduciary concepts—keeping the confidences of your client—but he had no choice. For Peckinpah's best interest, he couldn't permit the perjury to continue. It was obvious that Peckinpah's psyche had snapped. Gentry gave Jones an encouraging nod.

"Your Honor," Jones said. "There is evidence in Vail, Colorado, that links my client to the accidental death of a prostitute—one Ms. Kelly Parker—who happened to be in the federal witness protection system. There is evidence also that Mr. Scarlechek was involved in the death. We have evidence to prove that Mr. Scarlechek has been blackmailing my client with photographs of the incident. At first, Mr. Scarlechek's aim was to be named President of Western Town Production Company, but when my client walked in on Mr. Scarlechek and Ms. Lane ..."

Jones paused, choosing his words carefully. Scarlechek sank low in his chair as his eyebrows drew closer to his nose and his lips curled. DeeDee's eyes filled with the tears of vindication. Her intuition told her that it was going to be all right. Gonzalez sensed it too and grabbed her hand, covering it with the warmth and strength of his own.

Jones continued, "Mr. Peckinpah saw Ms. Lane being raped at knife point. My client has testified in a sworn statement as to this. Mr. Scarlechek's extortion then required my client to give false testimony in this case. My client has admitted he lied in his deposition in this case. I have here a copy of his sworn statement, and the photographs which Mr. Scarlechek sent to my client to blackmail him."

"Let me see them, please," the judge said gravely.

Scarlechek snarled at Golumbo in a low voice, "Do something! Can't you stop this?"

"No. I can't," Golumbo snapped back in disgust. Even he was surprised and, for the moment, unable to resist the desire to distance himself from his client.

The bailiff took the statement and photos from Jones and handed them to the judge.

Before the judge began reading the statement, she studied the seven pictures. Then, gesturing to Peckinpah, she asked Dr. Brooks, "Will he be all right?"

"Your Honor," Brooks answered. "With your permission, he should be checked into a hospital immediately—I can call an ambulance.

"Please do so at once," Judge Wozynski ordered. When the judge finished reading the statement, she looked up and glared at Scarlechek. He glared back with the unadulterated look of a spoiled child having a toy taken away.

"I assume, Mr. Jones, there has been an immunity deal worked out for Mr. Peckinpah?"

"That's correct, Your Honor, not only with Ms. Gentry and her boss, but with the D.A.s in Colorado and Phoenix. My client gave a proffer late yesterday afternoon, just downstairs, and the officials were all satisfied. I have been unable to speak with my client all morning, and I believe he's had a mental breakdown between yesterday and his testimony today. Your Honor can understand my client has much to lose."

"Yes," the judge said, stroking her chin. "The question is what to do now."

"Well, Goddammit! While you're deciding that, I'm outta here!" Scarlechek suddenly shouted, as he stood and moved toward the gate. "This is ridiculous! Call me when you figure it all out!"

Bam! came the judge's gavel. "Stay right where you are, Mr. Scarlechek! Sit down! ... Bailiff!" She motioned with her head. The bailiff moved quickly. In a brief moment, Scarlechek was back in his chair with the bailiff towering over him.

"Ms. Gentry, do we have probable cause?"

"Yes, Your Honor."

"Very good. Mr. Scarlechek, you are under arrest! Bailiff, take him into custody please. Ms. Gentry, will you read him his rights?"

"Yes, Your Honor."

"Request immediate bail!" Scarlechek hissed to Golumbo as Gentry began the Miranda recitation.

Adel stood astounded at the podium. An emotion overcame her—guilt issued forth from the sudden realization that it had been her episode with Scarlechek that had indeed led to DeeDee's rape. She felt horrible that she'd taken up the company's defense, guilty that she hadn't acted in the best interest of womanhood and truth. It had been her desire to pull for her firm that had blinded her. She turned to the judge.

"Your Honor, I have a confession to make ..."

"Ms. Blair, is this appropriate?"

"Your Honor, I'm not confessing a crime. Perhaps it's a moral crime. Your Honor, I was involved the night of March 6."

DeeDee leaned forward in her chair, as did Gonzalez. Scarlechek snarled, wriggling to achieve comfort in his cuffs. Tiyona wondered what change had come over her friend.

"Your Honor, on the day of the rape I was involved in mediation of a sexual harassment case involving Western Town—the Sorenson case you heard about briefly. Mr. Gonzalez represented Ms. Sorenson. The case settled. Afterwards, Mr. Scarlechek invited me to dinner along with Ms. Morgan here, and an in-house attorney by the name of John Laughlin. We dined, but after dinner Mr. Scarlechek told me he had another case for me, and that he wanted me to come back to his office with him to get the file. It was about eight o'clock in the evening. When we arrived at the legal department, he acted as though bright lights hurt his eyes, so he dimmed the lights to his office."

DeeDee's eyes widened. Gonzalez's and Tiyona's weren't far behind.

"He led me to his couch with the new file and sat close to me. Then, he approached me sexually … it was to be in exchange for all the work that he'd send to my firm. I was insulted and got up to leave. He tried to persuade me to stay and participate in his illicit, sexual deal, and he touched me in an inappropriate manner and place. I kicked him in the groin and hit him in the jaw with a right hook. My blows knocked him over."

Smiles exploded onto all faces in the courtroom but two—Peckinpah's and Scarlechek's.

Adel continued. "I left. This was about eight-thirty. It may very well be his anger at me that triggered the rape of DeeDee, I don't know. But I feel horrible." She sighed as she turned to face DeeDee with pleading eyes. Then she turned back to the Judge.

"Your Honor, I did what I was legally required to do, I believe. I disclosed my possible witness status and possible conflict to my client—John Laughlin at Western Town. I obtained written consent to my representation. I even obtained a subsequent ethical opinion justifying my representation. Mr. Gonzalez was not misled in any way—I think he'll agree—he simply did not ask enough questions to find out what happened just before the rape. Your Honor, I should have put all this together long ago. I just didn't know about the extortion. I wanted the work so badly for my firm. I feel terrible for Ms. Lane."

She stopped and turned to DeeDee again. "I'm so sorry, DeeDee."

DeeDee erupted into more tears, and Tiyona joined her. Even Gonzalez was visibly shaken.

"Your Honor," Adel continued, turning back to the Judge, "I've learned that we must be sensitive to causes. We cannot stay so focused upon ourselves that we ignore reality. It's not in our own self-interest, nor in the interest of community. We each must take up the cause of fairness. I have failed to recognize this—but no more. I cannot do this any longer. Your Honor, I move to withdraw as counsel for Western Town!"

"Not so fast, Ms. Blair! It's clear to me you have learned a valuable lesson, but you're being too hard on yourself. You're also being too soft: don't ignore your duty to counsel your client. I'll reserve ruling on your motion to withdraw until I tell you otherwise. They need you now more than ever. You're still fully in this case—do you understand?"

Adel looked down.

"Now," the judge continued, "I'm declaring an indefinite recess in this proceeding. It seems to me that Western Town is a ship without a captain at this point. I want you, Ms. Blair, to determine with your client exactly what will be done regarding Mr. Scarlechek's employment status. You'll need to get someone in the company with full authority, if Ms. Morgan here doesn't have it. Now, I'm telling all of you, and you can take this as gospel, as a sermon from the bench—I want this case settled! I don't want to embarrass my jurors any longer with these sordid details. I want it settled quickly and satisfactorily, to Ms. Lane's agreement. And I want you to do it, now! Mr. Scarlechek will be dealt with by the state authorities ... Do you understand?"

"Yes, Your Honor," a joint answer rang out.

"All rise," the bailiff commanded. "Ms. Gentry," the judge added, "go call whomever you need, and my bailiff will relinquish Mr. Scarlechek to them."

"Yes, Your Honor."

As soon as the judge exited, the room erupted. There was happiness from all except Golumbo, Scarlechek, and Peckinpah, who remained in a trance as paramedics arrived to take him away. Gonzalez and DeeDee hugged each other as though they'd just won a huge verdict. Tiyona was interceding to congratulate DeeDee. Mohawk Jones shook Adel's hand as they greeted one another. The bailiff shoved Scarlechek down the aisle toward a small room as Golumbo sullenly followed. Then, Adel rushed over to DeeDee, who was by this time beaming with Tiyona. They hugged, and the little tow-headed DeeDee squeezed Adel's torso so tightly, that Adel almost lost her breath.

"Thank you," DeeDee whispered. "I saw your eyes."

"Thank *you*," Adel replied.

CHAPTER 108

"My client pleads not guilty, Your Honor," the criminal lawyer said, with Golumbo by his side. An associate of Golumbo's, he forced an immediate arraignment and bond hearing with the circuit duty judge late that same afternoon. Scarlechek had been booked and now sat in an orange jump suit with hands still cuffed behind his back. His cheeks drooped like the skin of a rotten orange.

"Bail will be set at five hundred thousand dollars," the duty judge declared.

"My client can meet that, Your Honor," the lawyer said. "We need to make a phone call to his bank, and it can be wired into the registry of the court. The banker is standing by."

"Very well," the judge said, surprised. He'd expected a request for a hearing on the amount, but Scarlechek had made it known to his lawyers that he wanted out immediately, and that he had the money. "The clerk will process your papers while you make your call."

Scarlechek sat there with his head lowered. It wasn't shame—it was rage. He wanted to get the bitches that had caused his downfall—Adel Blair and DeeDee Lane. They had said "no" to him in a way that he had never before experienced. There'd be no riches, no power, no fame, no Western Town presidency, and he would have to flee the country. His mind was already calculating how. But first, he'd get them both.

. . . .

Later that evening, after Adel had contacted and briefed Landis and John Waverly, the lawyers reached a settlement in DeeDee's case. Gonzalez wanted to demand more than the company's latest offer of one and a half million dollars, but DeeDee wouldn't allow it. All she truly wanted was to have her job back and to have Scarlechek fired. Landis made the pronouncement—Scarlechek was terminated, and it was music to DeeDee's ears. It took a considerable amount of time to draft it, but the parties signed a settlement agreement, and DeeDee Lane became a rich woman that very night, in more ways than one.

CHAPTER 109

Adel needed to exercise after the extraordinary day. She was tired of thinking and going through rollercoaster emotions. She craved the mantra of the rowing stroke to ease her mind and to relax. But it was too late to row, so she elected once again to go to the boathouse to erg.

Ergometers were the friends of competitive rowers, and Adel needed a nonhuman comrade that night. She was tired and only wanted to sit on the erg and row a steady ten thousand meters. It would take about forty minutes at her pace of five hundred meters every two minutes. Then, she'd stretch, go home, and shower.

I'll call Dave and Michael again after I shower, she thought, having previously tried to reach them on break while the settlement agreement was being typed.

The boathouse was locked and the boats were tucked away for the night when she arrived. The air was heavy, and heat lightning lit the horizon. The water was calm; and the ducks had already climbed onto the dock to rest in the darkness. More lightning from a thunderstorm across the lake bolted, and thunder clapped many seconds later. Adel heard a tree frog croak and the Cypress crickets buzzing as she punched the combination to the boathouse and the electric roll-up door hummed and squeaked.

She flipped on the lights in the main bay, leaving the door open so she could feel the night as she erged. Walking to the other end of the bay and turning on the classic rock 'n roll radio station, she sat down on the erg, adjusted the flywheel for resistance, and strapped in her feet.

The flywheel gave off a low-pitched whine as she began the familiar mechanisms of the stroke. The old chain rattled as it skimmed over the metal frame of the erg, setting a drone-like rhythm that drowned out all sound save Jim Morrison and The Doors on the radio, playing the long version of "Light My Fire." It was perfect—she wanted to drown out everything.

As she warmed up, her muscles and limbs became more flexible, and her intensity increased to the steady pace that she could maintain for the full ten thousand meters. The mantra of the rowing strokes began its opiate effect, and Adel relaxed as her mind faded into the meandering paths of the organ and guitar solos in the song. She relished the relaxation, and wished she'd later be able to keep the day's events from her thoughts when she tried to sleep, knowing it wouldn't happen.

"Thunk!" A loud noise overhead sounded from the tin roof. *A boathouse cat,* she thought, *nothing to worry about.* Or, it was a pine cone from the overhanging trees that a squirrel had discarded. She continued her piece without stopping.

She could see the approaching thunderstorm on the other side of the lake. The rain was light on the tin roof at first, sounding "rat a tat tat tat," like an old, sporadic machine gun. The elephant-ear leaves of the wild taro plants by the dock bent and bounced to the weight of the rain and rising wind. Then came the downpour; flooding the boathouse with white noise as thousands of raindrops bombarded the tin roof. She watched and listened to the rain as she erged—it was mollifying.

Adel thought about Peckinpah, and hoped he'd be all right. She wondered what would happen to him, and how the company would be affected. She prayed his wife and family wouldn't suffer too much. The thought of suffering brought Lou Scarlechek to mind.

I hope that man gets what he deserves in the end, she thought. *Nothing is too harsh.*

Then she thought about DeeDee. *I'm so happy for DeeDee,* she thought. *She'll find happiness. She'll be wealthy and perhaps still work at Western Town. She has an incredible amount of heart. I'm proud of her. From now on, I'm going to fight for the little people ...*

Maybe it's not too late for Michael and me.

Forty minutes later the piece ended. Dismounting the erg, she walked to the drinking fountain by the door. The rain had lessened its intensity, but still came down steadily as two new thunderheads were converging with the one that had already deluged the boat-house. Adel stretched her lower back as she walked. She bent over and drank the water, enjoying its coldness on her throat. She let the cold pain in her craw subside, and watched the rain dance on the lake. A curtain of heavy precipitation charged across the lake to the boathouse, like a Mongol horde. She drank again.

Adel suddenly felt a chill, and it wasn't from the water. She turned to peer into the shadows of the fours bay. But there was nothing for her to see in the dark. There was no one there. *Just the eeriness of being alone late at night*, she thought. She had felt that way many times before, and refused to let the sensation unsettle her now.

But Adel heard a sound coming from the darkened fours bay over her shoulder; it was muffled by the rain battering the roof. She walked slowly to her right to see what it might've been. Suddenly, a wailing, guttural, "we...ooow," came from the shadows and startled her as a wooden board atop a sign toppled. Something small, lost in the shadows, scampered away farther into the fours bay.

Damn cats, she thought. The new downpour hit, and she walked back to the erg and laid out a mat on the floor. She lay down on her back and brought her arms over her head. She stretched hard, and felt her back muscles cramp slightly—it felt good. With her long frame stretched to its limit from the tip of her toes to fingers stretched far above her head, she struck a vulnerable vision in tight cotton shorts and a skin-tight halter.

Alone except for the wild cats, she didn't feel at risk. Yet, this night, an uneasy feeling wrapped around her and refused to depart. She continued stretching, changing positions from time to time on the blue mat—drawing her right leg straight up in the air, then her left; then drawing her right leg back, heel to bottom to stretch her quads, then her left.

She shivered although it was a humid, steamy night. Placing her hands on the mat, she pushed, drawing her legs to her chest and planting her feet in a full squatting position. She wrapped her arms around her knees and collapsed her back into relaxation. Holding her arms around her knees, she pulled her torso up—stretching her lower and middle back.

At first she thought the sudden pressure in her back was a spasm—one that she'd never felt before. A new ache ... a new twinge to catalogue with the many she'd experienced from her ultra-demanding sport. But it lingered, and increased in intensity, the pressure becoming cold and hard against her bare skin, and piercing into the right side of her spine.

"Don't move," a low voice commanded.

Despite the command, Adel looked around and saw Lou Scarlechek. His mouth was twisted, and his eyes burned fiercely. She could smell his breath, its fetid odor intruding upon her senses.

"I said, don't move!" he shrieked. He didn't like it when Adel moved suddenly. He pressed the barrel of the .38 harder into her back. "You're an intelligent girl; you can feel what I've got in your back. Be good, now, little girl."

He laughed. "Be good—you'll be good. I'm going to take you, Adel Blair. Right here on your own turf. Then, I'll get little Miss Goody Two Shoes. Now stand up!" His voice rang with hatred, and hung heavy in the boathouse air.

Adel hung her head and slowly rose first with her back, as though still stretching. With her hair drooping over her face, she looked to the side and spied a twelve-inch crescent wrench on the tool table. She rose up fully, with the wrench only an arms length away.

"Now, I'm going to do what I should've done long ago. Move without me telling you, and I'll put a hole in you. I'll put it in a place where I can keep you alive—so I can put *more* into you. Got it?"

Adel didn't speak. The wrench handle hung over the edge of the table. Adel realized that he'd kill her that night—after playing with her. She knew he'd do the same to DeeDee, and the thought chilled her. She felt helpless and wanted to cry out. But no one would hear a scream—the rain on the tin roof drowned out every noise. DeeDee would have little chance. It had to be her— she had to stop him now.

Stay cool. Watch for an opening.

She felt his fingers move up her left arm and run over her shoulder. She knew what was coming—realizing it may be her best chance. His hand parted her left arm from her side and moved to her breast. She felt the pressure of the gun in her back recede as he groped for her breast through her sports bra.

"Yeah!" she heard him utter lasciviously. *The wrench,* she thought. *Now?*

"Sweaty and gross!" he snarled as he continued, his hand moving back and forth between her breasts and feeling the warm wetness from her workout. "That's the way it should be for you, bitch!" His hatred became his distraction, for she felt the gun barrel growing even more slack against her back.

The wrench—she glanced to her right again, moving her head only slightly. *I need that wrench.* The situation required a moment of diversion. *My foot—the move in the office—dare I with a gun in my back? No. Distraction ... I need a distraction!*

"We ... ooow!" came the loud, bone-chilling noise. A boathouse cat wailed at another coming in out of the rain, from behind Scarlechek on the left.

He spun his head around, startled. Adel lunged, grabbed the wrench with her hand, and snapped it up with a rapid twist of her right arm. Whirling, she raised the tool high and lowered it with all her strength. His head was turned, searching for the source of the noise in the shadows. The wrench crashed square on the backside of his cranium—it pounded and momentarily stung him. Scarlechek staggered to the side.

But he reacted before the blow took full effect and fired his gun.

Pow! The shot echoed through the hollow boathouse, but the noise of thousands of raindrops muffled it.

The attempt was wild after her wallop, and missed. Then, Adel's strike took effect and his legs wobbled, and he stumbled to the left. He staggered, grabbing his aching head, yet he didn't go down. Instinctively, Scarlechek managed to level his weapon for another shot.

Pow!

But this time, Adel had already ducked out the side door. Scarlechek cursed and followed her as blood trickled down the side of his neck.

Lightning fired up the sky. Outside, Scarlechek spotted Adel thirty yards off. She was sprinting across the back parking lot, her long, muscular legs at full stride, and her shoes sending water from the puddles everywhere with each step. He pursued, gun in hand.

Chasing her out of the parking lot and onto the side of the road where she turned toward a closed convenience store, he realized he'd never catch her on foot. Out of breath, he turned back to get to his car, which he'd parked next to Adel's on the grassy lakefront by the boathouse.

Adel stole quick glances behind her and slowed her pace. Seeing him turn back, she ducked out of sight into a roadside thicket.

Got to call the cops. Got to warn DeeDee! She needed to get to the cell phone in her car. Creeping back through the brush to where she could see his vehicle, and crouching low behind a bush, Adel saw Scarlechek drive out of the lot. He screeched left and zoomed north onto the road.

She waited a couple minutes, scared that he'd return. Her heart pounded. Then shock hit her like the cool precipitation. *Calm down!* she thought. *Focus! ... That's enough time ... he's not coming back.*

Relieved, she took off running across the lot once again to re-trieve her keys from the boathouse keyboard. The cops had to be dispatched to DeeDee's home immediately. Her mind racing, she wondered how she could find out DeeDee's address and be on her way, too. *Perhaps 911. The cops would know.*

The fours bay was still dark. Light from the eights bay cast long shadows from the boats, but guided her to the keyboard where her keys hung. She could call from the boathouse office, but she decided to call the police from her car, where she could be out of the rain, safe, and on the move.

She snatched her keys off the board, turning to leave in the next instant.

"Gotcha!" she heard, as a wet arm wrapped around her neck. It was Scarlechek and this time, he had Adel headlocked. The familiar metallic pressure point separated her ribs. Scarlechek had guessed correctly. He'd noticed Adel's keys earlier and knew that she would need to return for them. He'd doubled back and snuck in from the side.

But it was raw adrenaline, explosive and violent, and void of thought, that caused her left elbow to nearly separate his rib cage from his soft belly. For her, the movement was simple, as though she were yanking on an oar. Scarlechek hunched down, involuntarily extracting his arm from her neck. Adel slipped out of his hold and raced through the dark fours bay toward the front of the boathouse.

Pow! On reflex, Scarlechek shot—not well, but it hit. The bullet pierced Adel's right lat muscle as she ran. Searing pain caused her to stumble, as the flesh exploded from under her arm. A high-pitched guttural noise escaped from her and she staggered to the right, falling onto the hull of a yellow, four-person racing shell. Her blood splattered onto the boat.

"Don't move!" he yelled as he lunged after her, toward the fours in the darkened bay.

If she'd thought, she would've complied. But Adel was incapable of thought now; her competitive drive took over. Just as Scarlechek reached her, she surged forward again, with him right behind. As she'd done thousands of times, she ducked a boat rigger off another four above the yellow four as she moved away. He was at full speed, every muscle in his body twitching. He didn't want to shoot again, because he didn't want to kill her ... yet. He saw her accelerating body, but didn't see what Adel saw. It was too dark and she was too tall. And then, there was nothing but a rigid metal rigger and oarlock filling the space in front of him.

"Thunk!" The hard metal smacked him right between the eyes! His legs wobbled like a KO'd prize fighter for a split second, and then Scarlechek went straight down, his legs crumpling beneath him. Scarlechek was out cold, taken down by a boat rigger.

Adel turned to look. Scarlechek was down and out on the concrete. With the realization that she was safe, she began shaking with pain and, though relieved, allowed herself to wail as she hobbled to the oar racks in the singles bay and retrieved her handcuffs off her oars. Reeling back to Scarlechek's limp body, she cuffed his hands behind his back. Excruciating throbs emanated from her wound, but still she drove on. She looped his ankles with a four-foot stretch of rope and wrapped his legs together as tight as she could with a double clove hitch.

Scarlechek was still out.

With her blood dripping to the floor, she staggered to the office phone and dialed 911. Then she collapsed to the floor. She wheezed, "Please … come … th' boathouse … Lake Fairview … been shot."

Weak and drained of blood, she couldn't hold onto the phone any longer, so she let it drop to the floor. In her last moments of consciousness, she clutched a dirty rag off the floor and compressed the hole through her lat. Then she passed out onto her wounded side, the weight of her body helping retard the sanguine flow.

CHAPTER 110

It was Saturday—Independence Day—and two days after Scarlechek's attack. The first face Adel saw when she regained consciousness was Michael's ... then Dave's ... then Tiyona's. The nurse had predicted Adel would awaken that afternoon. The trio had waited patiently, knowing Adel was going to be okay. And she was.

"Hello, beautiful," Michael said.

Adel stretched her left arm forward, petitioning an embrace. Her right side craved to participate, but pain caused her to grimace at any attempt to move.

"Take it easy, Adel," Michael advised, leaning over and dodging IV tubes, and hugging what he could of her for a prolonged moment.

Adel felt whole—the unconditional support from Michael buoying her traumatized spirit, just as he'd supported her when she'd found him waiting on the steps. He was always there when she needed him most.

He kissed her cheek. "I love you," he whispered, gazing into her eyes.

"You too," she breathed, and smiled through her tears. It was the first time in their topsy-turvy relationship that this sentiment had ever been expressed.

Dave McKerrin looked on, as prideful as a father. Tiyona's eyes filled with tears, and she laughed, embarrassed by her own display of emotion.

None of Adel's visitors knew exactly what had happened in the boathouse. Adel had been too weak, in and out of deep sleep, to speak to anyone. They only knew what the Orlando police officer had found: an unconscious Scarlechek, handcuffed and hog-tied, his forehead bleeding profusely, with a .38 Smith & Wesson by his side. The technicians had confirmed that the pistol had been fired three times. They found only Scarlechek's prints on it. Two bullets, which matched the ballistics of the gun, were found lodged in two different wood beams in the boathouse. The third bullet had passed through Adel and the thin graphite hull of the yellow racing shell. They found blood on the boat, which they identified as Adel's.

The nurse popped in just then and, seeing that Adel was revitalized, allowed the visitors to stay.

Much had happened at Western Town the Friday following the trial. Tom Peckinpah had recovered sufficiently to hold a news conference, with his wife by his side. He'd announced Waverly's retirement and the appointment of Sandy Yates as the new president. Then, he announced his resignation as CEO. He refused to answer any questions about Vail or the Lane case.

Yates held a press conference that same afternoon to announce the settlement of the Lane case for one and a half million dollars, DeeDee's reinstatement to her position, Lou Scarlechek's firing, and the future implementation of meaningful policies and procedures to prevent harassment and discrimination in general. Yates stated that the policies and procedures would be designed to eliminate "artificial glass ceilings" within the company that held back women and minorities from advancement. Yates also announced Tiyona Morgan's promotion to executive vice president of Equal Employment Opportunity: and that her mission, reporting directly to him, was to eliminate discrimination and harassment in all forms.

A black news reporter had asked Yates, "Are you going to guarantee the elimination of stereotyping and discrimination in Western Town in general?" Tiyona read to Adel a news clipping of Yates's response:

"You know ... when you're dealing with people—in general— you can't guarantee anything. My personal feeling is that the way people use the word 'stereotype' signals that what they mean is sort of the evil flip side of a generalization. While I believe generalizations can have an element of truth to them, you can never assume the applicability of a generalization to anyone, because they more often are fraught with mistruth. It leaves too much to chance. White men can't jump, for example. Did you know that at forty-five, I can slam dunk a basketball?"

Laughter broke out at the press conference at Yates's remark. Tiyona continued reading Yates's response: "But, in general, there is a small element of truth to that generalization. All I really know is this: there are good people and bad people in all walks of life—in each sex, each race, each church, each political party, and so on. The trick is to treat all people fairly—with fair chances. Minorities and whites must live and work together. Women and men must live and work together—each with their individual strengths and weaknesses—in fairness and toward a common good. This is Tiyona Morgan's job now. I trust—and have always trusted, from the moment I met her, in her judgment. I can guarantee this: she will have the power, authority, and support she needs to accomplish her mission. That's what fairness dictates. One more thing: harassers, sexual or otherwise, are nothing more than selfish rapists—they rape the soul. This company will not tolerate harassment of any kind. We are taking the first step toward smashing glass ceilings to bits by elevating Tiyona."

Tiyona paused and looked up from the paper.

"Oh, Tiyona …," Adel said weakly. "I'm so happy for you."

"Well, you helped bring it about."

"Not me, it was DeeDee."

"You helped too—you stood up for what was right in your own way. And, DeeDee … I'm proud of her too. She overcame her weakness. She gave me the chance to fight for people."

"Yes, she did," Adel said. "Dave … you're so quiet."

"I'm just very proud, Adel," Dave said, his voice breaking.

"Well … I won't be into the office for awhile. Think you can manage?" she asked, reassuring Dave that all was well.

He smiled broadly and said, "I knew you'd use this as some feeble excuse."

CHAPTER 111

Later that evening, Adel received another visitor. It was DeeDee Lane.

"Adel, thank you so much for what you did in court. It meant so much to me," DeeDee said.

"It's all of us that should be thanking you, DeeDee. You know, I always had the nagging sensation I was on the wrong side of the case. I'm just glad I finally figured it out … a little late though, I suppose."

"But you did realize it. That's all that matters to me … what happened to you at the boathouse … Adel, you are so good and strong. You saved me, I know it. He would have come after me, too. You're my mockingbird."

Adel gazed at DeeDee, not quite understanding her meaning. But she was too weak, so she let it pass. "No, you're the strong one. I just did what comes naturally to me. You're the one who overcame your weaknesses. You're the one …" Her voice trailed off.

"That's how I feel," DeeDee said. "But you inspired it. It was Scarlechek's frenzy over you that caused my rape and helped me find my strength. You set the pace for me to follow, in my own way. And you were with me in the trial, I know it."

They smiled at each other, and DeeDee leaned over and they hugged. As DeeDee left, she said, "Adel, if you ever need a new legal secretary, I want to work for you. Keep me in mind."

Adel smiled again. She nodded with assurance of things to come.

CHAPTER 112

There was no bravery behind the act of pushing the cold barrel of the twelve-gauge Browning shotgun into his mouth. The man was taking back what was his—the right to manage his own life. He'd felt out of control ever since the day Lou Scarlechek entered his life. It'd only gotten worse.

Others had invaded his province—Mohawk Jones, Charles Mix, Cookie Albertson, Marian Brooks, Adel Blair, Janis—they all had the nerve to tell him what to do. He was exhausted and unwilling to take it any longer. He'd show them. He was the quarterback, the leader, and he called the plays. He was about to call his last.

It didn't matter what it would do to the others. He couldn't really comprehend it. His wife and daughter, his mother. What mattered to him was all that really mattered.

He had driven far into the desert and now stood alone at the base of a reddish mesa. He was beyond all coherent thought and numbed by his compelling purpose. As the cold steel slid fully into his mouth, stretching his lips wide, his only fear was that the angle was too low and he'd miss his brain. He levered the barrel upward by pulling down, using his teeth as a fulcrum, feeling the tip of the barrel against his upper palette. He drew his last breath as he secured his thumb on the trigger, and then he squeezed.

On the hot, dry, desert dirt and rocks, the body of Thomas Armstrong Peckinpah lay lifeless, blending with the silence and time-lessness of the desert, and awaiting the coyotes and the buzzards.

CHAPTER 113

Ann Gentry and Heath Robero had been at their best, prosecuting Scarlechek for the State. DeeDee and Adel both testified, as did Cookie, Janet Watson, Deputy Edwards, Steve Gonzalez and even Richard Golumbo. It'd been more difficult without Peckinpah's testimony, but in the end, it didn't matter. Scarlechek denied the rape and claimed self-defense all the way through his sentencing—to twenty years in the state penitentiary. He threatened malpractice actions against his attorneys if they didn't continue to fight on appeal. His wife, Marsha, filed for divorce.

When Scarlechek was imprisoned, he was issued an ill-fitting, orange jumpsuit. They buzzed off his dangling dark hair, which he had always flipped about so proudly. His new hairstyle accentuated his large nose, and if he ever was handsome, he certainly wasn't anymore.

When the guard first led him down a long corridor of steel and concrete cages to his cell, the inmates chanted, "Fresh fish ... fresh fish!"

But all he could worry about was whether his cell was better than the others, that is, until the guard opened Scarlechek's cell and he beheld a massive, ugly man with only half of his teeth. The man grinned at Scarlechek in a strange fashion. His tattoos glistened with sweat. Scarlechek immediately feared his new roommate, and wondered what the look imported. He didn't know that he would soon learn the meaning of getting it in ...

The End